KATHERINE'S ARRANGEMENT

SHENANDOAH BRIDES ~ BOOK 1

BLOSSOM TURNER

WILD HEART
BOOKS

ISBN-13: 978-1-942265-26-9

For my dear son Joshua and my lovely daughter Ally(sha),
who, despite knowing my faults, love me unconditionally.
You have both believed in my writing and challenged me to follow this
dream.

Thank you for being my biggest fans and life's greatest joy.

"And now abide faith, hope, love these three;
but the greatest of these is love."

1 Corinthians 13:13

PROLOGUE

"*K*atherine. They're coming." Pa swung his rifle over his shoulder and grimaced. The gun slipped to the floor. With jerky movements, he retrieved the weapon.

"Pa, your shoulder."

"Go, girl, and do exactly as we planned."

Through the window, the smoke from the neighbor's house, a cloud of ominous black, darkened the distant horizon. She glanced back at her pa, torn between helping her ma and sisters and him. Her heart leapt into her throat as he fumbled with his rifle. What could he really do against a group of soldiers? He could barely hold a gun.

"Katie, get moving. I'll be on the porch."

She shot forward, stumbling on the hem of her dress as she ran toward the kitchen. "Ma, we gotta go." She snatched up her trusty rifle hung above the back door, and felt for the revolver she kept hidden under her dress.

Ma was stuffing a pillowcase with food. A loaf of bread fell

1

through her trembling hands and tumbled to the floor. Katie's sisters huddled close with wide eyes and tears streaming down their faces.

"Ma, come on." Katie picked up three-year-old Gracie, put an arm around her ma's shoulders, and steered them toward the door. Her three other sisters followed on her heels.

Gracie squirmed, fighting to get down.

"Beckie," Gracie howled. "I need Beckie."

"There's no time," Ma said.

Katie thrust Gracie into Ma's arms. "I'll find it. We can't have her screaming."

Katie placed her hands on both sides of Gracie's small round face and leaned in. "I'll get your doll if you promise to obey Ma and do everything she says. Understand?"

Gracie whimpered. Her thumb went into her mouth.

"Ma, take the girls. I'll find the doll."

Katie raced from room to room. She swallowed hard against the knot of fear rising in her throat. *Where is that doll? God, if you're up there, please ...*

No sooner had she voiced her prayer than she spotted the arm of the doll poking out from underneath her sister's bed. She swooped it up and ran out the door.

The smoke in the distance billowed into a thick black cloud. Katie picked up her skirt and darted across the yard. The Yankees were closing in.

She headed for the hedge that lined a small section of the dusty drive. The boxwoods, her ma's prized token of a childhood in Richmond, would serve them well today. A thick blackberry bramble sprawled directly behind, preventing any rider from coming that direction.

Ma and her sisters huddled in their makeshift shelter dug into the ground. Five sets of frightened eyes looked up at Katie as she approached.

She tossed the doll to Gracie and looked at her ma. "I'm not leaving Pa alone." She knelt down and grasped the leaf and twig covered board they had prepared to conceal the hiding spot.

"What about you?" Fifteen-year-old Amelia held out her arm, her dark eyes saucer wide and brimming with tears.

"I'll join you as soon as I can."

"Ma, stop her," Amelia said.

"She knows what's she doing." Ma nodded her approval.

A knot twisted inside Katie's gut. Ma so easily gave in. As usual, she treated Katie different from the others. Regardless, she wasn't about to leave Pa to fend for himself. If they tried to harm him, she would use her gun and they would pay. With her sharp aim, she would be able to take out a few of them before they got to her.

The board wobbled in her hands as she pulled it into place. A quick glance assured their hideaway looked like the surrounding area, and the pipe buried for air supply was carefully hidden in the brambles.

She moved further down the hedge away from the hiding spot and settled into the perfect ambush site. Lying low with her Springfield rifle held in one shaky hand, she pulled out the small six-shot revolver pocketed in her dress, the one she'd removed from a dead Yankee earlier that year. The metal took on the chill of the cold October morning and bit into her fingers, but nothing was as cold as her heart towards those Yankees who had killed her twin brothers.

Her heart pounded so loudly, she feared it was audible. With a deep breath, she worked to calm the thumping. The revolver lay loaded and ready as backup. Katie fit the rifle into the curve of her shoulder and shifted to find comfort on the uneven ground.

She clenched her teeth as her mind darted in and out of the horror of the past few years. Pa had warned the war would get uglier before it was over. He was right. Sheridan's troops were now systematically eliminating the Shenandoah Valley as a source of grain and livestock for General Lee's army—one field and one house at a time. The neighbor's place devoured by flames looked like a beast from hell had feasted.

Her vision blurred, and she brushed away tears with an angry swipe.

She spied movement on the road. Her adrenaline spiked as she peered through the sight on her gun. A Yankee. Perched ramrod straight on his steed, a soldier turned into their yard. Hatred washed hot, but it cooled at the sight of the man's face. The young officer reminded her of her twin brothers. He had the same wispy hair, angular cheekbones, and deep-set eyes. The urge to rise up from her hiding spot lifted her torso until the blue of his uniform caught her eye. She sank back, shaking, until hate once again gave her courage.

A swarm of soldiers followed the young officer to the front porch. They trained their muskets upon Pa.

"State your business," Pa said. The Enfield he held loosely at his side looked more like a toy than a weapon.

Still mounted on his horse, the officer spoke. "Surrender your gun, and we'll spare your life."

A soldier stormed the few steps and knocked the rifle out of Pa's hand. "Come on, old man. Got any fight left in you?"

Katie gripped the gun so tightly that it bit into the soft flesh of her shoulder. She set her sight on the pig-headed soldier. Her finger itched to pull the trigger.

"Take whatever you want. Just please don't burn the house."

The officer hesitated. "Sorry, old man, but an order is an order. You'd better get your family out of the cellar."

"Hope you got a pretty one for me," another said.

A group of them laughed. Their lewd intentions were clear Even from the distance, the lust smoldering in their evil eyes was obvious. She knew all too well what that meant.

Pa shook his head. "What did you say?"

"This crazy old buzzard's gone mad."

"Can't understand simple instructions," another said.

How dare they make fun of her pa. Turmoil roiled in her stomach, and she fought the nausea down. "Leave him be," the officer said. "When we start burning, he'll understand."

He barked out a few short orders, and the soldiers jumped into action, scurrying about like dungeon rats. The officer dismounted and went into the house with a few of his men.

Pa collapsed into the chair on the porch. His head fell into his hands.

They piled straw around the barn and drove Blossom, their milk cow, and old Sam, the mule, inside. The doors slammed shut, and they lit their torches. The flames danced into action licking up the sides of the barn. Katherine's insides churned into a ball of fear.

She lowered her gun and shoved her fist into her mouth, biting down hard to stifle a cry as Sam's bellow reached her ears. Next, the hay field Pa had worked so hard to plant was set ablaze. Their last few chickens were thrown into a sack and the little bit of cured meat left in the smokehouse taken. How would her family survive without food?

The screen door slammed, and the officer and his soldiers carried out Ma's preserves, fresh bread, and a sack of root vegetables.

Katie's fingers interlaced the gun with one trembling finger, ready to take back what was rightfully theirs.

"Come on, old man. Off the porch." The officer grabbed Pa's arm and lifted him from the chair. He dragged him down the steps and into the yard. The house was lit. They stayed just long enough to ensure the damage would be complete. The whole episode took less than fifteen minutes, before the soldiers turned and rode out of sight.

Pa sank to his knees in the dust.

CHAPTER 1

*J*osiah cantered into town and swung from his stallion. He liked to get in and get out without much ado. One of these days, if he ever hoped to remarry and have a family, he was going to have to change his loner personality, but not today. He tethered his steed on the hitching post outside the general store and took the steps two at time. He had one hand on the door and the other removing his hat, when a woman's shriek split the air.

He whirled around. Was that trouble coming from the saloon again? Sure enough. But usually the girls in there didn't put up much of a fuss. Curiosity got the best of him, and he headed in that direction. He picked up his pace as the scream intensified.

The swinging doors pushed wide as he entered. It took a moment for his eyes to adjust to the dim lighting, but when they did, one fist clenched, and he straightened to his full height. The other hand cradled his gun in the holster.

"Unhand her this minute."

Two unsavory men swiveled around at the sound of his voice. A feral glint danced in their eyes. "What's it to you. We're just having a little fun."

"Perhaps you boys don't understand what a scream from a lady means. Usually, it means she's not enjoying your company."

Josiah looked into the brilliant blue eyes of a black-haired beauty and a memory twigged. Was that the same girl he'd rescued long ago?

"Let me go," she said, confirming his suspicions.

His hand stayed steady above his gun.

She pushed her way free, but one of them grabbed her arm. "Not so fast."

Her brows flew up, and her eyes doubled in size as Josiah's gun flipped from his holster. He aimed it at the man.

"I will shoot, and they didn't call me Bullseye in the war for nothing." He held his hand steady and calm.

One of them twitched.

"Both of you will be on the floor before your hand touches your gun, so don't even think about it. Now let her go."

The one who had the hold ogled her up and down. His stare, a mixture of lust and evil, crawled over her. Josiah itched to pull the trigger.

"She's a fine one. But not worth a bullet." His wiry grip unclasped.

She scurried across the room to Josiah's side.

"Go on. Out of here."

To his surprise she bent down and pulled a small six-shot revolver from her boot and pinned it on them. "We will back out together."

He loved the spunk, and his heart tripped a beat. That had not happened in a long, long time.

"After you, my lady."

They backed out. She slid the gun back into her boot. He

kept his eyes on the door, just in case, then turned to her. She was halfway down the street before he caught up to her.

"Wait."

She did a half turn but kept on walking. "Just because you got me out of a bind doesn't mean I owe you anything."

"A thank-you would be sufficient."

"Thank you," she said over her shoulder before turning down a side street.

He found himself pursuing her without understanding why. As his long strides caught up, he touched her arm.

She flinched and turned with fire in her eyes. "Are you like all the rest? Can't keep your hands off?"

"I just wanted to introduce myself."

"I know who you are, Mr. Richardson. Everyone knows who you are. You don't go about being the richest man in the county and people not know your name."

He raised his eyebrows. "And your name?"

"We've met."

"So you *are* that same girl—"

"I'd rather not discuss it."

"Seems I have a penchant for rescuing you. Katherine, isn't it?"

"Seems you men can't keep your hands to yourself, or a girl wouldn't need rescuing. If I could've got to my gun first..." She gritted her teeth, and her tiny fists balled at her side.

"Ah, yes, you do know how to use your gun."

"Doesn't help much when a girl can't even go about her work without being manhandled."

"Were you working in the saloon?"

She raised her chin. "I was cleaning the place. It's all the work I could find, and my family's in a bad way—"

He raised his brows at her. "Your pa let you work in an establishment like that?" Surely, her family couldn't approve.

"I told my pa I got a cleaning job, just not where I was cleaning. Oh, never mind. You and all your money would never understand."

Frustration stirred inside him. "But a girl like you cannot safely work in a place like that."

"What do you mean, a girl like me?"

"Well, you don't exactly blend into the background."

"The curse of being born looking like this strikes again." She swept a hand from tip to toe, and a sheen of tears filled her eyes. "I thought I could handle myself, but how can I when they attack from behind as soon as the owner steps out for a few minutes?"

A mixture of sensations warred inside him. He hated seeing a woman cry, but he also hated being lumped in with those hooligans in the saloon. "Not all men disrespect women."

"I know. And I really am thankful for your help. Once again, I'll ask that you don't tell my pa." A lone tear slipped down her cheek, and she brushed it away.

Without thinking he stepped forward and folded his arms around her. For a brief moment, she tucked her trembling body into the warmth of his hold. The smell of rain-washed roses and the softness of a woman's body stirred long forgotten senses.

But then she wrenched free and took off running.

This time, he didn't follow.

Whatever had possessed him to do that? He hadn't held a woman since his beloved Georgina died, nor had he wanted to. But this beautiful enigma somehow reached in and touched his soul.

He took his hat and dusted it against the side of his leg, then plunked it back on his head and turned toward the store.

What would it be like to be so desperate one had to risk one's life—one's body—to work in a place like that? A surge of protectiveness rose from deep within. How could he help her?

❧

10

*K*atie squinted into the afternoon sun. Dust billowed behind a lone rider. Was that who she thought it was? Of all the luck. She'd only just chosen to escape the stifling heat and sit on her aunt's front porch and stitch up a frayed hem. Why did he have to appear when she could not stay hidden?

A tremor took to her hands. What did he want? The urge to dart inside welled up, but it was too late. His eyes were pinned upon her. She forced herself to stay put, but wove the needle into the fabric so she wouldn't prick her finger. Thankfully, a slight breeze lifted the hair on the nape of her neck to cool the heated flush. She had to get over the past. Today was as good a day as any. She jutted her chin in the air. The only thing moving were her hands, which nervously thread material through her fingers.

Smile. Stay calm. A tiny bead of sweat trickled down her spine.

He swung from his horse and tethered the reins to the porch rail.

She took in a cleansing breath. She could do this. She was a civilized young woman, no longer traipsing unchaperoned about the countryside nor needing his rescue—again.

He climbed the steps and made his way toward her. An irregular beat thumped inside her chest as he moved with sure steps, his head held high.

A wavy russet-brown curl fell across his brow when he removed his hat. The flattened hair sprang to life as his fingers raked through the thickness. Peppered gray tinged his sideburns.

"Good afternoon, Miss Williams." His eyes crinkled with friendly warmth.

She mumbled an obligatory hello and dropped her gaze to her lap.

"I'm here to have a conversation with your father and hope that my request will meet with your approval."

Her head snapped up.

He flashed an easy smile.

Katie's mouth went dry.

He slipped his hat back on and took a step back.

She gathered the strength to lift her head and meet his gaze.

His smile softened. "We'll talk soon enough." Light danced in the depths of his steel-gray eyes.

A prickle of awareness nipped at the back of her neck. "What do you want to talk to Pa about?" Katherine blurted out the words before her head had time to catch up to her mouth. "If it's about the incident—"

"Goodness no." His face fell. Silence filled the air as he stared down at her.

Why was he looking at her like that? Like he expected her to know his mind.

She shifted in the rocking chair, then jumped to her feet to relieve the intensity. She brushed against him and took a quick step back. The rocker swayed, and she stumbled forward as it hit her in back of the legs. He reached out to steady her.

She breathed in a woodsy mixture of pine and leather. A tingling sensation worked its way up her arms as the warmth from his large but gentle hands penetrated the thin cotton sleeves of her well-worn dress.

Abruptly turning, she moved across the porch. "If you'll excuse me, Mr. Richardson, I'll fetch Pa, I mean Father, for you."

After she informed her father of their visitor, Katie was thankful for the safety of the small cabin as she helped in the kitchen, away from his unsettling stare. What did he want? Her hands trembled as she peeled the potatoes for supper.

Ma fussed about as if the king had come for tea. She pulled

out Aunt May's best dishes, serving tray, and good cutlery. Her constant prattle set Katie's nerves on edge.

"How embarrassing we don't have tea. That blasted war is not over, even when it's over." Her grumbles grew louder. "When will we be able to get decent supplies again?"

Katie rolled her eyes. Why all the bother?

"Katie," Ma said, "set the sassafras to steep on the stove. Amelia, fetch me a few springs of mint from the garden. May, do we have any of your tea biscuits left, or did the kids eat them all?"

Aunt May wrapped a gentle arm around Ma's shoulder and smiled. "There's a few left. If we don't help ourselves, there will be enough for the menfolk to have one. Now, take a deep breath, Doris."

Aunt May squeezed Ma's shoulder, then moved to the counter. She lifted the checkered cloth that covered the few tea biscuits and placed the plate onto the tray. "Doris, why don't you go sit with the men, and I'll bring everything out when the tea is ready?"

"I won't meddle in men talk, and they asked specifically that Katherine serve the tea."

Aunt May swung around. Her eyes widened when Ma gave a slight nod.

Something was up, but what?

Ma turned to her. "Katherine, go use the mirror in Aunt May's bedroom and tidy yourself up. And fix your bun, you look unkempt."

"When have you ever cared what I—?"

"For heaven's sakes, is there ever a moment when you do as I say and don't argue with me?" She threw up her hands. "Go."

Katie dropped a half-peeled potato into the basin and huffed out a deep breath. She wiped her hands on her apron and headed for the only room with privacy.

"And change out of that old work dress. I'll bring your Sunday—"

"Mr. Richardson saw me on the porch when he arrived." She faced her mother. "If my dress was good enough then, surely it's good enough now." She slipped into the bedroom before Ma could say another word.

After she'd fixed her bun, Katie returned to the kitchen, where Ma and Aunt May stood side by side at the sink snapping off the ends of fresh beans. Little Gracie and their second-youngest sister, Lucinda, were running around in a game of tag with their youngest cousins, Jacob and Nathan. Jeanette—the middle daughter—sat in a chair with her nose buried in a book she had read many times over, and fourteen-year-old Amelia was surrounded by material draped over the kitchen table. She had her ears covered with both hands.

"Ma, can't these kids play outside?" Amelia said. When Ma didn't answer or even indicate that she'd heard, Amelia threw her hands in the air. "I'm trying to concentrate on my sewing, and there's so much noise." She sent Katie a look that pleaded for help.

Katie nodded and moved closer to get Ma's attention.

"We can't live here much longer." Ma kept her voice in a low murmur as she spoke to Aunt May. "We've imposed upon your family enough. This house barely fit the four of you without adding the seven of us, and now that you have another young'in on the way—"

"God will provide, Doris. Maybe, just maybe, provision sits on our front porch as we speak."

"What does that mean?" Katie asked.

They jumped apart and whirled around.

The light of excitement in Aunt May's eyes faded. "Katie girl, you scared us sneaking up like that." Her forced laughter filled the room. "You always did have the stealth of an Indian brave."

"I don't need stealth in this chaos. Can't the kids play

outside?"

"We're trying to keep the noise contained while the men talk." She motioned toward the counter. "The tray is ready to go. Could you be a dear and take that out?"

Katie frowned, but picked up the tray. Maybe she could rush in and out without notice. She swung open the screen with her head high and a charge in her steps. Unfortunately, she miscalculated the weight of the door and it crashed against the house before slamming shut. Not exactly the invisible presence she planned to project.

Pa and Mr. Richardson stopped talking. She could feel their eyes upon her, though she refused to look up. She set the tray gingerly on the small table between them.

"Thank you, Katherine," Mr. Richardson said.

She chanced a look his way, and he boldly captured her attention with a full smile that showed off a row of straight white teeth.

Propriety demanded she answer. "You are most welcome, Mr. Richardson." She forced a slight upward curve to her lips.

"Can you pour us each a cup, Katie girl?" Pa asked.

This was something she had done a thousand times before, yet a fluster pressed in. She lifted the pot and spilled a bit of the first pour onto the saucer. She gave that one to Pa, hoping Mr. Richardson hadn't noticed. One sideward glance told her his eyes were still pinned on her.

Determination held her steady as she poured and passed the second cup. Their hands brushed, and the slightly rough skin of his work-worn fingers felt far too intimate. She pulled away as if she had touched hot coals and started for the door.

"Come sit with us for a few minutes," Pa said.

She kept walking. "I have to help Ma with supper. You know how she is when I shirk my work." She slipped inside before he could protest.

Soaking in the safety of the cabin, she blew out a deep breath as the door slammed on its hinges behind her. There was something about Mr. Richardson's familiarity that unnerved her. Not to mention the breadth of his wide shoulders over his thick, barrel chest. He was tall. And big.

Too big.

Ma and Aunt May were huddled together in the far corner of the kitchen area as close as an apple to its skin. They stopped their chatter as she reappeared, and Aunt May moved toward her.

"I think you have an admirer, Katie," Aunt May said with a twinkle in her eyes.

Katie's mouth dropped open. "You can't be serious. He's almost as old as Pa."

"Don't look so surprised, girl," Ma said. "Why, with your comely looks, what man wouldn't be interested?"

The all-too-familiar disapproving tone and set of her ma's chin told Katie she was in for a fight if she tried to set her mother straight.

"I'm too young for him. What about the widow Laurie up the road? She'd jump at the chance to marry, with her brood of children and no husband to run the farm."

Ma's lips formed a tight ashen line, and her eyes narrowed. She moved in close, her voice hushed but stern. "You'd do well to remember that there's a very influential man sitting on our humble porch. I will not have you embarrassing us with your haughty ways. All I know at this point is that the conversation concerns you, and you will show nothing but respect. Do you hear me?" She clenched her teeth and wagged her finger so close to Katie's face she could feel the fan of a breeze.

"Fine."

She wouldn't argue. But neither was she going to try to impress any man, especially Mr. Richardson, with whom she had nothing in common. When she did marry, it would be for love. Her heart would skip and melt like it once had for Charles.

CHAPTER 2

*A*s Josiah plodded along, the cadence of his horse's hooves lulled him into deep thought. He leaned forward and patted the mane. "Home, boy." Fireball picked up speed.

He had been hoping, no, expecting, more friendliness from Katherine. After rescuing her a second time, he'd thought she would show more than a rush to get out of his sight. She had even trusted him with a quick hug before. Why the coldness now? By the look on her face, she longed to be anywhere but in his presence.

Truth be told, since that day a month before, he had thought of little else. A thaw had begun inside his cold and protected core. She was in his head, under his skin, and had even wiggled her way into the heart he'd thought was boarded up and closed down. Could this be what people referred to as love at first sight? Did such a thing even exist?

He hoped his offer would be met with her approval. That she would be happy to get out of the cramped quarters they lived in, and help out her family at the same time. Obviously, if she had accepted a job to clean the saloon, things were pretty desperate.

He could save her from such dire circumstances. He could give her a life she'd never dreamed possible, a life most every available girl in town would clamor for.

And since she was the first woman since Georgina who showed enough spunk to catch his attention, why not take the leap? His plan would solve a problem for both of them. She would have a home and future, and he would have a wife and family. Then, all his hard work in building the best horse ranch in the valley would have meaning. His cousin Tom back in Williamsburg didn't fit as his beneficiary. His views on the plight of the black people were decidedly different than Josiah's, and he couldn't risk someone not loving Abe and Delilah as much as he did. No, the legacy he dreamed about passing down had to go to a strapping son, or a brilliant daughter, who would have the opportunity to learn anything his or her little heart desired.

He chuckled. With the likes of a spitfire beauty like Katherine, life would be anything but dull. He had better act fast before some younger man snatched her up. A nagging jab churned in his gut. Was he too old for her? He pressed down the worry.

He *was* falling for the girl, there was little doubt. For the first time in a long time, he allowed a full grin to split free. He had the where-with-all to make it happen, so why shouldn't he?

∽

"*He* what?" Katie paused with the stack of dishes she was removing from the table to the washbasin. She swung around so fast the top plate went flying, landing on the floor with a thud.

"He wants to marry you." Pa eyed her, his expression impossible to read.

"He doesn't even know me." She slammed the stack of dishes down and bent to retrieve the plate.

"He told me you've met a couple times, and he found you both intriguing and interesting."

She straightened with the dish. "Since when do people marry for intrigue or interest?"

"His offer is generous."

"Offer?"

"He would supply a house for our family and work for me farming his land. And, as a wedding gift, he's offered the orchard and all the proceeds, so I can pay him back for the house in time. Do you understand what this means?" The excitement built in his voice. "You would live in luxury. A big house. Maids. Beautiful clothes. Anything your heart desires." His toothy grin grew wide.

"Anything my heart desires except love."

Pa's smile dissolved like sugar in a teacup. His gaze hit the floor.

Katie turned from him. She would rather run down the streets of Lacey Spring naked than get forced into an arranged marriage. Mr. Richardson was too old for her. Had Pa lost his mind? No wonder he'd cleared the cabin of everyone so they could talk privately.

"So, that's why he showed up out of the blue a few days ago all friendly and sure of himself. I wondered what brought the high and mighty Mr. Richardson to our humble door." She intentionally flashed Pa a stormy scowl. "Apparently, I was his reason."

Katie slammed the last stack of dirty dishes into the wooden tub and grabbed the dishrag. She stomped to the table and scrubbed with all her strength. The walls of the cabin room pressed in around her, much like the marriage arrangement her pa had just presented. How could she give him the answer she knew he wanted? She drew deep breaths past the knot in her chest. A loveless marriage couldn't be the only solution to their dire situation. There had to be another way.

19

"You're twenty-one. Don't you want to marry and have a family?"

"I want to marry, but not a stranger. I would've married Charles in a heartbeat." The thought of the strapping young man she had kissed good-bye brought instant tears. She turned away and squeezed her eyes tight, refusing to allow the flow.

"Charles is gone." Pa's warm hand touched her shoulder.

She moved out of his reach. "I know he's gone. But that doesn't mean I'm free of him." Heat filled her cheeks at admitting something so personal. "Besides, you and Ma have always talked about how important both friendship and love are in a marriage. I'll have neither."

"Katie girl…" The crack in his voice pulled at her heart strings. How could she deny him?

"I wouldn't ask if there was any other way." He brushed his hand through his thinning hair as the crevices deepened on his furrowed brow.

"I'll find another job and give you and Ma the money."

He remained silent. His soft brown eyes filled with sadness.

As quickly as the feeble solution surfaced, it dissolved. Room and board in trade for work would be hard to find, but to earn cash would be nearly impossible. Even if she could take care of herself, it wouldn't change the dismal picture for the rest of her family.

Pa lifted his hand toward her. "Can you give this opportunity some thought? He would like to be married by month end—"

"Month end? Opportunity?" Katie threw down the dishrag. "You call this an opportunity?" She sank onto the wooden bench. Her trembling hands pressed her face, covering the tears she could no longer hold back.

The solid strength of Pa's calloused hand squeezed her shoulder. He slid down beside her and placed his good arm tenderly around her shoulders. "I'm so sorry." He drew her head to rest against his wiry frame as if she were seven again. She sank into his embrace. She shuddered and pressed a hand to her mouth to still the scream that lay just below the surface.

Pa pressed a handkerchief into her hand, and she dabbed at her eyes.

"Talk to me. Tell me what you're thinkin'."

"I remember the day they lowered the age to seventeen and the twins enlisted." She gulped back a sob. "They looked so strong and proud straddling their steeds and spouting off about how they'd whip those Yanks into surrender and be back before we had time to miss them. I was so jealous, Pa. I wanted to join in the adventure and hated that I was a woman and had to stay behind."

He squeezed tight.

"When they never came home, I thought the Yankees had taken everything we had. But no." She shook her head. "Their looting and burning took our home next, and now it's demanding my life, my freedom, my opportunity to find someone who loves me." She crumpled against him.

"I'll find another way, Katie girl—"

"There is no other way. You and I both know it." She wrenched free of his arms and pushed up from the bench. "I suppose Ma finds this arrangement more than acceptable? Where is she, anyhow? Thought for sure she'd be in this discussion making sure I agree to this marriage."

"I asked her to stay out of this until I talked to you. The two of you seem to argue about most everything."

"No matter what I do, I'm not good enough."

"It's not you."

"That's what you always say, yet she doesn't treat the others the way she treats me."

He looked away.

Katie stood and crossed to the small window and stared out. The yellow calico curtains fluttered in the breeze. Their cheery color mocked Katie's abysmal plight. All hope of a future with true love was disintegrating as fast and ugly as that Yankee-built fire had destroyed their home.

She squared her shoulders, lifted her head, and turned to her pa with a jut to her chin. "I need a week to decide."

"He's a good man. Otherwise, I wouldn't ask this of you."

Her fists tightened into balls as she stomped back and forth. "Is he? Why do you think he chose me? He knows nothing about me except what all men see and want." She pointed from her face down her body. "I loathe the way I look. It's brought me nothing but sorrow."

His expression crumbled and the lines on his weathered face deepened. Katie rushed to his side. She'd said too much. Again. It wasn't his fault they were homeless.

He stood and held out his arms.

She fell into his warm embrace. "I'm sorry, Pa. I just need a little time to get over the shock."

He soothed a weathered hand down her back. "I understand."

She wanted to help her family, especially Pa, but where would she find the courage to marry a stranger?

"You know how much I love you, don't you?"

Katie nodded, relishing the arms that had always protected her.

"And that will never change. Even if...your answer is no." Pa leaned back and looked straight into her eyes without wavering. "I couldn't bear to see you unhappy." He enfolded her in his arms again and held on for a long moment before pulling back. "I'll leave you alone to think." He walked across the room, and without turning around the door clicked shut behind him.

The silence lasted but a moment. The rest of the family crowded back into the cabin. Her ma, her sisters, Aunt May, and young cousins filled the small room. Two sets of expectant eyes stared intently at Katie—Aunt May and Ma. Their expressions held a question for which she had no answer. A flicker of hope lit Ma's despondent gaze. The weight of her impending decision loomed heavy. With nothing to say and cooped in like a hen surrounded by a gaggle of chicks, she brushed past them. The swish of her homespun dress swirled around her ankles as she rushed out. The hinges groaned and the door slammed shut, much like the future of her dreams.

CHAPTER 3

*K*atie could think more clearly in the fresh air. The hills beckoned and the trees in the copse welcomed her into their private sanctuary. She walked as fast as her dress would allow. Nervous energy coursed through her veins, and she smoothed a hand over the knot that twisted in her stomach. Normally, she would feel guilty about leaving the chores behind, but not today.

"Mrs. Richardson...Mrs. Josiah Richardson." The name slipped miserably from her lips. If she followed through with Pa's plan, she'd be bearing that name within a month.

She screamed into the blue. "Why me?" There was only one plausible reason Mr. Richardson wanted her. The same problem she'd experienced from childhood up—her beauty was her curse. The looks. The stares. The comments about her unusual eye color and natural ringlets. The unwanted touches on her face and hair until she grew older and the boys wanted to touch a whole lot more. Mr. Richardson knew nothing about her, yet he wanted her for his wife. The mere thought sent a shiver up her spine.

The wind moaned a forlorn song through the towering

pines in tune with her brokenness. The one boy who had captured her heart and whose genuine friendship had stirred her soul now lay in the cold, dark earth, never to return, just like her brothers.

Life was cruel and bitter. Finally, the war was over, and the valley was beginning to return to some level of normalcy. Why did Mr. Richardson have to come along and snuff out all hope with his arrogant plan?

How could she be happy saying no to her family? Or worse yet, saying *yes* to Mr. Richardson? Pa's words of pleading haunted her. They were like hands upon her heart slowly wringing life out.

Katie found a log to sit on and turned her face to the midday sun. With a shake of her head and the determined jut of her chin, she chose to turn off the world. She unlaced her tattered walking shoes and kicked her feet free. Her toes danced deliciously through the cool meadow grass. Her eyes fluttered closed, and she soaked up the one small pleasure no one could take from her. She peeled the straw bonnet from her head, which allowed a gentle breeze to tug at the bun. The pins went next. She yanked them from her silky strands and shook the long locks free. Where the warmth of the sun and the fresh air normally melted her difficulties, today the depressing thoughts held firm.

The majestic flight of an eagle caught her eye, and she imagined what it would be like to soar high above the complexities of this life—to escape duty and obligation and fly far away from the weight of this decision. Try as she might, the foreboding pressed in.

She had no freedom. Instead, she was faced with an arrangement set to bring everyone benefit except her. True love didn't factor in. The happy engagement she had always dreamed of would be a one-month ordeal where two men hashed out the details. Her gift would be a loveless marriage. Tears clotted her lashes, and an ache rose in her throat. She fought the urge to cry, too stubborn to give in to the weakness.

She focused on the honeybees that drifted lazily and listened to the birds chirp their happy song. She breathed in the scent of wildflowers and lifted her eyes to the trees stretched heavenward. She gloried in the sun that warmed her face and kissed her skin.

Aunt May's words echoed in her head. "The reason you feel so close to nature is because God uses creation to speak to people."

Katie had scoffed then and was scoffing now. Neither nature nor God was helping. She felt not a whit better. And if God loved her, as Aunt May kept spouting, then why would he allow this to happen?

She huffed out an angry breath. There was no time for whimsical thoughts of God. She had a decision to make. She wouldn't find an answer spelled out in the wispy clouds or hear God speak in the wind. She, Katherine Anne Williams, had to decide her own fate, and she'd do well to keep her mind on the task at hand.

The waning afternoon sun and lengthening shadows made her aware of how long she had sat there. She rose from the log and slipped her shoes on without tying up the laces. With her hair knotted into a sloppy bun she plunked on her bonnet and began the trek home.

The way she saw it, life had thrown her another painful circumstance. Try as she might to process the positives and negatives, the end result would remain the same. She had little choice.

~

*J*osiah hated the days he had to run into town for supplies for the same reason that he stayed clear of church and public gatherings—the women drove him plumb crazy. But, with all the tension in town between the white folk and the newfound freedom of the black slaves, he could no longer safely send Abe. It was no secret the men resented how Josiah had refused to own slaves and had paid his help, but, because of his wealth and standing in the community, few took him on. It made his blood boil just thinking how their ugly behavior poured out when he was not around, all because of the color of Abe's skin.

With the women, he had a whole other problem. They flocked around him like birds to a feeder. It didn't much matter if they were married or not—they loved being seen talking to him. Each trip was made much longer and infinitely more boring than it had to be.

As he plodded down Main Street on his steed, one particular woman with flashing blue eyes came to mind. It had only been a few days since he talked to Jeb, and he couldn't wait to hear her response. He chuckled under his breath. Now, if that girl wanted to steal a portion of his day, he'd be happy to oblige. He'd give her the whole day. He couldn't keep the smile from his face at the thought of her sassy spirit and how interesting life would be living with her.

"Hello, Mr. Richardson." A high pitched shrill pierced the morning air.

Josiah took a deep breath in as he swung from his saddle. He tried to ignore Widow Anne marching across the dusty street. Her large frame and equally generous skirt stirred up quite the dust cloud.

"What brings you into town?" She adjusted the low-cut neckline of her dress, drawing attention to her voluptuous bosom which was giving him more of an eyeful than he wanted. He turned away.

"Just the usual need for supplies. Don't mean to be rude, ma'am, but I best be getting at it." He tipped his hat and hurried up the steps into the Alston General Mercantile. No sooner had he stepped inside than two other ladies headed his direction. He pinned his eyes on Winnie, the owner's wife.

"Is Robert in the back?"

Winnie nodded toward the far curtain and winked at him. "Go on in." From previous conversations, she understood how much he hated getting tied up with boring discussions.

He waltzed right by without making eye contact with the two who called out his name. "Sorry, ladies. I'm in a bit of a hurry today." He threw a quick look over his shoulder.

Happy to have escaped the drivel, he entered the storeroom. "That wife of yours, Robert, is an absolute gem. She could read my mind without—"

There *she* was.

Katherine stood in front of Robert, laughing about something he must have said. They both looked at him when he entered, and Katherine's smile vanished like the sun behind a storm cloud. Just seeing her tied his tongue in knots.

"Josiah, meet my good friend, Katie."

"We've met." They both said.

Katherine caught his stare and looked away. "I've got to run, Robert. Say hi to Winnie for me."

"But you just got here. She'll be most disappointed if—"

"Pa is waiting."

"I'll walk you out." Josiah offered his arm. "I'd like to say hi to your pa anyway." There was nothing he wanted more in that moment than to be with her.

"I'm quite capable of walking myself."

Her words shattered his confidence, and he dropped his arm.

"Carry on with your business." She waved her hand and slipped out the back.

Robert lifted up his hands. "What was that? Katie is not one to be easily run off."

"She must be busy." He couldn't very well tell Robert he had offered marriage. If she didn't agree, he'd be humiliated. And by the way she hightailed it out of there, the chances of her accepting were slim to none.

Robert hit his arm. "Not your usual response from a woman. We're usually trying to help you fight them off." He laughed. "Now you know what us mere mortals face every day."

Josiah offered a weak smile, but the gnawing of uncertainty dug a deeper hole in his gut.

"Sorry, my friend," Robert said. "But Katie has been off limits to everyone since Charles died."

"Charles?"

"They were close friends who would've grown into more. Then the war. He was one of the first to go. She hasn't looked at a man since, and trust me when I say that she's had ample opportunity."

An icy wind blew across the plains of Josiah's heart. The very woman he would love to have spent time with was the only woman who wasn't interested. He'd been counting on her accepting his marriage proposal and had let himself dream, hope, plan. The realization that she may decline his offer brought a wave of loneliness and grief he'd not experienced since Georgina passed away.

The thought of the other available women in the valley caused an immediate yawn. He could not abide the tedious boredom. He would rather be alone.

*K*atie placed the last plate on the table and looked to see what was missing. "Where are the preserves for the pancakes?"

"We're plumb out. With all these kids needing the milk, we don't even have butter. We just had enough to fry the pancakes up." Aunt May threw her hands in the air. "Butter is a scarcity these days. We'll have to make do. Can you call the others? Breakfast is served."

She flipped another pancake in the fry pan, and Katie's stomach growled at the buttery scent wafting her way.

"The boys are in the yard playing, your ma is gathering eggs, and your pa and Uncle John are in the barn. Put a rush on it. This eating for two has me famished." Aunt May laughed as she rubbed the ever-growing mound.

Katie yelled up to the loft. "Come on, sisters. Up and at it. Breakfast is served."

"Well, I could've done that, girl. Thought maybe you'd have a gentler approach."

Katie smiled. "Gentle? Me? You've got the wrong Williams girl." She opened the door. "Jacob, run and tell your Aunt and Uncle that breakfast is on, then y'all get on in here."

Her aunt chuckled. "I love your spunk and your plucky spirit. I shall so miss you."

Katie's voice warbled as she fought back the sting of tears. "So, you assume like the rest that I'll marry Mr. Richardson? You were the one person I thought…"

Her aunt bustled to her side and pulled her into a warm hug. "I'm so sorry, honey. I just meant…"

The door opened and Ma walked in with a basket of eggs. She harrumphed. "What now?" Her crisp, no-nonsense voice held not a smidgeon of warmth.

Katie pulled away and turned from her ma's intense stare. She brushed at the tears.

"We were talking about...the situation," Aunt May confessed.

"It's not a situation, it's a chance of a lifetime." She slammed down the basket of eggs none too gently. "Mr. Richardson is a fine man with an upstanding reputation, and the very fact he'd choose you should have you jumping for joy." She pointed in Katherine's direction. "Furthermore, after all I've done for you, the least you could do ..."

Aunt May touched Ma's arm, jerking her head sideways toward the girls climbing down from the loft. Ma let out a huff but pursed her lips shut.

Katie fought the pain that clawed at her heart. It was not the first time that remark, *after all I've done*, had been thrown in Katie's direction. What exactly had her ma done other than be a mother? And why was she cold and stern with Katie but warm and affectionate with the rest of the family? That familiar ache of somehow not belonging washed through her as she gathered around the table.

To win Ma's approval, she would have to live a lifetime with a man she didn't love.

Ma stomped back and forth, dropping the cutlery and smacking down a plate of flapjacks with such force that Katie jumped.

"Katherine had better get used to the situation and fast. Mr. Richardson is coming for a visit this afternoon, and I expect her to be on her best behavior." She talked loudly enough for the whole household to hear, but directed the conversation to Aunt May. "And if she thinks she's the only one who has suffered the ravages of this war, she can think again. We've all had to make concessions. You don't find me a constant watering pot."

Katie whirled around. Her body shook, and her chest ached. She had to get out of there before she lost control of the tears once again. "I'm standing right here. You don't have to talk as if

I'm not in the room, but I'll gladly vacate." She walked out the door and slammed it shut.

Pa stepped onto the porch from the yard. "I thought breakfast was on."

"I'm not hungry." She marched past him to the barn.

CHAPTER 4

*C*urled up in the loft in a bed of hay, the barn gave her the privacy she needed. She stroked her old cat Tabby, who rubbed up against her. A thick darkness coiled around her soul.

She had grandparents in Richmond. Maybe she could find her way there. But her parents never talked about their life in the city, nor did they have anything to do with her grandparents.

Nothing fit. Every idea she had for escape filtered in, then out. A getaway plan was about as likely as grabbing a handful of mist.

She scooped her cat into her lap. Tabby circled and plopped down. Her purr deepened as Katie smoothed her hand over the soft fur.

The deepest part of her heart spoke the truth. She had no choice because she cared about her family. Mr. Richardson's generous offer was nearly impossible to turn down. Her parents would once again have a home, their independence, and a renewed sense of hope.

She had it within her grasp to give Pa the gift of doing what he loved most—working the rich Shenandoah soil. The thought of him walking proudly out his door able to supply the needs for his family pulled on her heart strings. She could put a smile back on Pa's face, give much-needed room for her sisters to grow, and win Ma's love. What else was there to decide?

Mr. Richardson had offered Pa a house in trade for the small chunk of land her father had owned and farmed. What did he want with Pa's farmland back in Dayton, miles from his ranch in Lacey Spring? She aimed to ask him tonight. If they gave up that land, it would leave her parents nowhere to rebuild if the whole arrangement fell apart.

And why would Mr. Richardson want her? There were other attractive women far more suited to his lifestyle. He was a successful rancher with a large spread who had a solid reputation in the Shenandoah Valley. He could have his choice of any woman. She often overheard talk of the mysterious Josiah, the handsome and wealthy loner who needed love. The other wistful ladies would do anything to get his attention. She was too inexperienced and unsophisticated for the likes of him, and her humble roots were far beneath his station. It made no sense other than that he was out for what every man wanted.

Her stomach flip-flopped. The mere thought of his presence set her nerves on edge. She bit down hard on her lip. The memories of his timely appearance in the woods and then again in the saloon burned vividly in her mind. Instantly, heat rose from her neck to her hairline. She had to hand it to him, though. He'd kept his promise and hadn't spilled the beans to Pa. For that she was grateful.

Her stomach twisted like a washrag. With deep breaths, she worked to calm the knots. She was about to marry a stranger— someone she knew little about. The first time she'd laid eyes on him and his wife had been in Lacey Spring. They'd made a handsome couple. And now she was supposed to be that lady of elegance at his side? Fat chance. He had no idea what he was getting himself into, and he would be sorry. It would serve him right, after pressuring the situation. She was no Georgina.

But as she left the barn, Katie squared her shoulders and lifted her head. She could do this. She had to.

~

*J*osiah took the steps two at a time and rapped on the screen door of the small cabin. It had been one of the longest weeks of his life, since Jeb had told him Katherine wanted a week to think. The invitation could only mean one thing—she had decided. Worry had him on edge, especially after her cold reception in town.

Jeb answered the door and slipped out onto the porch. "Have a seat." He pointed to the nearby chair.

Josiah slid onto a wooden seat too small for his large frame, which creaked under his weight.

"You need to understand one thing," Jeb said. "I will not force her. Katie has a mind of her own. She hasn't told anyone what she's decided, just said she wants to talk to you."

A bead of sweat formed on Josiah's brow, and he swiped it away. Jeb's words could mean only one thing—she was letting him down gently.

"I'll go get her." Jeb opened the door and called for Katherine before coming back to sit across from him.

A moment later, Katherine's regal beauty caught his breath as she glided across the porch with her head held high. Her dress accented the iridescent hue of her eyes, turning them a deep vibrant blue. She settled on a chair, her back as stiff as an over-starched collar. A quick smile came and went but never reached those beautiful eyes.

The clip-clop of his heart beat hope into his soul. He was confident he could win her love if only she would agree to marry him.

She turned to him. "Mr. Richardson, I will accept your arrangement, but I would like to go for a walk so we can talk privately."

His mind spun in crazy circles. Chaotic. Confused. Had she just agreed to marry him?

She waited for his response, but his tongue felt stuck to the roof of his mouth. He swallowed. "Of course." His heart kicked into a gallop, and finally, a wide smile split free. Not what he expected.

She offered a slight curve of her mouth in return.

"Katie girl, are you sure?" Her pa's brows arched.

"It's a sensible plan for our family, but I have a couple of questions I'd like to ask Mr. Richardson privately." Her eyes flicked to the door.

Arrangement. Sensible plan. These were not quite the words he longed to hear, but what did he expect? He'd hardly taken the time to court her. She was right. His decision to secure the marriage was indeed a wise arrangement and a sensible plan.

"I'll tell the women folk to hold the tea. We can visit after you talk."

She stood. "We'll be back shortly. Tell Ma to keep the kettle on." She headed down the porch steps and started up the dusty drive.

Jeb opened the screen door and nodded in Katherine's direction. "You'd better go. One thing you'll learn about Katie is that she's as headstrong as she is kind."

Josiah took the steps two at a time. With the stride of his long legs, he didn't take long to catch up with her. He slowed to match her gait. "What did you want to talk about?"

She shook her head. "Not yet."

One glance back told him why they walked in silence. Her family now congregated on the porch. She wasn't about to have them within hearing range.

"I love the outdoors," he said. "How about you?"

Her eyes lifted to his, and, for the first time, he witnessed a genuine smile.

"Mr. Richardson, it looks like we may have one thing in common after all."

"My name is Josiah."

The smile vanished, and she looked ahead. "I have three questions."

"Only three?"

"Only three that matter right now." The way she said it, she sounded hopeless.

"This is not a death sentence, Katherine. You do have a choice in the matter. If you don't want to marry me—"

"Why do you want that farmland Pa owns in Dayton? What will you do with a piece of land so far from your home?"

He pulled off his hat and raked his hands through his hair. He had to be careful how he answered. The last thing he wanted was to insult her pa. He twirled his hat in his hands before plopping it back on his head.

"I need to know." She stopped walking and grabbed his arm. Even the touch of her fingertips on his shirt set his heart to bucking.

He looked down, and she jerked her hand away. The wind kicked up and tugged at tiny sprigs of hair, working them free of the tight bun. The urge to brush a curl from her face itched beneath his fingertips.

He swallowed hard against the knot forming in his throat. "Most every man wants, more than the air he breathes, to provide for his family. And when that ability is taken from him, it's demoralizing. Your pa had the worst of the war thrust upon him. I can't imagine losing two sons, my home, and my livelihood.

"I traded that property with him so this arrangement"—he tripped over the word she'd used—"wouldn't feel like a handout. Thought maybe, if one of your sisters gets married in the future and needs a head start, we could make it a nice wedding gift. And keep it in your family."

Katherine's chin quivered, and she looked away.

"Does that make sense?"

She nodded. One tear snaked down her cheek.

"Why does it make you sad?" He longed to gather her in his arms and comfort her, but that would only frighten her.

"I'm...surprised. That was most thoughtful of you." She brushed the tear from her cheek with a quick swipe and started walking again. He fell in beside her, waiting for the next two questions.

"Why me? You could have any woman in the valley you want."

He'd been expecting this question. "Why not you?"

"I'll tell you why not me. I'm not cultured or poised. I know nothing about being rich, having servants, or dressing up for dances and dinner parties. I'm a plain, hard-working farm girl."

"And I'm a rancher, and I hate entertaining. We'll make a good team. Besides, I would not call you plain." The compliment set her eyes blazing.

"You're just like the rest. I knew it."

"What does that mean?"

"It doesn't matter."

"Of course, it matters. I can see I've upset you."

Like a mask pulled over her face, all emotion vanished. "I'm fine, Mr. Richardson. Let's turn around now. Ma will have tea and biscuits ready, and I know she's hoping you'll stay for supper."

Josiah wasn't fooled. He'd said something to offend her.

Katherine spun back toward the house, lifted her head high, and picked up speed.

He matched her quick gait. "And the third question?" He was afraid to ask, but more afraid not to.

She laughed as if she didn't have a care in the world. "Do you like cats?"

"Cats?"

"Yes, cats. I have an old cat named Tabby who miraculously survived the Yankee burning, and I'd like to bring her with me."

"I love cats." He didn't even have to feign his enthusiasm.

"Really?" She threw him a sideways glance. For the second time that day, he caught a glimpse of a real smile.

He nodded. "The one pet my mother allowed while growing up was a cat. They bring back fond memories. My barn is home to a number of strays."

"I'll introduce her to you after tea. She lives in the barn."

She hurried them back, and the grim set of her jaw sent doubt nibbling at the edges of his mind. Could he really win her love? Or would she pretend for the sake of her family, much like she was doing at the moment?

CHAPTER 5

*K*atherine hated the nervous tension that filled her during Josiah's weekly visits. But to keep up the façade to her family that she was at peace with her decision, she had to endure his presence.

"He'll be here soon." Pa's chair squeaked as he rocked back and forth. A slight breeze blew across the porch, bringing much needed relief from the heat. "How are you doing, Katie girl? Are you getting to know the man?"

She searched for a way to keep from lying. "Well. It takes time to get to know someone."

"Yes, 'tis true. But the two of you seem to be hitting it off real fine. Love will grow." He leaned forward and patted her knee.

She twisted her fingers in her lap so firmly, her knuckles turned white. Ma and Pa believed what they wanted to believe. The thought of sitting for another afternoon tea, faking pleasure, made her stomach churn.

The urge to do something finally got the better of her, and she pushed to her feet. "When he arrives, tell him I'm in the barn saddling up Uncle John's new horse. I want to go for a ride."

"You can't take that horse."

She glanced back at Pa. "Why not? I can ride most anything."

"Your uncle got it for next to nothing because that horse was mistreated in the war. It's going to take time to simmer that one down. Any little noise, and you'll be bucked right off."

"Bucked off?" Josiah's rich timbre voice interrupted their conversation as he skipped up on the porch.

She hadn't noticed his arrival.

"I left my horse in the shade of the barn. Hope that's all right?"

Pa nodded, then motioned toward her. "Seems Katie wants to get out for a ride, but the one horse we have is—"

"Never mind." Katie threw out her hand. "It was just an idea to do something different."

"That girl really knows how to ride." Pride resonated in Pa's voice.

Josiah smiled. "I know."

"How would you know that?" Pa scratched his head. "We haven't had a horse for her to ride since before the war."

Heat crawled from Katie's neck to her hairline. She was extremely thankful when Josiah didn't answer.

He moved across the porch until he stood beside her chair. "Come on, Katherine. If you want to ride, we shall ride. Fireball is more than big enough for the both of us."

The thought of doubling up with that huge man made her heart pump right out of her chest. "No. I don't need—"

"Come on. We'll ride for a bit together, and then I'll let you take him for a gallop."

She rose to her feet. The thought of a good gallop on his beautiful stallion versus the sheer horror of having him so close... Oh, that was a tough one. She pursed one finger to her lips. "Give me a few minutes to change."

A slow easy smile split free. "Take your time." He eased into the chair she'd just vacated and stretched out his legs in relaxation.

41

How could she have been so stupid? Did she really want to be in such close proximity? She stewed while she changed into her old dress and slipped a pair of cut-off dungarees underneath. After one step into the kitchen, she swung around to reverse her decision.

"Good heavens, what are you up to now?" Ma asked. "Don't you know Josiah is here for a visit?"

That was all it took to make up her mind. Ma's disapproval rankled. "We're going riding."

"In that? You look like—"

"Like what? Like I'm poor? That's because I am poor. It's why I've agreed to marry the man, because we're all poor." She stomped across the kitchen and slammed the screen door behind her.

"Come on, if we're going." She gestured toward Josiah, who smiled in response, which only annoyed her. She looked like a ridiculous rag-a-muffin, and he was acting like he didn't notice.

They walked across the yard in silence. "Front or back?" He pointed to the saddle.

"Front for sure. Then I have the control."

He grinned. "Agreed."

She swung up into the saddle, surprised at the height of the magnificent horse as he pranced beneath her weight. At the slight tug of the reins and a gentle word, the horse settled.

"You do have the touch."

She smiled inwardly at his praise...until he swung up behind her and placed his hands securely around her waist.

Then, fear took over.

"Off we go," he said into her ear. "You have control."

The warmth of his large hands penetrating her muslin gown set her heart to racing. She kicked the flanks of his horse, and they shot ahead.

"Whoa, we're not in a hurry. I rather like sitting this close to you."

She turned and shot him a scowl.

He laughed out loud. "Never seen such a pretty frown."

She ignored him, but her feelings tumbled one over another —from panic to pleasure and everything in between. A slight breeze cooled the heat at the nape of her neck. Dappled sunlight filtered through the overhead trees. The sound of a babbling brook and the cadence of the beautiful stallion stirred an unfettered pocket of joy. She almost forgot her troubles until the arms wrapped around her middle tightened. Then all pleasure faded.

"Head to the creek. We'll stop a bit and give the horse a break and a drink." His breath tickled her ear. "Then you can take him for a gallop. He'll like that."

When they reached the water, she pulled the reins, and the stallion instantly stopped.

Josiah swung from the horse and, with both his hands raised, encircled her waist as she slid down. She tried to control the tremor through her body, but could not. He lowered his head within inches of her lips, and she froze. The longing in his eyes was not difficult to read.

Maybe he recognized her fear, for he pulled away, grabbed the reins, and led the horse to the creek. He removed his hat, dipped both his hands in, and lifted water first to his lips, and then to his hair. The russet-brown color glistened in the light of the sun. "Ah, that feels better. It's a hot one today."

She tried not to stare as he unbuttoned his crisp white shirt halfway down.

"Come on. I know you like the water. At least get your feet wet."

That was all it took for her to peel her boots and stockings free, lift the hem of her skirt, and step into the cool clear water.

He joined her.

A bubble of laughter slipped free.

"What's so funny?"

"Never thought I'd see the high and mighty Mr. Richardson enjoying the simple pleasures of life like wading in a creek."

"That's because you don't know me. If you did, you wouldn't call me high and mighty."

"Yet you want to marry me?" She unpinned the coil at the nape of her neck and flipped her long braid back.

"We'll have a lifetime to remedy that."

He stepped out of the water and pulled on his boots. "I have a great swimming hole on my property where you shall be able to swim to your heart's content."

"Really?"

"Really. Now, are you ready to take Fireball for a gallop?"

She nodded, trying to keep her excitement from showing as she laced up her boots, then swung up on his magnificent steed.

"Do come back for me." He laughed as he leaned against the oak, slid to the grass below, and tilted his hat to shade his face.

At last, she lit out. Now, this was joy. For the first time in a long time, she laughed into the wind. At least two good things would happen when she married Mr. Richardson. She would be able to ride again, and she'd be able to swim.

∼

*T*he household bustled in excited anticipation of the wedding. Katie noticed smiles on her parents' faces for the first time in years. Her sisters chattered excitedly about no longer being crammed together in the loft with their young cousins. Aunt May and Uncle John couldn't help but show a measure of relief, and Katie couldn't blame them.

At every turn, she offered to do jobs that took her as far away from the family as possible. At least when she was alone, she could wipe the pasted happy off her face. The barn was the perfect hideaway. She fed and watered the chickens, hauling water from the nearby pump. Then she raked fresh straw around the stall that belonged to the scrawny bay gelding. Thankfully, he was out in the pasture, being the ornery suspicious type. Would Uncle John ever be able to bring him back to a place of trust? The gelding and she had a lot in common. Pecking at the ground with the rake like a lost chicken looking for its next meal, Katie's mind raced. Only a week until the wedding. Her body broke out in a cold sweat just thinking about it. But who could she confide in? She'd always found it easy to talk to Pa, but this was different. If she spoke the truth, it would steal his joy. And Ma hadn't looked this happy in years. On more than one occasion, she'd given Katie an awkward hug. It had been so long since Katie had experienced that kind of warmth, it served to heighten the deep ache of loneliness.

"God, if you're really in this world like Aunt May believes, why do I feel so alone?" Katie murmured into the dusty rafters of the old barn. As if on cue, the moment she said those words, a shaft of light streamed through a crack in the weathered roof and encircled her. Had the sun peeked out from behind a cloud the moment she prayed? She looked up at the dancing particles of dust that shimmered gold. An odd sensation of warmth enveloped her, like the presence of more was in the barn.

"There you are, sis. Can we go for a walk?" Amelia stood in the doorway.

Katie pulled herself from the quiet moment. "Help me finish gathering the eggs. I kinda got sidetracked. Let's see who can find the most."

"You're on," Amelia said. "Probably be the last time we..." She cut off her words, but tears shimmered in her kind eyes.

"No, you don't, Amelia. Because if you start, I'll start. Let's get the eggs. Ready. Set. Go." Katie threw herself into the task and marveled at the difference between herself and her sister. Amelia was a gentle soul, ladylike, and cautious. Katie was the direct opposite—impulsive, daring, and adventurous.

In a crowd, Amelia was often overlooked. Her straight

brown hair, brown eyes, and pudgy frame with rosy round cheeks blended into the background. She was sturdy and strong, a mirror image of their ma.

From the time Katie was a child, people had oohed and awed about her unusual eye color, her porcelain skin, and her beautiful wavy hair. The remarks had always annoyed Ma. Then, when the curves came and boys buzzed around like bees to honey, Ma insisted she bind up her chest so tightly it hurt, wear dresses one size too big, and keep her hair in a tight bun. Oh, how she had longed to be a boy and have the freedom of her brothers, for she was far more comfortable in a saddle and britches than in the kitchen.

"Done," her sister yelled. "Who cares who got the most? Let's get out into that sunshine."

Katie laughed. "See, that's the difference between us. I was already counting my basket."

Amelia waved her hand. "I'll run the eggs in, and then we'll make our great escape."

Katie waited for her return, and they giggled like they were ten again as they lit out running for the nearby copse of trees. Once safely out of view, they slowed and drew in deep breaths. How desperately she'd needed these moments of abandon.

Amelia threw her arm around Katie's shoulder and gave a quick squeeze. The warmth quelled the deep loneliness that had earlier pressed in. Was it a coincidence that Katie had said that small prayer one moment, and her sister had arrived the next?

They walked in silence, through the trees and up the hillside, each lifting their face to the warmth.

At last, Amelia pulled her to a stop. "You're not all right, are you?"

Katie turned from her sister's perceptive gaze "I'm trying. I truly am." She pointed down over the valley. "We walked quite a long way."

"Don't change the subject. I need to know."

"What's the point of discussing it?"

Amelia's arms encircled Katie's shaking shoulders and she drew her close. "I know you better than that, Sis. Please talk to me."

A lone tear slipped free, and Katie brushed it angrily from her cheek. "I have no choice in the matter. However, Mr. Richardson has no idea what his money is buying." A cold chill spread over her, and she shivered in Amelia's arms. "He can make his plans, but he can't buy my love."

"Let's run away together." Amelia pulled back. With a determined look she raised her head. "Then there'd be enough room at Aunt May's—"

"Don't think I haven't thought about running, but then I think of Pa, and I know what I have to do. Besides Pa would never make me marry Mr. Richardson if I hadn't agreed."

Her sister's big brown eyes filled with tears. They rolled down her cherub cheeks. "But it's not right."

Katie pulled away.

"Surely you don't intend to follow through with this?" Amelia's eyes widened into huge saucers. "Just tell Pa how you feel."

"No, and you have to promise you won't breathe a word. The war taught me one big lesson—life is not fair. At least I'm still alive, whereas Scott and Jonathon gave everything, and they're no longer here to help Pa. I need to do this. Does that make sense?"

Amelia's hands twisted in the folds of her dress as giant tears coursed down her face.

Katie pulled a handkerchief out of the pocket of her calico skirt. "Here." She held out the lace-trimmed rumpled ball.

Amelia took one look. "I'll make do."

Katie giggled. "Goodness, I guess it's been well used of late."

"I can understand why. If I had to marry a man I didn't love, I'd be a mess too."

"I love you, Amelia. And I'm so glad you'll be living next door to me. Mr. Richardson told me that the home he's giving our family is within walking distance. For that, I'm eternally grateful, because we'll still have each other." She placed her hands on each side of her sister's cheeks. "Promise me you won't tell anyone what I shared today? I need you to be that one person I can talk to. It makes this bearable. Can you do that?"

"I promise." An unladylike snort followed as Amelia tried to hold back a sob and talk all at the same time.

They burst into laughter. Katie locked her hand into the crook of Amelia's arm. "We better get back, or Ma will be in a dither."

~

Katie pulled the blackened biscuits from the oven and slammed the pan on the bread board. "Ma, I need your help," she yelled out the window to the porch. She had been determined to master at least one meal before becoming Mrs. Richardson, and what an abysmal failure.

The screen door squeaked and slammed behind Ma as she bustled in.

"It's too late to learn. I'm hopeless." Katie pointed at the pan. "Look at my biscuits, and I'm trying to stir this stew, but the bottom half is sticking to the pot."

"Move it over here." Ma slid the hot pot to the other side of the stove. "Remember, I told you not to cook above the area where you put the wood in. And never add wood just before cooking. The heat from coals is more manageable."

Katie threw her hands in the air. "Too many things to remember." She tried to stir the stew, but it slopped over the edge.

"Gently." Ma's hand rested over hers and slowed the pace.

"That's better." She patted Katie on the shoulder. "You're getting it."

Her gentleness irritated Katie. She had so rarely experienced this side of her mother. It didn't seem fair for her to start now. "Amelia is far more prepared for marriage than I am. She wouldn't be burning a simple stew right now."

"Your sister liked the kitchen. You liked the farm animals, the outdoors, roaming about the countryside with your brothers, more than—"

"Yes, but now I'm expected to be someone I'm not."

"Mr. Richardson has servants—"

"But isn't the lady of the house supposed to manage the household? What do I know about any of that?"

"You're a smart girl. You'll do just fine, and Mr. Richardson will not expect—"

"How do you know what he'll expect?"

"Pa and I had a talk with him, we discussed your limitations."

Katie threw the spoon into the pot, sending a spray of hot liquid onto the floor. "That's embarrassing. The three of you discussing what I can't do. Did you tell him this is your fault? You didn't mind my tomboy look, nor the fact it got me out of your hair. Yet you taught the others to be cultured and ladylike. Even Lucinda, at eight, knows more about being a lady than I do, and little Gracie at five has impeccable manners."

Ma's face crumpled and she stepped back. A heavy sigh slipped from her lips. "I know I failed you."

"No, Ma. You just didn't care." Her voice softened. For years she had struggled with the way ma treated her differently.

"I did care, but you were headstrong, and it was easier to give in than to fight a battle I couldn't win."

"You're forever saying that Lucinda is a spitfire with a throwback to our Irish ancestors. And yet you find the energy to teach her."

The door opened, and the family poured in. Aunt May

laughed. "I kept the troops out of your way while you cooked, and now you have a starving bunch."

"Hope they like charcoal flavored biscuits and burnt stew." Katie took off her apron, threw it on the counter, and marched out the door. With the churning of her emotions, she'd have trouble being civil.

She walked to the fence and looked out at the ornery gelding. He lifted his head and tossed his mane to the wind. With a glare and a snort, he kicked up his hoofs and took off at a run. "Yeah, you got it right," Katie murmured. "Run. I wish I could do the same and never look back."

It wasn't her fault she didn't have the knowledge needed to suit the distinguished man she was about to marry, and it served him right that he was about to get...her. If he'd taken the time to court her like a true gentleman, he would have discovered her deficiencies. But no, he was in such a hurry to marry her, and Ma and Pa were all too agreeable. Their need overrode hers.

And would he have wanted her if she were hard to look at? For years, she'd put up with the leering remarks and the head swiveling gawks from men. Her best defence was to ignore them, but now she was in a predicament she couldn't ignore.

~

*T*he night lay thick around Josiah. He tossed his covers clear of his body and tried to get Katherine out of his head. In a few short days, she would be sleeping by his side. The thought sent adrenaline rushing through his blood and a stab of doubt piercing his mind.

Could he really get her to fall for him? He loved everything about her. Their conversations when he went to visit her each week were insightful and engaging. Her personality was fiery. She wasn't one to bend to his every opinion. He really liked that.

The women in town bored him silly, falling over his every word in agreement.

She challenged him, ignored him, trembled at the mere touch of his hand, and yet he couldn't wait to go back for more. They were worlds apart—in age, in experience, and in social standing—yet his heart knew no barriers. He fell a little more in love every time he visited, even if her aloofness infuriated him.

There was something inside him that longed to protect her. He wanted to show her what a true gentleman was. If only her dire situation offered more time, he would woo her gently rather than rushing the wedding. But after finding her desperate enough to work in the saloon—and not telling her pa —he couldn't risk where her need to help her family's plight would take her. And if he didn't marry her, how would they all survive?

He laughed at the noble twist he'd put on it all, but, truthfully, he had pushed for an immediate wedding for fear she would never look his way and be snatched up by a much younger man. This pint-sized lady full of life and grit made the thought of having a wife, a lover, a life partner once again, burn within him. Katherine would bring purpose to building his horse ranch with sons and daughters to pass it on to. He couldn't let their *arrangement,* as she so bluntly put it, fall through. His heart had bought into the dream and would be crushed.

He rolled over and punched his pillow. She'd loved the ride on his stallion. The way she had come back with her cheeks flushed with color and a smile on her face... Well, he had the power to give her a beautiful horse and a whole lot more. Yes. He was doing what was in her best interest. He was the one man in the valley who could give her a life she never dreamed possible—a life every girl would love.

~

*T*he wedding day dawned bright and beautiful. The early morning rays filtered through the cheery yellow curtains that hung in the window adjacent to the wood stove. Katie had tossed and turned all night. With a sigh, she rolled over one more time on her straw-filled pallet and buried her head under the covers, but sleep would not find her. She envied Amelia, who lay still beside her, drawing in deep restful breaths. All around her, everyone slept.

Katie slid from the bed with care. A shiver produced goosebumps that had nothing to do with the briskness of the morning air. All week, she had been strong, but this past night, her head had ached as if drums were beating close to her temples. Dread sat heavily in her gut. She pulled her threadbare day skirt and plain shirtwaist over her unmentionables. Her warm shawl hung on a hook by the door. All she had to do was pick her way over her sisters and cousins, creep down the ladder without stirring her parents, who slept in the living area, and slip outside. She needed time alone.

She let out a deep breath when she managed to open and close the screen door without the hinges creaking. She tiptoed across the porch and down the stairs, then ran. If she just kept going...

Her lungs screamed by the time she reached the top of the nearby ridge, but the exertion settled some of the nervous tension that flowed through. The sunrise grew and spread over the mist that draped the lower valley like wet cotton, and the cloudless sky opened to depths of enamel blue. The birds dipped and soared overhead, twittering and singing their morning song. The sugar maple trees were starting to turn that brilliant scarlet, and the craggy Massanutten mountain range rose majestically in the background. All was as it should be, except for one small devastating detail. She was about to step into a loveless marriage with a foundation built on nothing more than a rich man's eye for beauty.

Why could men not see past the outward shell? She had always dreamed of finding a man who would care more about her dreams, her fears, her heart, than the way she looked. Today was her wedding day, and the sad realization that the day she'd dreamed of would never come slammed in hard.

She bit down on trembling lips. Unable to stop the pool of tears that once again gathered on her thick lashes, she blinked them away. Their hot salty flow trailed down her cheeks despite the fact that she had promised herself she would cry no more.

With her face set in stone she chose anger instead of sadness.

"God, if you're up there, take this as a promise. I'm going to go through with this fraud of a marriage for my family, but Mr. Richardson shall rue the day he let his eyes take over common decency."

CHAPTER 6

"Where is that girl?"

Katie could hear her ma's disapproving tone clear across the yard.

She swept through the screen door with a jut to her chin. Her capability to express anger without words was a skill she had honed. Was she not entitled to one last morning alone?

"Where have you been?"

She remained silent.

"You've missed breakfast, and we need enough time to get you ready."

"Ma. Stop." Katie threw her hands in the air. "I couldn't eat if I tried, and you'd be the last one I'd expect to encourage I spend time on the way I look. Before Josiah came on the scene, you spent a lifetime demanding the opposite of me."

The room went silent. Even Gracie stopped the chatter to her doll.

Katie dared a look at Ma. She never cried. Even when the twins died, Ma showed little emotion. But there she stood with tears glistening.

Katie had failed to notice the signs of age creeping up. The years of war had taken their toll. The rounded shoulders from years of hard labour, the speckled gray in her bun, the wrinkles around her mouth, collectively told the story. The pain in her dark eyes sent a wave of regret over Katie. She should have kept quiet, but mulling over her plight had brought the hurt close to the surface.

Ma turned and stumbled out of the door, and Pa followed.

"Out. All of you out. We need a few moments of privacy." Aunt May shooed the kids outside and asked Amelia to watch them. She pulled Katie into her arms.

"There, there child," her Aunt May soothed. "Your ma is as prickly as a hedgehog at times, but she loves you."

Katie pulled out of the hug. "Always with me—"

"Yes, I know, but there's unhappiness from the past that gets the best of her at times. It's..." She wrung her hands and turned away.

"It's what, Aunt May? What have I done?"

"It's not you, honey, it's not you at all." She closed her eyes as if in prayer and turned aside for a moment, then lifted her head toward Katherine.

"My brother married your ma, who was way above his humble social standing. Their marriage was not accepted by society, nor her family. Truth is, your mother was once a pampered socialite in Richmond high society. She grew up surrounded by a wealthy family with servants at her beck and call. She was educated, primped, and taught the finer graces of life for one purpose only—to marry well. Then..." A troubled light stole into her eyes.

"Then what?"

"The fact she left Richmond and all that finery to farm with your pa in the Shenandoah Valley is nothing short of a true love story. As to the why your ma never talks about her family or has any contact with them, that's your mother's story. You'll have to discuss that with your parents."

"I've tried a hundred times, and neither of them will talk about it."

"Sadly, some things are better left unsaid. However, this one thing I can assure you—they love you very much."

"I would agree Pa does, but not—"

"Yes, your ma loves you." She placed her hands on Katie's shoulders. "I know she seems overly stern and harsh at times, but trust what I'm saying."

"Am I part of this unhappiness in their past?"

Her aunt's gaze grew wary, then lit up in response. "You were the only part of that sad time that brought joy. But I can't say more." She gave Katie's shoulder one last warm squeeze. "Can you find it in your heart to let your mother treat you special today? She wants so much to give you a nice day. Your disappearance just flustered her well laid plans."

Katie fought back the tears. "Go get her, Aunt May, and tell her I'm sorry."

Her aunt turned to leave, but stopped short of the door and whirled around. "You may not think so, but we all understand and appreciate the sacrifice you're making for your family today. And although you can't see it now, I've been praying up a storm, and, in that deepest part of my soul, I believe you and Josiah will find love."

Katie looked away. She was not about to believe that fairy tale.

~

The dress Mr. Richardson had dropped off earlier in the week, which Katie had not had the stomach to look at, now hung over Ma's arm. Huge butterflies cartwheeled in Katie's stomach.

Shooing everyone else out of the small bedroom, Ma shut the door firmly behind them. She laid the dress with care on the bed and turned toward Katie.

"Katherine—"

"Ma—"

They both spoke at the same time. Katie waved at her mother to go first.

"I'm sorry for my snappy ways. I love you very much, and want to make this day special." She moved forward and drew Katie into a rare hug. Katie soaked up the warmth.

"I'm sorry, too. This whole thing is..." Katie bit off her words. There was no point.

"Let's get you dressed," Ma said, pulling back. "You'll look as beautiful as that bouquet Jeanette created for you. Aunt May had some late blooming pink and cream roses and you should see what she did. That girl has an eye for arranging."

Clucking in satisfaction, she smoothed her hands over the creamy-white gown. "Why, that Mr. Richardson must have paid a pretty penny for this. I know he made a trip to Harrisonburg for the gown, but with supplies being what they are these days, I'm not sure how he found one so lovely."

Her ma's eyes danced in delight. "Just look at all this crinoline, and the layers of material in this petticoat." She ran her fingers up and down and lifted each piece for inspection. "You even have a new corset."

A faraway look entered her eyes as she held the soft material up to her cheeks. "If there is one thing I truly miss, Katherine, it's the feel of fine silk next to my skin. And I know my fabrics. This one is divine, absolutely divine." Her face beamed, making Katie realize how seldom her ma smiled. She looked twenty years younger. "I've made something for you."

Katie straightened. It was a rare thing to receive a gift from her mother. A slender vine of hope curled around the edges of her hurting heart. Could it be that she was wrong, that her ma cared more than she understood?

Ma turned away. "Don't peek while I lay them out."

Katie closed her eyes. The squeak of the dresser drawer opened, and the rustle of material piqued Katie's interest.

"All right. You can look."

She opened her eyes to a beautiful dressing gown, a camisole, and a set of lace trimmed unmentionables that lay spread out on the bed. "Oh, Ma, when? How? I was so embarrassed at the thought of him seeing the state of my—"

"A lot of stolen hours here, there, and everywhere, and the fact that you didn't mind the outdoor work helped a lot too. But to find enough material to sew this for you, let me tell you, that was a feat. However, I wasn't going to have my girl in anything less on such a special day." Ma's face lit up. "And I forgot how much fun it was to keep a surprise."

Katie picked up the soft cotton chemise and beautiful drawstring drawers trimmed in lace. She smiled and went behind the dressing screen to change. "What's next?" she asked as she stepped out.

"The crinoline hoop skirt." Ma already had it in her hands. They both laughed as they struggled to manage the huge bell shape in such tight quarters.

"Ma, if this is what the wealthy have to put up with every day, count me out. I much prefer my wrapper and apron."

"This is only for special occasions, and just wait before you make your final decision on the matter. They do make a dress look stunning."

Ma slid the dress over Katie's head, and the silk fell in a soft puddle around the hoop. She secured the many tiny buttons up the back and straightened the bow. Katie ran her hands down her sides to her waist, and, wonder of wonders, it was the perfect fit.

"How would he have known the size?"

"He asked me the day you accepted his proposal. I never saw a man so eager to buy a dress. I guessed about two sizes smaller than you usually wear, as you tend to wear things loose."

Katie held her tongue. There was no point in reminding her ma that long ago she had been the one who insisted on that practice.

"But isn't it the custom for the bride's family to—?"

"He knew we couldn't afford such a luxury. He insisted. You should've seen his smile when I finally agreed. He asked about your likes and dislikes, and, when I explained that you had not had much opportunity for finery, he took it upon himself to pick this out. Doesn't he have wonderful taste?"

Katie ran her hands over the gorgeous material that flared at the waist. Her fingers couldn't get enough of the softness.

"Look in the mirror."

Katie's breath caught at her reflection. "It's beautiful."

Ma laughed. "But it's you who make it exquisite."

Katie turned from side to side. Her full bosom filled the form-fitting bodice to perfection, the high neckline trimmed in lace, modestly covering what she had tried to hide for years. Intricately embroidered flowers with tiny seed pearls were hand sown onto the gown from the waist, over the bodice and shoulders, and around to a row of delicate buttons that ran down the back. Cinched in on her tiny waist, the skirt cascaded into three lace flounces with fluted ruffles at the bottom. The short-puffed sleeve would be ideal for the warm September day.

"It is perfect." But the words caught in her throat.

"Why do you say it like that?"

"I just wish he had put as much effort into getting to know me as he did in buying this dress."

"He did visit."

"A few visits hardly develop a relationship ready for marriage."

Ma's eyes clouded over. "Come, let's do your hair," she said with a forced gaiety in her voice. "When Josiah dropped off the dress, he asked if your hair could be left down. Hope that's all right with you."

"Don't much care." Katie tried to keep the despondency from her voice. He was already making demands.

Ma just kept talking. "The others will be going crazy waiting to see you, but I want to finish so they get the full effect."

A trickle of sweat ran down Katie's spine. She cared about only one question, but having never been close to her ma, it would not be easy to ask. Ma was almost done working with her thick tresses and still she had not voiced her concern. Better to ask Ma rather than leave it up to him.

"Your hair is so full. It looks so beautiful cascading down. And look at the pearls in the crown of this veil. I'm sure they're real." Ma stood back after putting the veil in place. "Oh my, you look so lovely. Mr. Richardson is going to absolutely love—"

"What do I do...you know...tonight?" Heat swallowed her face as she blurted out the words. "He's not even kissed me yet, and I'm..."

Ma's hands stilled upon her head. A weighted silence filled the room.

"Don't worry, Katherine, he'll know. After all, he's been married before. Now don't concern yourself too much, it's just one of those wifely duties we women endure to procreate."

"Endure?" A quiver of panic edged up her throat. How bad would it be?

Ma moved from behind and looked into Katie's eyes. A softness radiated. "To be honest, I was repeating what was told to me. Truly, it's as natural as breathing. You'll learn together and, well, it will even be quite enjoyable." A grin tickled her ma's mouth.

"Really?"

"There, there." She patted Katie's shoulders. "I'm going to

turn fifty shades of red if we keep discussing this, and so are you."

They both laughed, and Katie allowed some of her nervous tension out.

"Come." Ma pulled Katie to her feet. The hoop skirt made it difficult to move in the tight quarters, but she turned Katie toward the mirror with care.

"You look breathtaking, my girl, as every bride should. Do you like your hair?"

Katie gasped at what she saw. A total stranger stared back. Who was this lovely creature, so cultured and beautiful? She wore dainty matching gloves that covered her small work-worn hands and a form-fitting dress that accented her every curve.

She turned from side to side. The white veil stood out against the thick black hair twisted into elegant curls, kissing the side of her face. It cascaded free and wavy down her back. How different from the tight bun she typically wore.

"Are you pleased?"

"Ma, it's beautiful, but it's not me."

"Yes, Katherine, it is you. I've done you a great disservice to never let you see this side of who you are." Sadness stole into Ma's eyes. She sniffed and shook it off. "Let's go show the family."

Katie allowed Ma to lead her into the kitchen, where the family waited.

Gasps filled the room as they stepped through the doorway.

Gracie was the first to speak. "Katie's a princess, Mama."

"Yes, she is," Ma said.

Pa's eyes filled with tears as he walked over to engulf Katie in a warm hug. "My beautiful daughter."

Katie fought back the sting of tears and blinked hard.

"Now, Jeb," Aunt May scolded. "You can't make the bride cry after all the work Doris has done to get her ready. We have an hour ride to the church and forty-five minutes to make it on time." She broke up the hug and propelled Katie toward the door.

~

*K*atie usually loved the small town of Lacey Spring, but not today. News had traveled fast that Mr. Richardson had invited the whole community to the wedding and an outdoor picnic after. Word was that most everyone was up for a celebration after so much sadness during the war. Sure enough, as Katie and her family rolled up to the church, the area brimmed with hitched horses and buggies. Organ music floated out from the wide-open doors. Her family filed in, except for Pa, who waited outside with her.

Katie set her mind on not focusing. When her cue came, she held her head high and walked down the aisle on Pa's arm. With a deep breath, she looked straight past the large man in a suit smiling her way, past the preacher with his Bible in hand, and toward the stained-glass cross behind them both. She kept her eyes fixed there until the preacher said, "The ring please."

Mr. Richardson reached for her hand and pulled her to face him. They stood sideways, with the church packed to capacity looking on. Her heart raced, and her cheeks blazed hot. Everything within her wanted to run, run, run.

He lifted her trembling hand and did the oddest thing. Instead of slipping only her ring finger from the glove through the secret opening made for that purpose, he slowly, methodically, removed the dainty glove. Her first reaction was to pull away, to hide the rough skin that didn't match her pretty covering. But he held on with a firm, yet tender, grasp. He removed the ring from his pocket and slipped it on her bare finger. Then, he turned her palm upward and, with the light touch of his lips, he kissed each calloused finger.

A fluttery sensation bubbled in the pit of her stomach as he bent low so that only she could hear his words. "I never want anything to come between us, Katherine, not even a dainty white glove."

She couldn't stop her eyes from rounding, but she had no idea how to respond.

"Katherine, your ring," the pastor gently prodded.

She turned to take the plain band from her pa, then fumbled to push the ring on Josiah's finger. Heat flooded in and burnt her cheeks. His hands were large, warm, and too intimate. Her fingers took on a tremble. He came to her rescue, pushed the ring the rest of the way onto his finger, and placed his hands over hers as if to pray.

"Now, that's a great way to start a marriage, folks. I was going to leave the prayer to the end, but I think the couple is ready."

Everyone chuckled and bowed their heads.

The pastor droned on as if loving the sound of his own voice, but it gave Katie a much-needed moment to collect her wits. Until Mr. Richardson reached down and picked up her hands in his. The warmth of his skin penetrated the ice cold of hers, and, when the preacher was done praying, Mr. Richardson stepped closer.

"You may kiss the bride."

A shudder ran down Katie's spine, despite her best effort to remain stoic.

He gathered her in his arms and slowly pivoted his large back toward the crowd. He lowered his head toward her but at the last moment dropped the kiss on her cheek. The congregation hooped and hollered, none the wiser that the kiss had not met its mark. He turned to face the joyous group, keeping an arm planted around her waist. "I present to you my wife, Mrs. Katherine Richardson."

Whistles and claps filled the room and bounced off the rafters.

When he lifted his hand to the crowd, they stilled. "We invite you to stay for some good food and music, but please don't be disappointed when I whisk my beautiful bride away. We won't be staying long."

He whispered into her ear. "Smile. I won't drag this out. The least we can do is give the community a day of celebration."

She fisted her hands until her fingernails bit into the flesh. "I'll do it for my family, like I've done everything else so far today. Just don't leave me to deal with the crowds."

The creases in his forehead bunched, but he said nothing. His arm around her waist nudged her down the aisle and into the late afternoon sun.

Like a true gentleman, he stayed at her side. With a hand on the small of her back, he guided her from group to group and did most of the talking. She did most of the smiling. She worked hard to pretend all was right in her world, but not for much longer.

She didn't know how much longer she could keep the smile pasted in place when Josiah leaned down and said, "We're going to leave soon. Would you like to eat anything before we go? The church ladies put on quite the spread."

Katie looked at the long table laden with food in the shade of the sprawling oak. The people gathered around had plates piled high. Her stomach lurched. She shook her head. "You go ahead. I need to find Ma and Aunt May."

When she returned with her wedding dress minus the hoop skirt, he raised one brow and smiled. He didn't say a word, but popped the last forkful of apple pie into his mouth with a twitch to his lips.

Was he laughing at her?

She lifted her head with her nose to the sky. "A girl has to be comfortable, and the ride to the church with all this paraphernalia was torture. Glad I've been as poor as a church mouse if this is what the rich have to put up with."

He laughed full out, so loudly heads turned toward them.

A heated flush filled her cheeks. "Can we go?"

His lips curved into a wide grin, and he lifted his eyebrows. "I thought you'd never ask."

CHAPTER 7

*W*ell-wishes, hoots, and hollers followed the couple as they slipped into the awaiting carriage. Mr. Richardson spoke kindly to his driver, and they were off.

Katie lifted the curtain to sneak one more peek at her family. She waved with the last bit of happy pasted on her face.

The minute she dropped the curtain, she dropped the smile. Curiosity got the best of her, and she did a quick appraisal of the inside.

"Like it?" he asked.

"Fancy rig," was all she would give him. The padded seats were softer than anything she had ever sat on before. The frilly lace curtains that covered the small window filtered the afternoon sunshine. She longed for the day to end so she could fall into a deep sleep and shut off this nightmare. And then she thought about what the night ahead included. Her hands shook, so she stitched them together in a firm clasp on her lap.

The delicate wisp of the lacy curtains fluttering in the breeze annoyed her. She squeezed her eyes shut to block out the sunshine, the simple beauty of lace, and him. The trickle of fear became a torrent. She was glad for the bumpy road, hoping he would not pick up on the shudder that worked its way from tip to toe.

"I do believe you'll be happy with your new home, Katherine."

She refused to look at him, but he kept talking.

"The only reason it still stands is that the Yankees used it for their headquarters. For that mercy, I'm thankful. At least I didn't have to come back and rebuild as so many did. It's not yet restored to its former beauty, but nevertheless, I think you'll be pleasantly surprised."

Katie turned toward the window and away from him. "Hmmm."

"There's a lot of work to be done, but it's hard to find good help with so many of the young men gone." There was a choke in his voice. "I'm looking forward to working with your pa. It'll be nice to have another experienced man around the property."

Katie's emotions vacillated from fear of this stranger to red hot anger at her forced circumstances. She fought to gain control, but a taste of bitterness worked its way up from the pit of her stomach and into her throat. Words blurted out.

"It looks like the Yankees did you more than one small mercy, now didn't they, Mr. Richardson?" She flashed him an angry scowl on purpose.

His eyes widened, but held a spark of humor. "Well, well she speaks. I was beginning to think I'd married a mute."

"A mute, Mr. Richardson? You have no idea who you married."

"Please call me Josiah, then you may explain that remark." He let out a soft chuckle. "I must admit that my interest is more than a little piqued."

She couldn't believe he had the nerve to laugh. Her hands balled into fists, and her voice turned edgy.

"I'm just another one of those small mercies the Yankees afforded you, Mr. Richardson." She purposely used his last name. "Without that blasted war and their burning rampage, you wouldn't have had the leverage needed to force my hand in marriage."

The smile that had been pulling at the side of his mouth vanished. Hurt flashed in his eyes, turning them gunmetal gray.

She'd said too much. However, had he taken the time to get to know her, he would've known that her temper got away from her on many an occasion, and she was never short on opinions.

"I was not aware how you felt. The least you could have done was to be honest *before* the wedding. Hmm?"

She dared not look at him. He was right, but her family's need had silenced her.

"After all, I did visit, did I not?" His voice no longer held laughter. "Katherine, please look at me."

She shifted in her seat and raised her chin before meeting his stare head on.

"I'm not some young buck wet behind the ears. I anticipated that we would need to take time to get to know each other before this would grow into a loving relationship."

His eyes pierced right through her, but she was determined to not turn away like a coward.

"However, when your father told me that he wouldn't agree to the match without your permission, I assumed that we were both in agreement. Was I wrong?"

Katie melted under his burning gaze. She shrank into the padded seat and looked down at her hands. Best to be honest.

She lifted her head. "I shoot with a straight arrow, Mr. Richardson. I agreed to the arrangement to help my family, and I intend to fulfill my end of the bargain." Her face flushed with heat at the thought of what that agreement would include. "I'll be your wife, bear your children, and help out in any way I can, but I will not promise love. I cannot promise love." Her gaze dropped to the ring on her finger. She fidgeted under his stare and circled the ring around and around. "Love was never part of this deal."

~

*S*ilence filled the carriage after his bride's harsh words. Thick. Oppressive. Josiah could not believe the pickle he'd gotten himself into.

That incident in the woods had started this insanity. His overwhelming sense of protectiveness toward her had kicked in way back. Then, to find her working in a saloon in the presence of such unsavory characters... That sent his mind on a trip from which he had never returned.

The pluck of that girl was something special, something that bridged the gap between boredom and interest, so different from what the other women had to offer. She was someone he could see himself wanting to spend time with at the end of the day. The fact that her beauty was unparalleled could not be denied, but that brought out his need to protect, to provide, to propose. From honor to need, his motivation and thoughts tossed back and forth like a rowboat on a stormy sea.

He could not explain why his feelings had intensified and somehow had become as permanent as the skin on his bones. He hated the power his emotions had over him, and yet loved them, for he once again felt alive.

He'd chalked up her shy demeanor when he'd visited to inexperience. His ego had convinced him that she would react the same with any suitor. Little did he realize the resentment that flowed beneath the surface and the bitterness that brewed. After weathering years of loneliness, here he was wanting a life with someone who may never want a life with him.

~

*H*alf of her wished he would start chatting again, but the other half surmised it was better they'd had this discussion from the start rather than somewhere down the line. She comforted herself with the fact that, in their agreement, she didn't owe him anything more than she was prepared to give. The truth remained the truth. If he had wanted to marry for love, he should have picked someone in love with him.

"Look outside, Katherine." All humor had leached from his deep voice. His words sounded like a command. "I want you to see your new home. Because, if you thought your snappish words were a way out for you, you can think again. When I make a commitment, I keep it. I made one not only to you, but to your family as well."

A dart of guilt pierced her heart at the reminder about her family, the sole reason she had agreed to the arrangement. In her anger, she had forgotten, and yet he had remembered. One hand bunched the silk of her dress into a knot while the other pulled the curtain aside.

The carriage stopped as the driver hopped from his seat and opened the gate supported by two brick pillars. *Richardson* was engraved in a brass plate imbedded in one of the pillars. Richardson. The name of the richest man in town. Now, her name. The carriage lurched forward through the gate and stopped. This time, Mr. Richardson was out before the driver could dismount.

"I've got it, Abe."

This humble act of closing the gate both confused her and softened her heart. He jumped back in as if it was a normal occurrence. The rich and haughty did not treat their black hired help like equals, and yet Mr. Richardson did. He was not one of the many angry Southerners who resented having to pay their colored help or set them free.

The long road bedded with fine gravel curved up to a large

stone mansion perched on a knoll. A row of sturdy evenly spaced maples lined both sides, their leaves burnished a brilliant red. Captivated by the enormity of the house, she could not stop her mouth from dropping open. The stately two-story building made of gray brick was accented with smooth river rock at its base. The white colonnaded portico that skirted the base was like welcoming outstretched arms—to the rich, and the very rich.

"This is your home?"

"This is *our* home."

"You should've brought me here before we married." She shot him an accusing look.

"Why? That would have made a difference?"

"It would have made me realize that I will never, never be suitable." Her head swooned, and a wash of weakness flooded her. "This will not do. I should never have agreed. Take me home at once."

"You are home, Katherine."

"Take me back to my aunt's cabin." Her chest constricted, and tight bands of tension pressed in. "I...I don't feel well." She pressed both hands to her temples. Her stomach lurched and growled.

"What have you eaten today? You ate nothing after the service."

She shook her head, trying to get rid of the fuzziness. "I've had..." She couldn't think of anything. Had she really gone all day without food?

"Just as I thought." He exited his side of the carriage and hurried around to open her door.

"Come now, you'll feel much better after we get some food into you." He held out his hand to steady her as she climbed from the carriage, and he kept an arm tightly around her waist when she got her feet on the ground.

With a sweep of her eyes, she took in the slate roof and five chimneys, smoke curling from three. A quick look to the east assured her that the Massanutten Mountain range still loomed there, rugged and unchanging. Everything else around her felt surreal and disjointed. The lengthening shadows warned that the sun was about to slip behind the distant ridge, and darkness would soon hide that only familiar landmark. She was entering a world completely foreign to her. A chill climbed the ladder of her spine. Against her will, she sagged into his shoulder.

He pulled her close and, with no more fight than a kitten, she allowed the strength of his body to steady her. His warmth permeated the cold that seeped clear through to the bone.

"Abe, tell Delilah I'll look after supper, and introductions will be made in the morning." He nodded in Katie's direction. "This lady needs food now."

Abe came around to their side of the carriage and smiled at them both. A kindness rested there. "You just get your missus whatever she be needing."

Mr. Richardson propelled Katie up the steps and through the grand doorway. The entrance, cast in the dim late afternoon light, opened to a sweeping staircase and balconied upper floor. Without giving her time for further inspection, he drew her down a hall into the kitchen.

"Sit, my dear. Sit." He gently pressed her into a chair beside a scarred wooden table and busied himself at the stove.

Katie gazed around in awe. This one room was almost as big as her aunt and uncle's whole cabin, but the warmth from the crackling fireplace and the old beaten up table somehow brought comfort.

She stood. "I should help." The sudden movement made her head spin, and she swayed against the table.

He was at her side in seconds. "I have it under control. I'll get you some fruit. It seems to pick me up when I've been in the fields too long and not made time to eat."

She settled back down, and he shrugged out of his formal

jacket and rolled up his sleeves. The stark white shirt pulled tight across his broad shoulders and tapered to a lean waist. She averted her eyes to the long row of cooking utensils hanging from a shelf. She shivered at the thought of what that large body would feel like up close.

Distracted by her own weighty thoughts, she jumped when he placed a plate before her.

"Eat."

Slices of apple and a clump of grapes sat beside a thick wedge of cheese and a hunk of ham on a hearty slice of fresh bread. Her stomach growled and made her realize how hungry she was.

"Thank you," she said. "I guess I should've taken better care. I haven't felt that hungry as of late."

He arched one eyebrow before walking to the wood stove. He lifted the lid off a bubbling pot, and a heavenly waft of meat and vegetables filled the room. "Ah, you haven't lived until you've tried Delilah's stew."

Katie nibbled on the fruit and took bites of bread and cheese. She was mesmerized by the fact that Mr. Richardson seemed as comfortable in the kitchen as he did on his horse. He swallowed up the room with his presence. Her eyes followed him as he stirred the stew, gathered the bowls, and ladled out two steaming servings.

While he was preoccupied, she took the opportunity to stare. His skin, well-bronzed from the summer sun, indicated that he worked out of doors. Gray hair speckled his temples, giving him a distinguished, mature look. He did not have the facial creases and weathered look her pa had, which left her wondering how old he was.

"Do I pass inspection?" he asked.

Heat flushed from her neck up to her hairline as he turned toward her with two generous bowls of stew. "How old are you, Mr. Richardson?"

He set one of the bowls before her. "Call me by my name and I'll answer."

With some food now in her stomach, Katie had a renewed sense of spunk. "I do believe your name is Mr. Richardson, is it not?"

"To you, Katherine, as my wife"—he drew out the last word and pulled up a chair across from her and sat—"I'm Josiah, and I will not respond to anything else. You can decide if this is going to be easy or hard." He winked and picked up his spoon.

Katie thought for a moment, then smirked at a most ingenious idea. "Fine. Josiah it is. However, I prefer Katie to Katherine. I've been called Katie by those close to me all my life." She counted on the formal, socially proper Mr. Richardson not approving of such informality. Maybe this would make him as uncomfortable as she was.

He studied her before lowering his spoon back into the bowl. A smile split across his face. "Now, that's encouraging."

"What?"

He leaned back in his chair. "You said everyone who is close to you calls you that. That opens up a world of possibilities. I think I'll take it a step further and have a nickname for you —Kat."

Knots tightened in her shoulders as she forced herself to sit up straight and pretend his banter did not irritate her.

"I quite think Kat suits you," he said. "Much like the mountain lion. Beautiful, yet ever so dangerous."

She dropped her head and shoveled her stew in as if it did not bother her in the least that he had outsmarted her.

"Now, back to your original question, because I'm sure I heard a Josiah in there somewhere. I expected this question on that day you said you would marry me and wanted to ask three questions, but you were more interested in whether I liked cats. Today, my love for Kats grew exponentially." He chuckled.

She could not resist shooting him a glare.

"I'm thirty-five, almost thirty-six. That makes me fourteen years your senior. What do you think of that?"

She ignored him and finished every bit of her stew, the fruit, bread, and cheese. For the first time in over a month, she ate slowly, savoring every bite. How, on the day when she should have been the most nervous, had she found her appetite? Most likely, it was the fact that she was in no hurry to sample what lay beyond the kitchen door.

"What, has the Kat got your tongue?"

She tried to hold back a grin, then a giggle slipped out and she was laughing. "You win, Josiah. Enough of the cat jokes."

His laughter filled the room. "And?"

"And you don't want to know what I think about you being only seven years younger than my pa."

The laughter left his eyes, and his jaw muscles tightened.

Once again, she'd said too much. "Ma always told me to swallow my thoughts before they reach my lips, but I never quite mastered that one."

An awkward silent moment followed as he stared past her and ran his fingers over his mustache and through his neatly trimmed beard. "And my ma said, 'Don't ask if you don't want to know.' I'll have to keep that in mind around you." He stretched and sat up straight. "I guess it's about time to retire—"

"What, no dessert?"

His smoky-gray eyes held an emotion she could not quite figure. He pushed the chair back from the table and spread his long legs out in front of him. His huge frame dwarfed the chair he leaned back on, making her regret her hasty words about his old age. He looked anything but old and far from the father figure she had just likened him to.

"You have room for more food? Or are you trying to stall from your end of our bargain?"

Her heart hammered inside her chest, but she lifted her chin with determination. "Of course, I would like dessert."

He rose and sauntered to the sideboard, lifted a towel, and pulled out a freshly baked pie. He returned with a generous piece and slid it in her direction.

"Won't you join me?"

He cracked a smile. "Dessert for you, then dessert for me."

She gasped and shoved a piece of pie into her mouth.

"Just joking, Kat, relax." He eased back onto the kitchen chair and watched her finish every bite. By the time she was done, her corset cut into her flesh, and her stomach turned. She picked up the cloth napkin, dabbed at her mouth, and lowered it to her lap where she twisted it tighter and tighter in her hands.

"All done? Or would you like another piece?"

She shook her head, and he rose, lit the candle in the portable dish, and picked it up. The day was gone and the night upon them.

With an outstretched hand, he beckoned her. "Come, my little Kat. You're well fed, so let's get you settled. I won't bother showing you the house tonight. There will be ample time in the morning."

He waited for her to stand.

She was too proud to back down, remembering her earlier words and how she intended to live up to her end of the bargain. She stood with her spine straight and her chin up and placed her hand into his. A quiver took to her fingers as his large hand engulfed hers.

She wished with all that was within her that her ma had told her more of what to expect than just that he would know what to do. Such little comfort considering he couldn't even get her name right.

CHAPTER 8

$\mathcal{H}$e walked hand in hand with his trembling wife and almost laughed out loud. It was either that or scream. How could he have made such a foolish mistake? He had always considered himself a rather smart man, but today had topped the scale of foolhardy behavior—a day he had envisioned turning out so differently. Most women wanted to jump in his arms. Not this one.

He'd been prepared to take his time to get to know her before suggesting anything physical. But the last thing he wanted was for this jittery butterfly to flit away in search of an annulment because he hadn't consummated the marriage. He had stood at the altar and had only relaxed after she said, *I do.* He wasn't about to lose her now.

But oh, the blow to his ego. She viewed him as someone old enough to be her father, and the years were not something he could erase. He had never had to beg for any woman's affection, nor take what was not happily returned, but what choice did he have?

"Here we are." He swung open the door at the top of the

steps, and with a gentle press to the small of her back, propelled her inside.

~

*A*n elaborately carved canopied bed covered in a blanket of deep green and burgundy dominated the room. There was no doubt they were in his bedroom. Katie scanned the spacious area. Matching carved mahogany furniture, including two upholstered wingback chairs that sat on either side of the glowing fireplace. His wardrobe door was open, and she saw his clothes hanging within. That personal and intimate view brought heat surging into her cheeks. She cast her eyes to the floor.

"This area rug is beautiful," she said, desperate to still the twist and turn of her stomach. "And look at these curtains. What are they made of?" She stepped forward enough to cause his hand to fall from the curve of her back, then kept on walking toward the window. She lifted the heavy material in her hand and pretended to know her fabrics well enough to surmise the type.

He came up behind her, and the heat of his body radiated as he reached on both sides and drew the curtains shut. A blanket of intimacy enveloped them. His arms lowered slowly around her, and she shivered. He held her for a moment, easing her back against his chest.

"Relax, my dear." He breathed the words in her ear.

I'm not your dear. A flash of the diamond on her finger told her otherwise.

She held her breath as he lifted her long hair to one side and dropped a featherlight kiss on the back of her neck. His whiskers tickled her skin, and a trembling she could not control came over her.

He stepped away. "Come."

She turned as he moved across the room to a side door and swung it wide.

"This is your room. It will afford you some privacy on those days you desire to be alone."

Did he not know that every day, that room would be her choice? But her courage had not found feet, and she stood rigid and unmoving.

"Come, my little Kat. You'll like it." He disappeared into the room, and she forced herself to follow.

The first thing she noticed was her trunk with the few personal items she owned placed at the foot of a beautiful bed. That small familiarity brought a spike of comfort. She lifted her eyes to see a fresh bouquet of roses on the dresser. Someone had taken great care to prepare the room and even hang her sparse selection of clothing in the oversized wardrobe. The soft pink-flowered wallpaper drew her the rest of the way into the room, and she turned in a slow circle to take it in.

A gasp slipped from her lips. "Oh, my."

Shadows flickered from the glowing candle and fire crackling in the hearth. Warmth replaced the bite of anxiety that had been nibbling at her stomach all day. Soft light danced on the walls and reflected off the largest full-length mirror Katie had ever laid eyes on. She ran her hand down the ornately framed stand and caught his reflection smiling back.

She gave him a shaky smile before moving to the bright flowered pitcher and matching bowl, which rested on the washstand. She picked it up and held it next to the wall. "It matches the wallpaper. How pretty." She replaced it with care and ran her fingertips over the stack of fresh linen. "This is all for me?" she asked, turning to look at him.

"All for you." His face beamed.

Tears sprang to her eyes, and she blinked against them. "I've never had my own bed, much less my own room."

"I wanted you to have a place you could call all your own.

And you can change anything you like. The colors or fabrics or whatever you women like to fuss about. In other words, whatever your heart desires, you can have."

"Mr. Rich...I mean Josiah, this room is already perfect." She spun around with her hands outstretched. "More than any girl needs."

"You're not just any girl, Katherine, you're Mrs. Richardson, and you will grow to understand that affords you some of life's finer things. But you must be so tired. We've both had an exhausting day. It's time I let you unwind and settle in for the night."

He moved close. His gunmetal gray eyes grew smoky and flashed with something Katie could not understand. His jaw tightened, then relaxed. He lifted both her hands and gently stroked the insides of her wrists with his thumbs. A tingle worked its way up her arms as she bravely held his gaze. He lifted her hands to his lips and kissed the back of each. The air pressed out of her lungs, yet she could not inhale. No one had told her a kiss to the hand could feel so intimate.

His eyes bore into her with intensity. Heat flushed from her toes to her hairline. He bent his head, giving her ample time to protest. She didn't, just squeezed her eyes shut and waited. His warm breath fanned her cheek, then he dropped a light kiss on her forehead.

He released her hands, but she didn't dare open her eyes.

The adjoining door shut with a soft click.

Her eyes popped open. What was she expected to do? Was she to freshen up and go to him? The new clothes her ma had made hung waiting in the open wardrobe across the room. The thought sent her heart kicking. She could barely breathe. Surely, he didn't expect her to know how to proceed. How could she possibly unwind as he suggested?

She wanted out of the wedding gown, yet the thought that he might catch her half-dressed mortified her. She allowed her tired body to sink into the paisley chair. The longer she waited, the angrier she became. He should know she wouldn't have a clue what to do.

She popped up from the chair. She would change and slip into bed. If he wanted her to fulfill her wifely duties, he could come to her.

Tears filled her eyes as her arms reached to the back. There was no way for her to get out of the dress without tearing it off. Her ma had spent at least fifteen minutes doing up the row of tiny pearl buttons that ran up the back. In an exhausted heap, she fell across the bed and stifled a cry. She bunched the soft downy quilt into her hands and around her face and wept until she had no strength left.

Her eyes grew heavy, and she drifted into that wonderful place of nothingness.

~

*J*osiah took in the sight of her, sound asleep in her beautiful gown. "Kat, you must get into bed. The fire has died down, and your room is chilly." Josiah lifted her into his arms and pulled back the covers. "Why didn't you get ready for bed? You don't love the dress that much that you want to sleep in it." He put a little laughter into his voice, trying to gentle his concern. Why had she not readied herself for bed?

She jolted awake and turned in his arms. "Set me down." She pounded at his chest.

He gathered her fists in one hand so as to not get clobbered and lowered her to the floor. "Whoa, my little wild Kat. I'm just trying to help."

Tears pooled in her eyes and clotted her thick black lashes. His chest constricted at the sight of her red-rimmed eyes. An urge to kiss the drops away flooded through. He clasped his hands together behind his back to stifle the urge to pull her close.

She brushed at her tears with an angry swipe.

"What is it?"

"I…can't undo the buttons, and you left without saying anything and didn't come back."

His hand went to his forehead. "I'm so sorry. I didn't think. It's been way too many years since Georgina, and we had a whole lot more help back then. She had her personal maid to help her with all this finery."

What an idiot. He should have known. That must have been what Delilah meant when she asked if she should stay to help his new bride. "I'm truly sorry."

She turned her back to him. "Just get this thing off me already, and whatever else you're going to do to me, get it done."

He let out a deep breath as his large fingers fumbled with the tiny buttons. He wanted to tear the dress off, but that would scare her half to death. "Done."

The dress slipped from her shoulders. A deep shudder ran down her small frame as she caught the front from sliding any further. "The corset stays, could you…?"

Her body shivered each time his fingers brushed the softness of her creamy flesh. His heart kicked up to an all-out gallop, and blood thrummed through his veins like a wild stallion racing across the range. Goodness, he was not prepared for being this close to her and not acting upon the very thing he desired the most.

But, no matter what his body demanded, for all the best reasons in the world, he could not force his way into her bed any more than he could force his way into her heart. His wild Kat bride would have to be tamed and wooed. If she fled, then he would accept that she was never meant to be.

"Do you need any more help? I mean with these other layers."

"No." Her answer was swift and curt.

"I'm heading to my room, if you're sure you're all right."

Nodding, she turned toward him, clutching the dress to her chest with far too much of her creamy white flesh exposed. He almost lost all good reason, but he forced his gaze upward, only to find her iridescent eyes and ripe lips no easier to resist.

He swallowed hard against the lump in his throat. "I want you to know that this room is your own space. I peeked in tonight hoping to find you comfortable and fast asleep. Do you understand what I'm trying to say? This is your room and yours alone."

Her eyes widened and lifted to his. She was a vision of trembling lips, rosy cheeks, and skin so soft one could get lost, ever so lost. Unable to help himself, he brushed a knuckle down her cheek. The sharp intake of her breath and the stiffening of her spine did not escape his notice. If not for the fear radiating from her being, he would have weakened and thrown all restraint to the wind.

"Ma said you would know what to do. What I mean is... What about...you know?"

He smiled. "You mean your end of the bargain?"

She nodded, casting her eyes to the floor. A bright red flush covered her face.

His aching need screamed, but his love screamed louder. He just couldn't—no, wouldn't. Not yet.

"We have a whole lifetime for that. Let's get to know each other first." He bent his head, daring to touch his lips to hers in a quick kiss.

Her eyes rounded.

"Good night, Kat. Sweet dreams. You can lock your doors if it will help you sleep."

He shut the door between their rooms and waited. Silence. The click of the lock never came. He had won the trust of his young bride—a small but good start.

A walk to the creek and a very cold swim would be next.

∼

*K*atie stretched languorously. Why did her straw mattress, pillows, and quilts feel so glorious? She reached over to give her sister a morning hug like they had done for years and touched only air. Her eyes shot open. Where was her sister? Where was she? What time was it?

Like the rush of the Shenandoah River in the spring, reality flooded in. She was married. In a stranger's house, in a bed that was anything but straw, and, by the look of the light streaming through the gap in the heavy drapes, the day was well under-way. She jumped from the bed and stepped to the window. The sun was high in the sky.

"My goodness, what have I done? How did I sleep this long?" She poured tepid water from the pitcher to the bowl to wash in haste. The door to the wardrobe swung wide as she grabbed a plain shirtwaist and skirt and hurried to dress. She braided her hair and coiled it into a tight knot, stabbing in the pins in a harried rush.

She took one quick glance into the full-length mirror and stopped. She was not used to seeing her reflection, having never had the luxury of a mirror at her disposal. Wide troubled eyes stared back at her. Compared to the finery she'd worn the day before, her everyday clothes looked like rags. Most likely the maids had better clothes than she did.

With a jut to her chin and a flick of her head, she turned from the mirror. The day was half wasted. The least she could do was make herself useful. She had always been a hard worker. Maybe it would appease some of the guilt from not fulfilling her duty the night before. She had talked so big, but then… Heat flooded her face at the thought of how she had trembled like a leaf in the wind at the mere touch of his hands on her skin.

She swung her bedroom door open and froze. A look to the left then to the right did not set her bearings straight. The night before, when Josiah had led her to the bedroom, she had not been paying attention.

"Good morning, Missus Richardson." An older woman with a deep chocolate brown face and a cheery smile entered the hall from the adjoining room. "You're up. Mistuh Josiah said you'd be needing some extra sleep, so I kept real quiet."

She motioned to Katie. "Come, child. You must be starving. Let's get you fed. Why, when Mistuh Josiah told me you were a pretty one, he's not telling the half. You are just lovely. Just lovely indeed." Her dark brown eyes sparkled with merriment. "Just too skinny is all. Yes'um as skinny as a blade of grass." She chuckled. Her fleshy arms jiggled as her hands pointed to her generous girth. "Fatten you up to have babies nice and easy." She laughed as Katie raised her eyebrows.

"Come." She waved her hand and ambled down the hall. "Too soon for that baby talk, I reckon, but sure be right nice to have new life in this old house."

Katie followed, listening to her constant chatter. A warmth grew from the pit of her stomach. This kind lady made her feel welcome in the most unassuming way, and all the sleep she had received put a brighter light on her circumstances.

The woman gasped and wheeled around. Katie had to catch herself from colliding straight into her.

"Why, I do declare. I purt' nigh forgot to introduce myself. Just 'cause I know who you are, don't mean you know me." She gave a wide toothy grin. "I'm Delilah. Me and my Abe been with the Richardson family for years. His pa bought and freed us on the same day. We been working and living life as one big family ever since. Why, I helped bring that boy Josiah into this world."

Her face radiated both pride and joy. "Welcome to the family, Katherine." Huge fleshy arms engulfed Katie in the warmest of hugs. Delilah hung on much longer than Katie liked.

85

With a shake of her finger and a look of amusement, Delilah backed away. "I am going to teach you a thing or two about hugging girl, I truly am. But all in sweet Jesus' time. All in His time."

The fresh aroma of baked bread wafted through the air as they approached the kitchen. Katie's stomach growled in anticipation.

"Sit," Delilah said with a wave of her hand.

Katie slid up to the kitchen table and shifted in her seat. She was not used to being waited on. "Delilah?"

"Yes'um." She cracked an egg in the hot pan.

"What can I do to help? I'm not one of those fancy ladies who needs to be served. I'm not much good in the kitchen yet, but I aim to learn. And give me any work outside, and I shine."

Delilah moved about. "Mmmm." She sliced a few thick pieces of bread.

Katie waited, clasping and unclasping her hands.

Delilah slid a plate of eggs, ham, and fresh hot bread under her nose. "You show me you know how to eat, then I'll round up Mistuh Josiah for you. I be thinking you need to take that up with him."

"Good morning, Delilah. Did I hear you taking my name in vain?" Josiah walked into the room and planted a kiss on her chubby cheek.

She batted him with the wooden spoon and shooed him away.

"You keep them smooches for your missus now and let me fix your lunch."

Katie quite enjoyed their banter and marveled at the friendship between them. With the war just over, many Southerners would not take kindly to such familiarity.

"Good idea, Delilah, I do believe you have a point."

With measured steps, he walked to Katie's side and slowly

bent his head. Just inches from her cheek, he asked with a tease in his voice. "Who's supposed to kiss whom good morning?"

She had no idea how to answer, so maybe silence would be her best defense.

"I think we can start our own little tradition, don't you? In fact, I'll start one here and now. The sleepyhead in the family, whoever wakes up last, gets the honors." He leaned close with his cheek turned toward her and waited.

Determined not to run scared, Katie bent forward to peck the side of his cheek. At the last second, he moved so her lips found his. She jolted back. Heat spread from her neck to her hairline.

Delilah laughed. "Don't you embarrass your new bride, boy, 'cause you know full well I can still take a spoon to that behind of yours, if'n that sweet one says so."

Katie's smile split wide. She loved there was someone in the world who could put him in his place.

"Don't worry about her, Katherine," Josiah teased. "Her bark is most definitely worse than her bite."

"I'm not worried. I quite like the bark when it's directed at you."

Delilah let out a hoot and scurried over for a quick hug. "I do like the spunk in this one. We're going be the best of friends."

Katie lifted her head to Josiah with a defiant jut to her chin. "Friends indeed." A warmth filled her being.

His laughter bounced off the walls. "Come, my little Kat. It's time to show you around. Delilah, can you please pack up a lunch to go?"

"My pleasure."

He held out his hand.

Katie placed her hand in his as she rose, then quickly pulled it free. Why did everything have to be so big—his hands, his house, his land? She would never fit in.

CHAPTER 9

*W*hy couldn't she help Delilah in the kitchen? Katie wanted to be anywhere but standing beside her husband. Just that word, *husband*, sent a skitter up her spine.

"First the house, then the grounds," Josiah said. "I think you should be sufficiently rested for an afternoon ride."

"A ride?" She could not contain her smile. "That would be lovely."

"Thought the sleepyhead would like that as much as I do."

"I'm so sorry about that. It's not like me to fritter away the morning in bed."

He laughed. "Not a problem. I was glad you could sleep."

"Ma would be mortified."

"As Mrs. Richardson, your life affords you a few more luxuries than you're accustomed to."

"You won't tell her?"

"You're a married woman. The only thing that matters now is if I do a good job of keeping you happy."

Her head snapped up. "*You* keep *me* happy?"

He laughed. "Why not? Isn't that a husband's pleasure?"

An unfamiliar feeling stirred in her heart, one she could not define. She had agreed to their arrangement with the forgone conclusion they would have nothing in common and remain distant. But he liked riding and tickled her funny bone with his humor. And he was kinder than she'd expected. Her emotions tumbled, trying to compute this surprising knowledge.

"Are you ready? Because you're wearing the strangest expression."

"Lead the way." She swept her hand ahead.

Together they walked from the kitchen, down the hall, and through to the grand entrance. Her gaze flicked from the gilded framed portraits gracing the wall up the curved staircase to the balcony above and the lofty ceiling. How small and gauche the grandeur made her feel.

He pointed to the steps.

She stopped her ascent at the first two portraits. "Your parents?"

He nodded. "As you can see, I get my splendid looks from my mother."

Katie studied the average-looking but commanding gentleman and the stunning woman. Her gaze flickered between the paintings and the man at her side. His tone sounded as though he was joking, but his words spoke truth.

"I brought these all the way from Williamsburg. Our Virginian family roots go back to before the Revolution, which explains the many paintings." His gaze took on a faraway look.

"Is your family still back there?"

"No." A shadow of darkness flickered in his eyes.

She hadn't meant to cause him pain. "I don't need to know."

"It's not that I don't want to tell you, it's just difficult." His Adam's apple bobbed, and he looked up at the pictures.

"My parents, Cameron and Fiona, were killed in a stage-coach accident when I was eighteen. They were known for their unpopular abolitionists beliefs, and I'll always wonder at the legitimacy of the so-called accident that took their lives."

Katie instinctively touched his arm. "I'm so sorry."

He looked down at her hand, and she pulled it away.

His eyes lifted back up to the portraits. "Like my father, who didn't have the stomach for slavery, I wanted nothing to do with that lifestyle. Being their only child, I sold the tobacco plantation and moved here. At one time, the Richardson plantation was the largest and most prestigious in the area. But it had dwindled in size over the years, due to my father selling land to pay staff and maintain a lifestyle that he and mother had long been accustomed to."

"Was that hard, selling off the family home?"

He looked down at her. "Emotionally, yes. However, the actual ability to find a buyer, not at all. Sometimes, timing is everything. The surrounding plantation owners wanted to increase their holdings and were sure they'd be able to preserve the Southern way. I walked away with enough to purchase much better land in this valley. My one regret is that it wasn't far enough away to live in peace. When Virginia joined the Confederacy, I was torn. I agreed with the philosophies of the North that black people should be free but joined the South, not able to raise a gun against my old neighbors, family, and friends."

"That would've been a tough decision."

"The worst. I took a bullet to the leg early in the war, which turned out to be a blessing in disguise. Although not a coward, I didn't believe in what the South stood for. When I healed enough, they relegated me to looking after the horses and picking up the wounded. Even if this injury plagues me the rest of my days, a greater purpose was served."

He lifted his gaze to look at his father. "All that pain, all that death. Could we not have found a better way?"

She grappled for a way to change the subject. He was clearly upset, and her curiosity was to blame. "Were you and Georgina already married before you came here?"

He shifted his gaze to look into her eyes. "All I had to do was convince Georgina to marry me, leave her family and everything she had become accustomed to, and follow me into the unknown. No small feat, but somehow I was persuasive enough."

"Now, that's a surprise. I can't imagine you—" Her hand flew to her mouth. Maybe she should not be so blunt.

His eyebrows rose.

"I...just meant you have a way of convincing people to fall in line with your plans."

"I'm not sure if that's a compliment."

Why could she not pick a benign subject? She looked back at the wall. "Why is there no portrait of you or Georgina?"

"Time was not on Georgina's side." His voice cracked. "As for myself, all incentive died when she passed away."

She rested her hand on his arm and squeezed. "I'm so sorry, Josiah. I keep trying to change the subject to something easier, and it's going from bad to worse."

A watery smile filtered through. "Do you realize you said my name without hesitation?"

"I did?"

"You did." He offered his elbow before continuing up the stairs and, because her hand was already on his arm, it did not feel too foreign to slip it into the crook.

"Come, let's get the inside done so we can get out into the sunshine."

Room after room was opened. After a few, she said, "Why are so many sparsely furnished?"

"The Yankees used some of the furniture for firewood. Thankfully not all." He looked down at her. "I've thought about what you said yesterday, and I agree. I have much to be thankful for." He smiled. "With you at the top of my list."

The intensity in his gaze caused heat to rise and burn her cheeks. She cast her eyes to the floor.

He placed a finger under her chin and raised her head. "I'm thankful you agreed to marry me, whatever the motivation, and I aim to prove your choice a wise one."

Her stomach flip-flopped, and she gave him the best smile she could muster. His kindness touched a deep reservoir of unchartered emotion. She had spent a lifetime trying to win approval and, for the first time, someone cared about winning hers.

"We're back to our wing of the upper floor." He opened a room beside Katie's. A small bassinet, crib, and rocking chair graced the nursery. "Georgina and I never—" A momentary look of yearning came over his face, but he shut the door without saying a word, just looked down at her as if she was supposed to know what to say.

He wanted children. She could see it in his eyes. But the thought made her hands twist into the folds of her dress. They would have to do a whole lot of what she longed to avoid. Her hand fluttered to her throat.

He turned toward the steps. "Our bedrooms you've seen. Later, we can revisit them together." The tease was back in his tone.

He stopped for a moment to lean on the balcony rail and gaze down to the entrance. "This house is quite grand when you stop long enough to take it in."

"Grand and unnecessary, if you ask me."

"Ah, you're a practical girl. I like that." He swept his hand down the stairway. "Shall we, my love?"

As they descended the steps, she placed a hand to her heated cheeks. They must be red from his intimate remarks. She was not ready for endearments. Would she ever be?

He crossed the foyer. "This room I love." He swung open the double doors to an enormous drawing room. The rich oak floor gleamed in the sunlight that poured through the full-length glass doors that opened to the garden beyond. A huge chandelier hung majestically from a sculptured obelisk.

"Crystal," he said as she gazed upward. "This room transforms into a beautiful ballroom. Almost as beautiful as you."

He ran the back of his workworn knuckle down her face, and she shivered.

"Maybe this Christmas we'll invite the community and put this room to use. There's still so much division between neighbors regarding the freedom of slaves. We could offer something enjoyable to bring the community back together."

She walked farther into the room so he couldn't read her face. Parties? Dancing? Her worst nightmare. A cold sweat broke out on her forehead. She had to change the subject, and fast.

"So, why wasn't this place torched when they left, like—"

"Can't be sure, but I think there is truth to the story that a blue coat officer was stationed here and grew partial to the home's beauty. Rumor has it that he loved music, dance, and entertaining the ladies. Unlike me. I don't fall easily, but when I do..."

He moved close beside her. A faint woodsy scent filled her senses. When she braved a peek upward, his expression did not hide his longing. She found his honesty unnerving, especially when she felt nothing in return.

The coward in her took over. Her eyes darted around the room. "I've heard stories of a ballroom like this and dreamed of seeing one someday, but to think I live in a house with all this grandeur."

"The house is to your liking?"

"Honestly, Josiah. I can't deny its loveliness, but it overwhelms me."

A wide grin split his face, making him look ten years younger. "Look how far we've come since yesterday. You've used my name twice without prompting. Come, one more thing." Taking her hand, he pulled her into the kitchen. "But I need the oil lantern."

"Where are you taking me? To lock me in the dungeon for sleeping in and not fulfilling my part of the bargain last night?"

He laughed as he lit the wick. "I do love your spunk."

She followed him to a door that opened to a staircase down. "After you." He took her elbow firmly while she picked up her skirt to descend the steps. The dim, dank place they entered caused an instant chill. She was glad for the glow of the lantern and the warmth of Josiah's touch. The sound of trickling water and the moisture in the air had her curious.

"This"—he lifted the lantern to his full height, pointing to a cement-lined cistern—"gives us our own fresh water supply. The rainwater from the roof is collected into drainpipes and filtered into this tank. Delilah uses the pump in the kitchen with no need to haul water."

"How impressive. This would save so much work. You wouldn't believe how many hours I've spent hauling pails of water from the pump to the house, and you're telling me this no longer has to be done?"

"I knew a hard-working girl like you would value this. I couldn't take just any girl to the cellar and expect appreciation."

She grinned up at him. Their eyes locked in the flickering lantern light. Where had her anger from the day before disappeared to? Why did she feel more comfortable with anger than the unsettling thought of liking this man who was now her husband?

"Do you have riding wear?" he asked as they climbed the steps.

"I had my brother's dungarees, but Ma wouldn't let me pack them. She insisted that living with you, I would be expected to be a lady. Then she informed me that, after years of riding with my brothers, women are expected to ride side-saddle in a dress and bonnet. Can you imagine the agony? Why, I would land on my backside for sure."

"You mean you actually wore your brother's clothes?" His eyes widened as they stepped into the hall.

Heat rose up her neck, but her pride held her steadfast. "Not all of us are born into privilege, Mr. Richardson, and have fancy clothing for every occasion. Some of us are common hard-working people who have to make do with whatever works." She turned away from him and walked down the hall.

"Whoa, Katherine." He caught her and reached for her arm. "I didn't mean to insult you. But that day at the creek, you had your horse."

Katie nodded. "Yes?"

"You were wearing a dress, not dungarees."

She didn't want to remember that day, much less talk about it, especially with him. "I wore the dungarees under the skirt, for propriety's sake, but I sure haven't ever ridden side-saddle, and I'm not about to start now. And you might as well know, in those last years of war, when deserters and rogue blue coats roamed the countryside, I wore a complete outfit of male cloth-ing. It was the only way I could go outside safely and attend to the farm. From a distance, a passerby would take me for a young boy, and I was left alone. I learned my lesson that day in the woods." Tears pooled in her eyes, and she blinked them back.

"That was smart. Really smart. The war brought out the ugly in so many." He gathered her close.

She stiffened and backed away.

Both his hands flew up. "Sorry, I wasn't thinking. I only meant to comfort."

The touch of a man, any man, made her want to run. She'd had to work hard to become comfortable when Charles would respectfully give her a hug. They had never got beyond that point. And now, with all the strength she possessed, she forced herself to stand still and not bolt like a scared jackrabbit. She bit down hard to stop the quiver of her lips, and the taste of blood filled her mouth.

"There are going to be many things we don't know about each other," he said, the deep timbre of his voice steady, "but, in time, that will change. And even though you might surprise me, I want you to share your life with me, as I will with you. Does that make sense?"

She had no words.

"I know you don't want to recall that day in the woods."

She shook her head.

"And I promise I won't bring it up again until you're ready to talk about it. But you have to know, when I arrived on the scene, you were in a very compromising situation."

She could not bear to look at him.

"Do you know why I believed your story?" His hand tenderly slid under her dropped chin to raise her eyes to meet his. "I looked into your eyes, the way I am right now, and they shared your soul. I believed every word. Now, I'm asking the same of you. When I tell you that you can trust me with your life—past, present, and future, I mean it. I'll say no more, other than your mother should have let you bring the dungarees." He turned from her. "Let's head outside."

Katie stood for a moment without moving. His words penetrated deep into her heart. Were her assumptions about him wrong? She had no answer.

But she had to hurry to catch up, as he'd already disappeared through the door.

He stood on the portico waiting when she stepped out. "Ready?" He offered his arm.

"Ready." She slipped her hand into the crook. The sheer size and strength of his forearm felt strange beneath her fingertips.

"I'll show you my favorite first. The barn. I had it rebuilt because it burned down while the Yankees were using it as a field hospital. They then resorted to using some of the rooms on the main floor of the house. I can tell which rooms by the blood stains on the wood. Someday, all of that will be either replaced or refinished, but necessities such as this barn were the priority.

"I think you'll find it quite different from what you've seen. The design is something I brought home from my war days." He pointed out the two levels.

"This is so smart." She stood back and pressed a finger to her lips. "Built into the bank like it is lets you easily access both levels."

He beamed. "I keep farm equipment and the harvest on the upper level, and the horse stalls, livestock area, and a tack room on the lower. You'll see by the sheer amount of horse stalls what my plans are for the future."

She took in the rows of empty enclosures, dreaming of how they might be filled someday. "I love horses."

"Me too. I'll have the finest stock in the valley very soon. My good friend, Colby, is partnering with me. While he makes it here with the horses, I'll be rustling up the finest help around. Black or white, doesn't much matter to me. The best man for the job is who I'm looking for.

"I agree."

They walked and talked and, somewhere along the way, a switch was made from Katie having her hand on his arm to his hand supporting her elbow. The warmth penetrated through the well-worn sleeve of her day dress. She noticed the pressure increase when he was excited about one thing or another. A comfort settled over her jitters, and she found herself genuinely enjoying his company.

"Every household needs fresh eggs, thus the hen house, but watch out for old Strut." He pointed toward a cluster of the birds. "That rooster can be a mean one unless you let him know who's boss."

"His name is Strut?"

As if on cue, the rooster headed their way. He let out a shriek that hurt the ears and sent the hens darting for shelter. He proceeded to strut along the edge of his pen with his head bobbing back and forth and his comb in the air like a shooting flame.

Katie laughed. "Good name."

They wandered the grounds toward the summer kitchen. "The separate room keeps food smells and heat out of the main house in the muggy hot months. And Delilah loves the free-standing oven. Once the bricks are thoroughly heated, the ashes are removed, and food bakes inside."

She peeked in to take a closer look. "Ma would've loved this on those blistering summer days. But why so big?"

"It's a good place to do laundry, with the pump handy. Plus, the room is set to catch the cooling breeze from the north in the summer and has thick doors that can be shut in the winter. I won't bore you with all the details, but"—he turned his gaze on her—"it's important you know where everything is since this is your home. You're not just some passing guest. You're my life partner."

She turned from his intensity. What was she to say to that? He was far more invested than she was. A feather of guilt brushed across her heart, but she disregarded the message. "And what's that?" She pointed to a shed in the distance.

"That's the smokehouse, and the icehouse is over there." He pointed across the yard.

"Icehouse? Where do you get ice, and how long does it last in this heat?"

He smiled down at her. "I love your intelligent questions."

Her stomach fluttered at the compliment, and her heart picked up pace as he grabbed her hand and continued walking.

"There's a pond on the property, and we harvest the ice from there. Between the limestone brick walls of the icehouse, and the ice packed in sawdust and straw, the room is kept cool right into September. All our meat and dairy are stored there."

"We, as in you help with the work?"

"Of course. There's nothing on this farm I won't help with. I might not be the best, but I give a hand."

He kept talking, but all she could concentrate on was how wrong she had been about the entitled life she'd thought he lived.

"Come. I know the blacksmith and wheelwright shop won't thrill you, but I want to properly introduce you to Abe, Delilah's husband."

They rounded the corner of a sturdy log building and stepped inside. Abe looked up from his work, rose, and dusted off his hands on the sides of his trousers.

"This is Abe's home away from home," Josiah said. "The man is a genius when it comes to fixing just about anything—wheels, horseshoes, tools. You name it, Abe can do it."

"Don't be giving too much praise. It goes to the head. Then I'll get like you, too big for my britches."

The twinkle in his black eyes danced and the amusement in his voice caused a bubble of laughter to slip from Katie's lips.

"I see your new bride agrees with me." His friendly grin was hard not to like.

Katie moved across the room and extended her hand.

He hesitated, with a darted glance toward Josiah.

What had she done improperly?

Abe placed her hand in his. The warmth from his calloused palms engulfed hers as he gave a firm squeeze. "Most ladies don't shake the hand of my color."

"I'm not like most ladies."

He turned to Josiah. "You done good. I like this fine lady already." He turned back to her. "And you let me know if this youngin' gives you any trouble. You hear?" He nodded his head in Josiah's direction.

"From my perspective, I wouldn't be calling him a youngin.'"

Abe's laughter filled the room. "This indeed is the lady for you. She's not going to worship the ground you walk on like those silly town women." He pulled an old rag from his pocket and brushed a sheen of sweat from his brow.

"I do believe both you and your lovely wife Delilah are going to be my good friends," Katie said.

"And me?" Josiah asked.

She lifted her head with a saucy retort on her lips, but the look on the normally confident Mr. Richardson's face stopped her jest. A vulnerability filled his smoky-gray eyes. It was not a moment to tease. She nodded. "And you."

His smile widened to flash a row of straight white teeth.

Katie moved out of his intense stare and gazed around the shop. A collection of woodworking and farm tools hung neatly on wall pegs. A wheel was suspended between two sawhorses, and a fire crackled in a hearth against one wall. She breathed in the smell of sawdust, grease, sweat, and smoke. A sense of hominess enveloped her. "Hope you don't mind a visit now and then, Abe. There's something about this place I like."

"You're more than welcome anytime, girl. Anytime."

"Shall we?" Josiah offered his arm. "We'll stop by the house, pick up our lunch sack, and head out. As far as I'm concerned, we still have the best part to see—the land."

With one look back, she stepped into the sunshine. How would she ever feel at home in the big house when this humble shop drew her in? Under the heat of the sun, a shiver crawled down her back.

CHAPTER 10

*J*osiah could not pull his eyes away from his wife. He caught a peek of the britches he'd given her as she swung her leg over the mare and settled in.

She leaned forward and patted the horse's mane. "You're a good old lady. Yes, you are."

"Sorry, old Ella is far less horse than you can handle, but the Yankees owned up to all my prize horse flesh. That will change soon, and you'll be one of the first to take your pick."

Her eyes lit up, and her smile blossomed like an unfolding rose. "That will be wonderful." She straightened and sat tall and comfortable in the saddle. "But today, I don't care what I ride. It's just nice to be on a horse again."

He swung onto his horse beside her. Excitement brought a rosy blush to her cheeks and a spark to her eyes that were completely irresistible. His mind wandered to her very kissable lips. The wind brushed tendrils of wavy hair across her cheeks as she waited for his instruction. He resisted the urge to reach out but held onto his reins tighter than he should have. His stallion pranced backwards.

"Head on out." He pointed to the gate. His heart rate needed a moment to calm.

She nudged the flanks of the horse. With a soft voice and firm touch to the reins, she was off. His heart swelled at the sight of her. She was a mixture of wild and worry, happy and sad, confidence and shyness. Everything about her moved him.

He trotted down the drive after her. "Where did you learn to ride?"

"Pa had an unusual philosophy. He was raised a servant's son. When he broke free, he found he could learn most anything. He was insistent we all, whether male or female, have the opportunity to learn whatever we liked, and I liked riding and everything about horses. I also like math."

"Math?"

"Numbers fascinate me."

This woman continued to surprise him. "Well then, once you get settled, if you so desire, we shall see if you have an aptitude for bookkeeping. I know how to do it, but detest it, and it's one of the most important parts in running a successful ranch."

"Do you mean that? I would love to learn."

"Absolutely. You'd be helping me out enormously. Why would I say no to that?" And if he could give her something she enjoyed, all the better.

"That sounds great. I don't want to be bored."

Oh, he could think of lots of things to stem her boredom, but she was not ready for any of them. He worked at getting his mind back to casual conversation.

"When was the last time you went riding? And I don't mean when you had that short jaunt with me."

"Before the war. Pa and my brothers took off to war with our horses, and Pa came home with a donkey and, well...the boys never came home at all."

"I heard. I'm so sorry. Your pa told me you were close to them."

"Like skin to the body." She shook her head and turned her face away from him and into the afternoon sun.

He caught the glisten of tears on her cheeks and changed the subject. He understood the pain. When Georgina had died, his heart had been ripped out. He'd thought he would never love again, but Katherine had awakened life.

"With your obvious love for riding, a trip to the seamstress is on top of the list."

"Why?" She gave him a curious glance.

"For a riding habit, of course. I know you'll put it to good use."

She shot him a generous smile.

His heart kicked up speed. She had given him two genuine smiles in the past half hour.

"This is all yours?" She lifted her hand to the acres of prime farmland stretched before them.

"Ours, Kat. Ours. And yes, I plan to utilize every acre raising fine horses, enlarging the orchard, and planting corn and wheat for market. I have dreams, big dreams, for us, for our—" He stopped himself from saying *family*. She was surely not ready for that word. "And I'm not afraid of hard work."

"You're not just an entitled socialite?"

"Who described me like that?"

"The ladies in town had many an opinion, and you were often their subject of choice. Funny thing was, none of them described you as a hard-working farmer." She cantered a few lengths ahead of him and threw back a saucy grin. "Farmer Richardson. I rather like that."

He kicked the flanks of his horse and came up beside her.

"Don't tell me you found something about me you like, and in less than twenty-four hours. Things are looking up."

Her snapping blue eyes flashed his direction as a flush of color tinged her cheeks. If only he could read her mind.

With a jut of her chin, she changed the subject. "How do you plan to implement your dreams with just Pa and Abe? Neither of them is what you would call a spring chicken. Oh yeah, and Colby. How old is this fellow? Is he ancient too?"

"Meaning I'm ancient?"

"Oh." Her eyes widened. "I never meant to imply—"

He laughed. "Colby is younger than I am by quite a bit. I met him during the war, and we became good friends. Like a brother I never had. I was able to talk him into teaming up with me when the war left him alone in the world. He's gone west to settle his personal affairs and purchase the cattle and horse-breeding stock we need. Between your pa, Abe, Colby, and me, we'll have a great start. And I believe that, if you treat people right, white or black, the word gets out and others will come knocking."

"I like your thinking."

"I bet I can up the *likes* to three before the end of the day. What do you say?"

"You're pushing it now, Mr. Richardson."

"Back to the formal Mr. Richardson, are we? That makes me feel old."

"Well?" She lifted a hand in the air.

"How about I race you across the field to the apple orchard? And I'll show you just how young I am when I leave you in my dust."

Her eyebrows shot up, and she laughed into the wind. "You're on." She kicked the flanks of her old mare and lit out into a gallop. The picture she made flying across the meadow filled his chest with pure joy. Her wild spirit brought life and youthful zest to his world, which had been dead for way too long.

His horse could easily overpower the mare. He drew neck and neck, smiling at the look of sheer determination on her profile. If he let her win, she would think him old, but if he won, it would take away her pleasure. A tie might be the most prudent, so he reined in his horse. The look of delight that flushed across her face as they slowed the animals to a walk made his heart swell to twice its size.

"That was the most fun I've had in a long, long time."

He couldn't help grinning back. "Was I right? *Like* number three?"

"Yes indeed." She said without hesitation. "How did you know I liked to race?"

A laugh bubbled up from his chest. "Oh, there was little doubt."

He wouldn't tell her that, after that incident in the woods, he made a point of following her from a distance to make sure she got home safely. He remembered how his heart had stopped as she jumped the split-rail fence to her pa's land. She had sailed over it as if she'd sprouted wings and landed with the grace and skill of an Indian warrior. In that moment, two things had become clear. Her riding skills could rival any man's, and she was unlike any woman he had ever met.

"Let's stop here and eat a little of what Delilah made, or I'll have the wooden spoon taken after me."

She giggled as she swung her leg over and jumped smoothly to the ground. "You two have a wonderful relationship, don't you?"

"After my parents died, Abe and Delilah became everything to me. They're family, plain and simple. I know its unconventional. I hope that doesn't bother you." He spread a blanket on the ground and waved her over.

"Me, no." She knelt down beside him and opened the cloth that held the corn cakes, then offered him one. "Never been raised to think I was better than anyone. In fact..." But her words trailed. Whatever she hadn't said left a twinge of sadness on her face. She took a moment to speak. "I've heard talk from some white folk blaming the blacks for the war and their lost families. Sad to say, but there's a fair bit of hostility in this valley toward colored people."

He was surprised by her astuteness. "I agree. Abe, Delilah, and I are careful in public to keep things formal, but at home we're family. And if anyone tried to harm them—let's just say I would not stand idly by."

"Feeling that strongly, I would've expected you to have a discussion with me before we married." She bit into a piece of chicken. "What if I had been the type who thought—"

"I talked to your pa at length about this subject that first time I visited him. How your family viewed black people was of utmost importance to me. No matter how much I lo—." He caught himself just before the word slipped out. "*Liked* a woman, I was not about to jeopardize Abe and Delilah."

She nodded. "Hmm, that's good, and so is this chicken. I'll have to get Delilah to teach me how to make it like this." She licked her fingers, and his blood ran hot.

He rose in one swift movement, in need of space, and headed for the edge of the orchard. The apples hung ripe and heavy from the sagging branches.

"Would you like an apple?" He plucked one free and held it up.

She nodded, and he lobbed one her way. She instinctively lifted her hands and caught it. Her eyes danced with merriment. Everything about her filled the emptiness in his life.

As she bit into the juicy fruit, a look of pure enjoyment pulled at her lips. A spray of apple juice dribbled down her chin. He wished he had the freedom to kiss it away. The heat rose in his body, and his heart pumped faster as his mind wandered to places it could not yet go.

"What?" she asked. Her head cocked to one side with a question in her eyes.

The innocent had no clue what she did to him. How would he have the discipline to take it slowly?

"We better go."

He hated to share his new bride, but company was a safe option to the alternative.

CHAPTER 11

*K*atie could have ridden far longer, but she was thankful for the time Josiah had taken to show her around.

"Just through the trees, you'll see your parents' new home." Josiah pointed ahead as he drew up beside her.

The orchard opened to a clapboard house nestled in the arms of two massive oak trees on the edge of a field. A gorgeous sight.

And... Who was that person stepping from the house? As recognition took hold, Katie squealed in delight. In seconds, she was off the horse and into the arms of her sister Amelia. She soaked up the familiar scent of her sister, hugging her as if they'd been apart for years.

The door of the two-story building opened, and the rest of her family poured out. They flocked around her like chickens at the sight of grain. She picked up Gracie and twirled her youngest sister in a circle, relishing the giggle that filled the air.

She caught the gaze of her husband as she lowered Gracie to the ground. He was still astride his horse. His eyes held a wistful, haunted look. One that twisted in her chest.

Then he seemed to come out of whatever emotions had held him. "I'll look after the horses." He swung down and grabbed the reins of Ella, who chomped on a clump of fresh green grass. "Let your parents show you around their new house, and I'll be back to walk you home. Our place is just over the knoll. You'll be happy to know it's within short walking distance."

So close. A leap of something akin to joy shot through her. She smiled to thank him, but he had already turned to go.

Gracie pulled at her hand. "Come see. We don't have a ladder to our loft. We have real stairs."

"It's not a loft, silly," Lucinda jumped in. "They're real bedrooms."

Ma's face beamed. "Oh, Katherine, this is so much more than Pa or I ever expected."

Amelia threw her arm around Katie's shoulders, and they walked in together. "We even have a parlor to entertain." She giggled. "Imagine that. And the best part is we're close enough to visit each other."

The outside had hinted at the transformation from poverty to comfort, but the inside confirmed it.

Ma bubbled over the new cook stove in the kitchen, the seating in the parlor, and the privacy she and Pa would now have. Upstairs, the girls ran from room to room, laughing and giggling.

"Take a look. We can see your house from up here." Ma spoke above the noise of the girls and waved Katie over to a window.

A pang of guilt pierced Katie's heart as she looked over the knoll and spotted her stately home. Yesterday, she had not lived up to her end of the bargain, and yet Josiah had done his part. Just the thought of a man's kiss or hands on her body, after what happened in the woods, made a tide of goosebumps wash up her arm to the nape of her neck. How would she ever find the courage?

Ma's voice cracked, and tears glistened in her eyes. "I don't know how to tell you how much this means to Pa, your sisters, and me." She raised a hand and smoothed it down Katie's cheek.

Katie couldn't keep from stiffening. Ma had displayed this kind of affection with the other girls, but rarely her. Her touch felt as foreign as Josiah's.

"Please be happy, Katherine," her mother whispered, her eyes pleading.

Katie turned toward the window, unable to answer. It was a little too late for Ma to worry about her happiness.

Ma sighed and pressed her hands together. "Tea. I can serve real tea with real sugar. Can you believe it?"

They all piled down the stairs into their new kitchen. Katie took a moment to soak in each face—all the happiness and delight. Ma and Pa gave each other a quick kiss. The glow on Ma's face was bright enough to light up the room.

Aunt May's story from the Bible of Daniel in the lion's den came to mind. She would need that kind of courage to follow through with her plan that evening. Right there in Ma's new kitchen, with her family gathered around, she prayed in silence. *God, Daniel's God, will you help me? Will you give me courage to… well, you're God, so you know what I need to do.*

"Ma says that we can't bother you up at the big house, but I miss you already." Lucinda threw her arms around Katie's neck.

Gracie chimed in, "Why do you have to live in another house? This house is sooooo big." She spread her chubby little arms wide. "We'll share with you and Mr. Richie."

Ma, Jeanette, and Amelia all chuckled.

"His name's not Mr. Richie," Lucinda corrected. "It's Mr. Rich Man, cause he's very, very rich."

A giggle slipped from Katie's lips. "Girls, his last name is Richardson, like your last name is Williams. His name has nothing to do with how rich he is. And I'm married now, Gracie. Mr. Richardson has a house of his own that he wants me to share with him. I promise I'll visit you lots, all right, sweetie?" She hugged them close, then distracted them with a tickle to the ribs. "Guess who's goin' get you?"

The game was on. Squealing in delight, they ran circles around her chair, begging for the big, bad bear to catch them. "My goodness, the racket." Ma put her hands to her ears, but a smile split her face.

As Katie raced around the room after them, she grabbed Lucinda and threw her over her shoulder. She didn't hear Josiah and Pa enter the kitchen, but when she looked up to find them both watching her, she set Lucinda down with a plunk, which sent her sprawling.

"Ow." The girl rubbed her bottom as she scrambled to her feet.

Katie bent down. "Sorry, sweetie." She pulled her in to her side and hugged her tight. "The game is over for now," she whispered.

Tiny hands grasped the folds of her dress as they hid behind her skirt and peeked out at the stranger who had cut their fun short.

"Hope you two won." Josiah crouched down to their level.

Gracie stepped from behind Katie's skirt. "We playin' the big baaad bear game, and Lucinda gots caught but I didn't."

Lucinda ventured forward from the other side. "Do you want to play? I can tell you all the rules." Her eyes grew bright with excitement.

"Now, don't go bothering Mr. Richardson, girls." Ma waved the kids away.

Josiah stood. "I'd like to have at least one game. Don't want Katherine to have all the fun." He winked in her direction.

"Yes. Yes. Yes." The girls danced around them both.

"You're the big bad bear, then," Katie said.

"Last one caught is the winner." Lucinda ran behind Katie's skirt for protection, and Gracie scooted in too. Katie scooped them both up and ran from behind one chair to another, circling the table.

They narrowly escaped Josiah's grasp the first time, then his strong arms encircled them. He picked her and the little ones up with no more effort than if he'd hefted a sack of potatoes.

Gracie and Lucinda squealed in delight.

He walked to the nearest chair and sat with all of them on his lap. "I think I won."

The household erupted in laughter, and Katie jumped up with the girls still clinging to her. She set them down and smoothed wrinkles from her dress, even as her cheeks burned hot. Sitting on his lap in front of the whole family was far too intimate. "I'll help Ma make the tea."

"Why, that Mr. Richardson is a strong one," Ma whispered in her ear as they busied themselves in the kitchen. "And the girls have taken to him like butter to bread."

Katie turned to find one on each of his knees.

He looked up in amusement, then bent toward the girls and murmured, "Isn't your sister...?" She didn't hear the last part, but they looked at Katie and giggled.

How easily they climbed up on his lap. Laughed. Trusted.

Not her. She was a mess. So damaged. And he had no idea.

～

*T*hat evening, Katie lifted her napkin to the corners of her mouth and dabbed, hoping to project a confidence she did not feel. "Delilah, your cooking is absolutely delicious."

Delilah laughed. "To celebrate your wedding, I put a little effort into making it special. But you barely ate."

She didn't want to hurt Delilah's feelings, but her stomach churned at the thought of what lay beyond this celebratory meal. She couldn't fake another bite. "So many wonderful flavors."

"This past summer, we grew some right fine herbs."

Katie let out the air she'd been holding. At least she'd diverted the conversation away from her.

"And we didn't have those Yankee boys trampling them with their horses. I do declare, to see my garden treated so, well it purt nigh killed me. Abe and I appreciate what those men did in freeing our people, but land sakes they had no respect a'tall."

"Don't be getting all wound up now," Abe said. "This here's a celebration supper. We don't need no war talk to ruin it."

Josiah grinned and leaned in to Katie. "Those two really do love each other."

"What you be whispering about? Don't be filling her purty head with stories, lessen they be good ones."

"Now, Delilah, would I tell any other kind?"

"By Jupiter, yes. You say most anything to get a laugh." She waved her hand in his direction.

"Time for a toast." Abe raised his glass. "This here's one of the happiest times I remember in way too long. Josiah, we're as happy for you as a piglet in the mud hole."

"Tis true, tis true." Delilah clinked her glass against Abe's, then they both held theirs out to the couple.

Josiah cleared his throat. "To my beautiful wife, Katherine, who has made me happier than she could imagine."

Katie gathered the courage to look full in his face. His eyes flicked over her, then lifted to meet her gaze. She wanted to look away, but she couldn't give in to the coward in her. She forced a smile and raised her glass to meet his. "To us." The room went so quiet, she was sure she could hear the beat of her own heart.

His eyes changed from blue-gray to almost black. She had noticed that look in many a man as they stared at her. Didn't matter where she went or what she wore, the message was always the same. A ripple of fear sliced through and her stomach lurched. Daniel had no doubt been smarter and hadn't forced a meal before the lion's den.

"You two go sit in the parlor," Delilah said, waving her hand. "Abe can help me with the cleanup."

Josiah rose and extended his hand. "Shall we?"

Katie placed her hand in his and shivered against her will. They walked into the adjoining room, then sat on the settee in front of a roaring fire. He never let go of her hand. His eyes held her like a soft caress. She tried to hold his gaze but could not, instead turning toward the fire. His intensity unnerved her.

He began a gentle rub on the inside of her wrist with his thumb. Like the crackle and pop of the fire, her insides jumped. Even this simple touch unsettled her. She longed to give him something, anything, in return for all he had given her family, yet she couldn't find the courage to even look at him.

"Tell me?" she asked, pulling her hand free and turning to him.

"What?"

"How it is that we're practically strangers, yet you're so comfortable with me, as if you've known me for years?"

A long moment of silence followed as he studied her. His eyes didn't reveal his thoughts. "The war taught me to redeem the precious gift of time. Do I take from your question that you're not comfortable?"

"Do you realize you half answer my questions, then throw one back? Just like when I asked you why you wanted to marry me when you could have chosen anyone. You never did answer."

"Though you're very perceptive and intelligent, you may not be ready for the answer. How about we revisit both those questions when you can hold my hand without pulling free? Or allow me to kiss you without..." He leaned in close and wrapped an arm around her shoulder.

The heat of his breath fanned her cheeks as he bent his head.

His nearness was overwhelming, and she squeezed her eyes shut. The minute his lips touched hers, a memory surged with a shudder. Other lips had pressed hers, forcing, smothering her breath.

She popped her eyes open to push the images away.

He pulled back, a sadness cloaking his eyes. "Without shaking."

"I'm sorry. I—" She struggled for presence of mind, struggled to pull herself from the grip of that haunting memory.

His mouth formed a sad smile. "Don't worry, sweet one. I was doing that to prove a point." He straightened. "How about we start with friendship? You tell me three things you like and three things you dislike, as long as none of them are me." His chuckle sounded forced, and his eyes held a guarded look she couldn't read.

"Then," he added, "I'll do the same."

Friendship. Surely, she could manage that. "I love horses—"

"Nope, I already know that." He shifted to the other side of the settee, putting lots of room between them, then turned her way.

"All right then. I love all animals. The deer in the forest, my old cat you let me bring along, and everything in between. Except the skunk. I see no good reason for an animal that can make me stink to high heavens."

"This one I have to hear."

"You want the stories too?"

"Most definitely, Kat. Most definitely."

To Katie's surprise, their conversation flowed easily after that. She was surprised when he stood. One look at the dying embers in the fireplace showed how much time had passed, time during which she had fully relaxed.

He stretched. "As much as I've enjoyed this evening, sunrise comes mighty early. I'll be putting in a long day tomorrow. Your pa and I are going to plow the back field and get it ready for winter's fallow. Good night. Sweet dreams." He stepped near, but only dropped a light kiss on her forehead. "Most likely, I won't see you until the evening meal." He turned and walked away.

Katie sat without moving. *God help me, help me fulfill my duty.* The embers died, and the room took on a chill. Yet still, she sat.

CHAPTER 12

*J*osiah looked across the drawing room at his bride, who stood beside the fireplace pretending to warm her hands in a very warm room, rather than get too close to him. It was how every evening started until he waved her closer.

Their time together over the past few weeks had confirmed how interesting and intelligent she was. He made himself be patient, but the discipline was tougher than he imagined. The more time he spent with her, the deeper he fell. When she let herself relax, she would banter and challenge his opinions, depending on the subject. They were forming an actual friendship.

Now, his heart squeezed at just the sight of her as she fiddled with her hair. Her long thick braid hung down her back. She stuffed the pins in her mouth, then coiled it into another tight bun and started working the pins back into place.

He patted the seat beside him. "Come here."

She nodded her head in his direction. "I'll be right there, just have to fix this mess."

"Come." He waved her closer. "I'll help you."

Her brows lifted as she shoved in the remaining pins. "What would you know about hair?" At last, she made her way to him and sat, all prim and proper.

He put his hands on her shoulders and twisted her body away from him, ignoring the way she tensed under his touch. "I know how to make your hair look beautiful and be much more comfortable." He pulled a pin from her bun. Her hands flew to her head, but he gently lowered them to her lap.

With tender care, he removed every pin. Her shoulders lifted and tightened, but she didn't flee. For his part, having the chance to actually touch her felt like heaven. He untwisted her braid until her glorious head of hair fell long and free down her back. "Doesn't that feel better?"

The catch of her breath didn't escape him.

Such beautiful hair. Why did she hide it in that tight bun? The satin silkiness feathered through his fingers as he lifted the weight of the long strands. If only the tension in her body could be unwound as easily as the unplaiting of her hair.

He raised his hands to her temples and slowly massaged. Little by little, her shoulders lowered as she sank into the settee beside him. Her straight back curved, and, when he pulled her back against him, she didn't pull away.

His chest ached at the feel of her in his arms, leaning against him. How wonderful this was. But, oh, the agony. He lowered his face into her hair, and took a deep breath. The scent of rose water wafted up. It took all he had not to turn her luscious lips toward him.

"I was reading the paper this week and was shocked at the sharp lines drawn between the Southern Paternalism and Northern Capitalism. Do you think we'll ever get along?" Her voice sounded so unmoved.

He stilled his hands. She couldn't possibly be thinking politics when he was fighting to control the urge to turn her in his arms and give in to temptation. Did she feel nothing? He pulled away and swallowed the bitter taste of disappointment.

She turned to him, brows raised as she waited for his answer.

"I'll have to ponder that one." Later. Much later, when he could actually think.

"You know what I think?"

"Hmm?" He could barely breathe. A deep loneliness pressed in, sucking the air from the room. Was he destined to be considered no more than a nice man with whom she enjoyed conversation? That would mean no love, no intimacy, no children. The future suddenly looked bleak.

"I think both sides have their strengths and weaknesses, but unless we can admit the weaknesses, we'll never come together."

"You're most likely right." He stood and moved to stand in front of the fire. "I'm going to retire now. Don't forget we're heading into town tomorrow bright and early."

"But I don't need—"

He faced her. "You do need clothing." He spoke with more clip in his voice than he'd intended. "And what about the riding habit I promised you? Surely you won't deny me even this small pleasure." He struggled to keep his tone level, thinking of all the other pleasures he was denied.

"All right."

"Very well. Be ready by nine." He had to get out of there before he said something he would regret. "Good night."

He took the steps two at a time. With the decided click of his bedroom door just short of a slam, he ripped his hands through his hair. He would scream, except she would hear him. He fumbled with the buttons and tore his shirt from his shoulders, flinging it on the bed. With his head bent over the wash bowl he doused his upper body to cool the flame of anger…and a whole lot more.

~

*K*atie had disappointed him last evening. Her stomach still flip-flopped at the thought of his closeness. Thankfully, starting that conversation about politics had put an end to where things had been headed. Try as she might, she was not ready.

But she could do everything within her power to give him a nice day.

She climbed into the carriage Abe had pulled up to the front steps and offered Josiah a big smile. He gave her a watered-down version, and silence followed. His usual upbeat banter was absent.

After a while, she glanced his way. "Are you all right?"

"I'm fine." He patted her knee, then looked out his window.

She wasn't imagining it. He was upset.

Heads turned as they drove through Lacey Spring, and most everyone waved. Katie peeked out the window. "Is this how it always is when you come into town?"

"They're curious. Not much happens in this sleepy town, so if they want to stare and tip their hats, I'm happy to oblige in a friendly manner. Today, I bet they're trying to catch a glimpse of my beautiful wife."

It was his first attempt at lightheartedness, and she wanted to encourage the old Josiah back. "Or maybe it's the ladies all in a twitter over the handsome Mr. Richardson."

"You think I'm handsome?" His brows rose.

"One cannot deny the obvious."

He grinned. "Things are looking up."

The tension in her shoulders eased at his teasing.

Soon, a rap from above signified they had arrived.

Josiah swung out and reached for her hand as she stepped down.

"Mr. Richardson," a man called.

Josiah lifted his head and waved.

The rugged man sauntered across the street. When he reached them, he lifted his cowboy hat to Katherine and nodded. "Ma'am."

"Hank, meet my wife, Katherine."

She tilted her head in a respectable nod, careful not to invite more.

"Katherine, this is Hank, one of the best horse handlers in the country."

The man's sun-weathered face creased into a wide smile. "Thanks for the praise. I wanted to be sure you don't forget me when Colby gets back with those horses."

"You're at the top of my list."

"Sure glad to hear. Work has been hard to rustle up. Are you still fixin' to hire both black and white?"

Josiah nodded. "The best man for the job is my policy."

"I'd be happy to work with whomever, but talk about town is that if you intend to hire them there black fellows"—his eyes darted up to Abe—"and take jobs from the whites, there will be trouble."

Katie's heart picked up speed. Trouble?

"You know me." Josiah clapped Hank on the shoulder. "Never had much time for idle threats. You know how men talk with one too many a drink in their belly. But thanks for the warning. I'll be in touch the minute Colby is home."

Hank lifted his hat one more time in her direction and took off across the street.

She turned to him. "Trouble? What does he mean by that?"

"There's nothing to worry about. These cowboys are all big talk, no action." He whisked her into the nearby shop before she could ask any more questions.

She stopped just inside the door and gazed about the room, taking in the awe-inspiring selections. "I can't believe it. Look at all these choices." Bolts of fabric stacked in all colors and weaves cluttered every nook and cranny. Spools of thread, needles, measuring tapes, and scissors lay scattered on a large table. A woman appeared from the back and greeted them with a smile.

"Josiah, my dear." The older woman moved toward him with grace and class. She placed a kiss on each of his cheeks and did the same to Katie. "'Tis the French in me. I can't get used to greeting people any other way. I'm Clarisse, and you must be Katherine." She stepped back and surveyed Katie as if she were a rare animal in a cage. She moved all around. "My, Josiah, this bride of yours will be a delight to dress. Look at that tiny waist, and the fine form to fill out a bodice. And that hair and those eyes. *Magnifique.*"

Katie fought to keep from squirming under the woman's scrutiny.

"Stop with the compliments, Clarisse," Josiah said. "She's a shy one."

"My dear girl," Clarisse said to Katie, "you will have to outgrow that. Your kind of loveliness was created to be shared with the world." She ran a hand down Katie's cheek. "Look at these high cheekbones. You've been graced with regal beauty." She grabbed Katie's hand and pulled. "Come. We shall have fun." With the other hand, she waved Josiah off. "Out you go, and don't come back anytime soon."

Panic welled in Katie's throat at the thought of Josiah leaving her alone with this stranger.

Maybe he saw the look in her eyes, for he reached out. "I want her to have—"

"Don't you worry yourself with details. I'll start fresh. Undergarments, dinner gowns, petticoats, crinoline, hats, gloves, shoes—"

He stood there looking unsure. "Don't forget everyday clothes—skirts, blouses, shawls, and a riding habit and boots."

Riding habit, yes. She could do this for Josiah.

Clarisse laughed and shooed him away. "Katherine has a tongue in her head. We'll not forget a thing. Run along now."

~

*T*hat night in the drawing room, Katie sat on the settee near Josiah as they enjoyed their usual evening conversation. But, when he stood and turned to leave for bed, the action sparked a reminder in her. "Wait." She stood and moved toward him, then placed her hand on his arm.

His eyes widened at her initiation of touch and flicked to her hand. "Yes."

"I need…"

A flicker of hope filled his gaze.

She'd better hurry and finish before he got the wrong idea. "I would like some work to do during the day."

His eyes went dull and flat. He stepped away, pulling out of her reach. Without speaking, he turned and headed for the stairs. His response was answer enough.

"What?" She hurried behind him as he climbed the steps. "What's wrong with me helping out around here? And don't tell me again that I need to get accustomed to my surroundings."

He whirled around at the top. "You're not some common maid to be scrubbing and cleaning about."

Frustration welled inside her. "Then teach me the books, like you said you would."

"Until the horses come in and the buying and selling begins, there is little to do."

"Surely there are household expenses that would require some tracking. You have the maids, Annie and Ruby, helping around here, plus Delilah and Abe, not to mention my family. Surely there are expenses and I could learn how to do entries and—"

"No."

"Why not? I'm going stark raving mad with all this sitting around. Delilah is insistent I do nothing until you give the go ahead."

"This is not a conversation for the whole household to hear." He grabbed her hand and pulled her into his room, slamming the door behind them. Dropping her hand, he paced the floor before coming to stop in front of her.

"Soon, Kat. We have the complexities in our relationship to concentrate on first, and I don't want you so exhausted from daily chores that you—"

"So that's what this is about? You want me good and rested to fulfill my wifely duty—an area in which you know I have failed miserably." Now her frustration melded with fear. She would have to face the inevitable. But could she?

"Is that so wrong?" His voice sounded curt, but then he softened, his eyes gentling. "A man caring enough to not overwhelm his new bride, or a man desiring his wife—"

"Of course, it's not wrong." She fought the sting of tears. "I... just can't seem to get over...to get beyond..." Her body shuddered at the memory. "The thought of a man touching me..." Unwanted tears filled her eyes and toppled down her face.

"Can you talk about it? Does this have to do with that day at the creek or what happened in the saloon?" He reached out a hand, but then pulled back and dropped it to his side.

She motioned toward him. "See, I've made you afraid to even touch the woman who is supposed to be your wife. Don't you see? I never should have married you, or anyone, in this state."

"We can work through this, if you'll just talk to me, tell me what happened. I'm a patient man." His voice pleaded for her to believe him.

Poor man. He deserved better than this. "You have been patient. You've given my family everything you promised and I...I sit around here like a lady of leisure with no purpose whatsoever. I haven't even upheld my end of the bargain."

"I don't care about a bargain. I care about you." His voice was almost a whisper.

"That makes it even worse." She flung her hands in the air. "You're not the problem. It's me."

She ran for the door between the rooms and slammed it behind her. Ripping at her clothes, she stripped herself naked and stared into the mirror. *I should just walk into his bedroom right now and do whatever I'm supposed to do.* She marched to the door between the rooms and stopped. Who was she kidding?

She turned toward the bureau, slipped into her nightwear, and took refuge on the bed. Her pillow muffled the wrenching sobs.

Where was this God of Daniel who gave courage? Maybe He wouldn't show up for a coward like her.

CHAPTER 13

*H*er scream split the night air. Josiah sat up in bed, instantly awake. Should he go to her? Another scream, and his legs flew into action.

He found her thrashing on her bed. Fighting. Flailing. Furious. "No, no, don't."

He leaned over her and shook her shoulder. "Katherine, wake up. You're having a bad dream."

Her eyes popped open, and she grabbed at him, flinging her shaking body into his arms, dragging him down to the bed.

"It's all right, Kat, you're safe now," he whispered into her hair. "You're safe." She clung so tightly, her nails gouged his back. He held her until the weeping subsided. With a slow smooth touch, he stroked her back and rocked her in his arms.

His bare torso was getting cold outside the covers, so he moved to go, but she held on.

"Don't go."

Oh, dear God, help me. This was a tough one. She was in no condition to be touched in any other way than platonically, but his body was reacting to her nearness. The innocent would not have a clue.

He stood, thinking a little separation would give her room to think. Her fear would send him packing. But, instead of shrinking away, she held out her arms. He slid in beside her and gathered her close.

He dusted a thumb across her cheek to dry the flow of tears as she looked up at him with wide innocent eyes.

"Can you talk about it, Kat? I've had my share of trauma. The war accomplished that. It helps to share with someone."

She snuggled close and laid her head against his bare chest.

He could barely breathe as he folded one arm around her. There was not nearly enough clothing between them.

"I...haven't had that nightmare for a while." Her jaw still trembled. "Living with you makes me feel safe. I've slept so much better here."

He could not say the same, but he kept quiet, willing her to speak.

"I was back at the creek again, only this time you didn't show up." She shuddered against him.

He ran his hand up and down her back, soothing her. "What happened that day? Maybe if you could get it out, it wouldn't haunt you so much."

She was silent for so long, he looked down. Maybe she'd drifted back to sleep.

The movement seemed to restart the flow of both her tears and words. "The trouble began long before that day at the creek. Those boys were making a nuisance of themselves at school, which was one of the reasons I decided to quit. I was fifteen, and they kept vying for my attention. When I spurned them, it became a contest among the group over which one would make the ice maiden melt and get the first kiss."

He rubbed her arms. He could see her getting more attention than she wanted. "Go on."

"I was so naïve, I thought if I showed them up, humiliated them good, they would finally understand that I wasn't interested. I challenged Tommy Rowan, the ringleader, to a shooting match. I told him that, if he won, I'd give him a kiss in front of everyone. But, if he lost, then he'd have to promise they'd all leave me alone.

"Much to my horror, the competition became the talk of the school. Half the kids came out that Saturday morning to watch. I cleaned Tommy's clock, and he left humiliated."

A simmering anger was beginning to build in him, but he worked to suppress it, not wanting to scare her. But what had Tommy done to her? "A young man's pride is a powerful force to reckon with."

"I know that now. Being the fool I was back then, I didn't give it a second thought—until that day at the creek.

"My brothers and I were in the habit of traipsing around the back woods, and one of our favorite things to do was to swim in the water hole. They were my best friends, and the only ones who understood me. They didn't have any problem letting me join in what they did, so they taught me to swim. Ma would have killed me had she known I stripped down to my unmentionables and enjoyed a swim."

He searched the recesses of his memory. He remembered the day well, but not her brothers being there.

"That area was perfect for swimming because the water pooled into a deep eddy, and it was private, with the trees and rock formations at the mouth of the cave."

His chest ached at the memories, desperation welling in him anew. "I remember. I could hear your cries but couldn't see where you were. I had to work my way down the ravine."

"I believed it was safe to lose a few layers and swim like men do all the time. It irked me that a girl didn't have the right clothing or opportunity to learn how to swim. I always had an extra set of underclothing in my haversack to change into, the cave being the perfect spot."

He had to ask. "Where were your brothers?"

She swept the tears from her cheeks with the back of her hand. "I'd become too comfortable with our little hideaway," she admitted. "When my brothers didn't want to swim that day, I told them I was more than capable of finding my way home. That was not the first time they had left me to my stubborn ways."

The tears slid down her cheeks again, and he ached to brush them away. But he didn't dare move.

"I was too sure of myself. I was careless. If you hadn't come along—" A sob broke free. "What a fool I was." She hiccuped and buried her face in his chest. Her hair concealing her from him. "I'm so embarrassed remembering how you found me."

Her pain cut all the way through him. "Shh, my dear. We've all made mistakes." He lifted his hand and smoothed the hair from her cheeks. "It will help to finally get this out." *Lord, please soothe away her pain.*

A deep shiver ran up her body, which he felt against his skin.

"Tommy and the gang must have followed us that day, because it wasn't long after my brothers left, that the group of them emerged out of the trees. I was floating on my back, my eyes closed, when I heard my name."

"There was more than one?"

She started shaking, and he held her tighter, wrapped her close. "You're safe now. Trust me." He smoothed his hand up and down her back. "Let it out."

"I stayed under the water because I didn't want them to see me. You know how wet fabric sticks to the body, and I didn't have much on to begin with. My pile of clothes and my gun lay on the bank, but I couldn't figure out how to get there before one of them did."

Her trembling increased. "I can still hear their disgusting words, their leering looks. They dragged me out of the water, and each one took their turn at groping and slobbering all over me. I thought I was going to die. They said...they said they were going to start with a kiss, and then the high and mighty Katie Williams was going to give them a whole lot more."

Josiah worked hard to stay put as a spike of rage rose up his spine. His hands fisted.

"I fought. I screamed. But I was so weak against the pack of them. Tommy was already on top of me. His hands...the evil in their eyes... Had you not fired your gun from a distance they would've..." The tears coursed down her face as she gulped back a sob and tucked into a tight ball.

Wrath churned inside him. How dare they try to take what she did not want to give? What kind of animals would do that to a helpless woman—to *his* woman. He wanted to find them. Hurt them. Make them beg for mercy and then not give it.

He pulled in a deep breath. "I don't know what to say right now." She must have heard the anger in his voice, for she sat up.

"I'm sorry." She pulled the blankets up to cover her night-clothes, to hide herself from him as she turned away. "I was such a fool. You have every right to be mad."

"I'm not angry with you." He touched her chin, forcing his fingers to be gentle as they urged her to face him. When she did, he met her gaze. "Please don't think that."

After a moment, she rested against him again.

He inhaled a steadying breath. "But I wish I had done more. Had I known there was more than one, had I known what they intended, I would've used my gun for a whole lot more than a warning."

He'd been working his way down the ravine after hearing a woman scream. He'd fired his gun in hopes that whatever was going on would be stopped. That had happened, but it had also allowed them time to scatter. He'd caught only one, and when the young man had said they were just having a little fun, he had let him go.

"Fun, that's what he called it." He bit out the words. "I viewed the whole thing from different eyes. Two young people with too much freedom on a hot summer's day, and the young man got carried away. If I'd known there was a gang of them trying to..." He ground his teeth, not able to voice the words. And the way he had barked at her to get dressed and told her she should know better than meeting a boy alone, he hated himself for those words. Yet she had said nothing. He took in another breath. "Why didn't you tell me what had happened back then?"

"I was so ashamed." Her words were so soft, he barely made them out. "I couldn't tell you there had been more than one." But then her voice seemed to gain strength. "Somehow you believed me when I told you I had not planned to meet him." She pulled up from his chest to look at him. "I still don't understand why."

"At first glance, I noticed your neatly piled clothes and assumed you had willingly undressed. But one look into your eyes convinced me you spoke truth."

"And when I begged you not to tell my parents?"

"Everything inside me balked. I wanted to make sure you'd never swim alone again." He'd questioned his decision for months afterward. Years even.

"But you trusted what I promised."

"Yes." His mind was whirling with the information, though he tried to present a calm front. No wonder she could barely handle a man's touch. He couldn't believe she was allowing his nearness right now.

She seemed to relax further. "I've always wondered why you sat and talked to me that day. Remember how you shared some of the funny things you did when you were younger? It was as if you were trying to make me feel better about my stupidity."

"I was. At first, I wanted to ensure you were calm enough to ride home, then I found talking to you fascinating. You were unlike any woman I had ever met, and I believed you'd be more careful." His gut tightened. "But I had no idea there was more than one or how far their assault went. I swear I would've tracked each one down and beaten them within an inch of their lives. I'm so sorry."

She nodded, sniffing. "I believe you." Her hair rubbed against his skin like a curtain of silk.

Just that small movement heightened his awareness. Her nearness took the wind out of his lungs but he remained still. To have her relaxed in his arms was a milestone. He didn't want to ruin the moment with anything that would cause her angst.

"Go to sleep now. I'll stay until you drift off." He smoothed a hand down her back.

"Josiah?"

"Hmm."

"You need to know one more thing."

"What is it?" He rubbed his fingers over her hair.

"After what they did, I've been scared…of any man's touch. I'm so sorry for not being a real wife—"

"I understand. We have a whole lifetime ahead of us."

She snuggled up against him. "You make me feel so safe."

He kissed the top of her head, willing himself to remain strong.

Tonight had been one small victory in an ocean of turbulent waters. He wanted to kill the reprobates who'd traumatized his wife and caused the pain they now shared. He wanted to scream at her parents for not caring enough to keep a beautiful woman like her under their protective care. He wanted to poke out the eyes of every man who ogled and leered.

He was not blind to what she had to put up with. Every trip into town made him jealous enough to want to do damage. But mostly, he longed to nurture, to cherish this woman he called his wife, to prove that not all men were ruled by one thing only. As the waves of need pounded upon the shore of his soul, he took deep breaths in and out.

To hold her so close in bed, and not to act on the natural response, took supernatural strength…and so he prayed.

God, I don't know You in the way Abe and Delilah share so freely, but I know You're up there. I need Your help. We need Your help.

She fell asleep, but the opportunity to hold her close would likely not come again soon. He tucked beneath the covers and cradled her body against his. Peace washed over his soul. Perhaps God was pleased with his simple prayer. He smiled into the darkness, hoping beyond all hope that healing was possible, because to withstand this kind of torture was not sustainable.

CHAPTER 14

Katie stroked Gracie's hair, soothing away her sister's tears. She'd forgotten how wonderful it felt to snuggle the little ones. "There, there, you poor thing. You just need one of my special kisses to make it all better." She dropped a soft kiss on her sister's scraped knee.

Gracie offered a wobbly grin. "It feels aaaall gooder." She stood to test the limb, then her smile broadened and she skipped away.

"You'll make a good mama someday." Ma watched from her place at the kitchen work counter.

Katie forced a smile as she moved in to help peel apples for the evening pie. She may never have a little one if she couldn't handle her husband's touch.

"Maybe even now, my grandbaby grows." Ma patted Katie's flat stomach.

Katie turned away. Guilt burned her throat and her eyes filled with tears. "I have to go. Tell everyone goodbye for me." She dropped the knife and headed for the door at a good clip. On the porch, she collided with Aunt May and almost sent her flying. Her aunt's protruding stomach glared up at her, and one of the tears broke loose.

"Whoa, Katie girl, what's wrong?"

Ma came running. "What did I say?"

Katie shook her head, but couldn't speak.

"Seems I said something wrong again," Ma said. "No matter how hard I try—"

She struggled to push back the emotion. "It's not you. It's me. I...I can't..."

Ma's voice turned gentle. "How about I take Jacob and Nathan inside to play with the girls. You two talk." Aunt May nodded, and Ma herded the boys into the house.

Aunt May wrapped her arm around Katie's shoulder and gave a squeeze.

Katie worked for a smile, but couldn't find much of one. "You don't have to, Auntie. I'll be all right."

"Come, my dear. I have uninterrupted time, which is a gift to me. Your Uncle John has gone in search of the men, and your ma has taken the boys. Even if you don't think you can share, I shall get a walk with one of my favorite people in the world." With a kind smile, she turned Katie and ushered her down the steps toward the orchard.

Katie inhaled a strengthening breath as a soft breeze pressed her dress against her knees and rustled the leaves. A few drifted lazily to the ground. They walked between the fruit trees in silence but for the crunch beneath their shoes. The slightly pungent smell of apples on the ground filled the crisp air. All around them, the colors of fall were splendidly arrayed, but she couldn't appreciate the beauty.

Thoughts scrambled in her head. For years, she had craved a close relationship with her ma, yet it never happened. All this time she'd thought Ma was at fault, but maybe the problem was her. She couldn't love like she should, first her ma and now her husband.

"Can you tell me about your tears?"

Katie stopped and faced her aunt. "It's all so personal, so embarrassing." The words got caught in her throat.

Aunt May placed a tender hand on Katie's cheek. "It helps to talk."

Those were the very words out of Josiah's mouth. Had it helped? The pressure of expectation she'd put on herself *had* eased because of his kindness.

"I...feel terrible. I misjudged Josiah. First, I took my anger out on him, thinking he married me just for what I looked like. But, he's worked hard at getting to know me, being a friend. And then with Ma, Pa, and the girls so happy... I feel so guilty."

"Why?"

Heat raced to her cheeks and she dropped her gaze. But she pushed the words past the lump in her throat. "I haven't fulfilled my wifely duty. I'm so scared. I don't know how to approach him." She stopped and buried her face in her hands. "Ma said he would know what to do, but I think my reaction when he first tried to hold me has... I don't know. It's like he's waiting for my invitation, and I'm a coward." She blinked back a rush of tears.

Aunt May's arm closed around her, and they swayed back and forth. "There. It's going to be all right. I promise." Aunt May took a lace-trimmed handkerchief from her pocket and gently wiped the streaming tears. "My sweet one, marriage is not supposed to be so complicated. The way of a man with a woman is a beautiful thing God created for our enjoyment, as well as procreation. Usually, by the time a couple gets married, they can't wait to come together, but I can understand why you'd be frightened when you hardly know the man."

Katie couldn't bear to tell how much more complicated it was than that.

"But I want you to consider one thing," Aunt May said. "I've watched Josiah closely. The way he looks at you is the look of a man in love. Do you think you could try and open your heart to him? Then, the physical part of the relationship will naturally follow." She smoothed a hand down Katie's arm and gave a squeeze. "I've been thinking about my part in encouraging this marriage because I wanted more room for my growing family. I had selfish motives, and I'm sorry. Will you forgive me?"

Katie looked into the empathetic eyes of her aunt, and her nod came easily.

"There's a story in the Bible of a lady named Ruth, a sad story of loss, and yet a wonderful account of God's provision. Ruth opened her heart to the possibility of love in the strangest of places with an older man. A beautiful love story unfolds because of Ruth's obedience and courage. Do you have a Bible in that large, grand home of yours?"

She nodded. "Delilah reads one."

"Then promise me you will read the book of Ruth. Look for the similarities to your story and how God helped Ruth and will help you, even in the most difficult of situations."

Katie grabbed Aunt May's arm, pulling them to a stop. "I've tried to pray, Aunt May, and I still lack courage."

"Ah, yes, my sweet girl. Sometimes it takes stepping out. The strength is given in that moment of action. You have a patient man who is waiting for you to initiate. He has a level of respect for you that's impressive. It's no small thing for a man in love to wait for the physical connection."

Aunt May pulled her close. "I love you as if you were my own daughter. I know it was hard for you to talk about this. I'll keep it between you, me, and the good Lord." The hug grew tighter, and Katie held on, soaking in the warmth in her aunt's arms.

"I miss you girl. I had to twist John's arm to get him to bring me out here in my condition, but I'm sure glad I did." Her aunt placed her hands on the sizable mound. "Goodness me. This one's going to be a handful. I can tell by all the kicking."

Aunt May reached for Katie's hand and placed it on her swollen abdomen, then held it there.

The movement against her palm sent a surge of joy through her. "I think she's dancing."

"I hope it's a she. I love my two boys, but it would be so wonderful to have a baby girl. Just you wait. When it's your turn, you'll be in awe."

Katie gave her aunt a look. "First, I have to do whatever makes babies."

Aunt May laughed out loud. "You're right about that, Katie girl. Trust me. It's so amazing."

~

*K*atie snuck into the kitchen late that night. Her candle flickered, casting shadows against the wall as she scanned the area for the big black book. Ah, there it was, sitting on the edge of the table like it was waiting for her. She set her candle stand down and slid into the wooden chair worn smooth by years of use.

Aunt May had said to read the book of Ruth. She opened the Bible with care and turned to the contents. There it was, tucked between Judges and First Samuel, so few pages she almost missed it.

She was supposed to keep the similarities of their two stories in mind, so she'd brought both pen and paper. It wasn't long before she found her first similarity and started writing.

Ruth suffered loss, the death of her husband — I lost my brothers and Charles.

Ruth traveled to a strange land with strange customs — Coming from my humble roots, yes, this life is strangely different.

Ruth worked to support her mother-in-law — I married Josiah to support my family.

There were more similarities in this one story than she had thought possible.

Ruth was a beautiful woman who needed the protection of Boaz — I need the protection Josiah provides.

As she wrote that last line, the words jumped off the page. Josiah did make her feel protected and accepted for who she was. Now, after finding out the full truth, he was gentler than ever. She read on.

Boaz was a wealthy older man — Josiah is the same, though I'm not seeing him as what I would call old these days. The more I get to know him, the younger he seems.

Ruth was instructed by Naomi to go to Boaz at night and offer herself in marriage —

Katie's pen paused on the page. An ink blot stained the spot. Was she to go to Josiah? Was this what Aunt May was getting at? Well, that would be where the similarities stopped.

Ruth became a wife and mother — but I am a coward.

As she penned the word *coward,* a heaviness came over her soul. She slapped the book shut with far less reverence than she had opened it.

With a flick of her head to send her heavy braid to the back, she picked up her candle and the paper and went up stairs, her heart as heavy as her steps.

~

*J*osiah pushed his empty plate aside and pulled his weary body up from the table. He would pay a price, but he had to offer anyway. "Would you like to start learning the bookkeeping?"

The smile Katherine tossed him quickened his sorry heart.

"I sure would. But are you sure you're up to this after a full day of work?"

"You've been after me for weeks now, saying you need something to do. Do you really want to talk me out of it?"

"Certainly not." She jumped to her feet, a new light shining in her eyes.

He turned down the hall toward the library and puffed out a deep breath. *God, help me.* Ever since she'd spent that night in his arms, he could think of little else. Either he was battling anger at the degenerates who damaged her, or he was the one wanting the same thing they'd wanted. Neither scenario felt good or right.

Sure, he and Katherine were married, and he shared everything he owned with her. But why had he married her? He'd convinced himself it was noble and kind to help her family out of a tough spot and offer his protection. But when he looked deep inside where the whole truth lived, had he been any different than the rest? Absolutely, her wit and intellect were part of her attraction, but her beauty had stirred him, and her plight had made events simple to manipulate.

"Where do we start?" She waved her hand over the desk. "Are you sure you're not too tired?"

He didn't even remember sitting in his chair behind the desk. "No, I'm fine." But he was anything but fine, staring off into the distance like a lovesick idiot.

He opened up his black ledger book and began explaining the columns and rows. A faint smell of lilacs stole his concentration as she bent close. "How is your addition and subtraction?"

"Give me something to calculate and you can double check."

He stood and waved her to sit in his chair. In quick order, she added up the sum of three credits and subtracted five expenditures with a correct balance.

"I can see this won't be hard for you to learn. I'll look forward to handing this job off to you in no time."

She beamed at his praise.

Her pleasure sent a warmth through him. "Would it be too forward to say I married both the most beautiful and the smartest woman in the valley?"

She tipped her head to one side and pressed the pen to her lips. "Hmm. Would it be too forward to reply that I married the kindest and most generous man in the valley?" She pointed to the ledger. "You've helped Ma and Pa way more than you made out."

She was a quicker study than he'd expected. "Now you've discovered the main reason why I've stalled teaching you the books. I wanted to keep this private for your pa's sake. I have no doubt he'll pay it all back in time."

She stood and stepped into his arms. "Josiah Richardson, will I ever be able to repay your kindness?"

He encircled her petite body, pressed against him, with both pleasure and agony.

He didn't want repayment. He longed for love. For now, he would take the hug. Beggars could not be choosers.

CHAPTER 15

osiah followed Jeb and John into the Williams'
kitchen. Their long day of work had been produc-
tive. The hay of another field was harvested and
stored safely in the barn for the long winter months ahead.
John's help the past week had been a gift.

The door slammed, and Katherine and her Aunt May walked
into the kitchen arm in arm. His eyes followed her as she spoke
to her ma, then turned his way. His heart did a trip, skip, and
dip, as it always did when she looked at him.

"Smells mighty fine in here," Jeb said. "You got yourselves
some hungry men to feed."

"We've arranged supper together since this is the last day
before Aunt and Uncle leave. Hope that's all right?" Katherine
raised her brows in hopeful expectation.

She could have most anything she wanted when she looked
at him like that. Best he never let her in on that little secret. "No
problem on my part, but Delilah might have supper underway."

She smiled. "I sent Amelia over with a message for her
earlier. Abe and Delilah are going to join us. She's bringing over
the food she prepared, and we'll throw it all together."

Josiah tried to busy himself playing with the children, but he could barely keep his focus with the way Katherine's eyes followed him. The laughter and squeals while he played the role of Big Bad Bear didn't offer enough distraction from the burn of her gaze. Why was he suddenly garnering her attention? At dinner, she motioned him into the chair beside hers. Normally, she tried to place herself at arm's length—or further away.

After the meal, while the adults sat at the table and conversed, her leg brushed up against his several times. Sweet torture.

When she got up to help clear the dishes, he caught her staring again and lifted one brow in question. Instead of lowering her eyes like she usually did, she held his gaze. What had come over her?

He winked. That would send her back to busy, busy mode. But no. She lifted her head and sent him a grin that could almost be called flirtatious.

He almost spit out his coffee, struggling to swallow the gulp of hot liquid he had just taken. It was his turn to look away.

He had worked hard at keeping a respectable distance. That small feat would be impossible if she kept looking at him the way she was tonight.

God, have mercy.

There he was, praying again. She seemed to bring out the desperate in him. But did God really care about the minute details of life? He couldn't deny the power of Delilah and Abe's prayers. They'd been praying for a wife for him for a long time. And not just any wife, but a partner he connected with. Kat filled the lonely in ways he'd never expected. Without the physical they had become friends. Good friends.

She was carefree and relaxed in his presence, at least, until the time came to say good-night. Then, the tension would rise between them, his with desire, and hers with fear. But he'd realized something profound. Even if life never took them farther, he still wanted her as his wife. He enjoyed her company, no matter how difficult.

"Isn't that right, Josiah?" Kat's voice broke through his thoughts.

All eyes were on him. What had the question been?

"Yes." Did his answer make sense?

A knowing look curved the corners of her mouth upwards. "That is wonderful." She flashed him a radiant smile.

Had she just bamboozled him? Whatever he'd agreed to put that incredible beam on her face, and he wasn't about to squelch it.

"We'd better get going," she said. "As you've often reminded me, sunrise comes early. But could we walk back? It's a warm evening, and we won't have many of those left."

The thought of a walk through the orchard in the moonlight stirred his blood to a dangerous level. She, naturally, had no idea where his thoughts had just been, or where they would take him walking beside her in the moon's soft glow.

"Is that all right?" She looked uncertain. "I know you've been working hard all day."

Not hard enough.

"Sure." He infused his voice with as much calm as he could muster. "You're right. It's a fine night for a walk. The weather has been agreeable as of late." He pressed his lips shut. He sounded like a babbling idiot. But the last thing he felt confident about was a walk in the moonlight with her when he wanted so much more.

He couldn't help the pang of jealousy that shot through as she said good-bye and lavished hugs and kisses on her family.

When they stepped into the darkness, she grabbed his arm and slid her hand down to fold in the crook of his elbow. She gave a subtle squeeze and leaned in closer. They walked between the trees in silence, though she could surely hear the pounding of his sorry heart.

A three-quarter moon floated on the edge of the horizon through lightly scattered clouds. The glow cast a silvery shine to the fluttering leaves above them, and a warm breeze lifted the wayward strands of her hair as they drifted up to kiss his face. He had to pull away from her and fist his hands at his sides in order not to cave into the urge to take her in his arms.

A soft sigh escaped her lips, and she muttered something under her breath.

"Did you say something, Kat?"

"I want to be your wife," she whispered.

Did she mean what he thought she meant? His heart galloped like a thoroughbred. He stopped and turned toward her. "You are my wife." The words caught in his throat on their way out.

She met his gaze and stepped a little closer. "I have *not* been your wife. I don't know what I've been, other than a burden to you." Uncertainty filled her eyes. "You've been kind, gentle, and caring, in spite of my obvious fear. You've provided generously for me and my family. You've worked at getting to know me, and I thank you for that. But what have you gotten out of this arrangement?"

He stilled the flow of her words with the tip of his finger on her full lips. "Your company and our conversation has—"

She pressed up against him, and it drove the air right out of his lungs.

"Will you kiss me, really kiss me?" Her large, hauntingly blue eyes met his with a boldness, then her lids drifted closed. She stood on her tiptoes to reach him, her lips just inches from his.

He couldn't breathe. The invitation had the possibility of opening a thousand doors, and all he had to do was walk in. But did the innocent know what she was asking, and could he stop at just one kiss? Like being caught in an undertow with the power to suck the life right out of him, he had to force himself to take in air.

He cautiously placed his hands on her shoulders. "Do you understand what you're inviting?"

"Yes."

Resisting her was not an option. If she was frightened, it didn't show. He was the one trembling as he bent to meet her inviting lips. Fire burned in his bones, and he had to remind himself to take it slowly. When he lifted his lips from hers to draw away, she pulled his head back down, tightening her arms around his neck.

Need took over. He kissed her like a starving man given bread...her lips, her face, her eyes, the tip of her nose. He forced himself to slow down as his thumbs caressed her jaw and throat. He teased her mouth open, seeking out her response.

She mimicked touch for touch, but, when a sigh of enjoyment escaped her lips, he pulled away. The pull of her was growing too strong.

His voice thickened. "You've opened a door you'll never be able to close."

She offered a tempting smile. "Who says I want to shut it?"

He laughed at her boldness, but caught the look of shyness as she cast her eyes down. She shivered when he placed his arm around her waist and began walking to the house.

He had no idea if the kiss affected her even a smidgen as much as it affected him, but he wouldn't rush. As much as he desired her, the hope that she would fall in love with him outweighed all, and he wouldn't jeopardize that.

They reached the house, and he removed his arm, opening the door for her. After a quick glance his way, she headed for the stairs. His heart struggled to keep a steady beat as he followed.

At her bedroom door, she reached for the handle but didn't enter. Instead, she turned her gorgeous eyes, bright with questions, toward him. Her expression, soaked in innocence and invitation, swallowed him up. He couldn't move, and they stood there, staring at one another.

Since she had started the kissing, dare he risk one more?

He stepped toward her and took her in his arms. As his mouth descended toward hers, a flash of fear registered. He reined in the acute temptation to throw caution to the wind and gave her lips a quick kiss. It would be so easy to get lost in her loveliness, but he stepped back, and his hand brushed a line down her soft cheek. "Good night, my love."

~

*T*he click of his bedroom door brought both relief and disappointment to Katie. Had she not made it clear that he was invited? Should she have walked to his door instead?

Yet, though the intensity of his kiss in the moonlight had shaken her, was she ready for more? She entered her bedroom. A mixture of feelings, none of which she could sort, washed through her. An odd flush of emotion and a flutter of something beautiful danced in the pit of her stomach. Yet, fear of another place and time still haunted her.

She was proud of herself for pushing through the fear, and his kiss had been quite wonderful, so much more than she'd imagined. Yet, did she have the strength to encourage more? Her legs quivered. Could she, like Ruth, lie down beside him?

The wardrobe door opened with a tug, and she removed the white cambric nightgown that had been made for her wedding night. She slipped it on, allowing the soft folds to fall around her. A peek into the full-length mirror revealed her form beneath the gown. Heat slipped up her neck at the thought of standing before Josiah in so little. She wished with all her heart she was so in love with him that it would overshadow the embarrassment. If only she wanted him as much as he wanted her. The memory of that kiss and her response both frightened and beckoned her.

She walked to the adjoining door, the one she had never locked, and put her hand on the doorknob.

The coward in her turned back to the bed. She slipped between the covers and prayed that both God and Josiah would understand...for she was not Ruth.

~

*K*atie jolted awake as a groan split the night. The noise had come from Josiah's room. He sounded like he was in agony. Before she could stop to think, she threw the covers off, and was through the adjoining door into his room.

The light from the moon spilled through his open window, illuminating his form on the bed. The covers were twisted around his bottom half. His top half lay bare. Every detail heightened her awareness and drew her attention—the manly appearance of curly chest hair, the strength of his muscles, the breadth of his large shoulders. He really was handsome. She wanted to stare and run all in the same instant.

He moaned and thrashed. A pained expression filled his face, but she could barely make sense of his jumbled words.

"No, no. Forward, march. Retreat, Colby. Go. I'll cover you... God, help us."

He was having a nightmare. She moved closer, inching her way to the side of the bed, and reached out. "Josiah. Josiah, wake up." In the light of the moon, it was clear when he left that place of horror. His eyes opened, and his face changed from pain to pleasure.

"My beautiful, beautiful, Katherine." He reached out and pulled her into his arms.

She allowed her body to melt into his. The way he was moving, the way he was touching her—all so glorious. His mouth hungrily devoured her lips as his hands cupped her face, then slid into her thick hair. His hands moved over her body, and still he drew only pleasure. All fear vanished.

But when he reached for the tie of her nightgown, she stiffened, and a gasp slipped from her lips.

He pulled up. "Katherine, what are you doing here? I...I thought I was dreaming." His voice sounded drugged and ragged. A shudder ran through his body, one she could feel straight through to her bones.

He looked down at her, and a groan ripped from his throat. "You don't understand what you do to me." His eyes roamed over her and his stare grew hot.

She struggled with the ripple of fear that skittered up her spine.

He lifted his eyes to look into hers. "I am only a man. I want this more than I can say. But do you?" In the depth, beyond the desire, she glimpsed both his battle and his respect for her. If there was anyone in the world she could trust with this, it was him.

She reached up and pulled him down to meet her kiss.

He tried to pull away but her whisper stopped him. "I want this. Please let me be your wife." A tremor worked its way through him as he nodded.

Moonbeams spilled through the window. A soft breeze flowed through the opening, and the night-song of a thousand crickets filled the air. Everything but Josiah faded away.

～

*J*osiah awakened to find Katherine nestled in the curve of his warm body. He had not been dreaming. She was in his bed. He kissed the back of her head and nuzzled closer. He couldn't believe she lay beside him, her thick black hair downy-soft against his face. Although not much of a praying man, he murmured thanks.

He had tried to be gentle, knowing it was her first time, and was surprised by her genuine response. Her shyness and inhibition melted away with each tender caress. The only thing missing from an otherwise incredible night was hearing words of love flow from her beautiful lips.

He rose on his elbows and gazed at the beauty by his side. He had held back saying what he wanted to say the night before. With her asleep, he could whisper all the sweet words he so ached to tell her.

"I need you more than life itself. What a wonderful life we'll have together with children gathered around. And more love than you'll know what to do with. You complete me, my dear sweet, Kat. I love you more than words can say and hope someday soon you'll feel the same."

He longed to lie beside her all day, but her pa would be waiting. They were going to plow and prepare the last field for seed in the spring. Uncle John had said he would stay one more day, and Josiah couldn't miss the extra help.

He slid from the covers with care so as not to wake her and slipped out of the room with an extra bounce in his step. All he worked so hard for would now have purpose, and it energized him beyond words. Feeling twenty again, he whistled his way down the stairs.

~

The movement of Josiah nuzzling close pulled Katie from her slumber, but where she had been bold the night before, her courage vanished in the light of day. She kept her eyes closed and her breathing steady. She heard his sweet words and choked back the sob that filled her throat. The minute the door clicked behind him, she allowed her tears the freedom to flow down her cheeks and soak into the bedding.

He deserved so much more than she could offer. He deserved to be loved.

CHAPTER 16

*K*atie dressed in her oldest work skirt and plainest cotton blouse. Even if she could not love Josiah as he loved her, there was one thing she could do, and that was to support his dream of making the ranch one of the finest. This meant work.

She descended the steps with purpose. Her first order of the day was to team up with Delilah and find out what needed to be done. She would no longer play the role of a Southern Belle born into privilege. She was a hard worker, and it was time she started to take charge.

She rounded the corner into the kitchen and planted a kiss on Delilah's pudgy cheek. "Good morning."

"What you be so happy about, girl?"

"Work. I'm going to work today, and feel tired and fulfilled by evening. I'd like to start in the garden unless you have something more pressing for me to do."

"Land sakes, no! You are the lady of this home. Ladies don't get on their knees digging."

"But I love to garden, and the roses need to be pruned back, the weeds pulled, and—"

"No," Delilah said, shaking her head. "My Abe will get to them roses before winter. We just running low on time and energy with these old bones slowing us down. But don't you be worrying your purty head."

"Please. You just said yourself you have way too much. And why, with a house and grounds this size, where you should have at least twenty staff, do you only have Annie and Ruby and a couple girls who come in twice a week to help out with the clothes washing?"

"That's Josiah's business to tell."

"I am his wife." For the first time those words rang true. She was his wife.

"True." Delilah pressed a finger against her full lips. "With all the expenses of rebuilding after the war, until them horses start selling again, we're keeping things skinny."

Skinny? After all he'd done for her family? "Even more reason for me to help. Plus, you work too hard."

"Pshaw. Don't be concerning yourself with me." She placed both hands on her generous hips and stared Katie down. "I've been working this place for years now."

Katie twisted the bottom of her apron in her hand. How could she get through to Delilah? "Then I'll take it up with Josiah. You heard him yesterday at the supper table when he agreed it would be fine if I wanted to help. I'm thinking he will not be pleased if you can't find his wife even one little thing to do."

A crease furrowed her dark brow, and she put a hand to her well-starched checkered turban. "I don't think he was paying you any mind yesterday. But I could use a little help, I guess."

"You will not regret this." Katie rushed forward and hugged the plump woman. "We'll make a great team. You'll see." She pulled back and smiled into Delilah's chocolate brown eyes. "You are the queen bee, and I'll be one of your worker bees."

A wide toothy grin split free. "Don't be needing to be a

queen anything. No, ma'am. But truth be told, a little more help 'round here would be heaven to these old bones."

The men often took the noon meal in the outside cook hut as a matter of convenience, so they could get quickly back to work. Katie set out that meal early so that Josiah wouldn't wander in and catch her working. He'd said she could help, but he hadn't realized what all she planned to do.

The day passed in a whirl of activity as Katie joined in the work of the large, sprawling house. Every accomplishment energized her. The only caveat to a perfect day was the inkling that Josiah had not known what he agreed to at dinner. He had seemed rather distracted. Before Delilah started rattling on about all they'd worked on together, she had better talk to him.

She stuffed down her embarrassment regarding the night before and stood waiting to greet him that evening when he walked in the door. She would have to get comfortable with the fact that this so called "duty" between a man and woman was much more pleasurable than she could have imagined.

The door opened, and he stepped in.

She stepped toward him. "I need to talk to you."

He raised his brows. "My day was fine. Thanks for asking, dear wife." He dropped a quick kiss on her cheek and chuckled.

Heat washed up her neck. "I'm sorry—"

"I was just teasing, and you can greet me at the door anytime you wish." He threw her a pleased look. "Give me a couple minutes to wash and change, then meet me in my room." He bounded up the steps.

She couldn't help watching him go, every bit of his handsome physique on display for her. The memory of his muscles beneath her fingertips, the feel of his kisses on her skin, the touch of those large but gentle hands... She shook her head, forcing her mind elsewhere.

After leaving him a respectable amount of time to change, she tapped on his bedroom door and waited.

"Come in, my love." His deep voice rumbled through the wood.

She swallowed hard at his use of the endearment, but squared her shoulders and stepped in. She was surprised to find him in a state of undress. His trousers hung loosely at his waist, his suspenders dangling toward the floor. His chest was bare. She stood, mesmerized, as he bent over the marble topped stand and splashed water from the washbowl onto his face and hair. He grabbed fresh linens and straightened to dry.

His wide shoulders and rippled body took her breath away. The work of the day gave definition to his muscles. Would she ever get used to how petite she felt in comparison? The night before flooded in, the memory of how gentle he'd been. It didn't suit the strong man who stood before her.

"Talk away," he said, as the towel slipped from his face. He caught her open stare and grinned.

She dropped her gaze and walked toward the window. "Nice view," she said, needing a moment to regain her focus.

His arms circled her waist, and he drew her back against him. "I'm sure you didn't come up here to talk about the view, now did you, Kat?"

She lost her train of thought as he nuzzled the back of her neck. The smell of fresh thyme soap and the brush of his whiskers tickling her skin took over her senses.

"Ow. These blasted pins." He smoothed one hand up and down her arm as he pulled each pin from her hair with the other. They dropped with a ping onto the hardwood floor. Her locks fell free down her back. An involuntary intake of breath slipped from her lips as he tenderly ran his fingers through her waves. Like a sensual caress, the touch of his fingertips played a slow agonizing melody.

His ragged voice whispered into her ear. "I love your hair down." He slid his hands up to massage her temples. The work of the day melted away. She closed her eyes to the view out

155

the window and relaxed to the rhythmic motion of his fingertips.

When he turned her to face him, she was ready for the kiss, sweet and gentle, then tantalizing and needy. A heat stirred deep within until he stepped out of her arms. Her eyes fluttered open. She reached out to pull him back, but he had already turned from her and was pulling on his shirt.

She shook the hazy feeling from her head and stared at the man.

"Well, my dear, did you come up here to be kissed soundly, or did you have something to talk about?"

"I wanted to thank you."

He turned and raised both his eyebrows. A look of delight split across his face. "The pleasure was all mine."

"I mean…thank you for letting me help Delilah today. I felt like my old self. Useful, that is. The little bit of work you've been able to give me doing the books is just not enough." Still jittery on the inside from that kiss, her thoughts came out jumbled.

"That's what this is all about? So, last night at supper when my mind was elsewhere, I agreed to exactly what?"

So her suspicions had been right and he had not been paying attention. She couldn't help a smile. "Why, Josiah, you know full well I can't go on like some lady of leisure. It's not me. And with all the help you're giving my family, the least I can do is join in." She pressed her hands together. "If you give me some freedom, you'll find I'm quite resourceful. I can garden, help with the horses, learn the bookkeeping. I admit, I'm not a great cook, but I can help, and I love cleaning."

His eyebrows lifted.

"If you're not too good to do any job, why am I?" She deliberately widened her eyes to give him a pleading look. "Please, I need this. I want to work. It makes me feel like I belong."

"Maybe it wasn't the work that made you feel like you belong," he teased as he flipped each suspender into place.

She hit his shoulder. "It's just plain ungentlemanly of you to suggest otherwise. Don't unduly flatter yourself. The work is what made me—"

He dragged her up against him in one swift movement and crushed his mouth on hers. The pressure intoxicated her senses, and she found herself tingling with awareness and excitement. Her body melted into his embrace.

He pulled back with a wide grin. "Need I say more?"

Katie shook her head. He was bending toward her for more when Delilah's bellow filtered up the stairs.

"Come, you two lovebirds, da supper is getting cold."

He drew his face back, but kept his arm tight around her. "Saved, little one—for now. Delilah can get quite grumpy if her hard work is spoiled." Then he released his hold at her waist and grabbed her hand. As they left the room and headed downstairs, he didn't let go. Heat rushed to her face as they entered the kitchen, hand in hand. An immediate glance to their locked hands and Delilah's dark face donned a mouthful of pearly whites.

～

The next few weeks passed in a flurry of activity. The work energized Katie a little more each day. Delilah handed over the running of the household with the understanding that the kitchen was her domain, leaving Katie plenty of time to oversee the maids, keep up the books, churn butter, make candles and soap, and do the outside work she loved.

Josiah was slow to agree to her helping in the garden or with the farm animals, but she soon realized there was little he would deny her with a bit of pleading. She dug up the last of the potatoes, onions, and carrots from the garden and stored them in the cold room. She tended the overgrown flower beds and pruned the roses in readiness for winter. When Ma and her sisters headed out to the orchard to pick the last of the apples, she joined in. Each day, she worked with one purpose in mind— to ensure Josiah would have the best run home in the valley. She would see to it. If she couldn't be a wife spouting words of love, she would at least help him fulfill his dreams of family and a well-run ranch.

She smiled at the thought of the nights they shared. That time with Josiah was far more enjoyable than she had imagined, and the hope she would someday be a mother filled her mind with joy.

"What are you smiling about?" Amelia asked in the orchard one day as she climbed the ladder next to Katie.

Katie could feel the heat rise in her face. "I was just thinking how scared I was to marry Josiah and how different it all turned out than I'd feared."

"Things are good then? I couldn't help but hear the commotion a few weeks ago when you ran out crying."

So much had changed since then. She could actually answer with truth. Josiah was happy and, oddly, that mattered more to her than her own happiness.

"I'm better, much better. Josiah is a kind husband."

"Kindness is enough?" Amelia's eyebrows lifted. "Didn't you always say you wanted a true love story or no love story at all? I was the one willing to settle for a home, family, and a kind man."

Katie snatched an apple and plunked it a little too hard into her bag. "You know my circumstances. I'm making the best of it. The least you could do is cheer me on."

"You know I'm on your side. You have no idea how worried I've been about you."

Katie's chest twinged and she turned toward her.

"Here we are"—Amelia's hand fanned out over the orchard —"living a life of abundance while you pay the price."

"I'm fine." She forced as much cheeriness as she could into

her voice as she turned back to her work. She really was fine. Why was it so hard to say the words to Amelia?

"Are you? Look me in the eyes and tell me that."

Katie stopped picking fruit, but ignored the question. Her hands gripped the side of the apple bag slung around her shoulders so hard, the material bit into her skin.

"Ah, I get it," Amelia said. "You're putting on a brave face, even with me."

"You don't get it. I'm making the best of a difficult situation, and if kindness was good enough for you, why can't it be good enough for me?"

"Because you're nothing like me. Not even a little bit. And the older I get, the more I realize kindness would never be enough in a marriage. Now that I'm seeing Edmund, I want him to feel crazy, earth-shattering love for me, and I for him."

She couldn't bite back her frown. "Why do you bring this up knowing my—"

"I asked because I long for you to find happiness and love. My own guilt at having all we have at your expense eats away at me. But I see the way he looks at you. He loves you."

Katie stepped down the ladder and poured her apples into the nearby bin. "What's done is done, Amelia. And things are far better than I expected. I've had enough of this conversation. I'm going home."

Amelia scurried down her ladder and grabbed her arm. "Are things better? Do you think you'll grow to love him?"

"I don't know…"

Amelia drew her into a hug. "I hurt when you hurt," she whispered into Katie's ear. "And now I'm hurting for Josiah too. I really like the man."

Katie pulled back. "So do I." Unwanted tears filled her eyes. "Can't that be enough?"

Amelia held her shoulders, searching her eyes. "You tell me."

But Katie couldn't meet her gaze. She stepped away from her sister, then turned and walked toward home.

～

*O*ne evening later that week, Josiah took Katherine's hand as they retired to the parlor to sit in front of the fire. He loved their time of stimulating conversation, their time to catch up from the day.

"I expect Colby any day now," he said. "Wait until you meet him, you'll love him. He's like the brother I never had." He pulled her down beside him, and she leaned into him.

"Will he have the horses you want?"

"That's my hope. If he's successful, you'll be as thrilled as I am, and you'll have your pick." He wrapped his arm around her.

"You keep this up, and you'll indeed spoil me."

He laughed. "Would that be such a bad thing, a man spoiling the woman he loves?"

The minute he said the word *love*, her body tensed. She pulled away, but he left his arm cradled around her. He pressed hard against the pang of sorrow that threatened to rise within him. Why couldn't he just be happy with what she was giving? Why did he need more? Were a happy home, a friendship, and now even the possibility of family not enough for his greedy soul?

"Josiah."

"Hmm?"

"I wish I could say—"

He lowered his lips to hers, unable to bear the sound of her putting her lack of love into words.

As he kissed her soundly, he was almost able to press his disappointment out of his thoughts. He drew back enough to catch his breath. "Let's retire for the evening." He left off the endearment, *my love*, hanging on the tip of his tongue.

She came to him that night initiating a needy exchange, and he joined in, longing to get lost in the passion, where he would not have to think until after…always after.

He drew her close, and, as content as a kitten, she curled into his embrace. The ache began, as it did every night, the wondering if he would ever touch her soul the way she touched his. Did she come to him out of obligation? A need to earn his approval? The thought gathered like hot stones in his chest.

"Are you still awake?" Her voice was sleepy.

"Yes."

"Josiah, I love…"

He held his breath. A flicker of light touched that pitch-black part of his soul, and hope ignited.

"…sleeping with you next to me."

Daggers of pain shot through him. They cut into the fleshy part of his heart and carved out a chunk big enough to do damage. He smoothed her silky hair and kissed her head. He didn't dare speak for fear she would hear the pain in his voice.

He wanted to rise from the bed and scream into the night. Instead, he lay still. The steady rhythm of her breathing told him she had drifted off. Yet sleep would surely not find him anytime soon.

∽

Falling asleep in Josiah's arms became one of Katie's favorite things. There had been too many years with the men gone to war where she had slept with one eye open and her gun tucked under her pillow. Though she'd acted tough and strong, deep down, a frightened soul had lurked, especially after that incident in the woods, when her vulnerability as a woman had been made all too clear. The strength of his body curled protectively around hers gave her such calm. She snuggled in closer, her body nestled tight up against his.

"Good night, my love."

"Good night, Josiah."

A deep sigh escaped his lips. He kissed the top of her head and rolled away, turning to the opposite wall.

Not a day went by he didn't say he loved her in some form or another. Sometimes, he even sounded like he regretted the words immediately after they came out of his mouth. Though her silence with the words she knew he wanted to hear left her a bit lost and with a mountain of guilt, she couldn't bring herself to say such an important thing tritely.

Things were changing, ever-deepening between her and her gentle husband, but was it love or merely pleasure mixed with a sense of duty? She certainly didn't feel the crazy heart throbbing out of her chest, like the way it had been with Charles. Did she even understand what love was?

All she knew was that affection, loving actions, and words flowed effortlessly from Josiah toward her. Whatever she felt paled in comparison.

CHAPTER 17

$\mathcal{T}$he first rays of dawn barely peeked between the curtain panels, and Katie was wide awake. They'd planned their trip into Lacey Spring to pick up her new clothes today. Far too much extravagance for her back-country taste, but she hadn't been able to squelch Josiah's excitement. The riding habit was the one outfit she cared to lay ownership to. She tossed and turned on the bed, for it was far too early to rise, until Josiah pulled her back into the curl of his warm body.

"What's troubling you, Kat?"

How could she tell him she was fretting over the prospect of dressing up in fancy lady's wear? Or how silly she thought it was to own dresses that required help to get in and out of? Why would anyone want that aggravation? Until now, her lack of culture had been shadowed by the everyday work of life in everyday clothing. But, put her in a ballroom with an uptown dress, and her lack of sophistication would soon be evident. Her stomach clenched at the mere thought.

The way things had turned out, her family needed Josiah far more than he needed them. Letting him down constantly nipped at the back of her mind. What if he woke up one day to find whatever fascination he had with her was gone?

He pulled the hair back from the side of her face and kissed her cheek. "We're both awake now. Do tell."

"What am I going to do with not one, but seven, formal dresses? Not to mention the hats, shoes, and dainty parasols that go with them? You know I've never had much. I wish you had spent the money on the house or livestock or anything more useful."

"That's why it's such a pleasure. Most women would be screaming for new clothing, but not you."

"Unnecessary cost—"

"Don't be worrying about that either. Colby will soon be here, and our business will be off and running. I already have orders lined up. People can't get work done without good horseflesh, and our ranch will provide that much-needed service. Business will be booming in no time."

Katie slipped from his grasp and climbed from the bed. Instantly, she missed the warmth of his arms, but she padded across the floor, pulled on her wrapper, and stood before the mirror. She would never be enough. With a quick twist she unraveled her braid and brushed her waist-long hair with all too vigorous strokes. She closed her eyes as she worked and took in a few deep breaths, trying to still the insecurities that ran deep.

His hand on the brush stopped her movement. Her eyes popped open as he removed the brush from her clenched fist. "I'm sure bald is not the look you're aiming for." He smiled into the mirror as he gently smoothed the brush through her hair. "Besides, there is a motive to my madness. We can't host a winter ball with you in your everyday clothes, now can we?"

She turned toward him. "Then why host one at all?"

"It'll give Colby and me an excuse to sneak the men off to the stables for a look at our stock. Half the battle is won once that seed is sown."

"Hence the need for some frilly spectacle of a dress I'm supposed to wear to fit the part of a wealthy horse breeder's wife."

He laughed. "When you say it like that, darling, it sounds much more pretentious than I intend. Actually, most women love a dance and an opportunity to dress up and get together. Something to celebrate after all the sadness of the war. Don't you want that too?"

"I am not most women. In fact, you'll understand the mistake you've made when the uncultured Katherine is expected to dazzle the masses."

He kissed the top of her head. "Everything you've set your mind to do, you've excelled at. I know you won't disappoint me now."

"But half the clothes you bought me are unnecessary and impractical."

He leveled a gaze on her. "A few frilly dresses are not going to change who you are, nor do I want you to change. Don't worry. I'm not much of a socializer either, but once in a while we will take part in social events to give back to the community. Hopefully this will bring people together for a celebration instead of feeding their unrest."

He made a sad puppy dog look, which did not suit the strong, broad-shouldered man she'd married. She couldn't help but laugh.

"You win, but if I turn into a spoiled lady of leisure, it'll be your doing. Furthermore, you're going to have to hire a parlor maid just so I can get in and out of all that paraphernalia."

"Kat, the getting out of your dresses will be my pleasure indeed." A wicked grin pulled at the corners of his mouth.

She twisted out of his arms and shook a finger at him. "Not a chance. I remember how long it took you to undo the buttons on my wedding gown. You're not getting anywhere near my new dresses."

His laughter followed her into her bedroom as she walked away with a deliberate sashay of her hips.

~

The splendor of the valley spread before Katie as she and Josiah bounced along in the open buggy. "Aren't you glad I convinced you to leave the carriage behind so we could enjoy the day in the open air?" Down deep, she wanted to enter town with much less pomp. Perhaps this time they'd be ignored.

His look was full of tenderness. "Anything for my lovely lady."

She smiled at him with a genuine gratefulness. It was getting easier and easier to love this man who loved her so well. Her frozen heart was feeling the thaw.

The sun-dappled hills, clothed in vibrant fall colors of gold and scarlet set against a cerulean blue sky, brought forth the thoughts of a Creator. How could all this beauty just magically be? And why did a nagging need to respond call her name?

"How long is this valley?" she asked, hoping to remove the niggling presence of God. She shifted against the buckboard seats.

"It's at least a hundred miles from north to south. Have you ever had the privilege of traveling from one end to the other?"

"No, but now that the war's over—"

"I'd love to show you. The flowering meadows are spectacular in the spring. We could make it a horse trip and ride the trails close to those mighty Alleghenies." He pointed to the east, where the range rose.

She clamped her hands on his arms and squeezed. "I would love, love, love that."

A grin split his face. "Thought so. On the way back, we could circle around to the Blue Ridge Mountains so you can see that part of the valley and come back straight through the middle between the Massanutten and Alleghenies. Some unbelievable countryside, let me tell you."

She looked to the west at the craggy Massanutten, which rose majestically beside them as they meandered along the Valley Pike to Lacey Spring. She could remember many a hot summer afternoon with her brothers and Charles, enjoying time spent in the arms of its shaded forest.

The memory spiked a deep longing. She inhaled sharply. The pain still took her by surprise sometimes—the fact that she would never see them again. Charles had the most incredible smile, one she could not easily forget. Was she supposed to never remember him now that she was married?

"What is it?"

"Can you read my mind?"

He chuckled. "No. You just sighed and wilted against me."

She laid her head against his arm. "I was thinking of my brothers and..." The thought of hurting Josiah cut the mention of Charles's name. "And how we used to enjoy the mountains." She bit back the tears that gathered in her eyes. "Does it ever get easier? The loss, the memories that hurt so much?"

He took both reins in one hand and wrapped an arm around her. "It gets easier, Kat." He squeezed her shoulder. "The heart has a great capacity for love, far greater than I ever imagined. The grief becomes less acute, and, in time, if we allow ourselves to love again, the lonely crevices fill without ever forgetting or diminishing the memory of those no longer present. Your brothers will always be a part of you, but it won't always hurt so much to remember them."

"Seems those I love the most—disappear." Her voice caught at the thought of losing Josiah. "You won't leave me too, will you?" Fear skirted the edges of her mind.

"Does that mean you love me? You did say *love*." He squeezed her shoulders playfully.

"Stop joking." She picked up her gloves from her lap and swatted him. "Honestly, I want to let my heart love, but I'm scared."

He pulled her close. "I'm not going anywhere."

"I also want to be a mama."

He pulled the reins tight and stopped the buggy. The smile lines around his eyes crinkled. "Really?"

"Yes, really."

"That would make me the happiest man alive."

She gazed into the warmth of his eyes and pressed against his broad shoulder. Her heart skipped a beat, and her stomach fluttered as he bent to place an ardent kiss on her lips. "I wish we had a little privacy." His eyes danced, and his hand swept to the wide-open fields. "I'd like to start working on that prospect right here, right now."

She giggled in contentment and relaxed against him. Was this what being in love felt like?

A flash of Charles's smile flitted in her mind once again. His free spirit. His youthful vigor. Sadness followed, as it always did, along with a whole lot of confusion. She had to keep herself in reality and make her heart turn its allegiance to the living— the one so full of kindness, of generosity, of love.

❧

"We're here."

Katie stirred as Josiah's arm nudged her.

"Goodness me, did I fall asleep?" She straightened as their buggy rattled into the quaint town of Lacey Spring.

"You were up early fussing about your new clothes."

She grinned and turned away, focusing on their orderly town in hopes of calming the racing speed of her heart. They slowed to a crawl as they passed the stagecoach depot and post office. This was worse than the carriage, where she could duck behind the curtain. Everyone stopped and gawked. Josiah waved with nary a thought. She fought the urge to shrink, holding her spine straight.

They plodded past the diner, where three old men sat on the porch and lifted their hats, to the hotel, where a few widows gathered outside in a circle, talking. The minute one of them spotted Josiah, they all turned and waved without a glance for Katie. If one of them did look her way, it was only a glare they sent.

Piano music drifted from the saloon, and a few cowboys whistled at her, but immediately stopped. She glanced up at the man on the seat beside her. A deadly scowl was pasted on Josiah's face.

She nudged him. "It's all right when the widows flash you bright smiles, but not so much when the men direct anything my way?" A smile rose in her chest.

"You get it," he said. "I admit, that makes me jealous."

Sheriff Holden sat smoking his pipe outside the jailhouse. "Good to see you, Josiah," he yelled, "and your lovely bride. You caught one of the last beautiful days before winter hits."

"We did indeed."

"Make sure you come see me before you head back."

"I'll stop by later while Katherine and Clarissa are busy." Josiah tipped his hat as they rolled past.

Doc Phillips's house came into view. Katie looked up to the second floor, where he lived with his wife, and caught his wave through the window. She smiled as she raised her hand.

Josiah nodded. "Did you know they converted the bottom of the house to an office and set up a room for emergencies?"

"Ma mentioned it and said how happy she is I'll have good help when the babies come." The instant heat in her cheeks had nothing to do with the strong morning sun.

"Babies?" He squeezed her shoulders. "I do like the sound of that. And did I ever tell you how adorable you look when you blush?"

Katie scrambled for something to say. "Looks like this old town is coming to life. Nice to see the blacksmith, furniture maker, and wheelwright all hanging their signs once again."

"Hmm. Looks like my wife is trying to change the subject, so I'll be a gentleman and let her."

She bit back a smile.

A small one-room schoolhouse, where the spinster schoolmarm, Miss Barnes, ruled with stern authority, sat on the outskirts of town. Her cottage on the same property, surrounded with flowers, looked ever so inviting. The children were on a break, as squeals and laughter filled the morning air. Katie waved at a ragamuffin girl who stood apart from the crowd. Her heart lurched at the sight. The pain of being ignored by the other schoolgirls came flooding back.

They rode past the white clapboard church that stood like a sentinel at the end of Main Street. The arched stained-glass windows and copper gilded steeple glinted in the reflection of the sun. Reverend Jude and his wife Betty had their parsonage on the same property. Katie's mind went back to her wedding day. The scared, angry waif that had stood beside the tall, distinguished gentleman had changed. She'd been wrong. Josiah had been kinder than she'd ever thought possible. She peeked up at his handsome face.

"What?"

"Can't a girl smile at her husband for no reason?"

"I know you, Kat. Everything has a reason." His eyes danced with merriment. "But you're entitled to your private thoughts."

Josiah stopped at the livery, swung from the buggy in one quick leap, and tied the horse to the hitching post. Then, he came to Katie's side with his hand held out.

"A girl could get used to such chivalry," she said.

"That's the whole idea. You've never been spoiled. Don't you think it's high time?" He winked at her, then called to the man inside the stable. "Hey, Tom, can you give the horses a quick rub down and some water and feed? We'll be back in a few hours." Tom's head bobbed as he shuffled closer. "Yes, sir." His curly gray hair glistened in contrast to his dark skin, and crinkled laugh lines circled his sparkling black eyes. He grinned widely, revealing a row of uneven teeth. "They'll be rested and fed for the trip back."

"Thanks."

"Did you talk to Sheriff Holden yet? He say to be sure and let you know he wants to see you."

"I'll check in with him later."

"Good thing. Cause troubles abrewing. Some of the towns-folk are getting downright nasty about us doing the jobs we always done. Say we're taking jobs from them."

Katie didn't miss how Josiah nodded his head in her direction and widened his eyes at Tom in a message without words.

Tom nodded back. "We talk later, Mistuh Richardson."

"My lady." Josiah extended his arm. "Shall we?"

They walked arm in arm to the mercantile, and Katie blocked out the stares of far too many curious eyes. "Every time we're in town the word *trouble* comes up. Are things getting worse?"

"Just some angry town folk trying to put pressure on me to hire only the white when my horses come in. I don't give weight to their threats."

"Threats?" She squeezed his arm.

"Idle threats. That's why I think a community ball will lighten the mood and give people something fun to think about. Now, let's talk about anything else. I'm not going to let the town gossip ruin a perfect day."

"I'm looking forward to visiting Winnie again," she said. "The two of us were the outcasts from under-privileged families, and now look at us. She married the store owner's son and I married the richest man in the valley. Who would have ever thought? Not that I set out to snag the legendary Mr. Richardson. Truth be told, you scared the daylights out of me."

He looked at her, a twinkle lighting his eyes. "And now?"

She smiled up at him. "I know you're my gentle giant, Mr. Richardson. And as Delilah would say, I'm blessed to be your missus."

Josiah swung an arm around her waist and pulled her close. He planted a quick kiss on her lips.

"You can't be saying things like that in public, Mrs. Richardson, or I won't be held responsible for my unmannerly show of public affection."

She couldn't hold in her chuckle.

"Did I tell you Robert received a furlough during the war and raced home to marry Winnie?" she asked. "I remember at their wedding how he stood and told everyone that if he died, he would die a happy man. I've never seen such a look of pure love radiate from a man before."

"Hmm." His brows lowered as he studied her. "Wish you had looked into my eyes at our wedding, rather than everywhere but."

Her stomach flipped. "Our situation was different."

"For you, yes, but not for me." A shadow passed across his face.

He was right. She had ignored him as much as she could, and if she could marry him all over again knowing what she knew today, she would do things differently. If only her fears had not been so palpable and her anger so raw. If only her need to feel in love and memories of Charles had not been in her head. Was he still in her head? Just the thought of his name brought a kaleidoscope of feelings crashing in. She shuddered and shook them away. There were far too many *if onlys*.

He opened the door and ushered her in with a touch to the

small of her back. The bell tinkled above their heads, and Josiah had to duck to avoid hitting it with his hat.

Sadness filled the pit of her stomach with heaviness, and she looked around in an effort to rid herself of the gloom. Shelves stocked with buggy harnesses, saddles, and cowboy boots filled the air with the smell of new leather. One side of the store was set up for the men, displaying clothing, hats, and footwear. Tools and feed were available in the back corner.

The other side of the store displayed bolts of calico, cotton, silk, and wool. Notions of thread, buttons, hats, and footwear filled a corner. Dishes, baking needs, ripe cheeses, and a beautiful glass showcase at the front showed off the hard work of Winnie's touch. Jewelry, pocket watches, glass dolls, and serving dishes filled in every square inch. She gravitated to that side of the store and Josiah to the other.

Two women huddled in the corner spoke just loud enough for her to hear. "She thinks she's something now that she's Mr. Richardson's wife. But look at how she dresses like the commoner she is."

"Don't you worry, Laurie. He'll tire of her. Mark my word."

"Outward beauty only lasts so long, and the novelty wears thin when culture and sophistication are what a man of his social standing needs."

"He'll have his romp in the hay with the farm girl, and then you'll be there to pick up the pieces, as it was meant to be." Their titter filled the air as they lifted their heads and strolled by. They called out a welcome and waved to Josiah before stepping out of the store with a glare in her direction.

Katie's stomach twisted as she looked down at her plain clothes. What an embarrassment she must be to Josiah. No wonder he'd insisted on a new wardrobe.

He caught her eye and smiled, moving across the store to her side.

Robert emerged from the storage area. He slapped white

dust from his work apron without looking up and ran a hand through his thick, unruly mop. The powder from his hands streaked his hair gray and left a white mark across his bronzed cheek.

"Robert, what happened?"

His head snapped up. "Katie, I mean...Mr. and Mrs. Richardson, so glad to see you."

Katie moved forward and nudged his shoulder. "I'll always be Katie to you, and you know Josiah."

"I'd shake your hand, but I better not." He lifted his white palms. "I'll go get Winnie. She's been cooking up a storm for our lunch, so excited that you'll be joining us. I've been left to attend the store. None too successfully, I might add. I just busted a sack of flour."

Katie snuck a sideways glance at Josiah and stifled the laughter. The minute Robert disappeared behind the curtain that separated the storage room from the store, Katie and Josiah let loose, each trying to muffle the sound. Robert had looked hilarious covered in the powder. She looked up at her husband with laughter still bubbling out.

"You don't know how good it is to hear you laugh," he said.

She reached on her tip toes to plant a quick kiss on his lips. His eyes turned smoky gray with desire, and he bent his head for more.

"Well, well, Katie. I see married life agrees with you."

They jumped apart at the sound of Winnie's voice.

"I wasn't going to interrupt." She chuckled. "But it didn't look like the end was in sight. And"—she pointed to Hattie out the window—"the town gossip is making her way across the street. We don't want to start a scandal now, do we?"

Katie was shocked at herself. What had started out as a quick kiss had left her with little thought to her surroundings. When she glanced up at Josiah, he looked rather like a proud peacock.

The bells tinkled as Hattie burst in and slammed the door

behind her. "Why, I do declare." She panted heavily with her hands planted on both sides of her rotund girth. "I know you two are newly married, but that's just not acceptable." Her pasty white cheeks, covered in far too much talcum powder, puffed like a steam engine.

"Imagine, kissing in public." She pointed a chubby finger in their direction. "Mr. Richardson, you should be ashamed of yourself. That belongs in the bedroom, if at all." She clucked out her disgust like an old hen and lifted her head with a jut to her chin. "In the future, see to it that you remember where you are." She turned on her heels and, with a wiggle of her wide hips, flounced out of the store. She cast one more disapproving glare through the window as she passed by.

Winnie grabbed Katie's arm and focused on Josiah. "I'm stealing your bride for some ladies' talk. Try not to miss her too much." Her eyebrows waggled.

As they passed her husband, coming from behind the curtain, Winnie gave him a smile. "Robert, don't forget—I'm heading to the dressmaker with Katie this afternoon, and you have to man the store."

CHAPTER 18

*J*osiah pulled out his pocket watch and whistled as he pushed back from the lunch table in the apartment above the store. "We'd better get going. Clarisse will be waiting."

"I'll clean up." Robert waved them on. "You go enjoy."

"But the store?" Winnie said.

"Pa is fine for a few more minutes downstairs."

Josiah held out both arms. "Ladies, shall we?" As they walked down the street together, Katie's stomach churned. What did she know about dressing up like a lady? Those women in the store were right. Josiah had married way below his aristocratic lineage. Would he tire of her? A tumble of angst twisted and turned.

Josiah held the door open for the women and stepped inside as Clarisse approached. "Hope the clothes are ready as planned."

"But of course they are, darling. I never miss a deadline." She kissed him on both cheeks, then moved to the shop door and held it open for him to exit. "Come back in a couple hours to settle the account. Until then, no men allowed."

The girls looked at each other and grinned. "I love the way she takes charge with Josiah," Katie whispered.

"First rule, ladies," Clarisse said. "Never, never let your man see you in the finished gown until the dinner party and the guests arrive. It's all part of the mystery needed to keep our men on their toes. I assure you their reaction is worth every bit of effort. Come along now, Katherine. With the new supply of fabrics and the unlimited budget I had to work with, I do believe you're going to be more than pleased." She pulled Katie by the arm into an adjoining room. "Winnie, my dear, do follow. You'll be just the moral support she needs. She is much too shy for her own good."

Dread settled heavily on Katie's shoulders. She wanted to owe Josiah less, not more, and yet she didn't want to embarrass him.

Clarisse pulled a blue silk gown from the hanger, and Katie gasped. "That's for me?"

"Oui, oui, but of course. Do you like?"

Winnie and Katie ran their hands through the endless folds of soft tiered silk. "How absolutely gorgeous."

Clarisse laughed. "This one is the simplest of the dinner gowns I created."

Katie lifted her brows. "Oh my."

"I like to think that what Da Vinci did with paint, I do with fabric. Let's give it a try."

Katie slipped into the gown and waited as Clarisse bunched and fluffed, with pins hanging from the corner of her mouth, none of which she used.

"C'est magnifique, Katherine." She stepped back, removed the pins from her mouth, and smiled broadly. "I'll have more work than I know what to do with when people feast their eyes upon you."

Katie's gaze widened as she looked at herself in the mirror. Who was that stranger staring back at her?

Winnie circled around. "Oh, my goodness, Katherine. Would I ever like to see Josiah's face when he first sees you in this."

Katie swirled the fabric with a twist of her hips. "I barely recognize myself."

From dress to dress, the exquisite artistry increased, but Katie felt outside of her skin. She pulled up the bodice of a rose-colored gown. "Clarisse, this is beautiful but shockingly low."

Winnie and Clarisse laughed. "These latest fashions look fabulous on you," Clarisse said. "All the ladies will be wearing the same, but you will outshine them. Josiah will be so proud."

The least she could do after all Josiah had done for her and her family was to make him proud. She pulled at the fabric, trying to cover a bit more.

"If only you could give me a little of your extra." Winnie laughed as she motioned to her small bosom. "You look stunning. Josiah is going to parade you around with that same look he had on his face this morning after he kissed you into oblivion."

The heat rose from her toes to her hairline. She loved Winnie, but sometimes she said too much.

"Can I try on my riding habit now?"

"All this loveliness and you want your riding habit." Clarisse shook her head.

"I can't wait to see what the dark blue corduroy material looks like."

Clarisse snapped her fingers. "Very well. Come this way."

The outfit was more than Katie had dreamed. The nipped-in jacket accented her tiny waist. Even though she would have been more comfortable in a size or two larger, she had to admit it was perfect. Fitted trousers tucked into a pair of new knee-high boots and matching leather gloves completed the outfit.

Katie turned from side to side in front of the mirror with a look of delight. "Thank you, Clarisse. Thank you so much." She wrapped her arms around the startled lady. "This is by far my favorite."

Clarisse threw up her hands. "I spend hours and hours on those elaborate dresses and this"—she waved a hand up and down Katie's body—"is your favorite?"

Katie shrugged, and Winne giggled. "I'll take the dresses."

Clarisse chortled with her hands in the air. "J'abandonne."

Katie's confusion must have shown on her face because Clarisse said, "It means, I give up."

~

"Can you slip into one of your new gowns for supper tonight? I have a surprise." Josiah's eyes sparkled as he stood from the lunch table.

"There is no slipping into such finery. It is quite the ordeal."

"I've already checked with Ruby. She used to be a lady's maid, and she's ready and waiting to help you. You'll have all afternoon, my love." He looked down at her with such hope, she couldn't refuse.

"Tell Ruby to meet me in my room."

"And I left a necklace on your bureau. I hope it works with your dress." He dropped a kiss on her forehead and slipped away.

She chose the least ostentatious of the dinner gowns, which would go with the stunning sapphire necklace she found in a velvet encased box.

Ruby bustled into the room. Her plump cheeks bloomed cherry red and her eyes sparkled with excitement. "Mr. Richardson said I get to help you as a lady's maid this afternoon. Much more fun than cleaning the fireplace as I planned." She laughed and planted both hands on her hips. "Now, where shall we start? I see you've made a choice." She pointed to the dress laid out on the bed.

"Thank you for your help. I would never have been able to manage all these layers and endless buttons."

"Nor should you have to. I love this work, and I just happen to be good at it. Now step into this gown carefully and I'll pull it up."

Katie did as she was told. "Good thing I'm not expected to do this daily."

Ruby's fleshy hands smoothed out the folds. "You do look lovely, my lady. But don't look yet, I want to do your hair first." She moved the chair away from the mirror and pointed. "Sit, my lady, and enjoy the pampering."

Katie relaxed to the wonderful luxury of someone combing her hair. She almost fell asleep to the continual gentle touch.

"Now, take a peek," Ruby said.

Katie stood and turned toward the mirror. Who was that sophisticated woman gazing back at her? With her hair piled on the top of her head and the artistry of makeup and beautiful clothing, the transformation was undeniable.

"Ruby. You outdid yourself."

"It was easy working with your beauty."

Katie twisted from side to side. The bodice of the periwinkle silk gown molded to her curves, accenting her waist. She marveled at the yards of gorgeous material cascading in full tiers to the floor. The crinoline underneath enhanced the flare. Trimmed with a darker braid and tassels, the look was indeed stunning. The sapphire necklace added that touch of sparkle and distraction to the plunging neckline.

Katie slipped into her new shoes with a sudden bout of shyness. She was glad it would only be the four of them for dinner. She would get a chance to ask Josiah about the neckline, for her other gowns revealed even more. Gathering her skirt and her courage, she left the safety of her bedroom behind. Careful not to trip on the layers of material cascading around her, she descended the steps with care.

"Katherine."

At the whisper of her name, she glanced up from the steps. Josiah stood on the landing below, a look of raw hunger flaring in his eyes. His gaze fell to the bodice of her dress and the creamy white flesh spilling out. There was no mistaking the effect she was having on him. The heat of his intense stare burned hot. When she reached the landing, she twirled in a circle. "Do you like it?" She held her breath.

His answer was to crush her against him. His lips seared a path from her mouth to her neck, to her...

She pulled back. "Josiah, my hair. Ruby will be sure to notice if you mess up her work."

He stepped back and ran a hand through his thick russet curls. "Clarisse had a pretty good idea what effect she wanted to create when she designed this gown for you."

Katie smiled up at him.

"You are pure torture to a man in love." The dark passion in his eyes faded to a steely gray.

"You cut a dashing figure in your tailored suit as well, Mr. Richardson."

Obviously, those were not the words he longed to hear. A sad look crawled into his eyes as he took her hand in his and led her to the formal dining room.

They were indeed eating in style. Delilah had laid out the fine china and silverware with an extra place setting. A bouquet of late blooming roses mixed with wild Queen Anne's lace graced the center of the table. The profusion of color accented the lace tablecloth and added elegance.

She bent closer to inhale the sweet pungent fragrance. "Whatever is the big surprise, and why do we have an extra setting?"

"All in good time."

They waited for another half hour, sitting at the table chatting. Every time she asked what they were waiting for, Josiah put her off.

Finally, Delilah came into the dining room from the kitchen. "Dinner will be ruined if'n we don't partake soon." She clucked her tongue and shook her head.

Josiah sighed. "I thought our surprise guest would be here by now. He must have run into some problems. Call Abe, we'd best get started."

~

      *T*en minutes later, the brass door knocker sounded, and Josiah jumped from his chair. A rush of excitement pumped through his veins.

"I'll be right back." He winked at Katie. "Our surprise guest has arrived."

He headed for the door with a sense of pride. His wife—his beautiful wife—had finally stepped into the role of mistress of the house in every way. She looked the part far beyond his wildest expectations. Not that he didn't love her casual style with no pretense, but the woman he'd left seated in the dining room was commanding and gorgeous. She completed the picture to perfection. Everything was coming together—Colby's arrival, the horses safely in town, and his beautiful wife growing closer to him each day. Who could ask for more? Soon, she would declare her love, he was sure of it. Nothing could stop them now. A beautiful life lay ahead.

He swung open the door. "Colby."

"Josiah." A familiar grin widened on Colby's face.

He hugged his friend, then ushered him into the dining room with pride.

Nothing could have prepared him for the shock on his wife's face. Her eyes grew wide and her face drained of color.

"Charles." She stood, her legs looking a little wobbly at first.

Her expression looked almost dazed. Then she seemed to gather herself and skirting the table, almost running into Colby's arms. "I thought you were dead!"

Colby did not hug back, and she pulled away with furrowed brows.

Josiah's stomach dropped to the floor. She had never flown into his arms with anything even close to that level of exuberance.

Colby regarded her with a wary look. "You knew Charles? Charles Braddock?"

"Oh." She peered at Colby, and color pinked her cheeks. "You're not Charles." Her voice was flat, disappointed.

"He was my brother."

Her eyes were glued to his face, and she touched his cheek, then dropped her hand. "You...you look so much alike."

Josiah's temperature rose. What was she doing touching Colby so intimately? He placed his arm around her shoulder and squeezed. The touch finally broke the spell between his wife and his closest friend.

"Colby, this is my wife, Katherine. Most everyone calls her Katie."

She extended her hand politely. What a joke after having fallen into Colby's arms. Josiah worked hard to relax the muscles tightening his throat and to keep his voice level.

"Katie, this is Colby. My good friend I told you about. He spent most of the war looking for his brother Charles. You obviously knew him."

Katie rubbed her temples. "I need to sit." She returned to the table and sank back into her chair.

The tears glistening in her eyes cut into his heart. He wanted to comfort her and throttle her all in the same moment. Who was this Charles to her, and why had she never mentioned him? A memory slipped back to him then. Robert from the General Mercantile had told him about a Charles from her past. Was her Charles the same man as Colby's brother? He must be.

Her hands trembled as she smoothed them over the cloth napkin. "Charles was a friend, a good friend." She motioned for them to sit. "I'll explain."

Josiah plunked his body hard into the chair. He forced himself to remove the scowl he could feel bunching his forehead.

"Charles and I became friends at about the age of twelve. He arrived with his mother from...hmm I'm trying to remember." She was looking at her lap.

"Philadelphia," Colby said.

"Oh, my. You sound just like him." Her gaze flew up. "It's so odd, yet wonderful to hear..." Her voice trailed off.

"Katherine." Josiah gentled the voice that wanted to scream. "Tell me who this man was to you before I lose my mind."

"Yes, Philadelphia." She dropped her gaze again. "They lived with his aunt and uncle, the Warrens, and we met him at school. He was a couple years older, closer to my brothers' age, so he didn't stay in school long, but long enough for the two of us to hit it off. He often joined my brothers and me for an afternoon of fishing and swimming."

She'd been swimming with Charles? He could imagine the young man splashing and laughing and ogling her beauty. Josiah's blood boiled in his veins. Drums beat in his temples. He clamped his lips shut so he wouldn't say anything he'd regret.

Katherine looked at him as if to receive permission to continue.

"Carry on," Josiah said with what sounded like strangled encouragement even to his ears.

She offered him a forced smile and stared at the grandfather clock behind his head, as if unable to make eye contact.

"I cried the day he left to join the army. He promised to return, refusing to say good-bye." Her voice warbled. "I never saw him again." Tears slipped free of her thick lashes, and pressed her eyes shut.

Silence filled the room except for the tick of the clock. Josiah was doing everything he could not to get up and leave. He hated himself for being so jealous, so tortured, so not present when she was so clearly distraught. He dug in his pocket and handed her his handkerchief. It was the most he could offer.

She dabbed at the watery flow and twisted the square cloth into a tight ball. Her every nuance cried out pain. He felt the agony for a whole different reason. Would she cry if something happened to him? Maybe, but not the way she obviously still ached for this Charles fellow.

"My parents had a terrible marriage," Colby said. "Father's infidelity finally broke my mother. They came to an agreement to separate."

Katherine stared as if hanging on Colby's every word in a way that nearly drove Josiah insane.

"Mother told me she was going to visit her sister in the Shenandoah Valley, yet looking back, I realize the tears she shed that day... She took Charles and never returned."

Katherine gasped. "That must've been so difficult. I know Charles often talked of his older brother and how much he missed you. But he said he couldn't leave his mother."

"Father finally confessed. They'd agreed that I would stay and help him run the business, being the eldest, and Mother would take Charles, her baby. The two of us were separated without knowing it was to be a permanent arrangement. I'll never understand, nor forgive, either of them for that." His voice thickened.

Katherine reached across the table and squeezed Colby's hand. "I'm sorry."

Josiah fisted his hands in his lap. He should be consoling his friend, but he couldn't get his anger under control.

Colby gave them a sad smile. "Just before the war broke out,

I realized Charles and I could end up fighting against each other. There was no way I was letting that happen. So, I left before travel got impossible. I told father I wouldn't return until I found Charles. We argued. I told him what I thought of how he'd treated Mother. He called me a coward and said how ashamed he was of me."

"Why?" Josiah found his voice.

"He thought I was making excuses to run off so I wouldn't have to fight. I didn't care what he thought. There was no way I was lifting a gun against my brother. I tracked down my relatives and found Mother. But by that time, the war had started, and Charles had already enlisted. The only way to find him and not get shot on the spot was to join the Confederate Army. They never questioned me since my brother was already on the roster."

Colby looked at Josiah, his words flooded with affection. "That's when I met you, my friend. You were like my lost brother. In the midst of such horror, you held me steady. How will I ever be able to thank you?"

Josiah's anger melted, and guilt seeped in. How had he allowed jealousy to get the best of him? "You did the same for me, brother. You did the same for me."

"Did you find him?" Katherine asked. The way her eyes followed Colby, the compassion in her voice, and her inquiry of Charles, all rubbed like salt in Josiah's wound.

"No." Colby cleared his throat of the emotion. "Later, I learned that Charles died in those first months of war. My uncle said that Mother wrote me when she received notification of his death, but the letter never reached me, nor did the news that Mother died of diphtheria not long after."

"You lost your mother too?" Katherine asked. "I hadn't heard."

"And Father. It wasn't until the war was over and I returned to this valley that my uncle handed me a letter from Father's solicitor. He requested I return home to settle family affairs. My father had enlisted and not survived either." The pain in his voice leaked through.

"In the span of a few years, you lost your whole family?" Katherine's eyes filled with tears.

Colby nodded, his eyes showing the depth of his pain.

Josiah couldn't help but think how the same had happened to him, and he didn't remember her tears when he'd told the story. It seemed her heart immediately connected with Colby in a deep way.

CHAPTER 19

*T*he meal passed in a blur. Katie felt as if she'd seen a ghost. The face of her sweet, sweet Charles sat across from her. His voice spoke a story she didn't want to believe. She answered each question directed her way and nodded when it seemed appropriate, but her mind wandered miles away.

She couldn't sit across from Colby without thinking of Charles. A kaleidoscope of memories melted together, and she found herself wondering where her life would be right now had he returned to her. She went down a road in her mind she had not allowed herself to travel since marrying Josiah.

She had loved Charles. She had dreamed of becoming his wife and having his children. A mere glance in Colby's direction set the memories dancing and her heart fluttering. She tried not to stare, but the sound of that same rich voice resonated from the stranger across the table. Her mind tripped at the golden flecks sparkling in the same warm brown eyes that so resembled Charles's. Colby's handsomely rugged face drew her. She imagined that the horse-loving cowboy, with sun-bleached hair and bronzed skin, was Charles sitting across from her. Buried hopes and the dry bones of lost dreams found life once again.

"Katherine."

Josiah's stern voice bit into her musings. She'd forgotten where she was. She'd forgotten...him.

"Yes?" She turned from Colby and caught a look of intensity in Josiah's face she had never seen before. His eyes bore into her.

"I asked if you were ready to retire to the parlor. Colby's had a long day, so we'll let him bid good-night soon."

"Certainly, Josiah." Katie smiled in his direction, hoping to remove his sour look. A knot of anxiety twisted in her stomach. Josiah would have to be a fool to miss the way she'd been staring at Colby. And based on the glower on his face, he was fully aware.

She waited for Josiah to come around the table and, when he did, she looped her arm into his. As they moved into the parlor, he pulled as far away as he could without dislodging her hold. She sat in their special spot, but he did not join her, instead choosing a chair across the room. There was little doubt he was upset.

She worked hard to focus her gaze anywhere but on the man where it gravitated. She hoped the differences between the two brothers would become more evident as she got through the shock of seeing Charles's double.

She threw Josiah a look of tenderness, but he turned away, feigning a yawn. She'd hurt him. If only she had the words to explain just how difficult the remembering was. Maybe if he met a twin to Georgina, he would understand. The fact that she had never mentioned Charles may be adding to his distance.

A hollow grief settled in the pit of her stomach. What had been, would never be again. The past belonged in the past. Josiah was her future. He'd been good to her. She'd do well to set her thoughts on the living. But one look across the room, and the past came to life.

Her mind could not follow their idle chatter. She longed for solitude to sort out her thoughts. Relief slipped through her when Colby stood. "It's been a long day, and as you always say, Josiah, sunrise comes all too quick."

She rose while Colby hugged Josiah and slapped him on the back. "So glad to be here, my friend."

He turned toward Katie and smiled. "Josiah has done little else but write about you in our correspondence. I can see why. I'm so happy he's found a lovely lady to share his life."

Her eyes darted up to meet Colby's then turned to Josiah. "He's been writing about me, has he?" She put a tease in her voice, hoping to bring Josiah back.

"Oh yes, it started way back—"

"Now don't be telling all my secrets, Colby, or it'll go to her pretty head." Josiah moved close enough to place his hand on the small of her back.

"In the days to come, I'll look forward to sharing your memories of my brother with you, Katie. If you don't mind?"

"Of course."

The pressure of Josiah's hand upon her back increased.

"You're the one person who can tell me what he was like as a young man." A sadness flashed across Colby's face. He looked at Josiah. "Am I in the same bedroom?"

"You are. Welcome home, my friend."

"I do like the sound of that. Haven't felt at home in a very long time."

Josiah's smile lasted until Colby started up the stairs. Then, a frown harrowed lines across his brow.

They ascended the steps in silence. She walked into her own bedroom to change, and he into his.

She plunked her body on the edge of her bed and dropped her head into her hands. What damage had she done to allow her thoughts such freedom? What had Josiah seen in her eyes? Hopefully not too much.

She unpinned her hair and brushed it till it shone, allowing it to flow free to her waist, just the way he liked it. A splash of his favorite rosewater fragrance to each side of her neck, and she was ready to face her future and leave the past far behind. After a quick knock on the adjoining door, she walked in. He sat on the edge of the bed staring at the wall.

"Josiah, I need help with my—" Her words caught in her throat as he turned to her. What was that look? Like he was unsure, unsettled, uncomfortable. "Turn around." He responded as if miles away as he rose from the bed.

Katie turned, expecting his arms to encircle her, the warmth of his kiss on her shoulder. Instead he struggled with the buttons, just as he had on their wedding night.

"Blast these things. My fingers are too big and clumsy." The heat of his breath fanned across her neck as he puffed out his frustration. "I told you we needed to hire a lady's maid, but no, you fight me every inch of the way."

Feeling the release of the gown and the corset, Katie turned to him, holding her dress to keep it from falling to the floor. "What's wrong?"

"I'm tired." He moved away from her and slipped from his clothing before sliding beneath the covers. With a muffled good-night, he turned his back to her.

Katie returned to her room and hung her gown with care. As she slipped into her challis nightgown, she couldn't keep her mind from stewing about her husband. He had been so pleased to see her dressed up earlier, with a passionate reaction and whispers of what would happen later. Now, nothing. It did not take much to figure out what happened. She'd hurt him.

❦

*J*osiah balled his fists as he lay in bed. The way Katherine had said Charles's name that evening... had sounded like a caress. Charles had meant far more to her than mere friendship. He was the man she'd been meant to marry, not Josiah. Raw jealousy surged through his veins.

He tossed from one side to the other as he listened to her move about her room. He was no more tired than he could sprout wings and fly. He had been so excited to introduce her to Colby, but the way she'd leapt into his arms brought the ugly truth to the forefront. In all their time together, she had never displayed even half the emotion revealed in that unguarded moment.

He'd never had a problem with women falling for him, and he'd tried every kindness with Katherine, yet he was no fool. She didn't love him. She loved a ghost. A ghost whose twin now resided under his own roof.

The click of the adjoining door told him she was joining him, as had become their nightly ritual, but he couldn't face her. He couldn't think of making love to her knowing she might have someone else in her head.

As she slid between the covers and worked her way over to his side of the bed, he tried to feign sleep. His breathing became ragged and unsteady when she moved her arms around him and planted a kiss on his back. This was the first time she had initiated intimacy, and, although he wanted to be strong and not need her, he struggled. Conflicted emotions warred. He wanted to kiss her into oblivion—and ignore her, making her feel as insecure as she had made him. He wanted her love, not her obligation.

"Josiah, are you sleeping?"

He didn't answer.

Against his will, he shuddered as her hands circled around to the front, and her skin, softer than a doe's, rubbed up against him. How could she think he was sleeping? She obviously did not. When she brushed her foot against his leg, he flipped his body to face her. "I said I was tired."

"Too tired?"

Her coyness told him she was far more experienced than the scared little waif who had come into his bed a few months earlier.

His resolve crumbled like ancient pottery, and, when she pulled his head down to meet her lips, he responded. The thirst inside him could not be satisfied.

That night, for the first time, he squelched his words of love. The hurt burned a hole in his heart like a live coal searing through. Why hadn't she trusted him with the story of Charles? Only one reason made sense. She wasn't over him. And now Colby was here, stirring the embers, igniting memories he hadn't even known she battled. It all made sense now—her inability to love him.

He lay awake long after the steady rhythm of her breathing signified her slumber. He wished he could have resisted her for his own peace of mind. If for no other reason than to put some distance between her memories of Charles and their time together. But he was so weak. She unhinged him. She frustrated him. She stole the control he had always possessed.

But holding her in his arms, he made a decision. He would never again voice the feelings that were not returned.

CHAPTER 20

*K*atie hummed a tune as she scrubbed the grand banister wood to gleaming. A month had passed since Colby's arrival and her mind still wandered to Charles more often than she could control. She reined in the thoughts and the pain of loss that always swept in uninvited. With Colby around, the reminder came more often, but she was smart enough to know that she could not entertain the past if she wanted a future.

Thankful that things had been smoothed out between Josiah and her, she would not give the memories of Charles power. She cast them aside now and thought about Josiah's kindness and generosity instead. She was content and encouraged by their ever-deepening relationship. She was. Truly.

"There you are." Josiah rounded the corner. "You don't have to do such menial labor. Now that the horses are selling, we have more than enough income to hire more help."

"Work helps me feel part of this." She spread her arms. "Rather than a fixture."

He planted a kiss on her cheek. "Well then, what do you think of that idea of inviting the town of Lacey Spring to a

Christmas ball? It'll keep you busy, but we can hire extra help. Annie has a list of people she knows who are looking for work."

That familiar dread welled up. She hated to be the center of attention, and hosting a ball would certainly thrust her into that role. For Josiah's sake, she choked back her trepidation and smiled.

"Also," he said, "it'll help turn the tide of some of that negativity buzzing around town and infuse some celebration into the community."

"Negativity? Seems you hired a good cross section of white and black, and they're working well together. Are they not?"

"They are. But not everyone agrees with my decision to hire the best man for the job, despite skin color. Last week when I was in town, Sheriff Holden took me aside once again and said the rumblings of unrest were increasing. The best antidote to wagging tongues is to give them something different to wag about. A little generosity and something their wives beg to attend will simmer down the men folk. The power of the missus is a fine and wonderful thing." He gave her a crooked, charming smile.

"All right then." Her voice sounded weak, so she cleared her throat to give it more force. "I think it's a grand idea. The first Christmas after the war deserves a celebration. And I agree, if we can please the women, we'll have most of the battle won."

He slid his arms around her. "Does that mean all I have to do is please you and..." His lips met hers with crushing urgency.

She gave herself all into the kiss for a heartbeat, then pulled back. "Later." She threw him a grin that was supposed to be saucy, but felt more wobbly. "Come." She grabbed his hand and pulled him across the entrance into the ballroom. "Can we have a large tree to trim, and how about some fresh boughs above the fireplace?" She turned and cocked her head from side to side trying to imagine just how she would decorate. "I'll bring

Jeanette in on this. At thirteen, she already has an incredible eye."

His strong arms gathered around her from behind. "Anything your little heart desires, you just let me know. And thanks for helping me out. I know attending public functions is not your favorite thing."

She drew in a deep breath and leaned against him. It scared her how well he knew her in such a short time. He didn't miss a nuance or forget a conversation or fail to pay attention to far more than her words. How did anyone love that well? Her throat tightened to an impossible ache. She respected him. She was thankful to him. She was far more content than she had ever dreamed possible. But did she love him? A feather of regret flitted across her mind, but she brushed it away. She was doing her best.

~

*T*he Christmas ball was almost upon them. Josiah rounded the corner into the ballroom to check on how the decorating was progressing. Colby stood on the top of the ladder trying to fix the tree topper to Katherine's liking.

"A little more to the right, not the left."

"Oh, you mean my other right."

Colby moved the decoration in the correct direction, and her singsong laughter filled the air.

"Where do you get your craziness? Charles was far more serious."

"I got the funny," Colby said, "and he got the good looks."

"He was rather handsome."

"And you're agreeing I'm not?" Colby swiveled on the ladder to look down at her and caught Josiah standing there.

"Did you hear that? I think Katie just insinuated I'm unattractive."

Katherine spun and hurried to Josiah's side. She linked her arm in his and pulled him forward. "Do you like?" Her eyes sparkled as she gazed up at the tree.

Josiah nodded, but what he really wanted was to throttle them both. Their easy laughter, their teasing... It made him crazy.

"And she doesn't mean me," Colby said. "She means the tree."

Katherine laughed again and waved at Colby. "Get down from there before you hurt yourself."

"So, you do care?"

"I guess I have to, considering you're Josiah's best friend." She lifted her eyes to Josiah and threw him a smile, like throwing a bone to the dog.

How could he love and hate simultaneously? How could his best friend and his beloved wife strike up a friendship with so little effort, when he'd worked so hard to gain the small amount of ground he had? And why did their endless conversations always have Charles thrown in? It irked him to his core.

Jealousy would not look good on him, so he remained quiet. He swung his arm possessively around her shoulders and spoke to Colby. "I'll take over from here. You have men out there who need your assistance."

If Colby picked up on his undertones, he sloughed it off. "Sure thing, boss." He jumped the last few rungs of the ladder and picked up his hat from the table.

"I'm not your boss. We're partners." Josiah worked hard to keep his voice level and his expression blank.

"Sure thing, boss." Colby slapped on his hat and laughed as he headed out the door.

Katherine giggled at his side. "You did sound quite authoritative."

Josiah ran a hand around the back of his head and clenched his teeth.

*K*atie took special care to dress for the occasion. She wanted to do Josiah proud and give the catty women of town nothing to condemn her for. She chose the finest gown Clarisse had created. With the whole town invited and most everyone coming, she wanted to give Josiah back at least a little of the support he'd given her. Though it scared her half to death, she would work at befriending the women. And if Josiah could impress the men with his supply of fine horses, then this evening would be worth the endless hours of preparation.

The rosy-pink fabric contrasted dramatically with her shiny black hair, which Ruby had wound into an elaborate coiffure. Seed pearls attached to hair pins were dispersed through the heavy mass. The effect was stunning. However, the fitted bodice was even lower than she remembered. She tugged at the material to hide the generous display of cleavage.

"Relax, my lady," Ruby said. "Let your beauty shine. This is what all the ladies will be wearing."

Katie gazed at herself in the full-length mirror. "That's what Clarisse said when I questioned her. But I...don't like men gawking at me, and this will make it worse." She gave the material another yank upward.

"It will be fine, my lady. You look amazing."

Katie left her bedroom and waved at Josiah and Colby below. She gathered her skirt in her hands and descended the stairs with care, watching each step until she reached the bottom. A smile split free. "I made it." Her laughter stopped at one glance upward.

Where she had expected Josiah's approval and admiration, his eyes flashed with anger. The muscles in his jaw clenched, and his Adam's apple jumped. He grabbed her arm and ushered her none too gently into the nearby library and slammed the door behind him.

"Katherine, what do you mean by parading around, exposing yourself to the world?" His voice seemed barely restrained. "You have to change. Immediately, before everyone arrives. I can't have the whole countryside seeing you half clothed." His face grew beet red, and his fists clenched at his side.

Tears welled, brimming on the edge of her lashes. "But... Ruby and Clarisse assured me all the ladies are wearing their dresses this way."

"I don't care what the other women are wearing. They don't fill them like you do."

"I'm sorry. I didn't want the dress this low. I even argued with Clarisse about it." Her cheeks splashed wet as tears broke free of her lashes.

"What was she thinking? You'll have a different dressmaker next time, even if I have to travel as far as Harrisonburg."

"You can't blame her."

"You both should know better, but especially you with your past."

Katie couldn't hold back the sob. "I didn't want this." She waved over her dress. "But I didn't want to offend her, and she believed she was giving you what you wanted—the latest in fashion."

The clock on the mantle chimed, and he let out a deep breath. "There's not much time. Delilah will know what to do. Wait here, I'll go get her."

Katie could barely hold herself still as she waited for him to return. She should have known better. Her instincts had told her this bodice was too low. Why hadn't she put her foot down? She would go change now, except it would take too long to press the wrinkles out of the others and get through all the adjustments to the underclothing. Even now, she could hear the sound of a carriage outside.

Josiah stepped back into the room, followed by Delilah. The woman took one glance at the bodice of Katie's dress and nodded. "I know just how to fix that up pretty like in a hurry." She bustled out and returned with a needle, thread, and a piece of creamy white lace.

"Leave us, Josiah. Go. Greet your guests." She shooed him out, then turned to Katie. "You're going to have to trust old Delilah now, cause I'm going to stitch this on and try not to stitch you." She stifled a grin, and her eyes twinkled. "That man of yours is too jealous to be sharing so much of your beauty around." Her shoulders took on a shake.

"No stitching and laughing at the same time." Katie tried to make the remark sound lighthearted, but her voice quivered. "I didn't feel comfortable anyway. Hopefully Clarisse isn't offended when she sees the alterations."

"I dare say I did more sewing in my days than Clarisse and ten others put together."

Delilah's skillful fingers finished the job and, when Katie looked in the mirror, a smile split free. "Much better."

"Yes'um, even leaving a little to the imagination is still going to turn more heads than that boy knows what to do with."

"Thank you." She wrapped an arm around Delilah, but the woman shooed her away.

"Now, get on out there."

Katie scurried out to stand beside Josiah as more guests entered. Her eyes scanned the room for anything amiss. The ballroom was bustling with women dressed in their finery, and men strutting in tall hats and Sunday best. The group of musicians Josiah had hired from Harrisonburg were playing beautiful background music. Dance music would come later.

Jeanette had organized the decorating and, from the glowing tree with sparkling decorations to the boughs draped over the fireplace mantle accented with candles, all held a festive welcome. A long table of food sent tantalizing aromas wafting in Katie's direction. She was hungry after having spent every waking hour that day seeing to the final touches.

Josiah hugged her close. "I'm sorry," he whispered. "We'll talk later." He dropped a kiss on the top of her head. "Come. Let's present the opening toast."

He held his glass high until the roar of the crowd quieted. "We are survivors." His voice rang with authority across the room.

"Here, here!" said a man in the back she couldn't see.

Josiah smiled. "And I know, had it not been for the sheer luck of a Yankee officer liking this very room in which we congregate, I too, would be rebuilding like so many of you."

A voice boomed from the left side of the room. "Ha. The rich Mr. Richardson who sides with the black-loving Yanks. We know why this house stands—you traitor."

A gasp rippled through the crowd. Katherine stood on her tiptoes trying to see who had voiced that remark. All she could see was a nod from Josiah. Then a group of his men surrounded and escorted a couple men out.

She looked up at Josiah. "Who—"

"Smile," he said through tight lips. "We'll talk later."

He held up his hand to the murmuring crowd. "This is a night for celebration. Yes?"

The crowd clapped.

"All right then, we're not going to let the negativity of a few spoil our evening. My beautiful wife, Katherine, and I feel blessed and honored that you've graced us with your presence, and we want you to have a wonderful evening. Here's to friends and neighbors. Here's to life." He raised his glass to the crowd. The place erupted with cheers.

Music and dancing followed, and the crowd seemed to be enjoying themselves. For her part, Katie declined every offer to dance but her husband's. If her dress had brought on jealousy, she wouldn't add to it.

The widow Laurie and her friend, both of whom had talked unkindly about her in the General Mercantile, were sending daggers her way. *I guess I look too sophisticated for their liking now.* She lifted her eyes and smiled brightly at them. Their heads snapped away.

Hours later, when she scanned the room for Josiah, the widow Laurie was hanging on his arm, fluttering her eyelashes up at him. He smiled and said something that made her gush with laughter.

A wave of emotion Katie could not define twisted in her stomach and knotted in her throat. She marched over and slipped her arm around his waist.

"There you are, my dear." Josiah put his arm around her and pulled her close. "Meet Laurie Truvel, an old friend of Georgina's."

Katie extended her hand politely, barely holding in the glare she wanted to send the petite blonde. "Nice to make your acquaintance. Do forgive us, but I must pull my husband away." She emphasized the word husband and leaned in. "Come, my darling."

His eyebrows shot up, but he did her bidding.

Heat burned her cheeks at the use of the endearment—one she'd never spoken before. Guests were beginning to depart, so she led him to the entry where they stood to bid each family farewell.

In a spare moment, he leaned down and whispered, "I do like the sound of the word darling rolling off your beautiful lips."

She ignored him, shifting from one tired foot to the other. When the last gentleman struck up a conversation about horses, she interjected, "Do take him to the barn, Josiah. You must show him the strength and beauty of your stock. Talking doesn't do justice." She slipped from his arm. "Go, my darling."

He chuckled and sent her a raised brow look. She smiled in

return. Their spat was over. They were going to be all right. She rubbed the knot in her neck that had been building.

"I shall not be long." He planted a quick kiss on her cheek.

She followed them out to the portico and sank onto the rocker. The fresh air drifted over her in delicious waves, cooling her after the dancing and the heat inside. A heavy sigh slid from her lips.

Things had been off between her and Josiah for weeks, and she couldn't quite put a finger on it. He no longer said he loved her, even if he did say other very delightful things, especially in tender moments. Maybe if she could give him a son or a daughter, he'd relax a bit more in their relationship.

The thought of a child made her heart sing. She would love to be a mama, and what an enjoyable way to end the evening—working on that very goal. She smiled as she rose. A hot cup of tea to await Josiah's return, and then she could get out of this most uncomfortable dress. She headed for the kitchen, but as she made her way down through the entry hall a voice sounded from the direction of the ballroom.

"Great celebration," Colby said.

Katie turned to see him standing in the doorway of the ballroom.

He grinned at her, that familiar smile setting her at ease. "And you wouldn't believe how many men I snuck out to the stables for a *look before you buy* opportunity."

She relaxed as she walked over to him. "I'm glad it's you. I don't think I could've handled one more conversation with a stranger. Would you care for a cup of tea?"

"No, but I'll take that dance you promised me."

She laughed. "After what happened earlier, I thought it best to reserve my dances for Josiah only. He's a tad jealous."

"I get that. If I were married to the prettiest woman in town, I'd react the same way."

Katie smiled. "You'll find one prettier than me. Just you wait." She turned toward the kitchen.

"Wait." He grabbed her arm and tugged her back. "You're under the mistletoe."

She looked up at the branch hanging from the door frame. The couples had enjoyed a great deal of fun with it that evening.

"Merry Christmas, Katie." He leaned down and kissed her cheek.

She turned a friendly smile on him as he straightened, but an odd mixture of emotion was playing across his face. He released her as if she were a hot coal and stepped aside.

...just as Josiah entered the hallway. His scowl proved he'd seen the whole thing.

"Josiah, you're under the mistletoe." Katie reached out to pull him into the doorway to the ballroom, then wrapped her arms around his neck and pulled his head down. He didn't respond when her lips touched his, even though she pressed in.

A sinking feeling dropped in as she pulled back and exhaled. She did not have energy left for another misunderstanding. She lifted her head to find his brow still knit.

She needed to say something to distract him. "Do you remember meeting Anne, the Emmerson's oldest daughter?" Katie said. "She's so beautiful and witty too. Don't you think she'd make a wonderful wife for Colby?"

The scowl stayed in place, directed at Colby. "He definitely needs to find himself a wife."

Colby nodded. "That would be nice. Here's to hoping a beautiful lady like Anne would want a cowboy like me. Good night now." He turned and took the steps two at a time.

As she watched him dart away, a spurt of anger rolled through her. None of this should have happened. She turned a glare on Josiah. "You sure know how to wreck both the start and the finish of what could have been a wonderful evening." She started for the steps, and he followed her up. When they reached the top, she did not turn around, though he called her name. She pushed her bedroom door closed behind her with the intention of locking it. His hand caught the door before it crashed against the jamb.

She whirled to face him, and the insolent glare on his face only raised her ire more. "What has gotten into you? You're acting like a jealous little boy. It was a simple peck on my cheek, no more than Clarisse and a hundred other women planted on your face tonight, including the little blonde hanging on your arm, Laurie Trifle or Trivial or whatever her name is. And yet you act like we committed a crime."

"There is no *we* in this Katherine. Only *you*. I don't blame Colby one whit, but you...you dress to entice. Did you see where Colby's eyes were when you came down those steps? And you sweet-talk without any idea the effect you have on men."

She could not stem the tears that filled her eyes. "I dressed for you. I danced only with you. I stood by your side. I hate parties, but I worked tirelessly for weeks to prepare—all for you."

His frown softened, and he grazed his hand gently down her cheek.

But his touch only added another emotion to the mass roiling inside her. She pulled away. "Get out of my bedroom."

"I didn't mean what I said—"

"Out." She pointed toward the hallway as tears streamed down her face.

The lines of his shoulders sagged as he turned and obeyed her demand.

～

205

*J*osiah thrashed about on his bed. Her soft weeping whispered through the walls. Where had such jealousy come from? He'd never been that way with Georgina, but he'd known Georgina loved him.

What he witnessed—the sparkle of merriment in her eyes as she looked up at Colby with a look that should be reserved only for him. Where was the distinction, the favor, the love he craved? After listening to Katherine's memories of Charles when she shared them with Colby, he knew she'd been far more in love with him than Josiah cared to admit. Maybe she would never get over the man.

But what was fair to expect of her when he was the one who'd pressed her into marriage? Could he come to peace with something less? The something they had? Their growing friendship and the fact no other man shared her bed—was that enough? A weighty sadness filled his soul. Grief—different than what he'd experienced when Georgina died, but grief nonetheless—pressed in as he came to terms with the truth. He needed to accept what he could not change.

But one thing that was not in question was that he had been wrong tonight, and he had to set things right. His jealousy had been *jus-lousy,* as Delilah would say. He took a moment to pray, although he wasn't sure it would help. But he needed strength and the words to own his bad behavior and win back her trust. "Oh, God, I've hurt her. Help me."

Did God mind a simple heartfelt prayer? Hopefully not, for it was all he knew.

He threw the covers off and slipped out of bed. His slight rap on the door between the rooms brought no response. With a deep breath, he turned the knob and found it unlocked.

"Kat," he whispered into the dark. "I was wrong." He moved to stand beside her bed. "Please, forgive me."

A sob followed, then a hiccup. Her body moved beneath the

covers as she shuddered.

He eased down on the edge of the bed, unsure what to do.

"If…" The word drifted up from the covers, sounding half-strangled. "If you really believe I seek the attention of other men after all I've told you about my past, then you don't know me." He placed his hand on her back. "I didn't mean it. I was jealous and wrong to say what I did."

She turned toward him. "You're my husband, Josiah. I share my life with you. All I have, I give to you."

He pulled her close. "I know. I'm sorry." As he kissed her brow, she melted into his embrace. He lifted her in his arms and carried her through the door to his bed. After laying her down, he slipped in beside her.

She reached up to kiss his lips.

"Sleep now, my love. You've had a long day." He rolled her into the curve of his body and held her close, realizing he had called her his love when he had vowed not to. But how could he say less when that's what she was? His love. His heart. His personal agony.

CHAPTER 21

"*W*hy, you little cheater," Colby smacked Katie's arm as she laid down her winning hand.

Josiah looked up and laughed. "You're a sore loser, partner."

"I'm sure your wife looked at my cards when I got up to get a drink."

"Rule one, never drink and play at the same time." Josiah loved it when he and Kat ganged up on poor Colby. Every other time, Colby effortlessly took over the conversations, winning Katherine's attention with his quirky humor—all so very irritating. But game night, Josiah was solidly on Kat's side—and she his.

"Drat." Colby threw down the cards.

Kat smirked and winked at Josiah.

"I saw that wink. This time I did for sure." Colby popped from his chair and pointed at her.

"We've been pulling you along all winter." She laughed. "Do you realize how many times you get up in a game, go to the outhouse, get a drink, get something to eat. It's been so easy to look at your hand. Or Josiah will feign tiredness, get up to stretch, and stand behind you." She held up her fingers mimicking the sign language they shared.

Josiah leaned back in his chair. "Ahhh. Why did you tell him, Kat? This is the best part of my week."

"Because spring is around the corner and games will be no more when the mares begin foaling. I think it was time to put him out of his misery, don't you?"

He wished someone would put him out of his misery. He adored her fun-loving ways, how kind and attentive she was, their ever-deepening friendship, but still he waited for the words he wanted to hear more than life itself. And they never came. And the way those two teased back and forth was a constant source of irritation. Why did they have to hit it off so well?

"You owe me one game, Katie," Colby said. "Without the two of you working together. I need to know if I can whip you. I know I can beat this old man here"—he nudged Josiah's arm —"because I did it many times before you came into the picture, but you owe me."

"You're on."

Josiah cringed at Colby's term. Old man. He wanted to deck him one and show him just how old he wasn't.

Katie dealt the cards. Her brow bunched together, and she chewed her lower lip. Oh, how he loved that girl.

"You show him, Kat—"

"Boss. Boss." Hank barreled in. "One of the mares has gone into labor too soon. We have ourselves a problem."

Josiah jumped to his feet, his pulse thudding. Colby beat him to the door, and Katie was right on his heels. Josiah fell in behind them all as they headed to the barn.

The mare, Gloria, moaned and lowered her large head to the

hay. Katie smoothed her hand down the mare's mane. "Come on, girl, you can do this."

Josiah worked in tandem with Colby like they always did. They'd done this enough, words weren't necessary.

"That's it, Gloria, you're almost done," Josiah coaxed.

"Got him." Colby positioned the tiny foal in the hay. "We have ourselves a colt."

Katie moved in with blankets, ready to dry off the tiny foal.

As she dried the colt, Josiah rubbed the weary mare's head. "We'll stay with them to see if he can stand. We need to keep a small one like this real warm."

They watched the colt for hours, but the tiny animal never did learn to stand. Or feed. More than three hours had passed before Josiah shook his head. "Looks like we'll lose this one."

"Please let me take him into the kitchen and feed him." Katherine turned to him, her large blue eyes spilling with tears. "I'll do the work. I'll stay up. I believe this little guy can make it."

He didn't want to tell her what he'd seen too many times before. Even if the foal lived, the premature ones often grew with crooked legs because of their underdeveloped system. "Sorry, but there's little hope. Even if he survives, he most likely won't develop as he should."

"Please, Josiah."

Colby laid a hand on his shoulder. "I know I shouldn't say anything, but let her try."

Katie's eyes filled with hope. Josiah's hands clenched tight. How dare Colby contradict him and make an already difficult situation impossible?

"The worst that can happen is what is happening…the foal won't make it," Colby said.

Josiah's anger ruptured to full strength and he shoved off Colby's hand. "No. The worst that can happen is that my wife will fall in love with a horse whose end will be a bullet to its head."

Colby stepped back and threw up his hands. "You're right. Sorry I interfered."

"Go ahead, Katherine." Josiah did his best to rein in his anger, but the situation had festered too long within him. "Take that horse in. Try to save it. But when it dies in the next few weeks, or, God forbid, lives without the ability to walk properly, don't blame me."

He turned and marched away, angrier than he'd been in a long time. How dare Colby interfere? He made Josiah look like the bad guy. It was getting harder and harder to remain neutral about the unwanted influence Colby wove into their marriage. He would have a stern word with the man in the morning.

~

*M*aybe she should have followed Josiah's wishes, but Katie couldn't stand by and let the foal die without at least trying to help it. She had the tiny thing brought into the kitchen, and laid down old blankets for a bed and stoked up the wood stove. No matter what the outcome, she had to give this little one a fighting chance.

After hours of trying to get a dribble down his throat, of keeping him warm, the foal still didn't try to stand. Josiah was right. It was a lost cause.

In the deep of the night, a warm hand fell on her shoulder as she lay beside the foal. "Go get a few hours' sleep," Josiah offered. "I'll keep watch."

Her eyes brimmed with tears. "I had to try."

"I know. It's not over yet. I'll come get you if anything changes."

With a murmur of thanks, she dragged her weary self upstairs to bed. But she hadn't slept long when Josiah nudged her awake, his eyes bright. "Come, he's standing. Colby and I got him out to the stable with his mother, and he's actually nursing."

She popped from the bed and threw on her wrapper and an old pair of boots.

He waited near the door, watching her.

Standing there with the light framing his broad shoulders, he looked strong enough to defend her from anything. She should say something to smooth things over if she could. While she wove her hair into a quick braid, she said, "I know you were trying to protect me from more loss."

After she added her old straw hat, he slipped his arm around her, and they headed out the door. "That may still happen, but that's your decision to make, not mine. There's a lot to learn about this husband role, and the one thing I know for certain is how often I get it wrong."

She smiled up at him and leaned in. "Wish I could say I was the easiest person in the world to live with, but that would be a lie. We'll figure this out together."

"Together." He gave her arm a squeeze.

$\sim$

*C*olby and Kat's shared laughter spilled out the wide-open doors of the barn. A surge of jealousy flooded through Josiah and he stopped short.

"Look how good little Victory is doing. Even his knobby knees are straightening out." Her voice bubbled.

"You were the one who saved him, and now he only has eyes for you. Look how he's nuzzling in for a Katie hug."

"Come here, my precious," Katie said. "I'll snuggle you any time of the day."

"Who you talking to, me or the horse?" Colby chuckled at his own humor the way he always did.

Josiah fisted his hands. Was Colby flirting with his wife? How dare he?

"With all the attention you get from those girls in town, you don't need anyone else swelling up your head."

His easy chuckle wrapped around Josiah's throat and nearly choked him.

He wanted to hurt Colby. Jealousy burned in his soul, but he had to pull his emotions together. Katie was *his* wife, not Colby's. There was no need to be jealous. She shared his bed and his life. And he didn't want a repeat of what happened at Christmas. He inhaled a steadying breath.

But then Colby's voice drifted from the barn again. "Hey, I've been meaning to ask how you and Josiah met."

"Why do you ask?"

"Your age difference for one," Colby said. "I know age is no respecter of true love. Just curious how two people in totally different age and social groups would meet. After all, I have to find myself a wife."

"Yes, you do, and I've run out of fingers on my hands telling you the names of those interested." Her laughter flowed free, as pure as a babbling brook.

Josiah's heart squeezed tight in his chest.

"I'd like to be as lucky as you two," Colby said. "Any tips on how to find a love like yours would be appreciated."

Josiah took a sharp breath in.

"What did I say?" Colby's voice had shifted from amused to concerned. "You look like you saw a ghost."

Her voice wobbled. "Didn't Josiah tell you our marriage was arranged?"

"Really?"

"I see he failed to fill you in on that small detail."

Josiah's hands turned clammy. He should enter the barn and take over the conversation, yet he couldn't move.

"But you two are so in love. I would've never guessed."

"Josiah is in love."

Silence filled the space, and Josiah's heart dropped into his boots.

"I thought I was in love with Charles, yet that blasted war stole him from me. I wasn't in love with Josiah, but life forced us together."

Her words were like a razor-sharp knife chopping and dicing his world.

"The arrangement was made to suit everyone but me. I've felt like a pawn in the game of everyone's life but my own."

Josiah turned and fled the barnyard, unable to hear more. But shame dogged his heels. He'd married her to suit his needs. He'd arranged everything with the arrogant pride of one so confident he could make her fall for him. The cold, naked truth smashed in—a fatal blow to his heart.

He should've taken his time courting her, wooing her, allowing her to fall in love with him—or not. Instead, he set up a marriage deal that forced her hand. He'd been so afraid of losing her to someone half his age that he'd manipulated the circumstances to ensure she didn't have a choice.

Her feisty words on their wedding day often came back to him. "Love was never part of this deal, Josiah." She hadn't lied to him. In fact, she'd been brutally honest.

The good times they shared, the laughter, the friendship, the pleasure, had lulled him into thinking things had changed. Yet, she'd never declared her love to him. It was time for his delusions to end. He would no longer force his way into her life.

~

Something was wrong, but Katie didn't know what. Josiah had begun keeping far longer working hours than the rest of the household, missing supper hour on many occasions. Was his avoidance intentional? Had she done something to disappoint him? Maybe as the widow Laurie had said, he was indeed tiring of her.

When she tried to join him at night, slipping into his bed, he more often than not turned away, telling her he was too tired. She believed him, for he continued to work from dawn to dusk, and often beyond.

Loneliness pressed in. She missed their friendship more than she'd thought possible.

She'd endured weeks of his cold shoulder. But now it was time for a serious conversation. This could not go on. After another evening without him her frustration hit its limit, fueling the courage she needed.

At bedtime, she walked into his room unannounced and stood waiting for him to turn.

He pulled off his shirt, and the ripple of his muscles caught Katie's breath. He spun around at the sound of her intake. Her eyes collided with the molten gray of his.

"What do you want?" His tone was cold.

She gathered her courage and moved within arm's reach. "I want my husband back."

He let out a hot breath that fanned across her cheeks. The faint smell of hay, soap, and his earthy scent wafted her way.

"I miss you," she said, the truth of those words pressing a hard ache in her chest. "We used to be friends, and now...I don't know what we are."

He walked to the window, staring into the black. "I have enough friends."

Pain sluiced through her, churning into anger. Why would he talk to her this way? She bit back a retort and pressed her eyes shut to settle herself. Anger would not be the best way to find out what was happening.

She moved beside him and placed her hand on his upper arm. The muscle beneath her fingers tightened as he crossed his arms. "Well, I don't have enough friends." She kept her voice soft.

He wrenched free of her hand and paced the room. "No one marries a woman for friendship."

"I was more than a friend. I was your wife, we shared life, we made love."

He spun to face her, his eyes blazing hard. "Love. Did you ever make *love* to me? Have you ever said you loved me?"

She gulped back the knot of failure choking her words. "But, Josiah—"

"I don't need another friend, Katherine." His voice was as hard as his eyes. "And if you're in here out of some sense of duty, then I might as well go down to the local saloon."

She gasped, pressing a hand to her mouth as more pain burned her chest. "That was not what we had."

"You're right. It was not what *you* had, but unless you can tell me you love me, it was what I had. What I still have." A deep longing filled his eyes. "You don't get it, and I fear you never will."

His look nearly rent her in two. She reached out a hand toward him. "Help me, Josiah. I want—"

"You want what?" Desire smoldered hot in his gaze, and he shuddered.

"I want—" She couldn't say it. Did she even know what she wanted?

With a sigh and a curse, he hauled her up against his bare chest. "I don't have any problem knowing what I want. You're all I want." His mouth crushed against hers. His lips hard and desperate, hungrily sought the fullness of the kiss.

He picked her up and lowered her to the bed without taking his lips from hers. The usual tenderness was gone. In its place, a raw hunger, a desperate urgency, seemed to grip him. This time, there was little of the sweetness her husband usually offered so willingly.

At last, Josiah's anger seemed spent, and he rolled over with his back to her. "Please go." His voice caught. "In the future, I'd prefer you respect my private space as much as I respect yours. Don't come in here uninvited."

She'd never felt so raw and exposed as she slipped from the warm sheets and walked to her own room. Yet she forced herself to hold her head high.

Never again would she initiate or beg.

CHAPTER 22

SPRING 1867
ONE YEAR LATER

"*F*riend? Is that what we're still calling this?"

Katie looked ahead, unable to meet Colby's intense glare as he rode his horse beside hers. "You shouldn't have followed me. I told you I needed space to clear my head." She nudged her horse forward, but he caught up.

"You have a husband who has ignored you for over a year. There's been no intimacy whatsoever, am I correct?"

Heat spread from her neckline to hairline. She'd shared too much. Colby knew the exact state of her farce of a marriage. There was no point in lying.

"Katie, please. Can we be honest about this?"

"Why? What good will honesty do?"

"We could make a plan. Find a way."

When he used that gentle tone, it took every bit of her willpower to stay strong. But she had to, so she sent him a pointed look. "To what? Leave Josiah after all he's done for my family—and for you? We'll never do that."

"But, Katie, I can't help the way I feel about you."

Her chest ached. "Nor I you, but that changes nothing unless we're both prepared to betray Josiah and the last bit of goodness left inside our souls." She looked at him astride his horse, the handsome man, the friendly soul who had taken her in as a friend when Josiah had cut her out of his life. Her heart lurched. It would be so easy to give in to the flesh, the friendship, the feelings.

"So, you're just going to pretend—"

She looked away from him, staring into the distance. "I keep hoping to find the man I married. We had something special."

"It's been a year, and things have gotten worse, not better. What a waste of your life." His words came out drenched in sadness.

He was right, but that didn't matter. "I gave up my life the day I agreed to marry him." She had to resign herself. "This is not much different than the way I imagined things would go, I only thought I would at least have the joy of children to fill my days. My mistake was believing we were headed in the direction of having it all. That disappointment has been a long fall." She almost blurted out the one thought she had never shared with anyone. Why wasn't she a mother? Was she barren and inadequate in that area, as well?

"Every man in the countryside wants you except your husband," Colby said. "You deserve to feel loved. You're fun, kind, and beautiful on the inside—"

"Stop, Colby." She held up her hand and pulled back hard on her reins. The horse pranced back on his feet. "Sorry, Sugar." She leaned forward and patted the gelding's neck.

Colby turned his mount to come up beside her. His leg bumped hers as they steadied their horses.

She couldn't meet his gaze. "This is all my fault. I should never have confided in you."

His hand reached out and slid down the side of her cheek,

thumbing a tear away. "I will never regret our friendship, nor one moment in your presence, but I do want to kick Josiah to the moon. How could he waste such a beautiful gift?"

She shook her head. "See, that's the kind of thing you should never say."

"Why? Because it makes you *feel* rather than remain numb to the world?"

She glared and made her voice low and serious. "Don't follow me." The words took a monumental effort, but at least she got them out. She pressed her heels hard against her horse and lit off in a run.

After a while, she slowed her horse, letting him roam the hillside wherever he pleased. She had to break loose of her churning thoughts and feelings, and a long ride through the beauty of nature was her surest hope.

Yet she couldn't seem to find the clarity she sought. With a slap of the reins and a slight sink of her heels, she pushed the horse into another run. She sank into the glorious feeling, letting the exhilaration of speed consume her. Her long black braid flopped behind her as she tried to outrun her troubled thoughts. Like a woman possessed, she raced across the clearing, sailed over the wooden fence, and landed on the opposite side.

But no amount of speed could carry her away from her problems. At last, she reined in her horse and patted his mane.

The glorious smell of new foliage, grass, and meadow flowers drifted on the wind's cool breath. Their land stretched for miles around her, skirted by the rugged terrain of mountainous forest. The verdant pastureland dipped and rolled in a beauty all its own. The distant moo of cattle and the bleat of a newborn calf blended with the chatter of a mouthy squirrel in a nearby tree. Spring buttercups, hot pink lady's slippers, and purple violets dotted the hillside. All the little things that used to bring her joy now did little to lift her spirits.

She slipped from the saddle. All was as it should have been on a fine spring morning. Yet she clung to her only defense—to remain numb. Despondency helped her make it through one long day after another. If she felt nothing, she would expect nothing.

If only Colby had not challenged what worked. Not given voice to the solace she'd had in their...whatever it was that had grown between them.

Out in God's green open, with not a soul around, she allowed her walls to crumble. Pent-up emotion flowed free. Snippets, memories, feelings rose like a volcano inside her soul, forcing their way out. She let out the scream of a banshee warrior. The freedom to cry unchecked and uncontrolled poured out. The salt of her tears stung her wind-burnt cheeks as they spilled onto the thirsty ground. Cathartic. Cleansing. Crucial.

One by one, her cobwebbed mind released the emotions of the past year. She was powerless against their pull, and at last, she faced the darkness she had kept in the shadows.

Josiah. Dear, sweet, kind Josiah. What happened to that man, the one she first knew? She'd been so sure of his love for her and the stirring of emotion within her heart for him. And then, everything changed. What had happened to create this chasm? What had she done to deserve his coldness, his rejection? His complete withdrawal?

She'd not meant for this plethora of feelings for Colby to spring out of the dark thirst of her soul. Why had she so foolishly sought him out after Josiah seemed to turn away? In her loneliness, the need for a friend and a shoulder to cry on had outweighed wisdom. And over the past year, that friendship had developed too far. If she were honest, she had to admit she desired far more from Colby than friendship had to offer.

The duplicity was killing her. For the first time, she could finally admit the death of her marriage and the unpardonable fact—that she cared for someone else in a way meant for her husband.

Truth unwrapped the hidden, the secrets, the dark. She fell to the soft green grass and buried her face in her arms. Painful sobs rose up in her chest, forcing their way out to split the quiet.

What was to become of her? Could she really live the rest of her life like this? Maybe she should run away. Yet deep within, the truth burned hot. She could not run from herself.

Like a whisper on the wind, she gave herself the permission to let the memories of the past year blow across her mind. Full body sobs racked her being as she opened the door to truth. Why had she confided in Colby about her difficulties in their marriage? Why had she not pressed Josiah more? She should've demanded he tell her what went wrong. But, by seeking out comfort in a relationship with Colby, a shift had happened. She'd allowed a demon to insidiously slip into her life.

Though loneliness had driven her to Colby's open door, she'd never meant to give him her heart. But, as they shared conversation, laughter, and friendship, life had unfolded. Like a heavy mist, their feelings for each other seeped in and fingered out, spreading, living, breathing, until they consumed her. Guilt had also moved in, but it was fading. She cared far less about right and wrong than she used to. And that made her hate herself even more.

She and Colby walked a tight line, feeding a beast that could not be satisfied by mere friendship. A form of living hell created by their own foolishness ruled as they lived within inches of each other but were not able to act on the desires that plagued them.

And Josiah didn't care. He'd grown increasingly aloof.

"Oh, God, if you're up there, help me." Her words echoed through the pines.

⁓

*J*osiah had watched Katherine leave the yard mounted on her mare, and he'd watched Colby follow. Her desperate expression and Josiah's need to confirm his suspicions pressed him to shadow them. He didn't want to feel anything for her, but his sorry heart still picked up rhythm every time she came into view. He had spent a year fighting his love, to no avail.

He kept well back in the tree line and spied from a distance. They talked. It looked like Colby wiped tears from her face. And then she lit out in the opposite direction while Colby headed back. This had proved nothing.

She raced across the meadow and flew over the fence so fast, his heart jumped to his throat. Was she trying to kill herself?

He followed at a good clip and didn't breathe again until she slid from her horse. He moved as close as he dared, hidden in the stand of trees downwind from her. He didn't want the horses to pick up scent and nicker to each other.

Guilt surged at the way he was invading her privacy, but a force stronger than his will drew him forward. She was in a heap on the cold ground, weeping. Everything within him fought the urge to run to her side and comfort her. He longed to turn those tears into laughter and kiss away the pain as a husband should.

Instead, the memory that had held him hostage for a year assaulted his mind. Her description of their arrangement to Colby, after all he had done to reach her, had cut him down. Until that moment, he'd been so sure he could win her love. What an arrogant fool that man had been.

Today, however, witnessing her sadness and vulnerability, that memory lost its power. The mad obsession of not having her, yet not being able to let her go, had to stop. As he viewed her crumpled in a heap on the ground, sadness welled up.

Thick. Heavy. Oppressive. She didn't need his comfort. She needed her freedom. He would go ahead with his plan.

Wheeling his horse around, he left her, details spinning in his mind. He had gotten her into this mess, and he would get her out.

CHAPTER 23

here was God? Katie had called out so many times over the past few weeks, asking for strength to resist the temptation. But was that what she wanted anymore? If so, why was she waiting for Colby beneath the light of the moon? She shivered as both anticipation and guilt wrapped around her.

Colby's laughter compared to Josiah's grump, his stimulating conversation up against Josiah's rude silence—there was no contest. Colby didn't have to work hard to mesmerize her over dinner. The brush of his foot underneath the table stirred her blood. The lilt of his northern accent and his dancing golden eyes, the message he sent without the need for words, her abject loneliness... All of it made the impossible, possible.

She gazed up at the silver-washed glow of the moon, with only the crickets for company, and trembled at the thought of having him all to herself. The waiting made her jittery.

Like a shadow, he silently stepped into view, and they walked far beyond the view of the house. The stillness with nary a breeze, the dancing shadows, then the blackness of the night as the moon slid behind a dark cloud, heightened her awareness.

There in the black, he slipped his hand over hers for the first time. Her breath caught in her throat as a tremor of excitement and the foreboding knowledge of sin crept through her. The still, small voice of reason faded as she rationalized what she was doing.

He slowly ran his thumb up the inside of her wrist. She quivered under his touch. She could no longer think straight. Her foot caught on a stone and she stumbled forward. He grabbed hold of her and drew her up against him, his arms tightening around her like twin bands of steel. The rapid pace of his heart pumped hard beneath her hand on his chest.

A mere inch separated their lips. Her breath mingled with his, and the heat in his rapid breathing fanned her face. She closed her eyes and pressed up against him.

He groaned.

She breathed in the mix of aromas clinging to his skin, the clean smell of soap, traces of his horse, and his own manly scent. Pressed as close together as clothing would permit, Colby's pounding heart pressed into her, matching the racing of her own.

"Katie, what you do to me." His words came through hard breaths as he bent his head toward her lips.

Oh, how she wanted to give into the temptation. Her senses were singing. Her feelings for Colby overwhelming. But then, thoughts of Josiah crowded in.

She had to stop. Now. Or she'd never be able to.

"No." She wrenched back. "I can't do this to Josiah."

A swear word slipped from Colby's lips as they pulled apart. A canyon of pain filled his eyes. "I know you're right, but—"

"We need to stay clear of each other. This madness has to stop." She clutched her skirt in her hands.

~

*J*osiah threw the covers off his blazing body and stood from his bed. Thoughts of Katie had his mind tied in knots and his body responding in ways he would rather not. He wandered to the window and gazed through a narrow slit in the curtain. A movement flashed below.

His Katherine walked through the garden alone. She stopped and raised her face to the light of the moon. The silvery wash of her silhouette in the frosty glow took his breath away. There she stood. Lonely. Lost. Let down.

And he had created this life for her.

Could he start fresh? Should he make one more attempt to woo her before giving up? The way they were living was damaging them both.

Just when he decided to act on impulse and join her, Colby emerged from the shadows. She turned to him with her face in the light of the full moon. Her smile widened. Was that desire?

They both turned away from the house and walked into the blackness.

The suspicions that had been flitting in and out of his mind for months were confirmed.

A spike of anger rode up his spine and exploded into his skull. He smashed his fist on the wash basin stand, which sent the porcelain bowl flying. It shattered into a thousand pieces on the floor.

~

*K*atie ran for the safety of her room. She flung open her bedroom door and collided into Josiah.

"Whoa. You scared me. What are you doing in here?" She looked away, sure the guilt and shame screamed from her face. For even if she and Colby hadn't acted on their desires, their relationship was far from mere friendship. What could Josiah possibly want after all this time?

He didn't answer. Just stared at her.

She sidestepped to go around him, but he stepped in her path. She felt small staring into the barrel of his chest. Heat radiated from him.

He tipped her head up and forced her to meet his steady gaze. The gray in his eyes turned liquid, smoldering like blue-black flames. Dark emotions flashed across his face, from anger, to sadness, to pain.

He knew.

She tried to lower her gaze, but he kept his hand steady beneath her chin. They stood rigidly. The silence stretched into a long agonizing moment. She wanted to die under the scrutiny of his bold appraisal.

But he had brought this on. First with their arranged farce of a marriage, and then with his sudden rejection. He'd left her lonely and vulnerable. He'd created this mess.

Yet, no amount of justification could account for the hurt radiating from his eyes.

A strange jumble of emotions played inside her. She wanted to close the distance between them and resurrect the sweet, tender moments they'd once shared. And, at the same time, she wanted to run from the stranger he had become.

So she reached for anger. Something to protect her heart. "Why are you here? It's a little late to back up this train wreck of a marriage."

He groaned and lowered his lips to hers, his finger still under her chin. With over a year since they'd been intimate, Katie's heart leapt in surprise.

Gently, he coaxed a response from her. The pleasure, the tenderness they had shared in each other's arms, flooded back. His kisses feathered over her brow, her eyelid, her cheek, and her neck, then erupted into a heated rush on her lips. She melted into his embrace.

His body shook as he drew back, a question in his eyes. "Katherine?"

She nodded, and he swooped her into his powerful arms and lowered her onto her bed. With an urgency of time lost and wasted, they devoured each other. A seed of hope burst through the rocky soil of her heart as she lay spent in his arms.

He raised his head and stared down at her, a sheen of tears glistening in his eyes. His voice held a tremor. "Who did you see when you lost yourself in my embrace?"

Katie gasped, his words raising a pain that nearly stole her breath.

"No, don't answer." He dropped a quick kiss on her lips. "I don't want to know."

He swung off the bed and disappeared into his room.

Katie curled in a ball under the sheets, shaking. *What had just happened?*

For a moment, she'd had hope. Hope they could rebuild. Hope they could find the friendship they once shared. Hope birthed and crushed in less than an hour.

Tears spilled from her eyes and soaked the sheets. Too exhausted to fight, she sobbed into her pillow.

∿

*J*osiah tossed on his bed and slammed his pillow over his head so he wouldn't hear her sobs. His hands fisted at the weakness he'd succumbed to. He had meant only to confront her and hear the truth from her lips, but truth ceased to matter when he stood so close, smelled the rose-scented essence of who she was, and looked into her soft blue eyes. The minute he touched her, all resolve vanished like a vapor in the wind. He had wanted, needed, one more memory before setting her free.

An annulment for their arranged marriage should be easy to obtain. There was not proof of consummation other than what was imprinted upon his heart. He would give the excuse they had taken time to get to know each other, but had never fallen in love. Only he would know the lie in it all.

Katie wouldn't argue that last point and would be grateful for her freedom. The plan would keep her from the social stigma of divorce. It was the least he could do for her. He had stolen her right to choose to love whom her heart connected with, and he aimed to set things right. Colby, the brother he never had, was that lucky man, and although Josiah's heart hollowed at the mere thought, the truth remained the truth.

Dear God, you've helped me before. Please, give me the strength to let her go.

～

*I*t had been a week since Josiah touched her, and Katie had only seen him from a distance. Over the past year, she'd avoided her parents place as much as she could, to keep them from knowing how unhappy she was. But today she set out with a mission in mind.

The hinges on the screen squeaked as she pulled open the door. "Ma?"

"In the kitchen. Getting supper on."

Katie grabbed an apron from the hook beside the sink and fell into her old routine. She stood beside her mother, picked up a knife, and dug into the sack of potatoes. "I might as well help while we're talking."

"You haven't been here in so long," Ma said. "The girls keep asking about you."

"I know. Life has been busy. Pa told me you and Amelia are

going to Richmond to see Grandmother and Grandfather?"

"Yes, we leave next week."

"I'd like to join you. After all these years of silence from them, I thought you might appreciate some moral support."

"No." Ma's answer was immediate, and her voice quivered. "I want to see if they've really changed before I introduce them to my family."

"But you're allowing Amelia to go—"

"Your place is here with your husband, not traipsing to Richmond. Maybe another time."

Katie looked up from her peeling. Ma's response didn't make sense. There was none of the sternness she'd experienced growing up, more a desperate plea. "It would do me good to get away right now." Why had she said that? She pursed her lips shut.

"Why? What's happened?" Ma's burning gaze penetrated the front she was working hard to maintain, and Katie shuddered.

She'd almost revealed the shamble of her life. How could she tiptoe around the truth without spilling the beans? She wanted distance, and lots of it, from Josiah's coldness, from Colby's warmth.

She turned back to the bowl and grabbed another potato. "Nothing. Josiah is just so busy with the ranch, and I'd like a change of pace. I'm sure he won't mind. In fact, I'll ask him tonight."

"Go ahead and ask. I'm sure he'll agree with me." Ma's no-nonsense voice was back in place.

She didn't want to appear too desperate, so she let the subject drop. She was always the unwanted one. The burn of tears stung her eyes, so she slipped out of the apron and hung it on the hook. "All right then, I'll do that directly."

"You're not going to interrupt the man in the middle of the workday, are you? Stay and visit a bit." Both a tremor and a cajoling filled Ma's voice.

"I have things to do. I have to go." Katie swallowed against the lump in her throat.

Gracie came around the corner and squealed before leaping into Katie's arms. "You just got here, aren't you going to play with me?"

Katie swung her sister in a quick twirl, and Gracie giggled. "I can't stay, but walk with me to the orchard's edge." She brushed a wayward curl from Gracie's brow and kissed her silky-smooth skin. "I'll come back tomorrow, and I promise to play with you then."

She hugged her little sister tightly, pushing her body against the screen door to open it. An overwhelming urge to hold a baby of her own once again filled her being. She couldn't stop the tears from brimming.

"Why your eyes so wet?" Gracie's baby soft hand reached up to touch Katie's face. "Are you sad?"

Katie pulled her close as the weight of sadness nearly smothered her, but she kept walking. If she'd given Josiah a child, maybe he wouldn't have turned so cold. She had failed him there as well, although it was a little hard to have a child if one didn't... Her cheeks burned hot at the memory of the last night they'd spent together. What had that been about? She had been so hopeful, and then so crushed.

Her thoughts unraveled and swayed between her fault, his fault, their fault. Around and around they spun until her head ached. She shook the fog free. She had to get past the caring. It hurt too much.

She set Gracie down, and they walked hand in hand to the edge of the orchard. There, she bent down and planted a kiss on her sister's rosy cheek. "Off you go now. I'll watch how fast you can run back to the house."

Gracie spun. The jiggle of her chubby legs, the floppy braids, and the shriek of delight brought a tinge of happiness to Katie's heart, but the feeling faded as fast as it came.

CHAPTER 24

"Colby, hand me the halter," Josiah said.

"Sure thing, partner."

The words bit hard, and Josiah flinched. They shared the business, they shared the work, and now he would give up his wife. Seemed too big a leap. Were there not enough women in the world that Colby had to fall for his wife? And yet he needed Colby. There was no way he could run a ranch this size without his expertise.

For months now, he had both loved and hated this man. This brother. They worked so well together, it was unfathomable they had this unvoiced monstrosity between them.

All spring they had labored side-by-side in the birthing and nurturing of the new foals, the groundwork training, and the breaking in of some of the finest stock yet to grace the ranch. The operation ran seamlessly.

Josiah should be on top of the world. Instead, his life was crumbling. Everything that gave him purpose—wife, dream of family, hope of an heir to pass on his legacy—was gone. What was the point?

He had to hand it to Colby. He had a knack for the training.

His gentle dance of halter, then saddle, then the weight of his body came naturally. Horses loved and trusted him, much like Josiah's wife. At the mere thought, his hands clamped down on the fence rail so tightly, splinters pierced into the flesh. Fury filled his head and rippled down. He had to get away from the man or bust him in two.

"I'm heading to the house." Josiah plunked his cowboy hat back on his head.

"I thought we were going to work Victory next. You said you wanted to take charge of the colt."

Josiah turned and waved toward the horse. "All yours." As he walked away, he couldn't help mumbling. "Everything that matters will soon be all yours."

"Josiah." Jeb called out.

Josiah turned to see Katherine's pa barreling toward him. The last thing he wanted was a conversation with anyone, especially his father-in-law. He had to cool down.

"Do you have a moment? There's some things I've been meaning to tell you for a long time."

"Can it wait?"

"I'm afraid not. It concerns Katie's childhood. She's going to ask you if it's all right she travel to Richmond with her mother and sister. After I explain, you'll understand why you have to keep her here."

~

*J*osiah intentionally missed the supper hour that evening. He didn't want to run into Katherine for a myriad of reasons, the biggest being the need to remain far from her lure. He should never have touched her. What a fool. She haunted him enough in the day. With a mere unlocked door between them at night, he was going crazy. One minute he wanted to squelch all feelings and end his tortured marriage. The next, he craved anything she was prepared to give.

He slipped into the kitchen for the meal Delilah kept warming on the stove and slid into a chair at the table.

"Josiah."

He started at the sound of Katherine's voice and looked up to see her across the room. She must've been waiting for him.

"I need to talk to you when you're done eating." Her hands fidgeted with the front of her dress, clenching and unclenching the material. At what point had she reverted back to being uncomfortable in his presence? Why did it matter?

He swallowed his bite and forked another. "Go ahead."

"Amelia and Ma are going to Richmond to meet Grandmother and Grandfather Brunson."

"I'm aware of that."

"I'd like to go with them. I told Ma you wouldn't care, but she insisted I ask you."

"What makes you think I wouldn't care?"

Her face blushed beet red. "What I meant to say is that you're always working, and you wouldn't mind if I were gone for a few weeks."

"I mind."

Her hands lifted to her hips as she approached until she stood a mere foot apart. Judging by the color of her cheeks and the jut of her chin, her temper was about to flare.

"What does that mean?" she asked.

"It means just what I said. I mind." He was frustrating her, but he cared more than she would ever know. He cared that soon she'd no longer be his wife and he'd spend a lifetime missing her. He cared that she had more in her past than she could imagine. He cared that her parents, rather than face the truth, had lied to her for years. He shouldn't care, not with the paperwork he had sent away for, but he did.

The heat of her stare bore down as he shoveled his food in.

"Please."

He raised his head to a set of dejected iridescent eyes.

Her parents should never have placed him in this position. He would've given her the moon if he could've, especially when she looked at him like she was now. He choked on the words he was forced to say. "It also means no."

Teardrops pooled on her thick lashes. Her eyes, deep and haunting, blinked, and tears splashed down her fine alabaster skin. She looked fragile, like a bruised flower.

A mad sorrow squeezed his heart. He would have much preferred her anger.

The desire to gather her close and tell her the truth over-whelmed him, but, knowing the circumstances, he bit his tongue and shoveled another bite into his mouth. It tasted like sawdust. When he looked up, she was gone.

He slammed his fist on the table so hard his skin split open.

~

*K*atie ran into the evening rain, stepping through the mud puddles pooling in the yard. She didn't care. The hem of her gown turned as heavy as her heart.

She headed to the barn, and when she stepped inside, it took a moment for her eyes to adjust to the waning light. Her gelding nickered and lowered his head to nuzzle as Katie moved close. She threw her arms around his neck and let the sobs flow. Tabby circled around her feet, rubbing up against her.

She started at the weight of a hand on her shoulder and whirled around.

"Colby, you scared me."

"You're scaring me, running through a torrential downpour without a shawl. Come, we have to get you warm." He grabbed her hand and pulled her into the tack room and closed the door. He shrugged out of his coat and placed it around her shoulders.

The walls of the small room closed in, and the dwindling evening light cast them into almost complete darkness. He lit the nearby lantern and turned toward her. When he held out his arms, she walked straight in.

Since that night in the garden a month earlier, he had ignored her and she him. Without words, they both understood why. It was one of the reasons she'd wanted to leave for a while...to regain control and sort her jumbled feelings. How could she want Colby one moment and her husband the next?

She soaked in his warm embrace. With her ear pressed against his chest, she heard the hammer of his heartbeat through the muscled wall. They stood quietly for a long moment.

"I just wanted to go to Richmond with Ma."

"I know. I overheard the conversation." His hands soothed a gentle path down her back, and he pulled back enough to look into her tear-stained face. "Katie, it was strange. I walked in after you left, and Josiah asked me to go find you. He said you'd need comfort. When I told him that was his job, he told me he was no longer the one you needed. That I was."

Waves of guilt pounded through her tortured soul. "But we never talked about—"

He placed a finger on her lips.

"It's no use denying the obvious. We've skirted around the truth for too long now. Josiah knows how we feel about each other, and he doesn't seem to care."

The tension mounted as she raised her head to look deep into his eyes. Did Josiah really not care? Should she finally give in to the tenderness Colby offered? His head bent toward her waiting lips.

The door opened.

Katie's heart leapt to her throat at the man's form filling the frame. "Pa." She jumped back from Colby's embrace.

He stood without moving. His head dropped. "I see the apple

doesn't fall far from the tree." The sadness in his voice was palpable. His weathered brow bunched as he held the door open. He waved at Colby. "Out."

"Yes sir." Colby moved with lightning speed.

Katie's indiscretion burned like a live coal in her stomach.

"Katherine, you and Josiah have some business to discuss. Either you tell him, or I will." With that, Pa walked away, his shoulders slumped and his head down.

CHAPTER 25

atie waited for Josiah in the kitchen with her head in her hands. A week had passed, and she had not yet faced the worst conversation of her life. But she had to. Tonight. Pa would force her hand if she didn't.

At the bustle of fabric swishing against the hardwood floor, Katie lifted her head and breathed out relief. Delilah crossed the kitchen.

A warm, fleshy arm encircled her shoulder. "Katie girl, you've been unhappy for too long now." Delilah pulled her up into one of her warm hugs and didn't let go. Shorter than Katie, the starch from her turban brushed rough against her cheek.

"You know I love you, don't you?" Delilah pulled back, her dark almond shaped eyes piercing.

Katie nodded.

"Then I be honest. Sit." She pointed to the chair and plunked her large frame in the chair around the table corner from Katie. She spread out the palm of her workworn hands and enclosed them around Katie's. "You and Mistuh Josiah has not been doin' good for some time now. Not like in the beginning."

The understatement almost made Katie laugh. Delilah didn't understand the half of it.

"But I know he loves you."

She shook her head. "No—"

"I see more than you think. I see the way he looks at you when you you're not looking, and I see the way that Colby is looking too." Clucking like an old hen, she shook her head. "Not like a man should be looking at his best friend's wife."

A burst of anger spiked. "It's not his fault. He at least cares enough to be my friend. He's around in the evening, unlike Josiah. Look at what time it is, and my husband still hasn't come in for supper."

Her excuses sounded lame even to her own ears. How did she explain to this dear soul what she herself could not understand? Where had it all gone wrong? Though the marriage had started out shaky, it had turned better than she'd ever believed possible. She had even thought she was falling for her gentle husband.

And then, he turned cold.

"He avoids me and won't talk to me. We never..." Her face heated.

"You're not telling Delilah any secrets she doesn't already know. But it wasn't always this way."

"No, it was good. And then..."

"Find out what went wrong." She lifted her pudgy soft hands to both of Katie's cheeks and looked straight in. Her eyes were as soft and warm as melted chocolate. "Ask Josiah for the truth—"

"But I tried."

"Try harder. Make him put it into words. Men have a way of thinking we can read their minds."

She leaned forward and hugged Katie before rising from her chair. "You know I'm praying up a storm for you."

"Thank you." Her voice sounded as weak as the rest of her. Did she have the courage to do what Delilah asked?

"Be brave, my girl." With a final gentle smile, the woman turned and shuffled off down the hall.

Tonight would be the night. She didn't care how late he came in. Pa and Delilah were right—it was time to sort out this sad thing they called a marriage.

~

*K*atie retired to her room and waited. Sooner or later, he'd come to bed, and she aimed to get this conversation over with.

Finally, the faint sound of his door opening and shutting carried through the wall. She was ready. Although she hadn't prayed in a very long time, she whispered a petition for strength. She stood by the adjoining door for a few minutes until she could summon the courage to knock. Then she entered without waiting for an answer. She wasn't about to let him scare her off again.

His room had once been her safe place, but now it felt stifling, as if the walls closed in around her. As if his very essence accused her. He'd stripped to the waist, and her eyes fell to his sun-bronzed chest rippling with sinewy muscles.

The sight stole the moisture from her mouth and made her want to run to him. Or maybe run away. She spun. "I'll come back."

"Spit it out, Katherine. Then leave me be."

She turned again and stared against her will at his torso, where glistening drops of water clung to his chest hair. He grabbed his shirt from the back of the chair and worked it on.

The white shirt opened down the front and did the opposite of what she was sure he intended. Instead of covering, it accented the healthy glow of his tanned skin and emphasized the fact that he was half undressed. Her mind flew back to days past—happier times when he still wanted her, when he teased her, when he touched her.

"What do you want?" His voice sounded edgy and hard and brought her back to the present.

"We need to talk."

He sank into the nearby chair and puffed out a heavy breath. "I know. I was going to wait until I had the... Sit." He motioned to the bed.

She sat on the edge. This bedroom was not the best place for a serious conversation.

"How about I make this easy for you?" he said. "By the time I'm done, I'll have saved you the trouble of whatever you wanted to say." Though his eyes were cold, his Adam's apple bobbed as if it was difficult for him to say. "You don't love me, and never will. Colby is the man for you, and we both know it. If I hadn't run ahead and forced your hand—"

His words slammed into her, catching her off guard, and a gasp slipped through her lips.

"Don't look so shocked. A man would have to be blind to miss what's been going on between the two of you."

"But Josiah—"

"Let me finish." He scrubbed a hand through his hair, which bounced back into place with a curl that fell across his brow. She could only stare at the lock, steeling herself for whatever he might say next.

"It won't be long before you two can be together. I've filed for the appropriate annulment papers. All you have to do is sign them when they arrive. A lawyer friend of mine in Richmond is drafting them up as we speak. Soon enough, you'll be free."

She was glad she was sitting, for her shaking legs wouldn't have supported her. Was he ending their marriage? She'd failed him. And would she now lose him? She couldn't lose him. Desperation clawed in her chest.

"I'll keep working with your pa. I need him as much as he needs me, and of course all I've given to your parents and you for a wedding gift will remain yours. Just not this home. I'd like what Georgina and I built together to stay intact. In turn, I'll settle up with Colby so the two of you can build a house somewhere else on this big spread, far from my sight. Sadly, I also need him as much as he needs me."

Her mind was numb with all the details he was spewing at her. "What are you suggesting?"

"That small detail of consummating the marriage will be kept between the two of us. No one ever need know. It's not like you gave me any children."

Those final words struck like a knife blade, straight in through her ribs. She'd failed him in every way. Yet, she couldn't take this all on her own shoulders. "Well, it's not like you gave me anything to work with this past year, the way you've avoided me like the plague." She sent him a fiery glare.

As if she hadn't spoken, he continued in a level tone. "I'm doing this for your sake. It's relatively easy to annul an arranged marriage, and you won't have to carry that dreaded stigma of being a divorcée. After all, it wasn't your fault you got saddled with me." He slapped his thighs with his hands and stood. "And that about wraps up our sad little story. Now, if you'll excuse me, I'd like to drop my weary bones into those nice warm sheets."

He said it all with casual indifference, as if closing the last chapter of a boring book. The finality of his words pressed in on her. She rose with a wobble to her legs and made her way across the room to her door.

But Delilah's advice rang in her head. *Find out what went wrong. Make him put it into words.*

She whirled around, and it looked as if he was thumbing moisture from the corner of his eye. "I have just one question. Why?"

"Why, what?"

Her hands flew up. "Why did you love me one day, then turn me out the next?"

A muscle in his jaw clenched. "Any fool knocked down enough times will take the hint."

"How did I knock you down? I was trying. In fact, you meant more to me than any person ever had. You were my friend, my lover, the one person I shared true intimacy with." She couldn't seem to stop the tremor in her voice. "You...you promised to give me time, then you just went cold."

She propped her hand against the doorjamb, the truth of her own actions hitting like a blow. "I know it doesn't excuse how I turned to Colby, but I will not take this all on myself." She forced herself to stand straight and flashed him a stormy scowl. "You drove me away, and all I want to know is why."

His eyes turned from stone cold to smoldering black. "Do you want the sordid details of what shut me down? Or is this only so you can watch me bleed?"

She met the anger in his eyes with determination. "I deserve to know."

"Fine then. Do you remember a spring morning in the barn when you were discussing our little arranged marriage with Colby?"

Discussing...what? She had no idea what he was talking about.

"I guess I need to refresh your memory. You admitted to loving Charles and told Colby how you got stuck with me instead. You were only a mere pawn...with our little arrangement made to suit everyone but you." His voice took on volume with each word. "You emphasized how you were bought and paid for. Is any of this ringing a bell?"

The conversation came flooding back, but why would it upset him? If anything, the things she'd said should have encouraged him. Unless...

"At what point did your little eavesdropping escapade end?"

"What difference does it make? The message was all too clear. You didn't love me and never would. You resented the way I'd taken your freedom—"

Fury stormed within her. "If you're going to listen in on people's conversations, then listen in on the entire thing, because I have my suspicions you didn't stick around long enough to hear me answer my own questions."

"What more was there to say?" The fire washed from his eyes, leaving them haggard. His large frame crumbled as he lowered himself to the edge of the bed.

"There *was* more. But I'm so angry right now, I can't even talk." She turned and paced the room, gulping in a cleansing breath. How dare he eavesdrop and then not talk to her about his misunderstood assumptions. None of this would have come to be if he'd only asked her. What a waste of what could have been.

He remained silent, so she stopped directly in front of him. "I did question what love was, and I did tell Colby that I *thought* I had loved Charles. I told him our marriage had been arranged without thought or consideration for my feelings. That part you heard. None of that was a secret. The whole family knew it. The whole ranch. The whole town, maybe."

She could barely hold in her anger, but she forced herself to speak coherent sentences. "And I told Colby that I felt bought and paid for *at the beginning*. And then, I shared how many of my perceptions had changed from our wedding day. I told him how kind, gentle, and loving you had been, how you were teaching me what love was by loving me so well. I admitted I had a problem opening up because of the way my ma treated me, but how I trusted you with information I couldn't tell another soul."

Josiah's head dropped into his hands, and he let out a groan.

She grabbed his wrists and pulled them away. "I'm done with

you shutting me out. You need to hear this." She pulled in heavy breaths to still her anger as she waited for him to lift his eyes. A haunted look burned from his blue-grays.

"Do you know what Colby said? He said I was most definitely in love. He told me the way my eyes lit up when you walked in the room was practically worship." She dropped his hands and straightened.

There. Now, he knew everything. And the telling had leached not only her anger, but every bit of strength in her. "That's what you missed when you decided to shut me out—*me* loving *you*. Not loving an old memory of Charles. Not Colby. You."

His gaze held a question that made her chest ache.

"Don't believe me? Ask Colby. Go now, before you think I have time to collaborate the story with him, since I know how little you trust me." That last bit was a barb, but she couldn't help it.

She spun from him and strode across the room, wrenching open the adjoining door. With her hand still on the doorknob, she turned. "And if you think I'll allow our marriage to be annulled, you can think again. We made love. Heart wrenching, soul shaking love, and no one, not even you, can cheapen or take that from me. My biggest regret is that I never had a baby, your baby, to hold in my arms. Maybe if I had, I wouldn't have spent time with Colby, and you wouldn't have given up on me so easily. And, in case you're not sure, that was all I did with Colby. Spend time. Talk. Share my hurts, the hurts *you* inflicted."

He jumped from the bed. "You expect me to believe that?" As he marched toward her, the veins in his neck bulged like a bullfrog. "I saw you two in the garden, a romantic interlude in the moonlight. I wasn't born yesterday."

In the garden. She thought back, knew the night...

"That night I was waiting for you in your room. I was going

to demand the truth. But instead, fool that I am, I longed for one last memory before I filed for the annulment papers."

She dropped her jaw. "Memory? That was way more than a memory. That night..." She swiped her hands over her eyes to rid them of the tears. "That night, for a moment, I believed in a God of miracles. One that had been proud of the way I had run from Colby only minutes before. I wanted to give our marriage a second chance. When you came to me, I thought you felt the same. It wasn't until you took what you wanted and left me alone, tossing unkind words my way, that I realized we had no hope."

A shadow passed across his face. "What about your pa telling me to talk to you about what he witnessed in the barn. I didn't bother to ask because I don't care to know."

A shimmer of tears threatened to blink free. "Colby and I have been close friends. Too close. I will not lie about that. I was wrong to turn to him when I was hurt and vulnerable. He came to me that night in the barn at your suggestion. However, we never..."

His brows raised.

She threw up her hands. "Believe whatever you want. I can't stop you."

He took a step closer. She waved him away.

"If you want to divorce me, then go ahead. I will face what I am, a divorcée. All I ask is that you hold true to your word concerning my family. I want nothing more from you."

Then she turned and slammed the door between them. For the first time ever, she turned the key in the lock and flung her body across the bed. One thought kept cutting through the pain. If only he had talked, yelled, and screamed all those months ago. If only he'd done something other than turn cold.

CHAPTER 26

*K*atie couldn't bring herself to leave her room, no matter how many days passed. Even with Delilah and Ruby's coaxing, she had little will to do anything or even to eat. She didn't care that her body was shrinking before her eyes or that despondency and numbness had become her best friends. She couldn't summon interest in the usual running of the household, a place she no longer considered home. She lay on her bed or stood listlessly, gazing out the window.

The one thing she did long to do was get on her horse and ride, yet she couldn't take the risk of running into Colby. If he encouraged her at all in her weakened state, she wouldn't be able to resist his warmth, his friendship, his arms.

A slow burn developed the first week and blossomed into a full rage. If Josiah had loved her as he claimed, why had he not fought for her? Why had he believed the worst?

The second week, despondency set in. By the third week, the full bottle of laudanum she had snuck into her room called her name. She was ready to give in to anything that could stop the pain.

If truth be told, she was confused. Very confused. Colby

offered a soft landing, an easy friendship, an obvious attraction. But Josiah had been the one who restored her faith in men, who had taken her in and shown her true patience and love. She longed for that man back, the man before the jealousy. They had something she could not easily shake.

But there was no hope. Josiah had thrown her away like a worn-out dish rag. And Colby was there, willing to give up his dream of this horse ranch to be with her. Yet she feared someday, if she allowed that, he'd resent her. For the sake of both Josiah and Colby, she would not be the one to break up the partnership.

~

*J*osiah had to try one more time. The whole household was in a dither because Katherine was not opening her door to anyone. He knocked on the door adjoining their two rooms.

"Come on, Katherine. I know you can hear me. Open up. Everyone is worried."

"I can hear you just fine. Go away."

"You have to eat."

"What do you care?"

He wanted to shout that he loved her, and beg her to forgive him, but that would scare her off for sure. "I never stopped caring."

"You care so much you've made arrangements to end our marriage."

He gulped back the knot in his throat. Her words held too much truth. "Open the door so we can talk."

"Did you, or did you not, file for that annulment?"

Did she want a yes, or a no? He had no idea how to answer. Did she want to be with Colby? At this point, he just wanted whatever she wanted. Three weeks was a long time to stay holed up. His worry for her was eating him up inside.

"Answer me, Josiah."

"Yes, I did." Was that a sob coming from her room? He couldn't be sure.

"Then go. I'm no longer your concern."

Everything in him wanted to bust the door down and take her in his arms. Tell her she would always be his concern. Instead he dropped his head and turned away. It was too late. He'd failed her miserably. The one person who mattered most to him.

He headed down the steps for a late evening meal. He could care less about food, but he had to keep up his strength.

The day had been long and difficult. Not even hard labor helped erase the error of his ways. Josiah grabbed his meal from the edge of the wood stove and slipped into his chair. When he slammed his plate down, the metal clanged on the table.

A mad sorrow ripped through his aching heart. He had wasted over a year trying to avoid her because of a half-truth. He'd ruined everything, including their friendship. He deserved the agony he was feeling. She, however, deserved none of the sorrow he'd brought on her—not being pressured into an arranged marriage, not being shunned by the one who'd promised to show her what true love was, not the secret her parents kept from her, which would only bring more feelings of abandonment.

He cringed at the thought of giving her up, but he'd do anything right now to make her happy. Colby cared deeply for her and had been left to pick up the broken, confused pieces of her heart. And in the process, had found what Josiah had so freely given away—a kind, tender soul so easy to love. Josiah had no one but himself to blame.

He pushed the plate away and buried his face in his hands.

His head pounded. Would it do any good to pray? *God, what should I do?*

Then it came to him, a thought, a plan. Tomorrow he would put it into motion.

~

*J*osiah had Jeb and Colby just where he wanted them…together. He didn't call Jeb away from the farming aspect of the ranch that often, but he needed a good excuse for some uninterrupted conversation. A section of the fence had to be fixed, and he needed their help.

They rode in silence as they made their way to the spot.

"Where's that section you were talking about?" Colby asked.

"Coming up." Josiah pointed ahead.

"You would've had some better help than me had you grabbed a few of the ranch hands," Jeb said. "This shoulder of mine will never be as strong as it once was."

"There are two reasons I asked the both of you to join me. I wanted a chance to talk without any listening ears. And the fence needs mending. We can work and talk."

"Spoken like a true rancher." Jeb chuckled.

When they reached the fence, Josiah swung from his horse. The other two were right behind him.

Without words they spread apart and worked like a team. Josiah motioned to the downed section. "We'll flag where the posts need to be replaced and reinforce enough to keep the cattle in. I'll send some of the young cowhands out to do the tough digging."

Jeb nodded. "Sounds like a plan I can live with."

"Why are these down? The post isn't rotten, but looks like it's been chopped." Colby's brow scrunched.

"That's one of the things I wondered about," Josiah said. "You both think this can't be an accident?"

251

Jeb took a closer look at a few more posts. "Yup, this damage looks intentional."

Josiah's stomach twisted at the thought of broaching the two hardest subjects of his life.

"All right." Colby paused and swiped at his sweating brow with his handkerchief, then turned a steady gaze on Josiah. "What's going on here? And why the secrecy?"

Better to start with the easier subject. "We have trouble coming our way from some of the town folk. You know that Hinton Rowan, the big mouth at our Christmas party back when?"

"The guy who me and the boys escorted out?" Colby asked.

Josiah nodded. "For years he's ruled the roost around here with his huge spread and slave labor. He doesn't much like that I've hired both white and black workers and pay them all the same. He's tried to talk me into doing things his way, but I guess the fact I didn't capitulate has him angry. So, he's been going around town stirring up trouble. And because most people have been getting away with paying their black workers far less, our practice is not going over well. I'm getting some nasty threats to lower our wages or else."

"Or else what?" Jeb stopped and straightened with a hand to his lower back.

"This is the beginning...busting down our fences and stealing our cattle. Hank said his boys can't find all the stock."

"That could be any cattle rustler, couldn't it?" Colby frowned.

"I thought the same, and didn't pay them much mind until the threats started coming in the mail." And now the important part. "Sometimes including the names of our family members."

"Family members?" Jeb's voice took on strength.

"Yes. Delilah, Abe, and Katherine. And your girls too, Jeb."

The older man stepped toward him. "What can we do?"

"Sheriff Holden is aware and keeping me appraised of everything he hears in town. I've hired some extra cowboys, as you may have noticed, who'll patrol the grounds. And I'm going to schedule night watches."

He looked from one man to the other. "So, my question to both of you is, are you in? I have no intention of giving in to threats. I'll understand, Jeb, if you want to take your family and go stay with your sister until this dies down."

Jeb took off his hat and ran a hand over his hair. "If we give into fear and threats, they win. I have no doubt God will protect us."

Colby eyed Jeb. "Didn't think you were much of a religious man. Never heard you talk like that before."

"I don't know much yet. Learning a lot through reading the Bible. But when I took that one step of belief a couple months back, all I can say is the peace and love I feel right here"—he slammed a fist against his heart—"is more real than anything I've ever experienced before."

Josiah and Colby exchanged raised eyebrows.

"You two laugh away or say it's the ramblings of an old man. I don't care. I've been changed."

Josiah raised a hand. "You can believe whatever you want. I do think there's a God somewhere up there. I just don't think he cares much about the everyday down here."

"He cares." Jeb's brown eyes softened. "But that's enough preaching for one day, other than I'm going to ask you both to attend my baptism coming up. Hope it's all right that I've volunteered the use of our creek down by the swimming hole."

"You don't have to ask," Josiah said. "You know this place is as much yours as mine."

"I'd be honored to see you dunked." Colby turned to Josiah. "And I have no reason not to be in with your plan." He raised a rail back into place, then readied a nail to hold it there.

"That might change after we talk about my next problem."

Josiah took off his hat and dug his hands through his crop of hair.

Both heads turned his way, and the work stopped.

Josiah gulped back a knot in his throat. "It's about Katherine." He pressed on the knuckles on one hand until they popped. "She's been holed up in her room for too long now. I need one of you to go to talk to her. She's not talking to me or anyone else in the house."

Colby shook his head. "I'm not getting involved."

"A little too late for that, don't you think?" Josiah couldn't stop the clip of his voice.

Colby raised his brows. "If you hadn't neglected the best thing that ever happened to you, you wouldn't be in this state."

"You're a fine one to talk, when all you've done is flirt with her from the get-go." Josiah took a step toward Colby, hands fisted.

"And all you've done is act like a jealous oaf." Colby took up the challenge, moving closer.

"Stop." Jeb held up his hands and stepped between them. "This will solve nothing."

Josiah stared Colby down, wishing his friend would take a swing. Wishing he could start and finish the fight he'd been itching to have for weeks. Months.

But Colby shook his head and backed up. "I'm not fighting you, Josiah. As much as I believe you're crazy for giving up on Katherine and would love to knock you into next week for the hurt you've caused her, I'm done with this conversation." He scanned the land around them, ignoring Josiah's gaze. "I'll protect the ranch and work hard, but Katie and I are staying clear of each other."

"I'll talk to her," Jeb offered.

Relief seeped into Josiah's bones and he released a long breath. Someone had to get through to Katherine. He didn't even care if it had to be Colby. Her well-being mattered too much.

"Thanks. I'm worried about her. I messed up bad."

"Yes, you did." Colby's jaw hardened.

"Enough." Jeb pointed his finger at Colby. "You messed up, too."

The hardness on Colby's face eased, and he dropped his gaze, kicking the dust at his feet.

Josiah could not look his father-in-law in the face. Guilt pressed in. He deserved a talking to more than Colby did. If Jeb knew the extent of his blunder, the man wouldn't even want to talk to him.

CHAPTER 27

a knock sounded at Katie's bedroom door.

"Go away," she called out. "I don't need anything."
That response always sent Ruby, Delilah, and even Josiah packing.

"Katie girl, it's Pa. I plan to stand outside this door banging until you unlock it."

Not Pa. The shame of facing him after the way he'd found Colby and her in the barn burned hot. She buried her head under the covers.

"If I have to, I'll get Josiah, and we'll bust it down." Then his voice softened. "Please, let me in. I need to talk to you."

The pleading in his voice melted a corner of her heart. She'd never been able to say no to her pa, even when the farce of her marriage should never have taken place.

She rose with weariness and smoothed a hand over her matted hair. A glance in the mirror showed a sallow-cheeked, disheveled girl staring back at her. The glass didn't lie—dark rings around her eyes and pasty white skin hanging on bone. She pulled her wrapper tight and padded to the door.

When she opened it a sliver, Pa pushed in. He took one look

and sadness clouded his eyes. He gathered her close. "My sweet girl."

The warmth of his body seeped into hers, and the constant chill and shivers she'd been battling ceased. A new wave of tears burned her eyes and soaked the front of his cotton shirt. She had planned to send him on his way, but the familiar safety of his arms was more than she could withstand.

The facade of the past year melted away. She could no longer pretend. Josiah was divorcing her, and soon the world would know. She couldn't shield her parents from the truth. This marriage had been a terrible mistake, and it was time to stop living the lie. If only she felt like living at all.

Pa smoothed back the hair that had fallen across her face and led her to the bed. "Sit, my dear. We need to talk." He pulled up the chair she'd placed by the window and settled across from her.

"It's time for honesty." His warm eyes held the same love they always had.

"Pa, I never meant to start anything with Colby—"

"Katie girl, I didn't mean you... I meant me." He shifted. "This is difficult to tell, but I know the good Lord has been asking me to be honest, yet I've been a coward."

She scoffed. "The *good* Lord? I've tried to believe in a good Lord, but I rather doubt He exists. And if He does, then He's anything but good." She motioned around the room. "Just look at the mess I'm in. All I tried to do was help my family."

"Something we should never have asked you to do." Pa's voice was so much steadier than hers. A calming force. "I made a promise to your mother that I would always take care of her. And then I couldn't." A heavy sigh escaped his lips. "You became our way out of my abject failure."

"You never failed us."

"I did. In more ways than you can imagine. This goes way

back, and I need to tell you all of it." Creases furrowed his brow, yet he still looked calm and determined.

"My childhood started back in Richmond. I was just a servant's son, a poor lad living in the home of a wealthy and privileged family with two daughters. Emmaline, the eldest, grew more stunningly beautiful every year. By the time she was in her teens, she had most every man at her beck and call, but her heart was dead and cold.

"The younger sister and I became good friends, but the difference in our stations was ever at the forefront of my mind, even if not in the heart of the younger girl. When she was ten, she confessed her undying love for me and declared she would marry me some day. I, a young teen, laughed it off. I remember kissing her cheek, telling her we came from different worlds. She was destined for much better."

What did any of this have to do with her? Katie was having a hard time seeing the relevance, but Pa was so intense.

"Many said the younger sister was plain because she grew up in the shadow of Emmaline. Few recognized her inner beauty, me included."

He paused and drew in a long breath. "This next part is hard to tell." He stood and turned to the window, staring out. Moments of weighted silence hung thick in the room. He turned back and paced the floor. His lips moved almost like he was praying.

She wanted to prod the story out of him, but something held her quiet.

"The younger sister, true to her word, did love me. She never wavered, never faltered. All through her teen years, her love grew stronger. But I, the fool, got caught in the poison of Emmaline's web.

"Anything forbidden was a challenge Emmaline couldn't resist. When she found out her little sister was in love with me, she started a wicked game. She took delight in the chase.

Nothing stroked her ego more than to steal a man from another woman, even from her own sister."

Pa slid back into the chair across from her, but kept his focus on the floor. Whatever calm had cloaked his face before had vanished. "The attention she lavished on me felt real, exciting, intoxicating even. Every man in Richmond wanted the elusive Emmaline, and, somehow, she had picked me. We talked about running away and building a life of our own. I forgot the younger sister in the wake of so much attention. I really thought Emmaline and I would marry, and I did the unpardonable. I tasted all she had to offer, and she offered it all."

Was her careful, upright pa telling her he had a past? Maybe he was trying to acknowledge his own faults so she wouldn't feel as badly about what had almost happened with Colby.

"Emmaline's interest waned quickly. From the time we became intimate until she decided she was bored with me was no more than three months, just enough time for her to become with child."

Katie gasped. Did she have another sibling somewhere?

"I was banished from the house and kicked out onto the streets of Richmond without a penny to my name or the possibility of further employment. I was a disgrace to my family and a scourge to hers. I'd crossed a line between the common and the aristocratic class, *and* I was blamed for stealing Emmaline's purity. It didn't matter that I hadn't been Emmaline's first." A deep sadness weighed his words. "Even so, my behavior was shameful."

"Pa, they threw you out on your own?" Her heart ached for her father.

"They did. But the younger sister found me. She had talked to Emmaline, and they'd worked out a deal. Emmaline would go away long enough to have the baby and save face. The family wouldn't have to bear that embarrassment and social disgrace. When the baby was born, Emmaline, who didn't want anything to do with motherhood, would give the baby to her sister. The sister suggested we marry so this child would have a family."

He shook his head. "I still can't quite fathom the depth of such love. And so, the baby stayed in the family. Emmaline went on with her selfish life. I became the father I so longed to be, and the sister, although I didn't deserve her, became my wife."

Katie's heart raced. How had all that ended? Pa must have learned about her pending divorce and didn't want her going through the same kind of pain. "Does Ma know about this marriage?"

"Allow me to finish." Pa ran a hand through his thinning hair and breathed out a heavy sigh.

"Our plan worked except for the one factor we hadn't counted on. Her parents were furious and wanted nothing to do with us, especially her mother. They said she'd made her own bed and could now lie in it. They allowed her to take her clothes, the few pieces of jewelry that had been given to her, and her hope chest with the things she'd collected for her wedding day.

"We had a meager start, although things were a little better after we sold the jewelry. We awaited the arrival of the baby with Emmaline in a town called Charlottesville while I took work on the railroad. Following the birth of the baby, we traveled to the Shenandoah Valley and started our new life here. I worked for other farmers until we could afford that small scrap of land we called our own."

Confusion clouded her mind. What had happened to that wife, to that baby? She wanted to ask, but part of her...part of her feared the answer.

"Katie." Pa leaned forward and lifted his eyes to look directly into hers. He took her hands. His were chilled and felt weak against hers. His soft brown eyes glistened with emotion. "You're that baby girl."

Katie blinked. A jumble of colliding thoughts tumbled over

one another. It couldn't be. What was he saying? "Ma is…my aunt?"

He nodded. "And Emmaline is your birth mother."

Her mouth dropped open, yet she couldn't shut it. His words fell like a rockslide, crushing all she knew to be true. Covering her. Choking her. Suffocation set in, and she had to work to breathe.

The weight of all the lies, of Ma's unjust harshness, pressed in. "It…that…explains so much." Memories swirled back. "That's why she hated the way I looked."

"She didn't hate the way you looked, Katie. She feared that your beauty would take you down the same road it had taken her sister."

Too many thoughts and emotions churned inside her, and Katie pushed up from the bed, clutching her wrapper tight around her chilled body. "Let me get this straight. I've been abandoned by my birth mother, and never loved by Ma the same as the others."

"She does love you. It's the reason she refused to let this knowledge out. She always argued she had to protect you from Emmaline, knowing how wicked her sister was. She didn't want Emmaline showing up, or you wanting to find her. You were her daughter."

As nice as those words sounded, they didn't match her experience. "Say whatever you want, but we both know how I was treated."

He lowered his head to the floor. "I won't deny the truth any longer. I'm so sorry. Your mother's insecurity started way back when she was living in her sister's shadow. Her parents favored Emmaline, and your mother was always in the background. What I did to your ma compounded the problem. And you, my girl, have suffered many times growing up because of our sins." A network of worry lines etched the corners of his eyes. "I pray over time, you'll be able to forgive."

Forgive. She couldn't begin to wrap her mind around all the injustices. The thoughts brewed into a storm. "It still hasn't changed. Ma invites Amelia with her to Richmond but refuses my company, a prime example of how nothing has changed."

Pa's head snapped up. "You've got that wrong. Your mother needed to face her past alone before she could find the courage to be honest with you. Can you understand? It wasn't that she didn't want you there. She was just afraid of all the secrets, the lies, that hadn't been revealed. She hasn't visited her parents since you were born and wanted them to understand you're *her* daughter. She needed to be sure they would respect this. Also, she wanted to learn the whereabouts of Emmaline."

"Where is this so-called mother of mine?" The thought of the woman who'd given her away stirred a rush of anger in her chest.

"She disappeared to Europe with another lover before the war. No one has seen or heard from her since."

Good. One less complication. There were far too many as it was. The last thing she needed was a long-lost mother expecting something from her as well.

The memory of Josiah's refusal to let her travel slipped in. "Was Josiah in on this? Was that why he refused to let me go?"

Pa nodded. "I told him the truth and begged for some time for your ma to sort things out with her parents. He wasn't happy about the secrets we've kept." Pa's voice broke, and his weathered face crinkled as he moved close enough to brush his hand down her cheek. "I don't know if you can forgive me, Katie girl, but I'm sorry. So very sorry."

She let Pa wrap his arms around her. Let herself sink into his warmth. And with her defenses down, she couldn't hold back the tears that surged.

"Why tell me now?" Her body shook as sobs racked through. "You know things aren't good between Josiah and me. You know I'm struggling. Why now? It's all too much to take."

He guided her back to the edge of the bed, and they sat together with his arm around her.

"Since the time your Aunt May and Uncle John became Christians and I witnessed the change in them, I've been reading the Bible and talking to God. I gave my life to Him a number of months back and, though I know I've been forgiven for all my sins, that doesn't remove the consequences of what I've done."

She sniffed back the moisture still leaking onto her face. "You became a Christian?"

His eyes grew warm again. "And I have such peace for the first time in my life. I don't know how to explain it. I've told your ma, but she waves it off as if it's a phase I'm going through. It's real. I'm trying to figure out how to live by reading the Bible. I wish my sister lived closer so I could ask the hundred questions I have rolling around."

"I've tried praying sometimes, but..." She shrugged. God never seemed to answer.

"Life is a journey toward faith, not a lightning bolt hitting us from above." He leaned in and squeezed her shoulders. "And change for the better doesn't happen instantly, it takes time. But I tell you, when I walked into the tack shop and witnessed the closeness between Colby and you, I knew I had to come clean about my own sin. That remark about the apple not falling far from the tree—"

"I wondered what that meant, but never had the courage to ask."

"That was about my own indiscretions and what sin has brought into my marriage and into my life. I don't want that for you. I've caused your ma and you so much pain. I don't want my sins to be passed down to any of my children." His earnest eyes pleaded with her. "Please don't follow in my foolish footsteps. It'll lead to pain and years of hardship. I'm begging you to turn your heart from Colby to Josiah."

A new pain pressed in. "Oh, Pa. Colby is a temptation, but only because Josiah left me a long time ago."

"Left you?" Pa's eyes narrowed, and he regarded her a long moment. "I don't know what happened between you two. I figured, when your relationship started fizzling, it was because of Colby."

A shuddered breath slipped from her lips. "No. This can't be pinned on Colby. How about we start with an arranged marriage I wasn't prepared for, memories of Charles, expectations I couldn't meet, insecurities, Josiah listening to half conversations and abandoning me. Only then can you add Colby. It's so complicated."

Pa raised his brows in a pointed look, but the kindness still wreathed his gaze. "You're a married woman, Katie. You and Josiah belong together. There's hope if you allow your heart to soften instead of harden."

"Harden? It's not me who's hard." She let out a long breath. "There's no hope, it takes two to make a marriage."

"Josiah loves you. I know he does."

Her feelings were too raw, too exposed. And the fury, the hurt she'd been tamping down for weeks, erupted. She jumped up, and her father leaned back, eyes wide. "How come everyone is so sure of Josiah's love for me? He sure has a funny way of showing it. Did he tell you about the papers he's having drafted up to end our marriage?"

The shock on Pa's face said it all.

"End your marriage? But that can't be." His brows bunched together. "You and Colby haven't—"

"We haven't done anything. What you saw was the closest we ever got to even kissing, and then only because, when I was upset, my *husband* sent him out to comfort me. Colby has been more of a husband to me this past year than Josiah."

Pa shook his head. "I don't understand."

"Josiah and I were growing close. I shared his bed, his dreams, his life the best I knew how."

"Did you ask him why things changed?"

As she told Pa about the conversation when she'd confronted Josiah, his eyes widened and glistened with tears. He gathered her close and rocked her in his strong arms, and she rested in his warm embrace, letting his strength cover her. A whisper of words she couldn't decipher flowed from his lips. She didn't have much faith in prayer or God, but she couldn't explain the peace that filled the room and seeped into her tortured soul.

They stayed that way for a long moment. Then, with a tenderness, he pulled back and took her shoulders in his hands, piercing her with that knowing gaze. "Did you tell him?"

"Tell him what?" She had to fight to keep from nibbling on her lip under his scrutiny.

"Did you ever tell Josiah that you loved him?"

"I...I didn't. I was just figuring it out myself."

"That explains a lot. Here you are, this young, beautiful woman, forced into a marriage. Although he was determined to win your love, he had his insecurities too. When he heard you talking to Colby, could it be that jealousy got the best of him?"

Pa was right, no doubt. But it was too late. The sorrow in the pit of her stomach threatened to overwhelm her. If only... She glanced at the bottle of laudanum and craved the option of feeling nothing.

Pa followed her gaze and rose to his feet. He strode to the bureau. "I learned the hard way that the only one I can turn to when life is painful is God. You don't need this." He picked up the bottle. "You need your Heavenly Father. Talk to Him. He'll give you wisdom and strength. I promise."

"Pa, I'm so confused."

"I can't tell you what to do, but this one thing I believe. Josiah loves you, despite his hardened front. The way he looks at you when you're not aware, and his concern for you, shows someone deeply invested in your well-being. I suspect he's suggesting an end to your marriage because he thinks that's what *you* want. You're his wife, and I would bet my life that all he wants is to hear you tell him you would like to stay his wife."

Pa stepped close and kissed her forehead. "I'll be praying for you." Then he left…taking the bottle of laudanum with him.

CHAPTER 28

*T*he long grass swayed in the breeze, and Josiah's boot brushed the play of their green tips as they bent in waves over the sweeping expanse. Across the creek, a wooded rise with a steep rock-strewn slope opened to the rolling sun-dappled hillside. The land and the valley were the only thing in his life that made sense.

He sat rigidly in his saddle and looked at the group gathered below. Blast it. Why did he feel obligated to join Jeb for his baptism? These religious ceremonies were not his thing. At least he could keep a safe distance.

He moved closer so he could hear what was being said, and found Colby with his horse tied up under a large oak tree. Josiah nudged his mount forward. "Mind if I join you?"

Colby nodded. "Sure."

Josiah had heard the fire-and-brimstone sermons from these types of religious zealots a time or two. Would this message be the same?

He slid from his mount, tied his horse to the nearest tree branch, and leaned against the large oak. This spot on the bank just above the crowd was the perfect place to listen, but not be readily noticed.

"You're making a commitment," the preacher said, "letting the world know that you've accepted Jesus into your life. As I lower you into the water, it will symbolize the washing away of your sin and the beginning of a new life. The power to live free from the stronghold of sin will breathe within you. You won't be a perfect person, but you'll be changed. And your desire to sin will diminish as your love for God increases."

Colby removed his hat and ran a hand through his flattened hair. As the blond curls sprang to life, he looked at Josiah with sorrow in his eyes.

Josiah looked away. He didn't need a bout of conscience from Colby.

Where was the yelling, ranting, and raving he'd expected from the pastor? The man spoke with a strong, calm voice. An angry preacher would be better than these simple words that cut deep into his soul. At least with the hell-fire message, he could distract himself with a good laugh at the preacher sweating as if he were already there.

"Jeb, you'll be first. I'd like you to say a few words about what this means to you." The preacher motioned Katherine's father forward and slapped his back in encouragement. "You'll do just fine."

"Sorry. I'm so nervous." Jeb's laugh sounded forced. "Not much for crowds, just an old farmer working the land most days."

"You can do it, brother," one yelled.

"I'm a man of few words, but I do have something to say. I've sinned, and I am a sinner. Coming face to face with who I was, my weaknesses, the lies from my past I kept hidden, was the hardest, yet most freeing, moment of my life. To realize the good Lord loves a sinner like me, well I plumb near can't take it."

The crowd clapped, and *amens* were sprinkled throughout.

"Then to lose everything in a fire and humble myself enough to ask God for provision and have it handed to me"—he looked up the bank to Josiah—"I know I'm blessed beyond measure."

A look of sheer peace covered Jeb's smiling face as he turned toward the preacher. "Reverend Booth, I'm ready." He walked into the water with his head held high and his face to the heavens.

The preacher and another gentleman joined him, one on each side. As Jeb placed his arms across his chest and was lowered beneath the water, a jolt of awareness slipped through Josiah.

When Jeb was back on his feet, arms lifted toward the heavens in praise and a look of radiance on his face, a tremor slid through Josiah's body. Something much greater than he was present, and Josiah could feel the power. Sweat trickled down his back, and his shirt stuck to his skin. The crowd started into a song. Perspiration dried cold on his neck, and he brushed his clammy palms on his trousers. He'd never felt so unclean.

One by one, men and women spoke a few heartfelt words and were dunked below the water's surface, just as Jeb had been. Each time a person emerged with radiance on their face, an unspoken challenge called out to his lonely soul.

"For any of you out there"—the preacher scanned the crowd, then lifted his eyes up the bank to where the two of them sat in the shade—"who has a desire to know more about Jesus as your personal friend and Savior, come and we'll talk." His eyes, like live coals, burrowed into Josiah's soul.

Josiah was battling the itch in his own feet when Colby jumped up and slipped down the bank. At the bottom, he sauntered forward. The crowd split to make room, and the preacher moved forward with an outstretched hand.

"What? No fire-and-brimstone speech?" Colby chuckled, but the sound came out a tad nervous.

Everyone laughed, including the preacher, who shook his hand. "I'm Marcus Booth, but I answer to most anything."

Colby removed his hat, raked a hand through his hair, and shifted on his feet. "Colby Braddock."

"Colby Braddock," the preacher said. "Good strong name. And as for using scare tactics, I think that's been done a time or two, don't you?" A sparkle of amusement filled his kind eyes as he looked up to Josiah, as if to invite him too. He spoke in loud, clear tones. "Most people know that side of the story. I prefer to share how much God loves you. He sent His Son, Jesus, to die for you, and He awaits your decision."

"What decision exactly?" Colby asked.

The preacher smiled. Crinkles formed, cupping both his mouth and eyes. "God is a gentleman. He gives everyone the ability to choose. I guess just like we humans want real love, so does God. It's not something He demands we give to Him. Rather, it's something we *choose* to give to Him."

Josiah's heart pounded. Was that not what he desired from Katherine—spontaneous love, not something out of obligation.

"What do I need to do?" Colby asked.

The preacher circled Colby's shoulders with his creek-dampened arm. "All it takes is a simple prayer of faith acknowledging your sin and accepting the gift of Jesus's sacrifice for you. That begins the wonderful life with Christ." He smiled, first at Colby and then up the bank at Josiah. "Then the Spirit of God comes and resides in you. Changes will begin to happen. Don't worry though. God is gentle and won't overwhelm you with a thousand dos and don'ts.

"Just like that oak you were leaning against up there"—he pointed toward Josiah—"was once a young sapling bending to the slightest breeze. The roots took hold and grew, and now, that old tree is powerful and strong with roots that spread far and wide beneath the earth. Your relationship with the Lord is similar, and will take time to grow and mature. Just don't forget to nourish your soul as you would your body."

"I'm all for nourishment." Now Colby's voice came stronger as he patted his stomach. A few amused chuckles drifted through the crowd.

"You nourish your body by eating, and you nourish your soul by reading the Bible and talking to your Father daily. Also, surround yourself with others who can teach and encourage you." He waved a hand toward the crowd. "These people are your neighbors and will embrace you like family."

They nodded, hanging on the preacher's every word. Josiah was not so easily misled. This God was doing him no favors these days, and he felt no need for allegiance.

The preacher looked at Colby. "My brother, I have the distinct feeling God has been calling you for some time now. Am I right?"

Colby nodded. "I think so." He glanced up the bank at Josiah, then turned back to the preacher and spoke in a lower tone. "I know my sinfulness."

The reverend clapped him on the back. "Well then Colby, let's pray and baptize you right here, right now. There's no better moment."

Josiah couldn't make out more than a murmur as Colby spoke a quiet prayer, but he could easily see the repentance on his friend's face. Then he was dunked in the water, and when he came up, his face wore a broad grin. Jeb stepped forward and enveloped him in a big hug.

As everyone else gathered around them, Josiah had never felt more alone. He untied his horse, mounted, and lit out across the field. Yet no matter how far he ran, he couldn't escape the longing in his soul.

∾

*K*atie emerged from her dark bedroom, holding her lit candlestick as she padded down the hall. The soft glow cast wavering shadows on the wall. At well past midnight, she was safe to get a few bites to eat without running into anyone. Her stomach was giving her trouble, and the one thing that curbed the nausea were a few dry corn biscuits.

She entered the kitchen and started at the sight of Colby sitting at the table, his head bowed, his lips moving. He must have heard her gasp, for his head lifted. Her gown tangled around her ankles as she turned away.

"Katie, wait. I need to talk to you." The plea in his voice drew her.

She breathed out a heavy sigh. She did not have the strength to handle this complication. Her pa's words rang true. She wasn't innocent in her friendship with Colby. Far too many times she had wished she were married to him instead of Josiah. She kept her back to him, but by the scrape of the chair on the floor, he must have stood.

She tightened her resolve and didn't turn to him. "I don't think it's a good idea to be alone with you."

"I have to talk to you before I leave."

Leave? A pain pressed into her. Surely he didn't mean for good. For a few days? Katie smoothed a trembling hand over her long hair, cringing at the tangled mess.

"I asked Josiah to join me, but he said he trusted you."

She whirled around. "That's a laugh. And what do you mean you're leaving?"

He moved close enough to look in her eyes, but didn't touch her. "I have to."

"Where are you going?" Her voice wavered. "For how long?"

"Not sure where the good Lord will take me."

She pressed her fingers to her temples and rubbed at the throbbing headache his nonsensical words were giving her. Where was he going and why was he talking about the Lord as if he believed God would actually lead him?

"I must ask for your forgiveness, Katie, as I've already done with Josiah. I'm so sorry for encouraging a relationship with you that only belongs to Josiah."

She pushed down the guilt his comments stirred. "You know better than anyone that Josiah wants nothing to do with me. Why the sudden bout of conscience? It's not as if we did anything immoral." Yet, even as the words left her mouth, the lie in them clutched her throat.

He shook his head. "We did, though. The time we spent together, including our midnight walks in the garden, were not leaving room for reconciliation. I take complete responsibility. I knew you were struggling. I also knew that Josiah loved you, no matter how hard he tried to hide it."

Katie drew a sharp breath in.

"I relished your company and encouraged every moment you gave me. Instead of pushing you toward Josiah, I sucked up the attention like the sand in a desert rainstorm. I let myself love you, knowing full-well you belonged to my best friend. That was wrong...so very, very wrong."

"But—"

"Please, let me finish. You are, and always will be, a temptation to me. The Bible is clear about temptation, and God tells His followers to flee it. So, I have to leave."

Anger burned inside her. Maybe irrational anger, but she couldn't seem to stop it. "The good Lord, Colby? The Bible? Since when have you read the Bible?"

"I became a Christian the other day, and it's amazing how the Bible makes sense to me now." A smile warmed his face. "I'm at peace like never before."

A shuddered breath slipped through her lips. Colby was her last vestige of comfort, and now this God would take even him.

"Why can't you stay? Why can't we remain friends? Josiah needs you on this ranch." She stepped forward, but he stepped back.

"I can't speak for you, but I know in my mind I was way beyond friendship. We can never go back. I'm so sorry. Please, forgive me." Warmth and sincerity poured from his eyes.

Her heart lurched in response. But he was asking for forgiveness. If their relationship had been so wrong, then she needed forgiveness also. Yet she couldn't face that yet.

She turned away, holding her back straight. "I guess this is good-bye, then. Turns out, you're just like all the rest." Tears broke through her defenses, and she swiped at them fiercely.

"It's not like that." He placed a hand on her shoulder.

She shrugged it off. "You can have your God and this ranch."

"Please, try to understand."

She turned to meet his gaze. "I understand more than you know, and I've had a lot of time to think. You stay, and I'll go. I don't want to come in the middle of your partnership, of your dreams. If you go, Josiah will have too much to—"

"No." Colby's tone was sharp. "Josiah understands how he messed things up with you. Give him a chance. Besides, everything was fine until I arrived on the scene. So, no. I go. You stay. It's God's will."

Katie gazed up. Instead of the haunted look she had become so accustomed to, a peace and strength radiated on Colby's face. If only she could find such peace. She moved closer and placed a trembling hand on his cheek. "Be happy. Get as far away from me as you can. I don't bring happiness to anyone."

A rush of red filled his face at her touch, and he folded his hand over hers and lowered her hand away.

"I'll pray you and Josiah find love again."

"Love?" She couldn't keep the bitterness from her tone. "He won't even look at me."

"I'll also pray that someday you'll understand, and look back on my good-bye as demonstrating a far greater love than if I had stayed." He squeezed her hand, then released her. After crushing his hat on his head, he turned and walked out the door without looking back.

CHAPTER 29

*J*osiah flipped over on his bed for the hundredth time that night. His crumpled sheets and the summer humidity didn't help, but it was his racing mind that wouldn't let up.

He didn't know what to think of Colby's leaving. Part of him was overjoyed that the main point of distraction in his marriage would be removed. But another part of him knew it was unlikely Katherine would ever trust him again, so Colby's leaving was pointless. Now, he'd lost not only his wife, but also his best friend and business partner. And he couldn't risk the pain of another broken heart. It hurt way too much.

So why did he keep thinking about her? Why did he keep asking himself, if she would even want him after all this time? He had the papers, why didn't he file for the annulment?

He forced his mind away from Katherine, but where it settled was no better. Managing without Colby was like plunging over a waterfall in a canoe, not knowing how or if he would surface. Staff were coming at him during the day with more problems than he could handle. The only good thing about it was that he didn't have to think about her. Until the night.

Love and hate twisted together in rope-like strength. Josiah loved Colby like a brother, yet hated what had transpired between Katherine and him. He loved the man's work ethic. No one could ask for a better partner. But he hated that Colby could make Katherine happy when he'd failed.

He loved the new man Colby had turned into, so filled with Christian love that he would leave so their marriage would have a chance, but he hated Colby for ditching out on their plans to build the best horse ranch ever. And what was the point of that, anyway, with no heirs, no wife, no reason to slave the day away? Why did he bother?

Loneliness pressed in, sucking the air from the room. He missed Colby more than words could say. So maybe love burned stronger than hate.

He heaved his body out of bed and pulled on his clothes. Though still pitch black, he might as well get an early start to the day. Sleep was impossible.

∽

*K*atie stared into her full-length mirror as she combed her hair and twisted it into a bun at the nape of her neck. That talk with Pa, and then with Colby leaving, had shown her she must find the gumption to go on. She'd survived sorrow before, and she could do it again.

Her clothes hung on her frame, her dress now at least two sizes too large. She gave herself a long stare in the mirror. This moping about had to stop. The least she could do was help Delilah until the annulment or divorce papers arrived, whichever Josiah filed for. A shudder ran from tip to toe at the thought.

She didn't dare do the bookkeeping for fear of running into

Josiah. But she missed that job and the stimulation of her mind more than the rest of her chores put together. The fact that she was good at it and often found ways to save the ranch money only added to her loss.

No matter how Katie mixed the stew pot of her life, she came up with confusion. She'd been relieved to confront Josiah about their dying marriage, but surprised at the pain his suggestion of a divorce brought. Was her sadness the result of failure, or the loss of what could have been? To hear from everyone, including Colby, that Josiah still loved her—everyone but Josiah, that was—added to her bewilderment. How could he love her and part ways at the same time?

Fear nipped at her mind as she closed her bedroom door and headed down the steps. Where would she go? What would she do with her life once the divorce was finalized?

She entered the kitchen where Abe and Delilah were having breakfast. Her hands twisted in the folds of her work wrapper.

One look in her direction, and they jumped up and crossed to her. Delilah engulfed her in a warm hug, and she fought the urge to cry.

"We missed you, yes'um, we did." Delilah pulled back, tears sparkling in her black eyes. Abe stepped in for his own hug.

A corner of her broken heart mended, and she hugged back. "I want to help today." Her voice cracked. "It's not been good isolating myself like I have."

"Praise be to Jesus." Delilah threw her arms heavenward. "And these creaky ol' bones could surely use the help."

Josiah walked into the room as they drew apart, and Katie tensed. But she didn't expect the pained expression on his face, before his mask slid into place and he nodded quickly. "Good morning." He helped himself to a cup of coffee and left.

The slam of the back door sent a tremble to her hands. She hated she'd made him uncomfortable in his own home. That familiar dull ache returned. How long would those papers take? They couldn't go on like this.

~

*K*atie waited for Josiah to return from a long day at work. But the moment he walked into the kitchen, guilt washed over her. He looked so haggard. If Colby were still around, Josiah would not be working at this back-breaking pace.

But she had a plan.

Her hands clenched and unclenched as she followed him across the kitchen. A lump stuck in her throat, and she couldn't speak.

He grabbed his plate of food that warmed on the edge of the wood stove and turned to her. "What is it? I can see by the look on your face you have something to say."

She blurted, "Do you know where Colby is?" The question sounded wrong the moment it slipped from her lips.

His jaw clenched and twitched beneath his skin. His brow knit together. "I do not." He slammed the tin plate of food on the table, and his voice turned edgy. "Sorry to disappoint you, but I can't help you in your quest to join him." He dropped his large frame in the chair.

She massaged her temples a moment with her eyes closed. "I wasn't hoping to join him. I…just thought that if you were in contact with him, you could ask him to return. I'm the one who should leave. The two of you need to live your dream. I'm the part that doesn't fit here."

Nausea washed over her. She clutched at her stomach and pressed it down. This was an important conversation. Why did she have to feel sick again? But the sensation wouldn't go away. Instead, a surge of bile rose up her throat. She raced for the door and flung herself out, retching into the bushes at the side of the house.

He was right behind her. "Are you all right? Come, I'll help you." He gathered her close and almost carried her back indoors. "Sit, or do you want to lie down? I can carry you to your room."

The concern on his face was more than she could sort out just now. She shook her head and motioned to the bench beside the table. "Just let me sit."

When she settled, he still stood over her.

She motioned him back. "All this upheaval is causing an upset stomach." She smoothed a hand over her midsection. "It comes and goes. I'm all right now, and we need to finish this conversation." A new rush of tears threatened to fall, but she swallowed them back. The last thing she wanted to do was add weeping in front of him right after she'd gotten sick. She looked down at the floor. "Pa told me my grandparents in Richmond had invited me there. Maybe I could go and find work enough to earn my keep and stay with them."

"Katherine, you'll never have to go anywhere. This is your home until *you* choose otherwise." His voice sounded hesitant, almost strangled.

She stood to raise herself closer to his level, but she had to grab the table to steady her shaking legs. "But you said you wanted to separate?"

"I have no need. I'll never marry again. The divorce was what I thought you and Colby wanted. I have the papers if—"

"No." Her answer was swift, and surprised even her.

She gazed at the tall, gentle man in front of her, the man who had become the next thing to a stranger. A little more gray speckled the temples of his thick, russet-brown hair. A few more lines edged his steely-gray eyes, which now held that guarded look she so hated. He hadn't smiled in a very long time.

"I never wanted you to go." His voice gentled. "All I want is your happiness. This is your home as much as it is mine."

She fought to make sense of his words. "One moment you're talking annulment. The next thing, Colby is leaving—and it's all my fault." She rubbed her stomach as another wave of nausea hit her.

"It's not your fault."

The room swayed, and her vision darkened at the corners.

Josiah kept talking. "I think we can all own—"

"I need to…" She swayed on her feet.

Before she could protest, his strong arms wrapped around her, picking her up and carrying her up the stairs to her room. His strong body next to hers filled her with an awareness she didn't want to feel. He laid her gently on the bed. "I'm going to call Ruby to help you." Then he slipped away.

After the click of the door behind him, her thoughts tumbled one on top of another. He didn't want an annulment or divorce. Did he want to work things out? How far would they have to go to find their way back? Would that even be possible? How could she trust that he wouldn't turn her away again? How could he trust her after what she allowed between Colby and herself?

～

*T*he next morning, Katie rose from her bed with so much confusion that her head pounded. She was no closer to understanding what she should do, though she had ruminated most of the night.

As she crossed the room, the Bible Pa had dropped off a few weeks prior caught her eye. She paused beside the table where it lay. How could a simple leather-bound book under a thin layer of dust call her name? Her hands quivered as she picked it up and dusted off the cover. She moved back to the bed and sat down.

Hadn't God abandoned her like all the rest? Why should she bother? She flipped open the book. Her eyes fell to, *I will never leave thee, nor forsake thee.* The words gripped her, even as her mind spun. She dropped the book as if it were a red-hot ember, and it bounced on the bed. The pages flipped to a different place. A wash of gooseflesh traveled up each arm. She shivered. It was as if God Himself were talking to her.

She flopped on the bed and ventured another peek. Could God be speaking to her? She flipped the pages until her gaze landed on a note in Pa's handwriting. *This is a good scripture to memorize,* was all it said.

He'd marked the passage with thick lines. *I know the plans I have for you, declares the Lord, plans to prosper you and not to harm you, plans to give you hope and a future. Then you will call upon me and come and pray to me, and I will listen to you. You will seek me and find me when you seek me with all your heart. I will be found by you, declares the Lord.*

Katie slapped the book shut. She closed her eyes, put her arms over her head, and tried to think about something else, anything else, because the words cut into her soul in a way that scared her. They danced in her head like raindrops hitting a tin roof. *I will never leave you nor forsake you. I have plans to give you hope and a future. You will find me when you seek me with all your heart.*

All your heart.

She pushed up to her feet and slipped out of her room, determined to shut out the haunting message. With another bout of nausea hitting her stomach, a walk in the fresh air would be welcome. She made her way past the hen house and smoke house, then through the orchard until she was standing on her parents' doorstep. It had been a while since she'd visited. Not since before Pa's revelation about the woman who bore her. She was about to turn and leave when the door swung wide and Lucinda ran out to greet her. Trailing close behind was Gracie.

"Katie, Katie." Gracie jumped up and down. Lucinda threw her arms around Katie, and Katie soaked in the sweet hug.

"Ma," Lucinda shouted as she stepped back. "Katie's come to visit." Each girl grabbed a hand and pulled her inside and all the way to the parlor. A stab of guilt pierced her heart at the excitement on their faces. Why had she neglected them?

"You're just in time for some fresh apple pie," Ma said. "Come, dear. We're so glad to see you." The foreign endearment pricked at Katie's heart, and she couldn't mask her frown. Had Pa told her that he'd let Katie in on the secret?

A troubled light stole into her ma's eyes as she beckoned Katie into the warmth of the kitchen. "Our first crop of apples, and you know your pa. He had to have a pie."

Maybe it was best not to talk about it. At least, not now. Especially with the others around. She forced herself to focus on the apple pie her mother held up. Was September already here again? In a few weeks, she and Josiah would be married two years, if one could call it a marriage.

Hopelessness filled her heart. She needed to talk to Pa. She needed a future. She needed to know how to seek this God who could give her hope. If He really could do that. But if not, she didn't know how she would survive the long, dark winter ahead. If all the sunshine and warmth of summer hadn't lifted her spirits, then the cold, bleakness of winter would indeed consume her. A chill of concern swept through her thin frame, bringing a shudder she couldn't stop.

She endured her sisters' happy chatter. Her fork circled the plate, and she played with the dessert, unable to pull herself from the smothering pain.

"Katie?"

Pa's voice snapped her to attention.

"I'll walk you back to the house. The days are getting shorter again, and it's almost dark."

She nodded and rose from the chair, doing her best to

summon a smile as she kissed each sister on the cheek, then turned to Ma. "Thanks for dessert."

Ma's eyes shifted to the untouched pie and back to Katie. Without words, she pulled her into a hug, her embrace awkward yet sincere. "Come visit again soon. The kids and Pa miss you. I miss you."

Her stumbling attempt at showing she cared soothed the raw edge of Katie's hurting heart. She tried to smile through the gathering tears and nodded. "I will."

She'd forced her tears back into submission by the time she and Pa walked in silence through the orchard. The pungent smell of ripened fruit bit into the air. The moon crested in the waning light of a clear sky. The first star of the evening pierced the darkening horizon.

She remembered another walk in this very orchard, a first kiss, a warm embrace. Liquid warmth stole across her heart and settled in her soul. If only she could turn back the hands of time and change some of her decisions.

"What is it, Katie girl?" Pa asked.

She sighed. The time had come. She had to face this. "I don't know where to begin." She stopped walking and turned toward him. "I need God. I've made such a mess of my life."

A grin brightened his lined face and he pulled her into a hug. "I have been praying for this moment." He clutched her tightly as a chuckle rumbled in his chest. "I can't tell you how much I've been praying. We all need God, but it's getting to the point of acknowledging that fact that's so difficult." Pa kept his arm around her shoulder as they walked on. "Let me tell you a little about the God I've come to know…"

CHAPTER 30

*K*atie woke the following day with a lightness in her soul she couldn't explain. She slipped from her bed and swung open the curtains. The early morning light streamed in, and she welcomed it with a smile. Somehow, the weight of her troubles lifted as if she no longer carried them, and, although her circumstances were the same, nothing was the same. The constant despair that had nipped at her mind was gone, and joy bubbled inside her.

She should dress and go in search of Delilah. She couldn't wait to tell her.

Katie rushed from room to room in excitement. Where was that lady? And then, it came to her. Thursday morning was Delilah's bread-baking day. Katie picked up her skirt and ran to the summer kitchen.

Delilah's large frame was bent toward the oven as she slid the well-formed rounds of dough in.

"Delilah."

Delilah whirled around with her hand to her chest. "Land sakes, child. You scared me good. Why you up so early?"

"I have something wonderful to tell you. We now share the same Father."

Delilah's face brightened as if the sun shone right on it. "Well, I be jiggered. Praise be to Jesus." She lifted her arms to the heavens, then opened them to Katie.

She stepped into the warm embrace. The smell of bread dough and lavender soap filled her senses as Delilah held her in her fleshy arms. After a moment, she pulled back. "We're going to have a special dinner tonight. And you tell that husband of yours to show up. Don't you be taking no for an answer either." She raised her eyes heavenward. "Let the miracles begin."

"What do you mean?"

"Sweet Jesus can bring healing to your marriage. Yes, He can." She squeezed Katie's shoulders. "And it starts with that boy joining us for supper."

A new hope flared in Katie's chest. "I'll go find him straight away."

She couldn't explain the boldness, but she wasn't afraid to approach Josiah when she found him in the barn. "Supper is at six today, and I'd like you to join us."

His brows shot up, and she stifled a grin. "See you then." She turned and sauntered away with her head held high and a bounce in her step.

With extra care, she readied herself, requesting for the first time in many months that Ruby spend time on her hair. She needed more than the usual knot she did herself at the nape of her neck.

As Ruby fussed with Katie's rich, thick tresses she huffed. "You'll have to forgive me. I'm hopelessly out of practice."

"You'll do fine. Anything will be better than the way I've been looking as of late." She laughed as joy bubbled in her soul. She felt so alive.

~

*J*osiah was not prepared. The dress, the upswept hair—Katie's dazzling beauty sent him reeling. But her smile downright undid him. He hadn't experienced her genuine smile in so many long, cold months, and when she directed it at him like she was doing now, it felt like a hammer slamming into his frozen heart.

They sat in the formal dining area, and Abe, Ruby, Annie, Katie, and Delilah all looked as if they shared a secret he wasn't privy to. "What's the occasion. Did I miss a birthday?"

"No occasion," Katie said. "I've just made a new rule. Starting today, all those living under this roof will eat together. We're supposed to be a family, and it's time we start acting like one."

Was she so afraid he would throw her out that she was trying to resurrect a sense of family?

"As it should be." Abe nodded.

"Hallelujah," Delilah echoed. "And no more special meals kept warming on the stove. You don't show up for dinner, you don't eat."

Even Annie and Ruby's heads bobbed.

"I can see when I'm outnumbered." Josiah raised an eyebrow but kept his mouth shut. Whatever was going on, it was a change for the better. Anything that got Katherine out of her bedroom and brought life into her expression was worth the effort. "I'll have to make some adjustments in my schedule."

"Your bad habits, you mean," Abe said.

"Working like a crazy man has got to stop," said Delilah. They all nodded again like a bunch of puppets on the same string.

"This means every supper." Katie hit him with a dazzling look of tenderness that made his heart lurch. What was he to do with the wild thumping of his lonely heart? Make a good excuse...and fast.

"There's an awful lot to do with Colby gone, and with you

no longer doing the bookkeeping—"

"I'll gladly start back up. I've missed that work."

Oh, great. That hadn't gone the way he'd planned. He didn't want to be thrust working closely together with her, discussing the finances. He'd been glad when, months earlier, she'd refused to carry on with the bookkeeping. Suddenly, she wanted the job back. What was she up to? Why the sudden change of heart?

"Would that be a help?" she asked, her voice and eyes speaking both kindness and hope.

He nodded, but everything within him wanted to run. Weariness sank through him. How in the world would he keep a safe distance?

But why…? Understanding dawned in his tight chest. She hadn't expected Colby to become a Christian. His sudden bout of conscience and consequent departure had spoiled her plans. She no longer had a future wrapped up with Colby, so Josiah had become the default.

No, thanks. Sure, he had messed up, he was willing to admit his part. But he doubted he could ever trust her again or open his heart up to love. And he certainly didn't want to be second best.

She drove him stark raving mad, and he had to protect himself. He stood from the supper table with determination. "Supper's over. Back to work I go." He walked out without a backward glance.

~

Katie winced when the back door slammed as Josiah once again disappeared after supper, as he'd done for a week now. Delilah shook her head, and Katie sighed. "He simply cannot contain the joy he feels in our company."

Delilah harrumphed as she walked by with a stack of dirty

dishes. "Dear Jesus, help me. 'Cause I've plumb near run out of patience. I'm thinking a switch to his behind might be just what he needs."

Katie laughed. "If anyone could do it, you could."

"You run along to your pa's. Annie and I will finish up. That nightly Bible study is giving you the patience of a saint, and with him"—she cocked her head toward the door—"you're going to need it."

Katie sobered. "That's as much my fault as his. I'm truly sorry for all I've done to bring about this mess. I wish—"

"No wishing. You just pray, and he'll come around. And ask your pa to study First Corinthians chapter thirteen with you. It will help."

"Thank you." Katie planted a kiss on Delilah's chubby cheek and moved toward the door. "I'm learning so much, and now, Ma is even listening in. She keeps busy but is always within hearing range."

"That's how it happens, and the good news is spread."

Katie threw on a shawl and headed out. She loved her evening walk through the orchard in the fresh air. The only downside was that, every night, the memory of her first real kiss, of Josiah's arms around her, reminded her of all she'd lost. A longing to start over with Josiah as a Christian woman overwhelmed her.

You can start over, the Spirit whispered in her heart. *I am the God of second chances.*

$\sim$

"*T*ime for dessert." Pa slapped the Bible shut and rose from his chair in the parlor. "The girls have been waiting to spend a little time with you. They sure love that you're visiting more."

"I've neglected them this past year."

Pa swung an arm around her shoulders as they moved into the kitchen. "Never you mind that now. We can't look back, only forward." He pulled out a chair for her, then sat down in his usual spot at the head of the table.

Katie smiled at the instant uproar as the girls poured in. "Dessert time," Gracie said, jumping up and down before throwing herself onto Katie's knee. The longing for a little one of her own hit afresh each time she held her sister. She worked hard to squelch that longing. What was the point when she didn't even know if her marriage was going to survive?

"Ma, do you need help?" Katie tried to make herself heard above Gracie's all too exuberant chatter.

"Jeanette is helping. We'll have it ready in a snap."

"I was thinking we should try and get to church on Sunday in Lacey Spring, as long as the weather holds," Pa said. "The singing is a joy to behold. Want to join us, Katie girl?"

Her spirit jumped within her. "That's a splendid idea. You'll come too, won't you, Ma?"

She turned from cutting the pie and shook her head.

Katie rolled her lower lip out, and Amelia laughed.

"You know how I feel about all that religious stuff," Ma said. "When I lost the twins, I lost all hope God cared about what goes on down here."

Pa's face dropped, but he said nothing.

"I'll come," Amelia said.

"You just want to see your beau, Edmund," Jeanette teased.

Amelia turned a bright shade of red. "So what if I do?"

"Now, girls. Whoever wants to come can come for whatever reason they like." Pa winked at Amelia, and she smiled.

The chatter and love of family conversing and eating pie seeped into Katie's heart, filling some of her longings. The past year, she'd given up the dream of having a family of her own, but since she became a Christian, the idea kept pressing in. Did their marriage have hope?

She pushed back from the table. "Ma, you've got to stop feeding me all these yummy desserts every night. My dresses are getting so tight."

Her ma waved her hand. "Fiddlesticks, Katherine. You could eat until the chickens roost and you'd never gain weight. Just like your—"

"Nope." Katie placed her hand on her abdomen and pressed her dress in to prove her point.

Ma's eyes popped wide. She rose from the table and busied herself with cleanup.

"Should I walk you home?" Pa asked.

Before she could answer, Ma cut in, "Jeb, I need a break, and since you monopolize all the conversations with Katie these days, I'd like her to join me out on the porch to enjoy one of the last warm evenings before she runs away."

The girls got up to follow, but Ma waved them away. "Just the two of us." She pointed to the pile of dishes in the sink. "That'll keep you busy."

"Aw, Ma."

But Ma ushered Katie outside, and the screen door slammed behind them.

"How I remember those days." Katie laughed as she settled in a rocking chair beside Ma's.

Silence slipped over them, and Katie enjoyed the singing crickets, even if the breeze was a tad chilly.

"Did you want to talk about something, Ma? You had a funny look in your eyes, and I know when something's up." She smiled to keep things light and leaned forward in her rocker.

Something in Ma's sly smile gave her pause. "Could you be in the family way?"

The words slapped her backward. A baby? She shook her head. "I had hoped so long ago...but it never happened. And Josiah and I haven't been close for a long time. We uh... It's a long story." A heated flush washed over her. Good thing the lighting was dim.

"Have you been sick to your stomach?"

"My goodness, yes. A lot. But that's from all the turmoil in my life."

"Colby?"

Katie sucked in a breath. Was Ma suggesting that Colby and her...? No. "Colby was part of the turmoil, but we didn't... Never."

Ma's brow creased. "And you and Josiah haven't been together at all?"

A hand flew to her mouth as realization slipped through her. "There was one time a few months ago. But surely that wouldn't do it?"

"I'm a thinkin' it took." Ma giggled. "I know I shouldn't be laughing when obviously you're shocked, but I'm going to be a grandma, and I'm tickled pink." She reached over and smoothed a hand on Katherine's abdomen. "I assure you, with that decided bump on your slim frame, you're in the family way. I'd guess a good four months."

Her heart picked up speed. She'd missed her last few monthly cycles, but she'd blamed it on stress and lack of eating. She clutched at her ma's hand, her knuckles turning white. "You have to promise you won't say a word, not to Pa, not to anyone. At this point, I don't even know if Josiah wants me, and the last thing I need, is for him to pretend for the sake of a child."

Ma squeezed her hand. "I understand. Pa shared how difficult things have been between you two. I hope you don't mind that I know?"

"No, I expected him to tell you."

"I won't say a word, but you have to tell Josiah. Sooner than later."

"I will. I will. I just... I can't quite believe this." Katie rose and paced the porch. "I need time to wrap my mind around it."

"Sorry to say, girl, but time is ticking. Don't wait too long." Ma stood and gave her a quick hug. "I'll go get Pa to walk you home."

Katie soothed a hand down the front of her dress—over the bump. "Dear Jesus." She looked up to evening sky. "A baby? God, I want this child so much, but things are so messy. The timing is all wrong. Josiah is going to think I'm interested in the marriage only for the sake of the child. The truth is, I'm trying to love the man you gave me. I need help."

Her pa's steps came up behind, and she sent him a smile as they started walking.

The churning in her mind would take a while to sort, but there was one thing she knew she needed. "Pa, I haven't told Josiah about becoming a Christian yet. Can you pray for me? I'm not sure where he stands, and I was hoping to show him the changes in me rather than tell, but now—"

Her father turned a questioning gaze to her. "What?"

"Just pray for me?"

He slipped an arm around her shoulders. "Of course. I always do."

As they walked past the barn, a shaft of light poured through the crack in the door. The urge to talk to Josiah swept over her, and she stopped and faced her father. "I'll see you tomorrow."

He nodded and kissed her cheek.

After he left, she pushed open the entrance. The sweet aroma of fresh hay mingled with the tangy smell of horse sweat and leather. She moved toward the small tack room on the far end of the barn, where the warmth of light spilled through the open doorway. She gathered her shawl tight around her shoulders. A prickle of tension scuttled up her spine, and she shivered.

In the light of a lone candle, with a blanket around his shoulders, Josiah slept in an old wooden rocker. His face, devoid of expression, took on a little boy quality. The usual lines of fatigue and tension lay smooth and relaxed. The urge to wrap her arms around him welled up.

The fact that he wasn't comfortable in his own home brought a lump to her throat and tears to her eyes. How had their lives become so complicated? She remembered the days when he would hurry in from the fields to eat supper with her, and they would talk for hours. Now he slept in a cold barn, in a storage room, as far away from her as he could get.

God what am I to do? She breathed the prayer into the heavens.

Love him. As clear as an audible voice, the words penetrated her being. She stopped and listened.

Love him.

It didn't take much to realize that the command to love her husband lined up with the word of God, but what did this love look like?

Choose to love.

Love was a choice. How strange a thought. Wasn't love a feeling? Yet, the more she read her Bible, the more she learned how God's ways were so contrary to her previous way of thinking. She and Josiah could not go on as they were. One of them had to bridge the ever-widening gap. It might as well be her.

She dropped a feather light kiss on his brow, then turned and tiptoed away.

∽

*T*he sharp intake of Katie's breath woke Josiah from a light slumber. He was embarrassed that she had found his little hideaway, embarrassed to have been caught doing nothing more than sleeping. He kept his eyes closed so he didn't have to face her.

All was quiet now. Had she left? But then the swish of her dress and footsteps moved closer. His heartbeat banged nearly out of his chest. He willed his body to stay calm, but it tripped, skipped, and picked up speed. When she placed a light kiss on his forehead, he nearly gave himself away. The mere fragrance of her closeness stirred his senses. It took all his strength to remain still and not drag her into his arms. As her footsteps faded, his heart rate plummeted, and he wished that it would stop altogether. The pain was too much to bear.

Why had she kissed him? Did she care, or was he just better than nothing? But then why kiss him when she thought he would not know? None of it made any sense.

He couldn't begin to explain the change in her. It was as if someone had taken all her sadness, wrapped it in a sack, and tossed it to the bottom of the Shenandoah River. The new Katherine was confident, talkative, and peaceful. She'd been attractive before, but now—now she was beyond irresistible.

He couldn't sleep. He couldn't concentrate on his work. And he most definitely couldn't handle her intoxicating presence. He felt like a tongue-tied schoolboy when she was near. All the strength he had was used up in that one hour at supper. He would have made excuses to not join if he weren't afraid of her seeking him out and demanding an explanation. At least in a group, he had the power to resist her.

When he asked Jeb about the changes, he'd just smiled and told Josiah to ask Katherine himself. But how could he when he couldn't bear to be alone in her presence? For, try as he might, he had never stopped loving her. And like a mighty wave crashing over a child's sandcastle, one moment alone in her presence could crumble all his resolve.

❧

*I*n the past few weeks, the sweet agony had only increased. Josiah could not escape. He let out a puff of air as he headed in for supper. How would he continue to hold his composure together? He entered the house and slipped his hat on the hook. With determination, he took the steps two at time in a hurry to clean himself up before the supper hour. On top of everything else, he didn't want to take Delilah on.

His room, which used to bring solace, now brought memories of their time together. He slammed his hands down hard on the marble washstand as he looked at the haggard man in the mirror.

Why was Katherine seeking him out, asking his opinion on everything from Sunday church meetings to hairstyle preferences and supper menu ideas? It was bad enough the bookkeeping was a legitimate reason to thrust them together, but did she have to bother him with one decision after another on subjects she never would have concerned him with before?

He ripped a clean shirt off the hanger and threw it on, buttoning with fierce determination. He needed space and distance. Yet he found himself walking down the steps and slipping into his chair at the supper table, piling his plate high with food, and chatting as if nothing were amiss.

After a few minutes of quiet, Katherine's soothing voice brought his focus up. "No more working in the evenings, Josiah. You need time to unwind after a long day of physical work."

He glanced around the table to see what the others thought of his wife's sudden demand. Abe and Delilah nodded in agreement. Ruby and Annie each kept their gaze on their plate.

He raised his brows at Katherine. "I see you broach these subjects when you have reinforcement."

"When I have to." Her voice gentled. "Josiah, you're exhausted. And it shows. We're all worried about you."

He scanned the other faces again. None argued with Katherine's assessment. He remembered how she had caught him sleeping in the barn. How could he logically argue? The last thing he wanted was for her to bring that incident up in front of everyone.

"Fine." He gripped his fork and knife until his knuckles whitened as he ate the rest of his meal in silence.

When he finally pushed his empty plate away, Katherine rose from the table and came around to his chair. "Come, let's retire to the parlor." She held out her hand.

The thought of touching her brought a mixture of fear and longing inside him. He should stay far away from her, but with her standing there waiting for him, refusing would hurt her, especially in front of the others. Surely he could be strong enough to keep himself in check.

He enclosed his hand around hers and stood. The touch of her soft skin sent a thrumming through his limbs. He tried to pull away, but she braided their fingers together and led him to the settee. She sat close beside him, something she hadn't done in a long, long time.

His heart kicked against his chest as he drew in a deep breath, pulling in her scent. He almost reached out and gathered her close before he caught himself and jerked back, ripping his hand out of hers.

"No need to look so horrified." Her voice dropped, disappointment weighing her tone.

He caught a glisten in her eyes before she looked down and smoothed non-existent wrinkles from her gown.

He couldn't let her know there was nothing in the world he wanted more than her. He couldn't risk the pain of another broken heart.

She made that little inhale that meant she planned to speak again. He steeled himself for what else she might ask of him. "I want to let you know that I became a Christian not long after Colby left."

His jaw dropped, and he snapped it shut. "What is it with you all? First Jeb, then Colby, and now you? I believe in God, but I don't have to make a production out of it as if it's some kind of event."

"It's not a production, it's an everyday relationship."

He frowned. "I don't get it. God's up there. We're down here trying to do the best we can. No more is necessary."

"More *is* necessary. We need to make a choice to ask Him into our lives and then live—"

Her words had a familiar ring, one that settled a sour taste in his mouth. "Looks like you and Colby will have more in common than ever, he rattled on to me about the same thing. Why don't you go find him instead of hanging around here?" Even as he spoke the words, he dreaded her response. Would she leave him finally? Could he bear it if she did?

Her eyes shimmered with tears. "You're my husband, not Colby."

He couldn't seem to stop himself from spewing more bitter words. "This past year sure proved that, now didn't it?"

She stood. "I can see I've upset you. I'll leave you be."

Against his will, his hand darted out to catch hers before she moved away. "What do you want from me?" He looked at her upswept hair, her glowing cheeks and her oh so kissable lips. He wanted nothing more than to forget everything but the moment and take all she offered.

"Would it be expecting too much to ask for a fresh start?" Her voice was almost a whisper, and she looked at him with so much sincerity he almost gave in.

But that meant trust, and he couldn't give her that. If Colby returned for her, would she be gone in a flash?

He stood, pulling himself up to his full height so he towered over her. Emotion clawed at his gut. "I can't." He shook his head. "I just can't." He cursed under his breath and dropped her hand.

Tears swam in the depths of her hauntingly beautiful eyes. She turned and hurried from the room. He wanted to go to her, and he wanted to run from her, all at the same time.

CHAPTER 31

"It hurts more than I can say that he keeps shutting me out." Katie swallowed down the sting of tears as she peeled potatoes while Delilah prepared bread dough beside her. "That snow-covered Massanutten outside our door holds more warmth than he does."

Delilah punched down the dough ball a little harder than usual. "Yes'um. I'd like to take that boy out behind the shed and give him a straightening out like I used to." She picked up the ball of dough and smacked it hard.

They both chuckled.

"The one thing I'm learning," Katie said, "is that I don't need Josiah. I don't need Colby. I don't need anyone but Jesus to give me peace. I'm sad because of the state of my marriage, but yet at peace. And I've never felt more alive."

Delilah's black eyes sparkled as she turned her head to agree. "Wonderful, ain't it?"

"I wish I could thank Colby for leaving, for it woke me up. I wish I could tell him I'm sorry for running to him and pulling him in like I did."

"Katie girl, you be forgiven and free, and that's all the good Lord remembers."

"I sure know it. The Bible has come alive to me, and though I hurt, I heal all at the same time. It's like it's raining, but the sun is shining through. And the strangest thing"—Katie couldn't keep the excitement from her voice—"the Spirit of God keeps telling me to choose love and, in being obedient to Him, I think I've found the path to real love. I truly love Josiah."

"I knew this would happen." Delilah dusted the flour off her hands and spread her fleshy arms wide.

Katie walked into her warmth with happy tears clotting her lashes. "I have to thank you for leading me to First Corinthians thirteen.

When they pulled apart, Katie pressed a hand to her heart. "That chapter hit me right here. I thought love was the fluttery feeling of physical attraction. True love is all that but so much more. The amazing thing is that when I put those verses into practice, both the physical attraction and my feelings deepened. But now I'm in a real pickle, because I really want him." Heat flushed through her face.

"See, the good Lord knows best. He knew the work He would do inside of you before you got married."

Katie frowned. "Never thought that far back." An ache rose to her throat. "I've had to memorize that passage for the times Josiah snaps at me, which happens a lot these days."

"He's fighting against your love, he is. But like poking at a mama bear with cubs, he ain't ever gonna win."

Katie gave a weak smile. "I hope you're right."

"Of course, I'm right. You just wait and see." Delilah waddled to the nearest chair and sat. "I'll give this old back a rest, and you bless me with the Lord's words you've memorized." She closed her eyes.

"I like it to be personal. *Love is patient. Love is kind. It does not envy. It does not boast. It is not proud. My love will not act rude or self-seeking, it will not be easily angered. I will keep no record of wrongs, for love does not delight in evil but rejoices with the truth. My love will always protect, always trust, always hope, always persevere. Love never fails.*

"Beautiful." Delilah's eyes blinked open. "That boy better get off his high horse soon, cause his grumping around will be no example for the child."

Katie gasped. "You know?" What had she done to give away her secret? Maybe her dresses were pulling too tight.

"Of course. You don't keep that from my eagle eyes. Nothing doing."

She pressed a hand to her chest. "That is such a relief. I have so many questions, and Ma is not so good at these kinds of conversations." Just being able to confide in her good friend would be such a blessing.

Delilah laughed. "Ask away. I've brought many a baby into this world."

Katherine moved forward and touched her arm. "I wanted to tell you, but I thought it best I tell Josiah first. I've been waiting for him to come around and act like he halfway likes me before I broach the topic, but I can see that's not going to happen any time soon." A knot tightened in her chest. "I'm running out of time."

"I be praying, my girl. But in the meantime, I can alter some of those dresses so you're not busting at the seams around the middle."

∼

"Josiah?"

Josiah turned with a sigh from the correspondence he'd been sorting through. Now what did Katie want? Wherever he wandered after supper, she found him.

"I've got some important news to tell you. Can we take a walk in the orchard?"

There was no way he was going for a walk in the moonlight with her. "Here's fine."

"No, it's not fine." She crossed her arms. "I want some privacy."

"In the library then." He pointed across the hall.

"Just thought the nice days will soon be gone, and a walk would be lovely."

He dug deep and gave her his best scowl.

"Never mind." She attempted a smile, but the disappointment showed on her features. "Your library will do."

He led the way into the room and heard the click of the door behind them as he made his way to his desk. He had to keep busy. "What is it?" He didn't turn her way. Just laid the letters in their slot and stacked and restacked a pile of papers.

"Please look at me." Her words came out soft, like honey easing from a spoon.

He blew out an exasperated breath and faced her. He had to keep a strong façade or she would seep through his defenses.

She rotated sideways and pulled her dress tight around her midsection. He blinked, not wanting to believe what the very decided bulge might mean. He could only drop his jaw.

"As you can see, we're going to have a baby. I've wanted to tell you earlier. I've been waiting for you to…"

"To what?" There was no mistaking she was pregnant, but his mind refused to believe. A numbness had settled over him.

"To come around…to not… Oh never mind all that. You're going to be a father, Josiah." She smiled. "Are you pleased? I am." She dropped her hands from around the mound and stepped toward him. She looked at him as if she expected him to be happy.

Anger sluiced through him, a rage so strong he could barely

control himself. "That explains everything." One fist clenched, and he ran his hand behind the back of his neck with the other.

"I don't understand." A disturbed look flashed through her expressive blue eyes. Her smile faded.

"The kindness. The show of attention. Your constant attempt to wear me down." He should have seen through it.

"What are you saying?" Her eyes misted. "Is it wrong for a wife to desire her husband? I've fallen in love with you, Josiah."

A weight slammed into him, like a fist into his chest. Now she said it, when she needed something big from him. "This has nothing to do with love." He couldn't keep the anger out of his voice. Just the thought of those two together made his blood scream hot through his veins. "You're pregnant with Colby's baby, aren't you?"

Her eyes widened to twice the size. She shook her head. "No—"

"Don't try to deny it."

"I never...we never—"

"About the time you found out you were pregnant, Colby left."

"That's not true—"

"Come on, Katherine. I remember how you asked where he was."

"Not because I was pregnant. I wanted the two of you—"

"Cut the lies. When you couldn't find him, you decided to turn the charm my way and make the best of a dire situation. And now, after all this time, miraculously, you love me."

The color drained from her face. She stood silent.

Had she thought he'd be so stupid as to believe her now? "I bet you were hoping I would succumb to your flirtation long ago so I'd be in doubt as to who the father was." He stepped closer to her, towering over her, but she didn't cower. Instead, she lifted her head and stood very still. Giant tears rolled down her cheeks, and he tightened his breathing to keep the sight from swaying him. "You have nothing to say for yourself?"

"Would you even listen?" She looked him square in the eyes without flinching.

"Go ahead." There would be no reasonable explanation that would nullify his suspicions.

"In case you haven't noticed, there have been changes in me. As a Christian, I would never lie about something like this."

"How convenient, playing the God card."

She held up a hand. "I can see you have your mind made up, but give me the courtesy of allowing me to speak. Then, I will go."

He nodded. He could hold himself in check that long. Although nothing she said would change what had to be the truth.

"I stand before you and God with my head held high. Do you remember an evening in May when you came to my room, the very room you said would always be my undisturbed sanctuary?" Her eyes bore into his.

He looked away as memories surged. He'd lost control of his good sense that night.

"Do you remember asking to stay? Do you remember the passion that followed?"

He couldn't answer, not with the heat spreading throughout his body at the memory.

"I remember that evening well," she said. "It seems fitting we conceived our child in my room. That scared waif of a girl you took as a bride invited you into her haven, her safe place, and God was pleased. That very night, I had run from temptation. I chose our marriage over Colby. I believe this pregnancy is a gift. God himself sealed our marriage."

He turned back to her. What kind of hogwash did she expect him to believe? "So, you're trying to tell me that one time—"

"That's exactly what I *am* telling you, because I know it to be true. I will not allow you to smear Colby's name, nor will I argue the point with you."

He turned away and raked a hand through his hair. "Your story is a little too convenient." How could he ever know the truth?

"You'll see. When we have a child who looks and acts like you, you'll know. Until then, I'll choose to forgive your uncharitable words and accusations, but don't think for a moment they do not cause great pain." She wiped the tears from her cheek and walked out, leaving him with a storm of questions and raging emotions.

How in the world could this be?

~

*K*atie paced her bedroom. Were they so far gone that Josiah not only believed she'd slept with Colby, but that she was capable of lying about something so big? No wonder he was so cold and distant.

Three weeks ago, she would've slapped his face or given him a tongue lashing for an insult that big. It was amazing how God had held her steady. Composed. Calm. Collected.

Yet loving Josiah brought a new agony. She had finally found the courage to tell him she loved him, and he threw the words back in her face. Those words were not often spoken to her as a child, so saying them and meaning them hadn't been easy for her. His cruel response twisted her heart in two.

Oh, God what am I to do? This is far worse than I thought.

She sank down to her knees at the side of the bed and let her tears fall.

Be still and know that I am God. The Bible verse she'd read that morning came back to her and penetrated the fear churning inside her.

She lifted her tired body from the floor and slid into bed.

Somehow, God would help her remain obedient to loving Josiah no matter what. Being a Christian sure didn't remove the difficult from life, it only gave the strength to walk through. But oh, the peace. Sweet peace. She smiled into the heavens. *Thank you, Jesus.*

CHAPTER 32

*T*he doorknocker sounded.

"I'll get it." Katie stepped through the foyer and opened the door wide, then took a step back. A woman stared back at her—with startling blue eyes and black hair that made Katie feel like she was looking in the mirror.

"May I?" The stranger didn't wait for an answer, but swept in like the flow of the Shenandoah on a spring day. With determination in her eyes, and the bustle of fine silk, she carried a look of well-bred confidence.

"My, you were not easy to find and my parents were no help at all. You must be Katherine, for you're as beautiful as I was at your age. I'm dreadfully sorry to barge in on you like this after all these years," the woman said, "but I just had to see for myself if my daughter is healthy and well."

This couldn't be happening. Could it? "Are you—?"

"I'm your mother."

Katie's chest tightened. Not after abandoning her. Giving her away. "I know my mother. She lives across the orchard. I was going to ask if you're Emmaline."

The stranger's face fell, and she looked down. "I more than

deserve that. I never mothered you, but I was hoping to get to know you as an adult, and hopefully reconcile with my dear sister."

Katie's heart panged. How could she turn this woman away and call herself a Christian? And what would Ma say? She and Katie were just getting to the point they were friends, and this would hit her hard.

She inhaled a breath for strength and forced a smile. "This is a bit of a shock, to say the least, but do come in." She led Emmaline into the parlor on wobbly legs. "Would you like an afternoon tea?" She lowered her body to the edge of a chair and extended her hand for the woman to sit.

"I was thinking more of a bed. I'm exhausted from hours of traveling. I swear I shall not surface until at least tomorrow morning."

"You...you want to stay here?"

"If that's all right with you. I was hoping to spend some time and get to know you." Her hands swept around the room. "But only if you have space for one wee guest." She smiled, but the look didn't reach her eyes.

Katie sighed. She didn't need this right now. Why would God allow more drama when she was already stretched to the limit?

"I'll have to discuss a longer stay with my husband," Katie said, "but I'll get a room made up for you for a night or two. That should give you more than enough time to surmise that I am fine." Although she was anything but fine. A ripple of unease came over her. Why did she distrust this woman? Was it merely the coloring of her past? Was it fair to judge her without knowing her?

Emmaline's brows rose as if she were carefully choosing her words. "I will be ever so grateful for whatever time you share with me, dear daughter."

"I'm not your daughter, nor your dear." Katherine purposely

projected a firmness in her voice. "You made quite sure of that when you gave me away at birth and never looked back. So, please don't call me that."

Emmaline's gaze dropped to the floor.

"Follow me." Katie climbed the stairs. When she reached the upper landing and should've offered the guest room beside Josiah's room, she turned to the opposite wing of the house and chose a chamber as far from their personal space as she could. At the very least, this would pacify Ma. Emmaline would not be treated as an honored guest.

The door to the dust ridden room creaked open at their entrance, and Katherine waved Emmaline inside the cold bedroom. "Excuse the dust."

Emmaline's eyes swept the room with a look of surprise.

"We don't typically get uninvited guests." Katie hated that her words sounded curt, but was she supposed to feel something for this stranger who had the nerve to show up unannounced?

"Annie will be in with some water so you can freshen up." Katie stayed in the doorway. "She'll light the fire and freshen the room, but don't expect to be waited on. We all do our part around here. This is a working ranch."

~

*J*osiah had not even had time to hang his hat when Katherine rounded the corner. There she stood with her long hair flowing, the rosy glow that pregnant women carry, and her haunting eyes. He longed for the day when he would harden enough to no longer pick up on every nuance, every detail, every worry line etched on her face.

She was definitely worried now.

"Can we please talk privately?" She approached him with uncertainty swimming in her eyes.

Something must have happened. Or maybe she had something to confess. The thought churned bile in his belly, but he pushed it back. "Meet me upstairs in my room."

Her eyebrows lifted.

"Supper is on, and I have to freshen up. You know how Delilah gets when my tardiness spoils her hard work." He took the steps two at a time. Maybe he shouldn't have invited her into his personal space.

As he splashed water on his face and picked up the towel to dry his torso, hands, and neck, the door opened and closed. He didn't turn.

"Go ahead, talk. I'm listening." He pulled a fresh shirt from his armoire and slipped his long arms into the sleeves. When she still hadn't said a word, he turned toward her. This must be bad.

But the sight of tears pooling in her eyes as she looked around the room wasn't what he expected. "I'm sorry." She swiped at her eyes. "I'm so emotional these days. Ma says it's to do with the baby." She motioned around. "But I haven't been in this room for so long. All the wonderful memories...the moments of... Goodness me I'm blubbering." She walked toward the window and stared into the darkening sky.

"Katherine, what is it?" The urge to curl his arms around her nearly overwhelmed him. He needed her to say her piece and leave him alone.

"Emmaline, my birth mother, showed up today. I don't know what to do."

Her words were so unexpected, he could barely make sense of them. "She's here?"

"Yes." Her voice broke as she still stared out the window.

No surprise she was shaken and confused. What in the world did that woman want with her now? He threw better judgement to the wind and closed in behind her.

As he closed his hands around her arms, the warmth of her

skin, even through her dress, burned his palms. He eased her back against him as they had often done many moons ago, and the feel of her leaning into his chest was as close to heaven as he'd been in a long time. She didn't resist but relaxed into his embrace. He inhaled the sweet fragrance of rose water, and they stood that way for a long moment.

She didn't deserve more trouble. He'd given her a mountain, and yet she hadn't retaliated. This new Katherine had remained strong and loving, despite his accusations and prickly behavior. A shudder of remorse slipped through him, stealing away his good sense and leaving behind only the need to comfort her.

He placed his hands on her shoulders and massaged her stiff neck. She used to like that, and apparently she still did, as she melted into his hands. At last, he turned her around to face him. He needed to see her face. Needed to hold her.

She looked up at him with those luminous eyes drowning in questions. "What am I supposed to do? I feel nothing, and she… I don't know what she wants."

"It'll be all right, Katherine." He pulled her close. "Hush now, I'll help you."

She sank into his arms, and little sobs shook her shoulders as she clutched his waist. He smoothed his hands through her hair, inhaling her scent. Remembering… "We'll figure this out." He pulled away, patting her arm as one would a sister. He had to put some space between them.

She looked up with her soulful eyes burning into his. "Thank you." A step forward and a lift on her tippy toes, and her mouth touched his.

Fire swept through him. With a hunger so deep, so wide, so high, he allowed himself the enjoyment of a real kiss, a kiss where flame met fire, and her lips crushed against his, then opened to the sweetness within. Soul connected to soul. Bodies melted. Hands played in the dance. He moaned at the depth of his need.

He dragged his lips from hers. "Supper is waiting. We have to go." He could barely breathe, much less speak.

She smoothed a hand over her disheveled hair and tugged her dress back into place. Had his wandering hands done all that?

"I know we must." Her smile looked so vulnerable. "But I'd much rather not."

It took every bit of strength he had to open the door with one hand and place his other on the small of her back as he lead her out of his bedroom...instead of to his bed.

~

*E*arly the next morning, before Emmaline had even surfaced, someone was hammering on their front door. Katie set her coffee on the kitchen table and hurried down the hall.

When she opened the door, Ma swept in like a hornet disturbed from its nest. "Where is that despicable woman? The nerve of her to show up unannounced after all these years."

"Ma—"

"That's just like her, to think the world revolves around her and her agenda. Mark my words, this will not go well. She's up to something."

"Ma, please. Take a deep breath. People have been known to change—"

"Good morning. Is that my sister's voice I hear?" Emmaline flowed down the staircase like a princess to a ball. "Doris, is that you?"

Ma pointed a hard finger at her older sister. "Don't say a word, not one word, until I'm done speaking."

Katie had never witnessed her ma so outrageously rude.

"Let's go into the parlor." Katie waved her hand down the

hall and lowered her voice. "Out of earshot of the entire household."

The two women followed, although Ma sent at least one glare at Emmaline along the way. As soon as the door closed, Ma let loose. "You have no right to be here meddling in my family. You forfeited that right years ago. I want you to leave immediately. After all I've done for you, you owe me at least that much."

Emmaline opened her mouth and closed it again.

"Well, that's got to be a first." Doris braced her hands on her hips. "My sister at a loss for words."

Huge tears slid down Emmaline's cheeks as she dropped onto the settee and draped a hand over her forehead.

"Goodness, yes," Doris said. "It's all coming back to me now. The drama. The performance. You were a master at using tears at will, weren't you? I see nothing has changed. Don't even bother. We're all just a tad too old and too wise for that sort of nonsense."

The coldness in Ma's voice seemed to make Emmaline cry all the harder. *Oh God, help us.* Could there be any hope for reconciliation?

"Ma, can we not even try to settle the past?"

Emmaline stood with a practiced grace. A look of hesitant vulnerability streamed from her beautiful teary eyes. "All I wanted was a chance to visit my sister again, to meet my nieces and my daughter…" She choked out the last word as if over-come by emotion.

"Katherine is not your daughter," Doris spat. "And you will not be meeting my family."

"How can you be so cruel, Doris? What happened to you? I came to say I was sorry."

"That would be a first."

"I don't want to take your place as Katherine's mother. All I want is a chance to get to know the fine woman you raised. Is that asking too much?" Emmaline stared at Ma with the same set of iridescent blue eyes Katie had always wondered how she possessed.

Ma eyed her sister. "I want nothing more than to believe you, Emmaline. But truthfully, I can't."

Ma turned toward Katie with a plea in her gaze. "I'm sorry you're caught in the middle of this, but Emmaline is not welcome in my home. After hearing more of her trail of destruction over the years when I visited my mother and father, I don't trust her. I don't believe she's changed one bit. I hope you'll send her packing." She turned and walked out the door, slamming it behind her.

Katie looked at the stranger across from her, not at all sure how to navigate the day. Should she throw her out? Could she?

~

*J*osiah hurried in from the barn after seeing Doris stomp across the yard. Had there already been an altercation before he could even get the animals fed? He took the portico steps two at a time and slipped into the house.

Katherine's eyes spoke a thousand words as she met him at the door. "There you are." Her stiff shoulders dropped, and she placed her arm on his. "Ma insists we should send her away."

"I figured."

The woman, who could only be Katherine's mother, stepped from the parlor.

Help. Katherine mouthed the plea.

"I'm here now." He murmured the words just loud enough for her to hear. Just one look at Emmaline told him he didn't like her.

Behind her daughter's back, her eyebrows rose at the sight of him, and a coy, inviting smile pursed her lips. The minute

Katherine turned to introduce them, her eyes demurely glanced to the floor.

Had he imagined it? As the day wore on and he stayed close to Katherine, the scene played and replayed. She showed utmost interest in all Katherine said, but when Katherine turned away, the older woman kept staring at him as if he were a fresh piece of apple pie.

It wasn't hard to see what kind of woman she was. He'd met her type many times in the past. The gold-digger, the marriage wrecker, a woman who used her beauty to get anything and anyone she desired.

Well, he didn't want her, but neither did he want to squelch his wife's effort to get to know her mother. Maybe there was an outside chance he was wrong.

~

*J*osiah was about to round the corner into the parlor when he stopped short at the sound of Katherine's name on Emmaline's lips. That woman had worked her stay into a full week with no end in sight.

"Katherine was wondering why you haven't changed the sheets in her bedroom." He couldn't see her from where he stood, nor could he see who she spoke to.

"But, I did just yesterday, ma'am." That was Annie's voice. "My lady likes them done every week, and I never miss."

"My mistake." Emmaline's laughter filled the room. "At my age, the hearing must be going. Maybe Katherine said pick the beets, not clean the sheets. Never you mind. I'll get it sorted."

Josiah ground his teeth. She was digging for information about whether they slept together. He stepped forward and rounded the corner.

"Josiah. How lovely to see you this morning."

He ignored Emmaline's flirtatious smile. "Annie, can you go

find Katherine? Ask her to please come to the parlor straightaway."

Annie wasn't a second out of the room before Emmaline turned her attention his way with a look that made his skin crawl.

"Sit, Emmaline." He pointed to the nearest chair. It wasn't hard to make his voice stern.

Instead, she moved closer, her voice dropping to a seductive tone. "You poor man. You work way too hard. Why don't you let your slaves manage this little farm?" She flicked her hand towards the window as if shooing off a pesky fly. "A man of your prominence shouldn't have to do the menial work."

"I don't own slaves."

"I understand. With the war and all..." She opened her fan and waved it in front of her face, coyly batting her lashes at him. "I guess we now have to say they're free, but you know what I mean."

"I do not. I've never owned slaves."

"Your help then. The point I was trying to make—"

"Why are you here, Emmaline?"

Her eyes popped wide and she gasped with a practiced look of shock. "You know why. I wanted to check on my dear Katherine. What a shock to hear from your maid that she entered into an arranged marriage. Money aside, I must say she married very well indeed." She lifted her eyebrows.

Her flirting burned his insides, and he couldn't help a jab. "I married well too. Would you not agree?"

"Yes, but she's a rather boring child with all the Jesus talk. A man of your stature and sophistication must grow weary."

How dare she speak ill of her own child? "I'm not about to discuss my marriage—"

"I'm sorry to hear things haven't worked out, but it's hardly surprising." Her eyelashes fluttered up at him.

He stepped away from her. "What gives you that impression?"

"Come now, you two aren't exactly cozy, and though Katherine won't say much, she's an easy book to read."

He clenched his jaw, working to contain his anger.

"So sorry." Katherine swept in. "Annie caught me in the middle of cleaning out the fire grate in my room." Katherine brushed the soot from her hands. "Can I take a moment to freshen up before I join you two?"

Josiah moved toward her. "You know you don't have to do that kind of work, but I love it that you don't mind."

She smiled up at him.

"You have soot on your nose, my dear." He thumbed it free and dropped a kiss on her forehead. "Come, it looks like you could use a little help." He slipped his arm around her shoulders and walked her out of the room. He didn't look back as he escorted his wife up the stairs and into her room, although he could feel the burn of Emmaline's stare.

Inside her door, Katherine turned toward him. "What was all that about?" She flashed him an inviting smile. "Not that I mind."

"Emmaline seems to think we're not cozy and was asking Annie about changing your sheets. She's picking up on the fact things are less than perfect. I don't want her catching on—"

"Why does it matter?" Katherine pursed her mouth in a look of wounded curiosity.

"I don't trust her, nor do I like the way she looks at me." Coming out of his mouth, the words sounded a bit conceited, but he hadn't imagined Emmaline's behavior.

Katherine's eyebrows hiked up. "At you?"

"When you're not around, or not looking, she—"

Katherine laughed and slapped his arm. "What, another one who finds Mr. Richardson irresistible?"

He stiffened his shoulders. "I'm not joking. A man knows the look."

The teasing left Katherine's face, and her expression grew earnest. "Has she done or said anything inappropriate?"

"Not exactly. I know you want to believe that a meaningful connection is possible, but there's something wrong."

Katherine's eyes filled with compassion. "Give me one more week. I can't just throw her out. She told me she has no place to go, and I wouldn't feel Christian sending her away without giving her time to work out a reasonable solution. Plus, she needs Jesus and is asking questions and showing interest."

"Ah." He stepped closer and lowered his voice as he brushed the back of his hand down the side of Katherine's face. "You're too kind." He didn't have the heart to tell her Emmaline had mocked her faith.

"Just one more week. I agree that we don't want her here this winter. Plus, there's an easy way to remedy her misconceptions." A smile tickled her lips.

"What?"

"We'll have to get cozy."

The thought of slipping under Katherine's spell made his heart buck against the walls of his chest. There was nothing easy about it.

CHAPTER 33

*J*osiah safeguarded himself for another few days, forcing himself to be in that woman's presence through supper and every evening to support Katherine. Tonight was no different.

He got up and stoked the fire, then seated himself close to his wife on the settee. He draped an arm around her shoulder and pulled her in. She looked his way, and he smiled, bending his head close enough to whisper. "Relax." She sank into his embrace. It was killing him to be this close. The smell of her hair. The feel of her body melting against his. Her open smile and warm embrace.

Emmaline's shockingly low dress, the bright red lipstick, and the fourth glass of wine in her hand made his stomach turn. He ignored her chatter and spoke sweet nothings into Katherine's ear. She giggled and gave a smile that would warm a winter's day.

Emmaline huffed. "It's rather rude to conduct yourself in that manner in front of others."

"You'll have to excuse us," Josiah said. "We're not used to

endless company. We've been more than hospitable, but to be honest your visit has been quite lengthy."

Emmaline's eyes popped wide, and she let out an exaggerated gasp. "Well, I never—"

"The evenings are our private time," Josiah said. "I fear I've neglected my wife something awful." He stood and held out his hand to Katherine. "Come, my love. Obviously Emmaline prefers we go elsewhere."

She shot him a tentative smile and placed her hand in his. She was not taking this to heart, was she? They still had a mountain between them.

"Good night, Emmaline. Feel free to enjoy the fire while my wife and I search for some much-needed privacy."

His arm encircled Katherine's waist, and he guided her across the hall to his library. His head dropped to kiss her full on the mouth while he slowly shut the door behind him. He made sure Emmaline had plenty of time to view the cozy scene.

Katherine's giggle erupted beneath his lips the minute the door closed, and he pulled back. They both started laughing, their hands to their mouths to stifle the noise.

Katherine pressed her other hand to her chest. "Did you see her face and how she looked at me? She was jealous."

"I told you."

Katherine's expression sobered. "I wanted to believe she cared to get to know me. I'm sorry it's taken me this long to figure out she's only here to cause more trouble."

"You needed time to make sense of your past. I know how difficult it's been with your ma, and I was hoping I was wrong about Emmaline, that she'd realize what an amazing daughter she has."

She reached up and touched his face, and he froze. "Thank you." The look in her eyes warmed his insides.

His eyes closed, and he enjoyed the featherlight feel of her fingers caressing his cheek. He caught her hand in his to stop the agonizing, yet wonderful, sensation, and turned it toward his lips. He kissed the inside of her wrist. The intake of her breath urged him to fold her close.

She pressed her body against his, and it was his turn to take a sharp breath.

Her hands circled his neck, and his heart kicked into a gallop. The soft brush of her fingers along the clipped hair at the nape of his neck nearly undid him.

He gave into the temptation and brushed her lips with aching tenderness. Without hesitation her mouth opened to his caress. He was lost. He dug his fingers into her hair, crushing his mouth against hers. A blaze ignited inside him.

The creak of the library door opening frustrated him beyond words. Lost in the pleasure, he did not want to be interrupted. But he pulled back and they both turned to Emmaline's head peeking in.

A glower belied her upbeat words. "Just wanted to say goodnight." She stepped back and slammed the door shut.

A knot of anger curled in his gut. "Can you believe that woman?"

Katherine pulled out of his arms, leaving his body missing her warmth. He wrapped a hand around the back of his neck to keep himself from dragging her back into his arms. "She has the audacity to intrude upon our privacy. Unbelievable."

"That was good she saw us." Katherine still sounded a little breathless. "I'm certain she witnessed the opposite of what she thought she would see. We haven't exactly been affectionate in her presence, and she's thinking tonight a ruse." The flickering candlelight danced across her face, and her eyes smoldered in the shadows. "I wish we were more," she whispered. "Like we used to be."

He hung his head and turned away. He was so confused. The changes in her were undeniable. In every way she was loving.

But could he take on another man's baby? Could he accept being second choice?

He never wanted to face the pain of that kind of rejection again.

~

*K*atie didn't want their closeness to end. She would be willing to put up with Emmaline indefinitely if it meant she could go on holding Josiah's hand at will or snuggle as they sat together in the evening. She loved taking the opportunity to drop kisses on his cheek or place her arm around his waist as they walked from room to room. She had a few more days, and she would make the most of it.

"Ah, Josiah, you're first to supper. Such a wonderful improvement from days gone by." Katie smiled up at him as she moved in close.

She wrapped both arms around his neck as his eyes darted around the dining room.

"Where is she?" he asked.

"I don't much care." She pulled his head down to meet her.

An immediate response was her reward. His lips moved over hers, while his hands held her close.

"Um-hm." Emmaline stood in the doorway.

They jumped apart, and Katie smoothed her hands down the front of her dress.

A muscle in Josiah's cheek jumped. He ground out an angry breath and leaned close to whisper in her ear. "Please talk to her tonight. She has to go." He grabbed his hat and crushed it on his head. "I'm no longer hungry." He strode from the room.

Katie's gaze followed him out. Was he angry at her for kissing him? At himself for his obvious reaction? Or at Emmaline for the interruption? She had no idea.

"You two are sure acting different than when I arrived."

Emmaline took her place at the table. "A tad too unbelievable, if you ask me."

Katie's face grew hot. "First, Emmaline, our marriage is none of your business. And second, we both think it's time you go."

"Why dear, whatever have I done?" She dabbed at the corner of her eyes with her handkerchief, though no tears were visible.

"You've spent a lifetime manipulating situations, just as Ma warned. What is it you want? A free place to live, money—"

"I care about you."

Anger boiled in her throat. "You don't care about me. I'm not sure you have the capacity to care about anyone. Sad to say, I had hoped you would." Her heart ached knowing her birth mother would never fill that lost piece in her history.

"Josiah—"

"And every time we're together," Katie said, "all you want to talk about is Josiah, as if you have some fixation on him. You're making him very uncomfortable. I've insisted you stay because I believe you need Jesus, but—"

"Jesus? I'll never believe in that nonsense, and neither will your husband."

"You talked to him about it?"

"Of course we did. And a whole lot more." She arched brows, her voice dropping low and sultry.

"He wants you gone." Katie swallowed to keep her voice from wavering. She needed to show confidence.

Emmaline patted her arm as if comforting a dullard. "He doesn't want me to go. Let's be honest, Katherine. He feels obligated now that you're with child. He's torn. You see the way your husband devours me with his eyes."

"I see no such thing." Katie stepped away. "You're delusional, Emmaline. It's time to pack your bags. We'll arrange to get you to the train station in the morning. Help yourself to dinner. I'm no longer hungry, either."

As she walked out of the room Emmaline spoke in a low tone. "You're the delusional one. Just you wait and see."

~

*K*atie woke to sounds coming from Josiah's room. Another nightmare. She jumped from the bed, pulled on her wrapper, and opened the adjoining door. The smell of her favorite perfume scented the air, and a figure leaned over her husband—a woman with raven black hair spilling down.

Katie stood in a daze as her stomach pitched and rolled. Was that Emmaline draped over her husband? Had Josiah been tempted all along? A tremble took to Katie's limbs. Had he not begged her to get rid of Emmaline? It was not natural the way they'd been apart for way too long. Could Josiah have succumbed?

No. Tentacles of fury spread like fire through her veins. The scream that filled her lungs came from deep inside her body. "Josiah, what's going on?" Her voice pitched high with the anger pulsing through her.

He sat up and pushed Emmaline so hard that she flew off the bed and landed in a heap on the floor. He rubbed his eyes, looking from Emmaline to Katherine.

Emmaline stood, draped in a white dressing gown. A shaft of moonlight revealed the very gown Ma had made for their wedding night.

Katie gasped. "You stole my clothes and perfume?"

"These are yours? He asked me to wear them." She stared Katherine down without flinching. "Now, you can see with your own eyes what I tried to tell you earlier."

"Out!" Josiah yelled the word with a booming voice and pointed toward the door, his eyes shooting flames at Emmaline.

The woman's own eyes widened. She scurried to the door and slammed it shut behind her.

Josiah jumped out of the bed and turned his attention her way. "Katherine—"

She held her hands up. "I can't talk now. I can't." The shock made her voice jittery. She had to make sense of what just happened.

"I was asleep. I thought I was dreaming, and you came to me like you did long ago…"

She backed into her room and slammed the door. The turn of her lock clicked loudly in the dark. Bile rose up her throat, and she raced to the bowl sitting on the stand. She stood shaking, holding onto the edge of the basin as she worked to keep her insides from spewing. Tears slipped down her cheeks, and deep wracking sobs shuttered out of her.

He hammered on the door. "Please, Katherine, let me in. We need to talk."

For long minutes he kept knocking and pleading, but she held herself steady. At last, the knocking finally subsided, and she stumbled to the bed. Maybe Josiah was right, but she needed time to process.

Her body curled to cradle the little one moving inside her. "It's all right, wee one. Mama will take care of you. Even if it's just you and me in this world, I'll never leave you." Tears spilled down her cheeks.

And I will never leave you. The still small voice of the Spirit washed peace over her.

God, tell me one thing. How can I have a mother so evil, a marriage so tortured, and still feel Your peace?

I am with you.

The tears diminished, and she stretched out on her back, rubbing the mound with gentle strokes. The one thing she did not question was the truth of these words. God *was* with her.

~

*J*osiah hadn't slept a wink since he woke to find that vile woman in his room. The bed felt defiled, and the first thing he did when morning finally came was rip the sheets off. Even though nothing had happened, the thought of her in his bed made his skin crawl. What would he say to Katherine? Would she believe his innocence? As if they didn't have enough problems in their relationship already.

He found her that morning in the parlor with her knitting sprawled across her lap. His stomach twisted into a knot.

The blanket, which had a blue background and white birds decorating it, was almost done. She looked up from her work. "Good morning." Her face wore a look of peacefulness, not at all what he expected considering the night before.

"Not so sure what's good about it." He plunked himself down on a chair across from her. "You have to believe me. At first, I thought I was dreaming, and you had joined me like…like you used to. Next thing I knew, I heard your voice from across the room."

She set her needles down on her lap and looked at him, waiting.

"She was wearing your perfume and your gown." He let out a curse. "She's trying to destroy our marriage."

"Do we have a marriage? Seems you've been talking to her about me—"

"I most certainly have not." What had that woman been saying? He tamped down his rage. Katie didn't deserve to feel the brunt of it. "I've stayed as far away from her as I can. I haven't trusted her from the day I met her. But she's your mother. Who was I to deny your relationship?"

"I wish you'd told me you felt this strongly."

"I hoped I was wrong. I'm so sorry about what happened.

You've got to believe me. Last night, I thought it was you." He raked a hand through his hair.

"I do believe you."

He stood and paced. "Just like that, you believe me?" Maybe he shouldn't question her, but how could she extend such grace?

"I had time to think and pray, and I believe you."

"How could you, after...after how I treated you when you told me you were having a baby."

"I've chosen to forgive you because I'm confident in the truth. But as for last night, we have ourselves to blame. And I take as much responsibility as you."

"What do you mean?"

"If we had been living like a married couple, I would've been lying in your arms, not in another room. She picked up that things were rocky between us, and I took too long in telling her to go. I longed for some sort of connection between us, but what I found is that she's more wicked than I could have imagined." Katie breathed out a sigh and leaned forward to place her knitting back in her basket. Then she rose with grace. "I'm certain Emmaline has nothing and nobody. I pity her, and I don't want her to be homeless."

"After what she did last night?"

"I've prayed about this and I can't leave her destitute, not when we have so much."

"I sure can. We owe her nothing." He rubbed his hand over his trimmed beard. "How can you even entertain the thought of helping her?"

"Because it's what Jesus would do. He says to turn the other cheek, and if someone wants your tunic, give them your cloak too."

He gave her a pointed look. "Your Jesus is far too kind."

"Please, Josiah." She moved closer and placed a hand on his arm. A charge of energy shot up to his shoulder. He would do anything when she looked at him the way she was now, her eyes so blue they swallowed him up. As much as he longed to retaliate with not an ounce of compassion, he would do as Katherine asked.

"You need to stay right beside me," he said. "We need to present a united front and finality in dealing with her."

Katie nodded. "I'll get her. She's in the kitchen having a morning tea, as if last night didn't happen." She left the room, and a moment later, Emmaline followed her back into the parlor.

Emmaline ducked her chin in a penitent look. "Josiah, I—"

"Quiet. Not one word."

Her mouth formed a perfect O as she lifted a gloved hand to her lips.

Katie crossed the room and stood beside him, and her presence infused him with strength.

"Let's get something clear," he said. "I have neither liked nor trusted you from the first day. You're a spiteful tart, and those are your good points. You'll pack your things directly, and Abe will take you to the nearest train station."

She paled.

"The only reason you've been here as long as you have is due to Katherine's kindness, which I've respected. Had it been up to me, the minute you batted those devil eyes at me, you would have been gone. And after last night... You don't want to know what I would do if not for my wife holding me in check."

A spark of panic flashed across Emmaline's hardened face.

"We know you have no money and nowhere to go, but that's not our problem."

Her hand flew out. "Josiah, please—"

"Don't *Josiah* me." He locked his jaw to hold in the less kind words trying to force their way out.

She bit down on her lip.

"Out of regard for my wife's wishes and because her heart is soft, I have agreed to give you enough to last for six months, if you choose a frugal lifestyle."

Her eyes brightened.

"That should give you ample time to find honest work or another sucker. I don't much care which. However, the money is given on one condition."

She pulled her shoulders back and lifted her head with a jut to her chin. "And what might that be?"

"You never—and I mean *never*—show up here again. Am I clear?"

She nodded, and her lips pursed tightly.

"Funny how the promise of money can seal your lying lips, isn't it? Now go pack."

She turned without a glance backwards.

After Emmaline left the room, he looked at Katherine to find tears misting her eyes. He did what his heart wanted and opened his arms. She walked into his embrace and he clung to her.

CHAPTER 34

*J*osiah couldn't sleep with Katie's words echoing in his head.

I've chosen to forgive you, Josiah, because I'm confident in the truth.

He picked up his pillow and flipped it over, punching it in frustration.

I'm confident in the truth.

He threw off his covers and stared at the ceiling.

We have only ourselves to blame.

He climbed out of bed. His body shook as if he were shedding a skin.

If we had been living... He took a few steps toward the adjoining door. *...like a married couple...* He took a few more. *...then I would've been...* He was at her door. *...lying in your arms, not in another room.*

He put his hand on her doorknob. Her invitation had been clear, had it not?

He pulled away and paced the room. His head and body ached. He wanted to scream.

Their planned affection this past week had been slow and

exquisite torture. The subtle touch of her hand on his knee, the shared caresses, the needy kisses. And there he stood with an unlocked door between them.

No. He couldn't do this again without an understanding between them. A curse slipped from his lips. Though she'd been ever so kind for months, not once had she said what he most needed to hear.

But she has told you she loves you, and you spurned her.

Where had that thought come from? She hadn't meant it that time. She'd only said it because she was telling him about the baby.

Didn't she? She's shown you unconditional love every day.

She wanted to ensure she had a home for her baby.

Your baby.

What if the baby *was* his? What if she had meant those words?

His hands pressed to his temples. He couldn't even win a conversation with himself. He walked to his hall door and slipped down the stairs and straight into the cold November air.

~

"Josiah, come here."

Josiah looked up as Katherine placed her knitting aside and rubbed her growing mound. Her eyes sparkled with excitement.

He walked over to the settee and sat beside her. She took his hand and placed it on her middle. "He's been kicking. I think you'll be able to feel him."

"He?"

She shrugged. "I think our baby is a boy."

She kept referring to the baby as theirs. And the idea was becoming harder to resist.

"Right here." She moved his hand to a spot on the side. Her

delicate hand over his made his heart kick wildly. A gentle flutter played beneath his fingers, and surge of wonder shot through him. Then a good kick hit his hand. "How incredible."

"I know. Isn't it amazing?"

He looked into her shining eyes. She giggled, and he laughed as the little one gave another good kick.

"Does it hurt?"

"No, it's just a tad uncomfortable at times." She gave him a warm smile. "What names do you like?"

He'd refused to think of the child as his, so he hadn't given names any thought. "I'm not sure."

"What was your pa's name, or your grandpa's?"

"You're fixated on boy names."

"It's a good place to start."

"My grandpa's name was Seth, and I've always liked that name. But Grandma's was Eunice, and that's not an option."

She laughed. "I do like Seth."

"You do?" His heart bolted, and his pulse accelerated at the way she was looking at him.

"I do."

"How about Kat for a girl?" he teased.

"Ah, I've so missed that nickname." She touched his face. The gentle graze of her fingertips along his jaw sucked the air right out of his lungs, and he leaned closer. Her breath mingled with his.

She bridged the gap and her warm, pliant lips brushed against his. His mind, body, and soul entered into the kiss, and he was falling…falling…falling.

He groaned and tore his mouth from hers. Then he pushed up with a snap to his feet.

"Emmaline's gone now, Katherine. You don't have to pretend with me anymore." He turned on his heels and walked swiftly away. He had to get control of himself.

"Josiah, I'm not—"

He put both hands over his ears. He didn't want to hear, for then he would have to make a decision—to trust, to be vulnerable, to open his heart back up to love.

~

"*A*nother premature foal?" Josiah looked around the kitchen at the soft pile of blankets for the horse's bed. The wood stove was throwing more heat than necessary, too. "You realize you were lucky with the last one."

"I know," Katherine said, "but it's who I am...a softy for the ones who need me most."

"Is that why you're still hanging around here?" He should have resisted the jab, but it slipped out.

She struggled to lift her ever-growing body from her knees. He rushed to give her a hand.

When she was on her feet, she brushed her hands together and smiled up at him. "I stay because I want to stay."

His voice got tied up in his throat. He was the one who needed her most, but he could never let her know.

"In your delicate condition, I'm not letting you do this alone. I'll get Hank to assign one of the boys to help through the night, and if the foal makes it, we'll move her out to the barn."

"I don't want to miss the best part of seeing her get to her feet, like the last time." Her pleading eyes grew large and misty.

"There's no guarantee—"

"I have hope." She touched his arm. "I have enough hope for the both of us."

The way she looked at him, she seemed to be speaking about more than just the horse. He turned away from the intensity in her gaze. "Do whatever you wish, but help you shall have."

"I can agree to that." She leaned into him, and he gave her shoulders a squeeze, but didn't linger. Everything about her moved him—her kindness, her love for all living things, her joy in giving.

~

*J*osiah awoke to a crackling, popping sound coming from outside. He flew out of bed. Something was glowing through the split in the curtains. He ran to the window and swept the drapes open.

Fire. His barn was aflame.

His mind exploded in a thousand directions as he pulled on his pants. His stomach dropped into the boots he was yanking on his feet when he remembered Katherine was helping with the foal.

Had she come in to her room? He crashed through the door separating the rooms to find an empty bed. He turned and bolted into the hall, then took the steps two at a time. The foal's bed in the kitchen was empty, and Katherine was nowhere around.

He roared into the midnight air. "No. No. No." This couldn't be happening.

By the time he reached the barn, the flames were shooting into the sky, and a few of his workers held him back from entering.

"You can't go in there, boss. It's too far gone. We got some of the horses out, but not all."

"Katherine." He choked out her name. "Where's Katherine?"

They looked at him blankly. With brute force, he ripped free.

The searing heat intensified as he pressed against the inferno, dodging flaming rafters that crashed to the floor.

"God, if you're up there, save my Katherine. Save my baby." Somehow, in that moment, his stubborn heart melted. Of course, the baby was his. Of course, Katherine loved him. She'd been showing him for months.

He checked the first few stalls but came up empty. The roars and squeals from the trapped horses in the other end of the collapsing barn pierced the air. The acrid smell of burning flesh seared his nostrils. The intensity of the heat and his inability to breathe collapsed him to his knees. Two strong sets of hands, one on each side, drug him from the inferno and across the yard.

All he cared about—his child, his horses, his future—burning to the ground in front of him, and he could do nothing more than stare. More than all of that, though...Katherine. He dropped to his knees as a groan ripped from his lips. "Oh God, not Katherine."

"Josiah. Are you all right? Speak to me, my darling."

A torturous hallucination swept through his mind. Her sweet words and the touch of her soft hand on his shoulders felt so real. He forced his eyes open, and the sight of a person bending over him made his pulse beat faster.

That was Katherine's beautiful profile, outlined against the firelight behind her. He worked himself up to sitting. *Dear, God.* It was her.

He reached out and pulled her into his arms, crushing her to him. "You're alive. Oh, dear God, I thought you were in the barn. I thought I lost you."

"I'm right here." Her words muffled against his neck.

"I tried to save you, but I couldn't." He kissed her hair, her face, her lips.

She pulled back. "Josiah, you're hurt. We need to get you cleaned up and attend to your—"

"I'm fine, now that I know you're all right. But where were you?" All he could do was look at her, his hungry eyes feasting on the beautiful planes of the face he loved so much.

"Hank and I were on our way to the barn with the foal when we noticed some men with torches lighting the barn. He told me to call all the ranch hands and then get you, but when I got to the house, you were gone."

A new anger kindled in his chest. "There were men lighting the barn on fire?"

"Hank screamed at them, and they ran off. But they'd set hay all around, so it lit up fast. He got out as many horses as he could, but, Josiah, we lost a lot." Her voice quivered. "I'm so sorry." Ringlets fell around her face, freed from the disheveled bun she had twisted on top of her head. She looked like an angel.

He gathered her in his arms, holding on with all his might. "The rest can be rebuilt, but I thought I lost you...and our baby." A shudder ran through his body. What would he have done if he lost them both.

"Our baby is fine." She pulled back, and he laid his hand on the mound between them. "Had it been any later, I would've been in there sleeping beside that foal. But God had me in His hands."

"He saved you when I couldn't." He wrapped her in a fierce embrace.

"Yes, He did. But please, come in the house. I want to be sure—"

"I'm more than fine, now that I know you're all right." He kissed her lips again, long and hard, before pulling back. "I'll come in as soon as I can, but I have to finish out here with my men."

He glanced over at the glowing heap, at the men standing in shock. He needed to get over there.

"Go in now, my love. Get some sleep." He placed one last kiss on her lips. "I'll be in as soon as I can."

$\approx$

*K*atie waited in the kitchen, refusing to go to bed until Josiah came in.

A shake on her shoulder brought her awake, and she lifted her head from the table.

"Why aren't you in bed?" Josiah knelt beside her, worry marking his soot-streaked face. "You must be exhausted."

"I wanted to be sure—"

"We're all safe now. A couple of our men used to be soldiers. They set off after the bandits and tracked them down in no time at all. They were brought back here."

"How many?"

"Four. They're being taken into Sheriff Holden as we speak, but first we wrangled the answers we needed. They won't be moving too comfortably for some time to come."

"But who did this, and why?"

"Hinton Rowan, a big slave owner in these parts—"

Realization struck a chord in her mind. "You mean Tommy Rowan's father?" That memory of the creek came flooding back and she wrapped her arms around herself to still her shiver.

"The Tommy who attacked you is the son of Hinton Rowan?"

"Yes. And I doubt he's ever gotten over his hatred for me." Had any of this happened because of her?

"So, this could be about more than just their resentment of change. For some, the hatred never ends. I'm sure one of the names I heard the guys mention tonight was Tommy."

Pain pressed on her chest. "It must be him."

"Well, wouldn't that be justice after all these years, catching the likes of such a scoundrel and being able to lay a good beating on him before having him locked up." He smiled at her.

But then his frown lines slipped back. "Hinton Rowan has been badgering me to pay my black workers less than my white.

I refused and the unrest has grown. But I never thought he'd resort to such evil. In fact, things had settled down to where I was no longer on guard. I guess that was his plan. When I think what could have happened tonight... Thank God you're all right."

"And what about you running into a burning barn? I stayed up because I intend to be sure you aren't hurt. Let's get rid of this scorched shirt so I can assess the damage." She began undoing his buttons, and he just stood there. The sound of his breathing quickened with every touch of her hand on his flesh.

Her own hands began to tremble as they worked. She'd craved this nearness so many times. She nudged him to turn as she pulled the scorched fabric from his shoulders. His broad shoulders and sinewy back distracted her mind from looking for burns. She wanted to splay her hands and kiss him.

Instead, she said, "Sit."

"You're a bossy one in the middle of the night." He slid onto the kitchen chair. A faint grin twitched on his lips.

Her thoughts flushed her cheeks with heat, but she ignored them as she moved to the stove to retrieve the basin of water she'd kept warming. She placed the tub on the table beside him and rung the warm water from the cloth. With gentle strokes, she washed the soot from his strong hands, up his muscular arms, and around his neck. Back and forth, the splash of water, the warm cloth, the hot flesh.

His gaze followed her face, tracking her every movement, but she didn't flinch.

She reached his cheeks, and he closed his eyes as she smoothed the cloth over his forehead, to his eyes, to the roughened planes of his neatly clipped beard. She wanted to kiss every chiseled feature right down to his mouth, but she worked the cloth instead in tiny circular motion. Showing her love. Pouring her love into him as if she were an overflowing pitcher and he an empty container.

Please God, let him feel my love.

She ran her finger over his lips, and a groan slipped free. His hands settled on her waist and pulled her onto his lap.

His eyes met hers, a warmth in his gaze she hadn't seen in so very long. One of his hands reached up to cup her cheek. "I don't want to waste another moment not giving you every bit of love I have to give." His voice was rough and sincere, his gaze earnest as it held hers. "Will you forgive me, Katherine? Will you give this old grouch a second chance at loving you?"

She could barely contain the joy welling inside her. "Yes." She planted a kiss on his lips. "Yes." Another meeting of their lips. "Yes." After the final kiss, he lifted her in his strong arms and carried her up the stairway to his room.

The light from the soft glow of a lone candle and dying embers in his fireplace flickered across his handsome face as he set her on her feet. His eyes darkened, and his stare grew hot.

Yet there was one thing she had to tell him before anything more happened. She pressed a hand to his chest. "I have something to say that I mean with all my heart." She bit down on her lower lip.

He took a sharp breath in as his gaze lowered to her mouth, then rose again to her eyes.

"I love you, Josiah. I know you may find that hard to believe—"

"Shh." He placed a finger over her lips. "I've been blind. I've loved you for so long, yet I treated you harshly, letting my jealousy and my misconceptions get the best of me. Yet you've been showing me for months what real love looks like. Everything flashed in front of me when I thought I'd lost you." His voice hitched. "Your love for me has been so much deeper than what I've given you." A mist veiled his eyes.

She stroked a wayward curl from his forehead.

Josiah's eyes closed at her touch. When they opened again,

they smoldered. "And He's given you back to me when I thought all was lost."

"Kiss me, Josiah. I love you so much it hurts."

His lips found hers with aching softness. But then she pulled back. There was just one more detail to set straight. "I want to stay tonight and every night."

The smile lines around his eyes crinkled. "With pleasure, Mrs. Richardson."

~

*C*urled in the warmth of Josiah's arms, Katie snuggled even closer. She had no intention of ever letting go. She had held nothing back and gained everything.

She turned in his arms to face him and kissed his lips. He stirred and sluggishly opened his eyes. A pleased look split his face.

"So, it wasn't a dream?" He kissed her waiting lips and pulled back. "I've been so unlovable, and yet you're here."

She nodded and giggled. "God is a miracle worker."

He rolled onto his back with a sigh and snuggled her close, pulling her to rest her head on his strong chest. "Never gave God much thought beyond the occasional church service, until Jeb started yammering about Jesus. Then Colby, now you. The changes are undeniable."

"It's called peace."

He kissed the top of her head. "You know, I thought I could protect you. I thought I had everything under control. That burning barn made me cry out for mercy, and God answered. He kept you safe when I could not."

"There have been substantial losses—the barn, some of your best horses—"

He kissed her quiet. "If that's what it took to bring me to my senses and soften my stubborn heart, then so be it."

Her ear pressed against his chest. "I can hear the gallop of your heart."

"No secret there. I adore you. It's as if there was something bigger than I could understand drawing us together from the very beginning."

"There was. Though *I* didn't yet know, God knew the best possible soul mate for me."

He chuckled. "Soul mate? I do like the sound of that. I'm liking this God more by the minute."

EPILOGUE

FEBRUARY 1868

*K*atie lumbered through the house. With her hands to the small of her aching back, she eased her heavy body into the rocking chair in the parlor close to the window. She moved a hand to her midsection and whispered to the large mound. "You can come anytime now. Just not today. There's a storm brewing, little one."

The swirl of thick snowflakes fell outside, transforming the earth to pristine white. She enjoyed the hypnotic twirl. Her eyes grew heavy, and she gave in to the tug of her drooping eyelids.

She woke to warm hands around her. Josiah knelt beside her with his head once again on her swollen abdomen. She reached out to smooth her fingers through his russet curls.

"Hello, darling." He looked up at her. "How are my two favorite people in the whole world?"

She couldn't help a laugh. She loved the way he included the baby in their conversations.

"It's snowing again. So beautiful." She looked out at the accumulated layers of white. There seemed to be no end to the dance of snowflakes coming down.

"It's beautiful unless the baby decides to come tonight." His eyes filled with worry.

She smoothed a hand over his creased brow. "Relax, my love. Having a baby is as natural as time." Maybe the words could also soothe the twinge of angst needling in her chest. It was normal for a first time mother to be a little nervous about the delivery, right? But she knew beyond a doubt God would give her the strength when she needed it.

He planted a quick kiss on her lips. "Don't you be making light of it. It's not every day a man becomes a father."

"I'm fine. The baby isn't due for another couple of weeks. Besides, in a crunch, we always have Delilah. Didn't she bring you into this world?"

He rose to his feet and offered her a tender look. "Wish I had your peace of mind."

"I've been telling you Jesus—"

"I know. I know." He cut her short and bent to help her rise. "Supper is ready. Come."

He offered his arm, and they walked into the large kitchen that had become the common area for all the workers to join together for supper. Their growing spread had acquired many more ranch hands, and Katie loved to invite them in like family. She smiled at the rambunctious crowd awaiting their grub as she waddled to the counter to help Delilah and Annie serve.

She'd just picked up the bowl of beans when something seemed to pop inside her, and liquid ran down her legs. A pool of water gathered around her feet as realization slipped through her. "Oh goodness."

All chatter stopped as every eye turned her way.

Delilah moved in. "Land sakes, girl, let's get you off your feet. You're going to have that baby tonight, and you'll be needing your strength. Yes, you will." She turned to Josiah. "Boy, move on over here. Don't just stand there gawkin."

The place erupted in pandemonium as everyone rushed to Katie's aid. Embarrassment flooded her face, and she whispered to Josiah, "Take me to my room." Much to her horror, he swept her up in his strong arms and climbed the steps two at a time. Delilah followed, huffing and puffing all the way.

He laid her gently on the bed. "I'll ride out and get Doc."

Katie's hand shot out and grabbed him. "No. This child needs a father, and I will not have you lost in a blizzard. Do you hear me, Josiah Richardson?" Her hand shook as a wave of pain wrapped around her, and she curled into as much of a ball as her belly would allow. She clutched Josiah's arm tight.

"Ohhhhhh," she cried out as the pain intensified. She struggled to take a deep breath through the agony. "Promise me, you will not—ahhhhh. You will not go out in that storm." She rocked back and forth, anything to lessen the band around her middle.

Delilah removed Katie's hand from Josiah's arm. "Go get her ma. This baby is surely not waiting for no town doctor. I done brought one Richardson into this world, and Jesus and I can bring another."

A scream pushed out from her, and Josiah ran.

Within an hour, a lusty cry filled the air, and Katie had never been so exhausted. Yet, as Delilah brought the tiny bundle to her, a new strength flowed through her. A red-faced baby boy peeked out from the blankets, and she could barely breathe as she took in every perfect part of his precious face.

Josiah stepped into the room as Delilah and Ma left, and Katie could only beam at him. "Come see."

As he moved to her bedside, she drank in the sight of their son. "We have a beautiful baby boy who looks just like his papa." A patch of russet hair stuck straight up in a mohawk swath, his blocky solidness so like Josiah's. She grinned at his innocent face. "Your papa owes me a huge apology, little one, and I'll try not to enjoy it too much."

Josiah chuckled. "Had there been any doubt left, which there wasn't, one look would've cleared that up."

He pressed a tender kiss to her forehead with a smile as wide as the sea. "We're officially a family. And a happier man you couldn't find if you looked the whole world over."

Joy rose up inside her, overwhelming her as she stared at the tiny babe in her arms. "Welcome, my baby boy. Mama loves you so much." She snuggled the babe close and dropped a light kiss on his pink brow.

"May I?" Josiah held his hands out to take the child. She handed him over, then watched her strong husband hold their precious son in his thick arms. "My dearest son. I want some of the first words you hear to be your daddy telling you how much I love you and your mama and how sorry I am for ever doubting her love."

Katie smiled toward the heavens. "God, you are still a miracle worker."

Josiah's booming laugher filled the room.

~

Katie slipped into the nursery, sure she would find Josiah spoiling their child once again, as she had so many times in the past few weeks. He stood at the window holding baby Seth, wet streaks running down Josiah's cheeks.

Her chest pressed at the sight. "Josiah, what is it?"

He smiled and beckoned her closer. She slipped an arm around his waist as they gazed down at their child.

"I didn't get it until now."

"Get what?"

"What true peace feels like."

345

Joy slipped through her. "It's beautiful, isn't it?"

"You tried to tell me, but I was stubborn."

She smiled up at him.

"The night of the fire, a monumental shift took place in my thinking. God did care about our prayers down here. I just didn't get why it mattered to understand the sacrifice for my sins. But the gift of our son somehow makes the gift of His Son come alive. I couldn't imagine giving such a gift to someone else. He must truly love us."

She squeezed his waist and leaned into his shoulder. "Welcome into the family of God, my love."

He leaned into her. "Thank you for believing in *us* when I no longer did, and for showing me the difference between self-centered love and unconditional love."

She smiled up at him. "Isn't it amazing how God brought us together, knowing what we'd both need long before we did."

He tilted his head towards her and dropped a kiss first on her head, and then on the baby's. "How did I ever get so blessed?"

Did you enjoy this book? We hope so!
Would you take a quick minute to leave a review where you purchased the book?
It doesn't have to be long. Just a sentence or two telling what you liked about the story!

Receive a FREE ebook and get updates when new Wild Heart books release: https://wildheartbooks.org/newsletter

Don't miss the next book in Shenandoah Brides Series!

Amelia's Heartsong

CHAPTER ONE

JULY, 1868
SHENANDOAH VALLEY

"He what?" Amelia Williams's heart battered the inside of her chest cavity with a wild thumping. She slammed her teacup into the saucer, splashing hot liquid onto her hand. The pain of the burn was nothing compared to the sting of truth. Her other hand automatically mopped up the mess with her napkin, then lifted to dab at the tears that fell free.

"I wanted to tell you, rather than have you find out from prattling tongues like that of Hattie Mayfield." Katherine shook her head. "I'm so sorry, dear sister." Her hand reached across the small end table and squeezed Amelia's.

"But Edmund told me just the other day how much he loved me...I don't understand. Where did Josiah see this?"

"He happened upon them kissing behind the General Mercantile—"

"Who was Edmund with?" Her words came out strangled.

"The daughter of that wealthy railway builder who moved into town a few months ago. I think her name is Helen."

"I know the one. I've seen her strutting about town in her fancy clothes like she owns the place. And all the men buzzing around her like she was some kind of special. But Edmund?"

"Josiah said they didn't see him, but he sure saw them. He came home directly and told me."

"Where is Josiah? Is there any way he could've mistakenly—"

"No. I asked the same thing." Katherine placed her teacup down. "Just a minute." She stood, moved across the parlor, and called down the hall. "Josiah, can you come in here for a moment?" She returned and slipped her arm around Amelia's shoulder. The warmth curbed the urge to run straight out the door to Edmund's house and confront him.

Josiah rounded the corner, and Amelia lifted her head. The grim set to his mouth and the empathy in his eyes spoke volumes.

"I'm hoping you witnessed this from a distance and there's room for doubt."

He shook his head. "With the many times Edmund has visited your home, there's no mistaking him. And with all the hullabaloo over the Tysons moving into our area, and the way their daughter parades about town in her low-cut dresses—"

Amelia stood swiftly. "That two-timer...how dare he—" She paced the floor but got caught off guard by the way Josiah was swaying on his feet. "Are you all right?" She hurried to his side, leading him to a nearby chair.

Katherine rushed over.

He sank down with a hand to his head. "Don't know what that was all about. Felt a little light-headed for a second. It's past now." He brushed both women aside. "Give me room to breathe, ladies. I'm fine. Let's concentrate on the situation at hand."

Amelia walked across the room and stared out the window. "It's too late today, but I intend to take the buggy to his place first thing tomorrow and address this."

"You're not going alone. I'll come with you," Katherine said.

"I'll take you both," Josiah offered.

"Tomorrow it is." Amelia held back the tears stinging behind her eyelids. "Now, if you'll excuse me, I'll head home."

The buggy rattled along, and Amelia sat in a daze. A thin slice of sunlight fought its way through a patch of cloud-filled sky, mirroring how her heart felt. She must find the courage to have the hardest conversation of her life. The landscape blurred behind a sheen of tears.

All she had ever wanted in life was to find a love like her parents, get married, and raise a family of her own. She was a born nurturer and had so much love to give. She felt most fulfilled when encouraging the down-hearted or tending to the sick. And ever since she was a young child helping with her younger siblings, her ma had told her what a fine mama she would make some day. Was that dream about to be thwarted?

How could this be happening to her? How could her long-time friend double-cross her like this? How many times had her family and the community teased them both about when their nuptials would be announced?

But three years of courting had gone by and still she waited. Edmund kept going on about his big dreams of making it rich. He said he would not promise marriage before he could properly take care of his wife. Yet, just recently he had insisted it would not be long before he placed a ring on her finger.

They rumbled to a stop in front of Edmund's home.

Katherine squeezed her arm. "We'll be right here waiting, and if need be...Josiah will verify what he witnessed."

Josiah nodded.

Amelia jumped from the wagon. Her mind spun in crazy circles. Chaotic. Confused. She approached the house with apprehension for the first time ever. Knots crowded the space between her shoulder blades.

A light rap on the door and it was swung wide by Edmund's mother. "Amelia, dear. To what do we owe the pleasure this fine Saturday morning? Come in. Come in." She lifted her eyes and noticed Katherine and Josiah sitting in the wagon. "I have a batch of pancakes on, please invite your sister and her husband in. The more the merrier." She laughed and held open the screen door. It made Amelia want to cry. She loved Edmund's mom.

"I can't stay, but can you tell Edmund I need to speak with him outside?"

Her brows knit together. "I'll go get him. I do hope everything is all right, my dear?" She patted Amelia's shoulder before she bustled away.

Edmund came around the corner. He looked so tall and handsome, her heart squeezed tight. He took one look at her face and his smile faded.

"I need to talk to you in private. Can we walk to the barn?"

He nodded, grabbed his hat from the rack, and flopped it on his head of curls. "I've been meaning to talk to you too."

Amelia's stomach twisted and dropped to her shoes.

He glanced up at Josiah and Katherine and touched his hat, but didn't say a word. They walked in silence across the yard. He waited just long enough to be out of hearing range. "I gather you know."

Tentacles of fury spread their hot fingers throughout her body. Oh, she would not make it that easy for him. "Know what?"

"By the look on your face, I thought…well I assumed you heard—"

"Heard what?" He could darn well put into words what he had done to her.

"Uh, what I've been meaning to tell you for a while. I've fallen in love with someone else."

"Love." She spat out the word. "Seems you use that word loosely. "Not so long ago you were saying you loved me and we were talking marriage."

"I do care for you—"

"Don't bother with the platitudes, Edmund. You owe me far more than that."

"What can I say without hurting you?"

"You've already hurt me far beyond words. Imagine how it felt to hear from my brother-in-law that you were at the back of the store kissing up a storm with the new tart in town."

"She's not a tart. She's fun, intellectually engaging, and—"

"And rich. Let's face it Edmund, the only thing that has kept us from marriage is your obsession with money. And how convenient you can fall in and out of love at will."

"Her father is going to give me an opportunity to join his management team building the railway. And so what if I'm motivated by money? I have no desire to be a dirt-poor farmer—"

"Or marry a farm girl."

He looked at her with sincerity and sadness in his eyes. "Can we remain friends?"

She almost capitulated ,but then remembered what she had spent all night thinking about. "Friends do not do what you just did to me. The least you could've done is given enough respect to break it off with me *before* starting with someone else."

"It just happened. How would I know a lady of her caliber would take a shining to a nobody like me?"

"That's says it all. Nothing just happens, Edmund. We make

decisions every day of our life, be they right or wrong. And the fact that you think you're a nobody without the money her family totes around is sad. You were never a nobody to me."

"Ahh, Amelia…" He raised his hand and slid it down her tear-stained cheek. "I'm sorry."

She slapped his hand away. "I'm not. I'm glad I found out how weak you are *before* we were married. God has saved me from a lot more heartache than it could've been." With her head held high and starch to her spine she walked out.

Get AMELIA'S HEARTSONG at your favorite retailer!

BOOKS IN THE
SHENANDOAH BRIDES SERIES

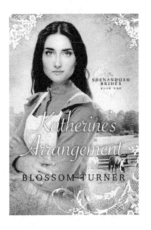

Katherine's Arrangement (Shenandoah Brides, book 1)

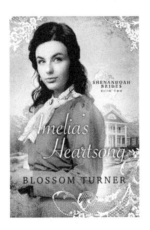

Amelia's Heartsong (Shenandoah Brides, book 2)

Lucinda's Defender (Shenandoah Brides, book 3)

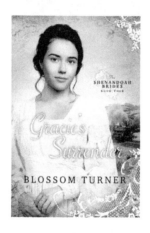

Gracie's Surrender (Shenandoah Brides, book 4)

Jeanette's Gift (Shenandoah Brides, book 5)

ABOUT THE AUTHOR

*I write because I can't **not** write. Stories have danced in my imagination since childhood. Having done the responsible thing—a former businesswoman, personal trainer, and mother of two grown children—I am finally pursuing my lifelong dream of writing full-time. Who knew work could be so fun?*

A hopeless romantic at heart, I believe all stories should give the reader significant entertainment value but also infuse relatable life struggle with hope sprinkled throughout. My desire is to leave the reader with a yearning to live for Christ on a deeper level, or at the very least, create a hunger to seek for more.

Blossom Turner is a freelance writer published in Chicken Soup and Kernels of Hope anthologies, former newspaper columnist on health and fitness, avid blogger, and novelist. She lives in a four-season playground in beautiful British Columbia, Canada, with gardening at the top of her enjoyment list.

She has a passion for women's ministry teaching Bible studies and public speaking, but having coffee and sharing God's hope with a hurting soul trumps all. She lives with her husband, David, of thirty-eight years and their new puppy, Lacey, named after the town of Lacey Spring, Virginia. Blossom loves to hear from her readers. Visit her at blossomturner.com and subscribe to her quarterly newsletter.

Don't miss Blossom's other book, *Anna's Secret,* a contemporary romance and Word Guild semi-finalist.

ACKNOWLEDGMENTS

I believe no book is a work in and of itself. There is always a support team behind the scenes...the "unsung heroes/heroines" to use a cliché, or "the wind beneath my wings" to use the lyrics of a well-known song. To the following I offer my sincerest thank you. My book has been elevated way beyond its original first draft because of your expertise.

I thank Karin Berry for her tough but honest critiques that improved my story. Karin you are awesome.

Erin Taylor Young, you challenged many a scene, highlighting only one line and encouraging me to expound on that sentence because all the action was hidden there. Your guiding hand was so appreciated. And Robin Patchen, your penchant for perfect grammar and patience explaining why it is so, taught me much. Thank you.

Misty M. Beller, the team co-ordinator and final editor, thank you and your talented design team for a cover that I am truly excited about. You have been amazing to work with on every level. A thank you does not hold enough gratitude.

To my critique partners, beta readers, street team, and writers' group, your encouragement has inspired me onward. And to my close friends and amazing family members who have continually poured out encouragement, love, and prayer support—thank you from my heart.

All glory to Jesus Christ who makes the impossible possible. Far beyond my wildest imaginings God has taken my writing and given it wings. Matt. 19:26

If you love historical romance, check out the other Wild Heart books!

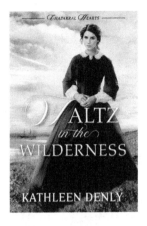

Waltz in the Wilderness by Kathleen Denly

She's desperate to find her missing father. His conscience demands he risk all to help.

Eliza Brooks is haunted by her role in her mother's death, so she'll do anything to find her missing pa—even if it means sneaking aboard a southbound ship. When those meant to protect her abandon and betray her instead, a family friend's unexpected assistance is a blessing she can't refuse.

Daniel Clarke came to California to make his fortune, and a stable job as a San Francisco carpenter has earned him more than most have scraped from the local goldfields. But it's been four years since he left Massachusetts and his fiancé is impatient for his return. Bound for home at last, Daniel Clarke finds his heart and plans challenged by a tenacious young woman with haunted eyes. Though every word he utters seems to offend her, he is determined to see her safely returned to her father. Even if that means risking his fragile engagement.

When disaster befalls them in the remote wilderness of the Southern California mountains, true feelings are revealed, and both must face heart-rending decisions. But how to decide when every choice before them leads to someone getting hurt?

~

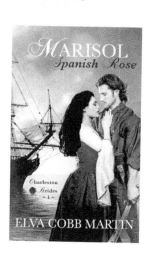

Marisol ~ Spanish Rose by Elva Cobb Martin

Escaping to the New World is her only option...Rescuing her will wrap the chains of the Inquisition around his neck.

Marisol Valentin flees Spain after murdering the nobleman who molested her. She ends up for sale on the indentured servants' block at Charles Town harbor—dirty, angry, and with child. Her hopes are shattered, but she must find a refuge for herself and the child she carries. Can this new land offer her the grace, love, and security she craves? Or must she escape again to her only living relative in Cartagena?

Captain Ethan Becket, once a Charles Town minister, now sails the seas as a privateer, grieving his deceased wife. But when he takes captive a ship full of indentured servants, he's intrigued by the woman whose manners seem much more refined than the average Spanish serving girl. Perfect to become governess for his young son. But when he sets out on a quest to find his captured sister, said to be in Cartagena, little does he expect his new Spanish governess to stow away on his ship with her six-month-old son. Yet her offer of help to free his sister is too tempting to pass up. And her beauty, both inside and out, is too attractive for his heart to protect itself against—until he learns she is a wanted murderess.

As their paths intertwine on a journey filled with danger, intrigue, and romance, only love and the grace of God can overcome the past and ignite a new beginning for Marisol and Ethan.

~

Lone Star Ranger by Renae Brumbaugh Green

Elizabeth Covington will get her man.

And she has just a week to prove her brother isn't the murderer Texas Ranger Rett Smith accuses him of being. She'll show the good-looking lawman he's wrong, even if it means setting out on a risky race across Texas to catch the real killer.

Rett doesn't want to convict an innocent man. But he can't let the Boston beauty sway his senses to set a guilty man free. When Elizabeth follows him on a dangerous trek, the Ranger vows to keep her safe. But who will protect him from the woman whose conviction and courage leave him doubting everything—even his heart?

Made in the USA
Monee, IL
22 April 2022